The Red Veil Diaries
Special Edition

Marianne Morea

Coventry Press Ltd.

Welcome to the hottest Vampire Club
in New York City!

The Red Veil

Vegas got nothing on what happens here.

Coventry Press Ltd.
Somers, New York

ISBN 13: 978-1732526211

Printed in the USA

Introducing
The Red Veil Diaries

Choose Me

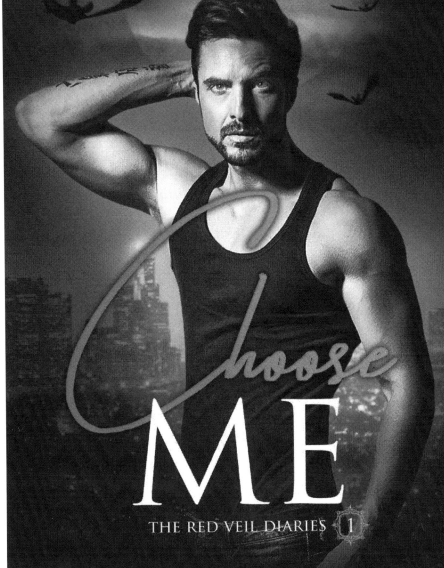

Choose ME

THE RED VEIL DIARIES 1

MARIANNE MOREA

INTERNATIONAL BESTSELLING AUTHOR

*"I think every woman
should have a one-night stand.
If it's done right, it can be liberating."*

~Rachel Perry

Chapter One

"*T*his place is off the chain!" Edie squirmed in her seat. "*The Red Veil*. My panties are getting wet just looking at all the man candy! Gimme a hardcore underground club draped in crimson and jet and the promise of hot sex and I'm in."

"Jeez, Edie." Rose Landry fidgeted with the damp paper napkin under her martini glass, curling wet strips between her fingers.

"What's the matter? Good looking men make you nervous, Ro?"

"Not at all. I'm around men of all varieties every day."

"Yeah, but none as mouthwatering as these." Edie drummed on the table. "The rumors about this place have done wonders for its publicity. The bar is packed! I heard the club is some kind of vampire mecca. They have secret backrooms and according to the Soho Chronicles, wild sex and fetish play is what draws the vampires and the fang-bangers."

Rose rolled her eyes. "Vampires? Fang-bangers? Gimme a break. More like downtown freaks who fancy themselves undead, but that's nothing a little reverse cosmetic dentistry and a stay on a psychiatrist's couch won't cure."

"Sounds fun even if it is bullshit. You're not even the slightest bit curious, Ro?" Her sister Cassandra asked.

"Backrooms and fetish play? I get that. But nocturnal predators roaming the streets of New York?" Rose shook her head. "We've got enough humans who fit that description to keep us busy. They file through my courtroom every day in orange jumpsuits and steel bracelets. We don't need to invent the supernatural variety, thank you."

Edie flicked a few drops of her martini at Rose. "You know, for someone who should be tons of fun, you're no fun at all."

"Edie..." Cassandra warned.

"Fat jokes this early in the night. *Hmmm.* You're consistent if not predictable, Edie, I gotta give you that."

Edie eyed her across the small table. "No offense Rosie, but you need to get out more. All work and no play makes for a dull girl, and honey your dreary is coasting toward epic."

Rose glanced at the stem of her martini glass. "Some of us crave something deeper than the thump, thump of heavy bass and a heartless bump and grind."

Ignoring her, Edie signaled the waitress for another round. "OMG!" She jerked around grabbing Cassandra's arm under the table. "Don't look, but the hottest guy at the bar is checking us out."

"Who? Almost every guy in here is underwear-model gorgeous."

Edie slid her eyes back from the bar. "The sexy Spanish looking one with the wide shoulders and long dark hair."

Rose casually lifted her hand to the side of her face to sneak a peek through her fingers.

As though on cue, he met her eyes in the mirror behind the bar and lifted his beer to his lips with a soft smirk.

"Nice, Captain Obvious. I said not to look, and now he knows we caught him checking out the goodies. He'll never talk to us."

"Goodies?" Rose made a face. "Do you even hear yourself?" She shook her head and got up from the small round table, her chair scraping back against the loud music. "I'm going to the ladies room."

Edie rolled her eyes watching her go. "More like *escaping* to the ladies room." She looked at Cassie and shook her head.

"Seriously Cass, why did you bring her tonight? She's a buzz kill. Plus she's old."

Cassandra watched her sister walk through the crowd toward the restrooms. "She's thirty-five, Edie. Not exactly ready for social security."

"Still."

"No. No still. Rosie's here because we're supposed to be celebrating my engagement. She's my sister *and* my maid of honor."

"Old maid is more like it."

"Stop it. She is more successful than you and I will ever be. She made Law Review her first year of law school and then went on to graduate in the top one percent of her class."

"So you keep saying."

Cassandra blinked at her friend. "If I didn't know better Edie, I'd swear you were jealous."

"Me? Jealous of her?" She glanced toward the crowd. "Please. Rosie's bush league and I'm pro."

"Sweetie, while I agree your bush is in a league of its own, I wouldn't throw the word *pro* around if I were you. People might get the wrong idea."

"Not funny, Cass."

"I thought it was," she smiled sipping her beer.

Edie glanced in the direction of the restrooms again. "What's wrong with your sister, anyway? She's not bad looking, that is if you can get past her rolls and the size of her ass. Plus, that old-school sense of style. *Ugh.*" She made a face. "I bet she hasn't had a date in years, or at least none willing to vent that furnace between her legs."

"Hey! Be nice."

"I am being nice. Generous, even."

"No, you're not. You're being a bitch. Rose is shy. She's always been more at home in a classroom or with her nose in a book. But that's just her way. She's more of an introvert."

"Tell me something I don't know. Did you dress her tonight? Because I haven't seen her look that put together in forever."

Cassandra gaped. "Of course not. You're making my sister out to be a cross between a train wreck and a nun, and that's not fair. She's a crackerjack attorney and her conservative wardrobe reflects that. She'd be the first person you'd call if you were ever arrested and you know it."

Edie snorted.

"You've never seen her in action. She can work a jury, like you work a stiff cock, but when it comes to men outside of the courtroom, she doesn't have a lot of confidence."

"Sounds to me like she's hiding behind her career. Or at least using it to keep her life at arms distance."

Cassie looked at her. "Wow! That's very profound coming from the winner of this year's Jersey Shore Wet Tee-shirt contest."

Edie stirred her dirty martini. "Hey, here's an idea. Let's get her drunk and then get her laid."

"Edie!"

"What? She'll thank us in the morning."

"No, she won't. She'd be mortified. Rosie does fine on her own, in her own way. She's not a barfly like you, and she's not interested in getting married like me. Or at least she's never said. There's nothing wrong with being quiet.

4

If I had a profession as challenging and rewarding as hers, I wouldn't be trolling the bars and neither would you. I'm proud of her."

"Trolling the bars? Please. We don't troll."

"Well, I don't. Not anymore…but come on, Edie. Look at the way you're dressed. All that's missing is a neon arrow pointed at your pussy."

Edie pursed her lips in an unhappy pout. "Well, this is turning out to be a waste of a Friday night." She turned back to the bar and raised her martini glass to her pink lips, catching the Spanish hottie's eye in the bar's mirror.

She took a sip and then lifted the thin toothpick from the glass, tonguing the salty, green olives at the end before dragging them into her mouth.

"Wow! Talk about taste central, Edie. Seriously." Rose shook her head taking her seat again. "If they ever make sucking nails out of a board an Olympic sport, you're our girl."

Cassie laughed. "Edie's got her own brand of elegance."

"Hmmm."

Yeah, well. Just because you two aren't interested in the wall-to-wall eye-fucking going on in here, doesn't mean I'm not up for a little fun and games."

"I have Michael, thank you very much, and he provides all the entertainment I need."

"Gimme a break. Just because there's no money in your pocket doesn't mean you can't window shop." Edie turned. "I guess that leaves you, counselor. Are you up for a game of chase that might lead to hide and seek the salami?"

"*Ugh.* I just felt my IQ points drop. There's more to life than hooking up, Edie. If you put as much effort into promoting your brain as you do your pussy, you might surprise yourself."

Cassie burst out laughing. "Promoting her pussy? What happened to my correct lawyer sister? Two martinis in and you develop a truck driver's mouth."

Edie frowned picking up her glass. "Two more and it might kill the bug that crawled up her ass."

Cassie pinched her friend under the table.

"Ouch, quit it! I'm sorry, but it's got to be said. No one wants her here, Cassie. Not even you!"

"I beg your pardon?"

Edie glared at the two. "It's true. Not that Cassie will ever admit it. You don't fit in, Rose. You never did and you never will. You were fat and invisible then, and you still are, regardless of how many degrees you have. It's no wonder you buried yourself in books. They were the only sheets you could climb between with your sad book boyfriends."

"Edie! That's enough!"

Rosie stood, her eyes wet and flashing. "Turn around, Edie. There's a nameless cock waiting at the bar to stuff your mouth so none of us have to hear your sad, jealous bullshit."

She turned on her heel and headed toward the coat check.

"Damn it, Edie! You took it way too far. You may not like Rosie and vice versa, but she has never disrespected you the way you did her."

"Cass...I'm sorry."

She shook her head. "No. I'm not the one you need to apologize to." She lifted her finger and pointed toward the exit. "Go. If Rose leaves without a sincere apology from you, we're done. A decade of friendship down the toilet, and I mean it."

Chapter Two

"*L*eaving so soon, *linda*?"

Rose turned and had to stop her jaw from dropping. It was the hot guy from the bar. "*Uhm*…I think you have me confused with someone else. My name isn't Linda."

He laughed. "Forgive me. My mother tongue slips into my English from time to time. *Linda* is the Spanish word for pretty. Which you certainly are."

Rosie blinked, ignoring the heat crawling up her face. "Do I know you?"

Stupid much, Rose? She just spent the better part of the evening ogling him from behind her drink, so yeah she knew him.

She blushed even harder, resisting the urge to drop her gaze to her feet.

He shook his head answering her question. "No, we've never met, but that is something I would very much like to change. I noticed you earlier while at the bar." He reached out his hand. "I'm Miguel León." Without warning he slipped the coat check receipt from her fingers. "…and I'm not letting you leave until you have a drink with me."

"Hey!"

"Rosie?"

Both sets of eyes turned.

"I'm sorry. I don't mean to interrupt."

Rose made a face. "Sure you do. What do you want, Edie?"

"I…" She licked her lips glancing from Rose's waiting gaze to the sexy Spaniard. "I wanted to apologize. Seriously. I was out of line and I'm sorry Rosie."

Miguel shifted his eyes to Rose standing speechless. "Were you named for the flower or the beautiful way you blush? Either way, it suits you."

Okay, what just happened? Did he really ignore Edie and compliment me?

"Thank you, but the answer is neither, actually. Rose is short for Generosa."

He smiled and her mouth went dry at how utterly delicious he looked.

"It's uncommon, I know." She shrugged, not knowing what else to say.

"I've always been attracted to the exceptional and the rare." Taking her hand, he lifted her fingers to his lips.

The scent of her filled him and his fangs tingled in his gums, itching to pierce the soft blue veins on the underside of her wrist. It was more than the smell of her blood. It was her. The fullness of her body and its untapped lust made his mouth water.

He wanted to taste her, tease her. Blood that sweet, that potent, would rush through her veins with arousal so powerful his cock hardened at the thought alone.

"Come, let me buy you a drink so we can talk more."

Edie's eyes widened even more than Rose's. "I'd love to have a drink with you, handsome. Point the way and I'll follow you anywhere."

Miguel looked at the obvious woman, his eyes trailing Edie's cliché man-eater clothing. "Thank you, but no. I have a small table reserved in the VIP section."

Edie opened her mouth to reply, but snapped it shut when he turned back to Rose, ignoring her completely.

"Shall we?"

Rose hesitated. "Miguel, I appreciate the offer but I'm here with my sister. We're celebrating her engagement." She pointed toward the bar. "We still have our table near the back if you would like to join us, instead."

"My apologies. I assumed your celebration was at an end since you were about to leave."

Her lips parted and she spared a glance at Edie, ready to explain her reasons for leaving, but changed her mind. Embarrassing the little twit was petty.

Miguel handed Rose her coat check receipt. "Generosa." He smiled. "Your parents named you well. A generous spirit inside a beautiful woman."

Was this guy for real? Who cares? He's hot! Then why is he talking to me?

Her brain went back and forth with every cynical thought she could conjure. Old habits begged her to walk away or go bitch squad on Miguel and call bullshit, but she wouldn't give Edie the satisfaction.

She slipped the little green coat check into her purse. "Why not." She smiled up into his face. "One drink more won't hurt."

ॐ

Pop! The waitress wiggled the top from their second bottle of Cristal before handing the cork to Miguel. The four had talked for over an hour and it was nearing midnight.

"*Deseo que usted y su novio mucha felicidad,*" Miguel said, handing Cassandra her refill. "One more toast to wish you and your future husband a lifetime of happiness."

"Fill'er up, honey. I love champagne," Edie added lifting her glass for the waitress to top off. "It's my go to drink. That or a good martini." She took a large sip and sneezed, dribbling and coughing at the same time.

"Now that's class." Cassie laughed, handing her a wad of napkins. "Proving once again, it's possible to look sexy and stupid at the same time."

Cassie clinked glasses with Rose.

"Hey!"

Miguel laughed. "It's okay, Edie" he said taking the glass from her hand, so she could wipe her face and neck. "The bubbles tickle my nose, too."

"Is that why you're not drinking?" Rose asked, her own head a little fuzzy from the wine.

He put Edie's champagne flute on the table. "There are many ways to intoxicate, and for me, most of them start and end with you tonight." Miguel's eyes locked with hers and Rose didn't dare look away.

"It sounds as though you have a challenging career. It must be rewarding to know you are responsible, in part, for taking predators from the street. Innocents are not always held as sacred, and they should be, regardless of circumstance. No one should ever walk in fear of what lurks in the shadows."

She stared at his mouth and the way emotion played in his eyes and his expression.

"You sound as though you've had experience with this. Are you a prosecutor as well?"

He laughed shaking his head. "No, unfortunately my nature is not as noble as yours, or at least not inherently, though I'm working on it. Perhaps you will be a good influence."

Pushing himself from his seat, Miguel trailed his fingers over her arm as he stood. "If you'll excuse me for a moment."

Three sets of eyes tracked him as he walked down the short set of stairs toward the dancefloor.

"If you don't jump his bones tonight I'm having your lady card revoked. He is so into you it's not even funny!"

Rose sighed, shaking her head. "Forget it Cass. It's a classic bait and switch."

"A what?"

Rose shifted on the couch to face her sister. "He's only flirting with me to make *hot pants* here feel rejected and vulnerable. That way she's easy to pluck." She jerked a thumb toward Edie.

"Easy? You can't get any easier than Edie. Talk about no effort required."

"Hey! I require effort."

Cassie snorted. "I hate to break it to you, but a bottle of cheap wine and a drive along the beach for a quick toss, does not qualify you as hard won."

She covered her sister's hand with hers. "I've never seen anyone less interested in Edie or anyone else for that matter, *or* more interested in you. Face it Rosie, he wants you."

I don't know, Cass. It's too easy. There's got to be a catch."

"Exactly," Edie interjected, but Cassie ignored her.

"What catch? If it turns out to be a one night stand, so what? At least you'll have a secret smile and something to dream about for the rest of your life." She squeezed Rose's hand. "Look at Michael and me. I thought he was a one night stand and now we're getting married."

"I don't know, Cassie. What if he turns out to be a creep or a psycho? I prosecute creeps every day, but they're in custody. I'm not sure I could handle one still on the loose."

Cassie waved her off. "You're always telling me I'm the one with the witchy genes in the family and my sixth sense is telling me he's good." She winked. "In more ways than one!"

Rose smirked, shaking her head. "Not buying it, Cass."

"Come on, Ro. I never told you this, but in middle school I would sneak your romance novels from your bedroom when you were in college and read them under my covers. No one else knew you were into them, but I did."

Rose exhaled. "My class load was mind-numbing back then. I needed something to sweep me away from all the dry reading and they were the perfect escape. They still are."

Cassie chuckled, lifting one hand. "Hey, you're preaching to the choir. I've been hooked ever since."

Rose let out a warm laugh. "You were what? Twelve? Mom would kill me if she knew."

"Classic. New York's up and coming Assistant District Attorney reads trash romance." Edie snickered draining her drink.

Cassie crumbled her napkin and threw it at her. "It's a billion dollar industry, smarty pants. Don't poke fun at it."

Edie clicked the inside of her cheek. "I don't know about books or industry, but I could certainly go for a guy with a billion dollars."

"Yeah, well. Try the subgenre on taming the billionaire. You might learn something." Cassie dismissed her, turning her attention back to Rose.

"You always spoke to me about life's *what ifs*. This is your chance to live your own spontaneous romantic scenario. If you let this opportunity pass, you'll end up regretting it. If only because you didn't let it play out."

"Speaking of fun and games, this place is a washout and I think it's time to leave." Edie looked at Cassie. "You coming?"

She nodded gathering her things. "Yes, but only so Rose has more room to maneuver. Three's a crowd."

"Three can be fun." Edie snickered.

"Hey, let's start with one and see where it goes."

"Wait...I haven't said I want this."

Cassie laughed getting up. "Oh, you want this, Rose. It's written all over you. Just relax and let it happen."

Leaning over she gave her sister's cheek a peck. "Call me tomorrow. I want details."

Chapter Three

"Are you both leaving?" Miguel asked passing the two girls as he walked back across the floor.

Cassandra nodded. "I've got work in the morning," she said, lightly elbowing Edie.

"*Uhm*...yeah. Early shift."

"What about your sister? Is she leaving as well?"

"Not yet. She wanted to finish her drink and wait for you to say goodnight." She paused, eyeing him. "Take care of her. My fiancé's a cop, and we'll find you if you don't."

He laughed. "Of that, I have no doubt." With a nod he turned and headed back toward their table.

Rose watched him approach. He was elegance in motion. Sinuous and graceful, yet there was something mysterious and dangerous about him. She couldn't put her finger on it, but it made her blood race.

"And then there were two," she said with a chuckle as he slid into the seat beside her.

He was so close she smelled the scent of his skin, the underlying maleness of him and her heart pounded with nervous energy.

Lifting the bottle of champagne, he poured her another glass. "You're uncomfortable," he said handing her the flute. "There's no need to be."

She shrugged, taking the glass from him. "I'm not used to all this attention. Even in the courtroom I try to keep a low profile. As you might have guessed, Edie is usually the one who attracts the men whenever we go out."

"A man would have to be blind not to notice her, but she's too obvious. I prefer the understated, and I can sense

14

the extraordinary in a crowd of thousands. Edie may attract most men, but I'm not most men."

Rose warmed to him. "I think that's an understatement."

He smiled almost sensing the shift. "We can sit here and talk all night if you wish, or we can find *other ways* to get to know each other."

He stressed the words in such a seductive tone it made her panties damp.

"The choice is yours, *querida*."

More than a little unsettled, Rose lifted her eyes from his intense gaze and focused on the beautiful music floating in from the speakers.

"What a lovely sound."

He smiled and in one fluid movement he stood, holding his hand out. "Dance with me."

She shook her head. "I don't think so, Miguel. I'm not what you would call graceful."

He took her hand and pulled her to her feet. "You'll be fine. Trust me, no one will even know we're on the dance floor. We are the only two that matter."

His words struck her as strange, but she followed him to the dance floor, her strapless dress fluid around her full curves as she walked. He circled the small corner of the dance floor with her before slipping his arm around her waist, spinning her with him to the beat.

A gorgeous melody played and the strains from a twelve string guitar filled her ears, leaving her as breathless as the feel of his chest and thighs.

As Miguel moved with her to the music, shocks jolted her lower belly making her panties wet.

Oh God, was she that hard up that a simple dance could send her crashing toward climax?

He tightened his grip and his lips found hers. He kissed her softly at first, but when she sighed in his arms, he bit her lower lip, sliding his tongue into her mouth to taste her, urging their kiss deeper.

Rose knew they weren't alone on the dance floor regardless of what Miguel said, but she didn't care. Her lower body pulsed with such need she pressed her body to his, aching.

"You're beautiful, Rose," he whispered, skimming one hand over her waist to gently caress the side of her breast, his thumb grazing her nipple before his fingers traveled to cup the side of her face.

He kissed her again, deeper. "I'm finding it harder and harder to resist you."

This was happening too fast and she knew it, but she didn't dare stop it. "Then don't," she murmured back.

She was leading him on, but she didn't care. Wherever this went, she would follow.

"Then tell me your deepest desire, what you crave, right here, right now."

His words rained over her and she gasped as images of their bodies entwined filled her head. No one had ever asked her what she wanted. Not like this.

"I want to be seduced, taken."

His hands roamed her full curves, gliding over the thin fabric of her dress, electrifying her senses as his teeth and tongue nipped and grazed her bare shoulders.

"Now tell me your deepest fear, your secret shame, right here, right now."

She sucked in a breath at the feel of his mouth against the hollow of her throat. It was as if she'd been hypnotized and Miguel had control. "That you'll reject me. Use me and discard me."

❦

Her scent overwhelmed him and Miguel bit back on the urge to drag her to the nearest dark corner. Even from a distance he sensed her longing and her discontented abstinence, and the combination was irresistible.

He hadn't fed in days, and the smell of her fresh arousal made his mouth water and his fangs tingle. One word echoed through his brain. *Mine.* He had to have her, even if it meant glamouring her into submission and breaking his own rule.

Miguel's body moved with hers, foreplay set to the music. He led her, walking her backward toward a door marked private at the back end of the club.

"Come. Let me be your fantasy, as you are mine tonight."

A thousand reasons buzzed through Rose's lust-clouded brain why she should say no. Why she should bolt and run. She ignored them, throwing all rational thought to the wind.

Miguel pressed his hand to a biometric keypad and the door snicked open. She walked across the threshold not knowing where it led.

She stood with him in a dimly lighted antechamber of sorts. He slid his hand from hers to grip her shoulders, caressing her skin.

"From here there's no going back. Do you still want this? Still want me?"

Throat dry, her only focus was the shape of his lips and the thought of his mouth and tongue on her body.

"Yes," she croaked.

His eyes darkened, and he led her through an arched doorway to a large circular room. Inside were luxurious compartments, each divided and hidden behind semi-translucent veils of sheer red silk.

Silhouettes of bodies entwined, and twisting met her wide stare and she froze. "What is this place? Where have you taken me?"

"The Red Veil." He paused. "The *true* Red Veil. This is the first of the infamous backrooms many whisper about. Here you can live out all your fantasies."

"The first?"

He took her hand and pulled her close. "There are many, many rooms. Some of which are off limits even to me. They are not for the faint of heart."

He kissed her once more before spinning her around in his arms. His sweet breath fanned against the back of her throat and the base of her ear as his hands slid over her breasts, stopping to pinch her already hard nipples.

"Look at their bodies, Rose. Hidden, yet a mere touch from us. See how they move and writhe in excruciating pleasure."

His hands released her breasts and slipped teasingly over her belly, gliding over her curves to the juncture between her legs.

"Inhale, *querida*. It's the tang of lust, tension and delicious release. Sex in the very air."

Rose reached behind with one arm fisting Miguel's hair. She lifted her face, turning to pull his mouth to hers. She devoured his lips, sucking in his tongue and when she ran her own over the sharp edged tip of his fangs, she drew back.

His dark chocolate eyes now held an aura of red and his pupils a cavernous black. She couldn't look away, and the taste of her own blood on her tongue suddenly seemed sensuous and primal.

"What are you?" she whispered.

"I am what you crave in your darkest fantasies, what you've longed for. I am what you've only dreamed could be...until now."

Her disbelief nearly paralyzed her, but not enough for her to stay frozen in place. "I...I...don't believe you," she whispered. "It can't be." She shook her head, but couldn't tear her eyes away.

His eyes searched hers, the tips of his fangs peeking from under his upper lip. He lifted his chin and let her watch them retract into his gums. No deceit. No secrets.

"The rumors are true. I am what you have heard, but I brought you here because I choose you, Rose. Of all the women here tonight, I want you and only you."

She exhaled, her eyes never leaving his. She had lied to Cassie. She was more than curious. This was a fantasy come to life.

He held his arms out and she walked into his embrace and kissed him again, only this time he dragged his fangs over her bottom lip, grazing the sensitive flesh enough to bleed. He sucked her lip into his mouth and groaned with the taste of her.

Miguel walked her to one of the rooms and parted the sheers. He stood her in front of an ornate floor mirror and let her see him in all his vampiric glory. His fangs, his red eyes and his need for her body and her blood, her wet juices and her sex.

"I am very real, *querida*. As real as you are." He pressed her hand to the bulge in his pants and then leaned in to whisper at the back of her ear. "As real as my cock is hard for you."

This was more surreal than she could ever imagine, and she was powerless to stop it even if she wanted. She was a freight train careening down the tracks.

Slowly he unzipped her dress, letting the loose fabric puddle to the floor around her high heeled pumps. Rose kicked it to the side, and catching her mirror reflection in just her bra and panties, she immediately moved her arms from his neck to cover herself.

"No, *mi amor*. I want to see you. All of you. I want you to see me love you, take you, feed from you. I want you to see yourself as I see you, as I make you come. I want you to see me as I empty myself deep within you."

He stripped, allowing her to turn to face him. "See me as I am. As I have been for nearly a century and a half."

Rose licked her lips at how beautiful Miguel was, not just his body, but his face and the glow in his eyes. He wanted her...truly wanted *her*.

She circled him, taking in his sculpted chest and strong thighs, his firm ass and long, thick cock. He was magnificent, and with the way his dark hair cascaded to his shoulders, he looked like a Latin Adonis. A dark lion.

"You find me amusing, *mi amor*?"

Rose shook her head. "I find you astonishing. Extraordinary and indescribable. Both, who you are and what you are. I should be frightened, and my rational mind rebels against what my senses tell me is truth, but I'm not afraid. Maybe I'm drunk with lust, or perhaps you've cast a spell on me, but I don't care. You said my name suits me? Well yours is you incarnate. You are a lion ready to strike and I am your willing prey."

At her words Miguel sucked in a breath and his cock jerked. His fangs lengthened fully and he licked his lips.

Excited fear spiraled into Rose's belly along with the unbearable ache to have him, and the combination sent her juices dripping.

"I smell your need, *querida*. Your panties are soaked with it. Take them off."

She did as she was told, unhooking her bra first and letting it fall to the floor. She then slipped her underwear down her thighs to her ankles and stepped out of them.

"Come." He held out his hand and led her to the plush chaise. He stood behind her again. "We all harbor secrets and passions that haunt us in the dark, which leave our bodies throbbing with unfulfilled want. Tonight I will quench that hunger in you as you will quench mine."

Miguel turned her toward the mirror again, and lifted her long hair to one side. He kissed her shoulder, feathering his lips over her skin, circling the pulse in her throat with his tongue.

She moaned and he trailed his hand low over her belly again, fingers splayed against her flesh until he cupped her slippery, wet sex.

Two fingers worked her slick slit while his thumb circled her clit, rubbing her hard nub.

He inhaled deep, and just as her orgasm exploded against his palm, his fangs pierced her throat. Hot coppery blood laced with sex and adrenaline filled his mouth as she ground herself further into his hand.

He lapped at her throat, drawing deep pulls from her vein until he threw his head back with a snarl. He licked her wound closed and bent her over the end of the couch, impaling his cock, balls deep, in her still convulsing sex.

Miguel rode her hard, his skin slapping against her ample ass. He leaned over, cupping her breasts with both hands, squeezing and working her nipples.

"Look, Rose. See how hot you are. Your white flesh is pink with lust and ready for more."

She turned her head toward the mirror and gasped at how wonton her reflection seemed with her knees apart and her ass in the air.

Her eyes met his in the glass. "I want you to spread me wide. To lick me and fuck me and feed from my pussy."

Stunned at her own smut, she bit her lip, reopening the abrasion from Miguel's fangs. Blood dripped from the cut and he groaned leaning over to lick it clean.

Shivering at the raspy feel of his tongue, she closed her eyes, tilting her head to offer him her throat again. Waves of pleasure from his thick cock and pain from his fangs washed over her.

Too many nights she spent in the dark alone, with only a movie, a bottle of wine and battery operated boyfriend to ease her loneliness.

This was real, regardless of how surreal it felt. She'd wrap her head around that tomorrow. Right now all she wanted was to wrap her legs around his hips and ride his cock or bury her pussy in his mouth, maybe both if she had the strength.

Releasing her throat, he resealed the wounds and pulled his member from her slick entrance. She protested, but he silenced her with a kiss before flipping her onto her back.

"Spread yourself for me. Show me your pretty pink pussy, shining and wet, swollen and waiting for more."

Miguel pushed her knees apart even farther, dipping his head to her juicy slit. He dragged his tongue from her ass to her hard bud and bit down.

Rose hissed, raising her hips for more.

Swirling the tip of his tongue, he dragged the taut nub into his mouth, sucking and teasing the tender flesh.

She dropped her head back, fisting his hair to force herself further into his mouth.

Miguel reached down to wrap his hand around his rigid shaft, gliding his palm over its engorged head.

He jerked himself, harder and faster. His hand moving in time with his tongue as he delved deeper and faster into her soft, wet folds. She tensed and he lifted his head and inhaled. This was it. She was ready.

He plunged his cock deep, holding her ankles wide to lift her hips. He pounded her pussy, until she cried out for him.

"Give it to me! Come!"

Miguel threw his head back, every muscle rigid and stretched until his body let go. With a snarl of release, he pumped jets deep into her sex, but the feel of her body's heat enveloping his cock drove him to the edge, again.

She slumped back against the tufted end of the couch. "I can't...put a fork in me, I'm done."

"But I'm not."

He pulled out, his still hard cock bobbing as he stepped back.

"On your knees, Rose. Open your mouth."

She climbed to all fours and crawled to the end of the chaise and cupped his shaft. She licked its sticky hardness and opened for him.

He fisted her hair and drove his cock deep into her throat. The warmth of her lips and the pressure from her tongue as he fucked her mouth was all it took, and he wrapped his hand around his shaft again and pulled back from her with an audible pop.

A feral rumble at the back of his throat was the only warning he gave and Rose lifted her face to the spurts as he came, lapping at the glaze on her lips and cheek.

Miguel cupped her chin and kissed her before pulling her into his arms, her face against his stomach. He stroked her hair and then laid her back on the couch, crawling between her legs again, only this time, tangling his with hers as they drifted into sated sleep.

Chapter Four

Late afternoon spilled across the bed in a fine stream, winking in Rose's face. Cracking one eye open, she pulled her covers higher and rolled over into the expanse of Miguel's back.

Both eyes flew open and she blinked, disoriented panic melting into sharp reality.

The night flooded back in detail, and she slumped against the pillows, her hand flung over her forehead. She muttered an expletive.

Maybe it was a hot dream.

Not a chance.

The soreness between her legs and the sticky feel of sweat and…she squeezed her eyes shut. *Ugh*. She let him come on her face.

Yup. Good morning sunshine.

She sat up, wincing with the effort. The bruised, raw feel in her lady parts a poignant reminder of just how real this was. That and the tenderness at her throat.

No. That part couldn't be real.

Miguel must have given her some kind of hallucinogenic or some new Spanish fly aphrodisiac street drug.

Yeah right, sweetheart. Try again.

"Miguel. Wake up. We need to talk."

She reached across and shook his shoulder, but jerked her hand back. He was cold. Ice cold.

Holy crap.

She rolled him over to peer at his pale face. His lips weren't blue, but he was deathly still.

Rose scrambled to her knees on the bed to check his pulse. Nothing. Oh my God. CPR? What was the rule? Two breaths to thirty compressions?

She lifted his chin and opened his mouth to check his airway. No obstruction. Pinching his nose, she blew two breaths into his lungs and then laced her fingers, pressing the heel of her palm against his breastbone, counting *One, two, three...* pumping in measured compressions.

She repeated the sequence, looking for the telltale rise in his chest, but it didn't budge, and his body was still like ice.

Vampires are immortal, right? So they can't die. Can they?

Minutes passed and sweat formed on her forehead and between her breasts as she tried to resuscitate him. Damn. Under normal circumstances she'd call 911 or the police or someone.

Come on, you're a smart woman for Christ's sake. THINK!

The Red Veil.

This was one of their backrooms. They had to know what to do. They could send for an ambulance or whatever they did for the unresponsive undead.

She blinked. Wait. This wasn't The Red Veil. The last thing she remembered was the room with the gauzy sheer curtains and private orgy cubbies.

Rose whirled around, her eyes taking in everything. The floor to ceiling windows with blackout curtains. The minimalist style of the furniture. The king-sized bed and sitting area. It looked like a hotel room.

But she didn't remember leaving the club with Miguel. Ugh. She was a living episode of Law and Order.

She pressed her fingers into her temples trying to focus. Okay...Hotel room equaled phone, phone equaled front desk.

Taking the sheet with her, she wrapped herself toga style and climbed off the bed for the night table on the opposite side. Bingo.

She picked up the receiver and dialed zero.

"The Mandarin Hotel, how may I direct your call?"

The Mandarin? Her hand froze on the receiver and she looked at Miguel's motionless form. The man had taste and means as well as skills in the bedroom. She finally met a guy who rocked her world and the universe takes him after a single booty call. She closed her eyes and exhaled at the sad injustice.

"Are you there? Hello? How may I direct your call?"

"Yes...I need you to call... I think my..." she hesitated. Her what? Boyfriend? No. One night stand? Uhm...hell no...

"Ma'am? Hello?"

"Yes... My friend is unresponsive. I can't wake him."

"I'll take care of it, ma'am. Hang tight and I'll have hotel management call you."

Rose hung up the phone and sat in the dim light chewing on her lip. How the hell was she going to explain this to whoever got there? She didn't even know if she had any clothes.

She glanced around and spotted her bag on the chair across from the coffee table along with her coat. Only she didn't remember returning to the coat check and she'd left her purse at the table in the VIP lounge.

How could she be so irresponsible?

She walked into the sitting area, shoving the cotton sheet under her butt on the end of the couch. Unzipping the top of her purse, she reached for her phone only to find it dead as well.

Figures. Poetic, even.

She exhaled, running a hand through her long dark hair. What time was it? What day for that matter. Cassie probably had the police looking for her by now.

The clock on the nightstand read 4pm. She'd lost an entire day, and once the police and first responders got here, she was going to lose a lot more in terms of dignity, not to mention a stint in Bellevue's psych ward if she mentioned vampires.

"Stupid," she murmured under her breath. How would she face her colleagues when this hit the papers? Her family?

Purse under her arm and sheet in tow, she stalked to the bathroom to clean up as best she could. This was not the romantic ending she envisioned. A sticky good-bye after a one-night-stand was one thing, or worse, facing your fantasy and realizing you don't want it to be good-bye. But this?

Rose closed the door and took inventory of her face in the mirror. Puffy lips and smeared make-up. Great. Add in disheveled hair, a bruised throat and a distinct post-sex stink and she stole the crown from Edie as skank of the month.

The first responders would most likely get here before she was done showering, so it was a top and tails whore's bath for her, and she frowned at how well it fit the scenario. Ugh. This was so much worse than doing the walk of shame with ruined panties in your purse.

At least she enjoyed herself for once in her life. The memory of what she and Miguel did and how they did it and the dirty talk that came out of her mouth, sent a crimson blush from her chest to her ears.

She'd never done anything like this before. In fact, she scoffed at girls who hooked up after barely making a guy's acquaintance. Rose Landry was too independent and had worked too hard to throw her reputation away on a seedy hook up.

Except, this wasn't seedy.

Last night was unbelievable and Miguel was definitely someone to haunt her dreams, even if she never got to say goodbye.

Tears pricked her eyes, but she brushed them away. She needed to be strong and emotionless. It was time to break out every lawyerly trait she'd learned over the past decade.

She opened the linen closet beside the toilet for a towel and washcloth, only to find her dress, bra and shoes placed neatly inside. Even her panties were clipped to a hanger, clean.

Either she did hand laundry last night or Miguel was truly one in a million.

Fresh tears threatened at the thought of never seeing him again. Never getting to ask the thousands of questions she had about his life, his existence.

She hated unanswered questions and loose ends. But this went deeper. She had been given a gift. Shown something amazing and she never felt more alive. What she thought would be a frightening and a psychosis-inducing scenario was actually thrilling and romantic, and it had been ripped from her before she had the chance to savor it fully.

If she thought she was lonely before, life was going to be hell now.

Rose dug out a washcloth and a towel and turned on the tap. She lathered the soap and washed the parts of her body that needed it most before using the hotel's facewash to scrub off last night's makeup. Rinsing, she groped with one eye open for the towel.

"Hey there, sexy."

Rose jumped, dropping the towel and knocking the tray of sample-sized toiletries clattering to the floor.

"Miguel!" she stared at his reflection in the mirror, afraid to move. "You're alive!"

"What?" He stared back at her clearly trying to reconcile her fear and confusion. It dawned on him then, she had awakened before dusk.

He flashed a sheepish smile. "Rose, I'm fine. Let me explain."

Scrambling to pick up the towel and spilled toiletries, she backed away clutching the damp towel to her naked chest.

"Explain? I did CPR on you, Miguel! I called for help. It'll be here any minute."

He shook his head. "No it won't."

Speechless, she opened her mouth but then closed it again.

Miguel was as naked as she, and he looked and smelled even better than she remembered.

A swath of early winter twilight illuminated the room from where he opened the curtains, and the purple light, highlighted his swarthy good looks.

"This has got to be a dream or a residual high from the champagne."

He shook his head. "This is no dream, and you didn't drink that much. What happened between us is very real. As am I."

"But you had no pulse. You weren't breathing."

"It's called death sleep. It's part of what I am."

"Death sleep?" Her hand involuntarily went to her throat. "I can't handle this, Miguel. I thought you were dead." She looked at him. "I mean dead-dead. As in, never waking again."

He didn't answer, but the look on his face spoke volumes.

With a high pitched whimper, Rose sank to the cold tile, her fingers knotted in the damp terrycloth.

Miguel took a step toward her and squatted down. He slipped two fingers under her chin and lifted her face. "Are you sorry we met? Sorry for what we did together? I'm not."

Slowly, Rose shook her head. "I had the time of my life."

He smiled, running the pad of his thumb over her bottom lip. "Me too. You're very special."

You're very special. She cringed inwardly. That was a guy's get-out-of-jail free line if she ever heard one. Like telling a date he's a nice guy or that it's not them, it's you, when you don't want to see them again.

When she didn't reply, he nodded, acknowledging her silence before straightening to his full height. "You must be starved. I'll order room service."

She looked at him, her face tilted up, studying him. "Why is help not coming if you didn't know I called?"

"Because." He held his hand out to help her up. "This hotel is operated by a friend. He understands my kind and their needs."

"Kind?"

"Vampires, Rose. It's okay to say the word. I'm not ashamed of what I am. I got over that a century and a half ago."

She swallowed hard. "You must understand how this sounds in the cold light of day. I accept what you are, but my rational mind is having trouble wrapping around it."

"Around what?"

"Vampires. The existence of the supernatural... and *us.* You have to explain."

"Explain what? Ask me anything."

"THIS, for one." She pointed to their naked reflections in the bathroom mirror.

Confused, he looked at her. "A vampire not casting a reflection is an old wives tale, Rose. It's an oral myth from when mirrors were backed with pure silver. Our aversion to silver is true, but the rest?" He shook his head.

He paused. "I can understand your hesitation about the supernatural, especially since we skate so far under the human radar…"

"That's not what I meant," she interrupted. "I mean me…*this*." She ran her hands over her body. "Why me?"

He put his hands on her shoulders and turned them both to face the mirror.

"You are a beautiful, desirable woman, Rose. I told you that last night. I chose you for many different reasons. Your humor, your humility, your loveliness." He pressed his stiffening cock against her ass. "See what you do to me even now? I can't get enough of you, and I don't mean just your blood."

Their eyes locked and when Miguel skimmed his hand around her waist and trailed his fingers to gently cup her breast, the same electricity jolted through Rose's belly as it did the night before.

"Nothing has changed for me, *querida*, and from the smell of you, nothing has changed for you either."

Heat crawled to her ears. "I tried to wash as best I could, but there was no time."

With a wicked grin, Miguel lifted his hand to cover her mouth. "That is not the scent I mean."

He slid his fingers to the juncture between her legs and stroked the quickly moistening flesh. Bringing his fingers to his lips, he licked her essence. "This is the scent I mean." He moved his wet fingers to her lips. "Open your mouth, Rose."

Her lips parted and he slipped his thumb between them. "Suck."

With a sigh, she drew his thumb into her mouth, swirling her tongue over the rough pad, tasting the salt of their combined scents.

Using his free hand, he cupped the full weight of her breast, squeezing and massaging the soft flesh, rolling her nipple between his fingers until her head lolled back on his shoulder and her jaw went slack.

He pulled his thumb from her mouth, leaning down to lick her bare throat and shoulder.

"If you wish to wash properly, the shower is right there," he whispered against her skin.

Rose shivered, opening her eyes to see his in the mirror. They held the same dark need ringed with a red aura as they had before. He was the predator and she was the prey once again, and she shivered, not caring in the least.

He stepped away from her to turn on the spray, letting the hot water run until the bathroom filled with steam.

Moving to sweep Rose into his arms, she balked at first, but he lifted her full figure into his arms with ease.

"Never try to hide yourself, *mi amor*. Never be anything but proud of your body, in your ability to please any man as well as yourself. You are a true woman."

He kissed her, stepping carefully into the hot spray before putting her down. Her soft curves skimmed his hard chest and thighs as he let her down, allowing her to feel every inch of him as he felt every one of her curves.

"In Spanish we have a saying," he whispered between kisses. "Bone is for the dog. Woman is for the man." He broke their kiss and locked his gaze with hers. "Do not fear me, Rose."

"I'm not afraid of you, Miguel. Maybe you're the drug and lonely women like me don't stand a chance. Maybe it's all the romance novels I read. Maybe I'm crazy, but I know one thing that is certain..." She wrapped her hand around his hard shaft and squeezed. "I want you, too."

He hissed, covering her hand with his, moving in unison as they both stroked his cock. "Romance is good for the soul, even if you're not sure you still possess one."

At that moment her heart clenched, and she wanted to wrap him in her arms and never let go, but she didn't.

She knew nothing about Miguel other than he was a sex-on-a-stick supernatural who rocked her world, and from the feel of his cock in her hand and the juice dripping down her thighs, he was ready to rock it again.

Impossible or not, I could fall in love with him. She chastised herself for the thought. "Oh, for fuck's sake!" *Be in the moment, Rose. Hot guy in hand. Literally.*

He froze, and she cringed at the amused look on his face, realizing she had spoken out loud.

"For fuck's sake to be sure," he laughed, spinning her around and pinning her back to the tile wall. "Having second thoughts?"

She spread her legs and rubbed her pussy against his hard sex. "I'm all yours."

He lifted her hips and pressed her shoulders to the tile, slipping his member inside her waiting slit. "Mine," he growled.

Her legs turned to jelly as she wrapped them around his back and he buried himself, balls deep. She hissed as tender, used flesh protested, stretching again to take the full length of him.

Shivers of pleasure and pain sliced through her body and her muscles clenched in a rapid-fire climax.

Hot water cascaded over them, their bodies slick and slippery as Miguel thrust, pumping high and hard. His fingers gripped her thick thighs, sinking into the soft flesh, shoving her further onto his cock.

Balls high and tight, his entire body tensed as he came as quickly as she, his release echoing against the tile.

Panting, he dipped his forehead to hers, and sucked in a ragged breath.

"You okay?" She nudged his head up.

His eyes were an eerie red and his lip was bleeding. She gripped the back of his neck and leaned in to kiss him, licking his blood from his lips, moaning at the taste.

He chuckled, letting her down slowly. "Don't be so surprised. Vampire blood is a narcotic. It's part of the lure."

He paused, dipping his hand to her sex, stroking her again. "But not as much of a lure as this...or this." His fingers trailed the thick femoral artery in her groin.

"May I?" he asked, his eyes dark with hunger. "I'll make it worth your while." he teased.

Taking her hands, he helped her to the floor, leaning her back gently. He kissed her mouth, her throat, her collarbone and the space between her breasts, working his lips and tongue across her skin until he buried his face in her crotch.

He spread her legs wide, using the warm water gathered on the shower basin to tease and massage before dipping his head to her sex. She moaned at the feel of his tongue, but when he pulled his mouth away and slipped his fingers inside, she tensed.

He licked her inner thighs, kissing and teasing her flesh as his fingers worked her pussy. She gasped and lifted her hips on the crest of another climax and that was his moment.

With a moan, his fangs slid into her groin, piercing the thick artery. Potent blood rushed straight from her racing heart into his mouth, the force of her pulse almost too much for him.

He pulled from her vein, pacing himself as each orgasmic spasm hit her, and when she arched, exploding full against his palm, he drew deep.

Visceral lifeblood thick with carnal endorphins hit his throat, and he groaned with the sheer pleasure of its taste, but held back from taking too much.

Rose slumped back as exhaustion claimed her and he licked the wound, sealing it completely. Miguel wrapped her in his arms, and they laid in the warm water pooling at the base of the large shower.

"You good?" she asked.

"Perfect." He kissed her nose. "What about you?"

"A little light-headed, but I'll be okay." She paused. "I will, right?"

He laughed. "Of course. We'll get you fixed up good as new and ready to go home in no time."

She nodded, but a shadow fell at his words.

"There's no reason to be sad, Rose. This was an amazing adventure, no?"

With a sigh she nodded again. It was too good, to be true. "This was…"

He placed his finger over her lips. "Wonderful, like you."

"You don't have to placate me, Miguel. I'll be fine. I'm just not used to being a one hit wonder."

He laughed. "One hit wonder? At last count I tapped this fine ass at least eight times since midnight." He grabbed her soft ample flesh in a playful squeeze.

"You know that's not what I meant, but it's okay. No regrets."

"You speak as though we'll never see each other again." He leaned over her. "Is that what you want?"

She sat up, her eyes searching his. "Of course not."

He shrugged. "Then why speak of it. I have no intention of letting this be the last time I taste you or take you."

The need to possess and claim made his mouth water and his fangs lengthen, but Rose wasn't ready, so he tamped down on the feeling. "We have much to learn from each other."

She smiled. "Yes, we do."

He put his finger over her lips again. "Much to learn and much to choose."

She nodded and then looked away, playing with the swirl of water near the drain. "Miguel, this vampire thing. It's exciting, but it's scary..." Rose chewed on the corner of her mouth.

He sighed silently. She let him take her body, her blood, but she wasn't ready for him. Not truly.

"Look at me, *mi amor.*"

She turned back to him and he cupped her chin and blew into her face. Immediately her eyes glazed over.

"Here." He pierced the pad of his thumb with one fang and slipped it between her lips.

She licked the blood that pooled and drew the digit into her mouth. Miguel made a fist and squeezed, letting his blood puddle over her tongue, and she swallowed. An immediate peace settled over her and she sighed.

He pulled his thumb from her mouth and squeezed his fist again, only this time he spread her legs and circled her sex, marking her inner walls with his blood, letting it mix with his essence.

"We had one hot night and you'll remember it always. You'll remember the ordinary man who opened you to sensuality, to raw pleasure and to acceptance. And when we meet again, I will be that ordinary man. No more than that. Ordinary."

He cupped the back of her head and kissed her, tracing the shape of her full bottom lip with his tongue.

Rose's eyes fluttered open and she smiled.

"Miguel."

He met her smile with one of his own.

"You dozed off."

She sat up and rubbed her face with her palm. "I guess. I feel so funny. A little light-headed." She smirked, running a hand through her wet hair. "I suppose it's because I haven't eaten anything but you in almost twenty-four hours." She reached over and teased one finger across his cock.

"Bad girl."

She laughed. "Come on. Let's dry off and get some food. I have to get home soon. My sister has probably reported me to missing persons."

She stepped out of the shower and wrapped herself in a towel, tossing one to him. "Hey, tomorrow is Sunday. Why don't you come to my place, early? I've got a great apartment with a terrific view of the river. Lots of sun exposure."

He glanced at the water swirling at his feet. "I can't...at least not until much later. Maybe we can have dinner and see a movie."

She nodded with a smile and the beauty of her pierced him to the core. *His.* For all time. And if time is what it took, then so be it. What else did a vampire have but time?

Chapter Five

Rose kissed him goodbye, waving as she climbed into the cab. "Call me later!"

The door closed and he stood alone on the curb.

"You glamoured her, didn't you?"

Miguel shrugged watching the yellow cab merge into the midtown throng. "I had no choice, Trevor. Her doubt and fear were palpable."

"I heard she thought you were dead."

Miguel smirked, but then turned to his friend confused. "Yet, she let me take her blood as well as her body."

"Humans are fickle creatures, especially when their passions are high. They lose their balance in the heat of the moment."

Miguel gave him a resigned laugh. "What would you have done? Keep her and let her anxiety grow or wipe her memory so there might be a chance she could love you?"

The wind blew and the two vampires walked back into the hotel lobby. "I would have kept her in a constant state of arousal. That way, she'd never question."

"Not funny. Especially since your wife is undead and you don't have to deal with the drama."

"No, but certainly fun to think about." Trevor laughed. "And undead or not, Margot is still female. Drama is part of the luscious package." He clapped his friend on the shoulder. "Come on, I'll buy you a drink."

They both turned as a yellow cab stopped short at the curb, tires screeching.

The rear passenger door flew open and Rose scrambled from the backseat.

Stunned, Miguel ignored Trevor's discreet goodbye and walked curbside to meet her. "Are you okay? Did something happen?"

She nodded. "You happened. I couldn't leave things the way we did."

"I don't understand." He shook his head. "I thought we were seeing each other tomorrow?"

Rose grinned. "We are, but I have something to ask you first."

Miguel braced himself. "What?"

She lifted her face and planted a quick kiss on his lips. "Can you pick up a large bottle of B-Complex vitamins before you come over tomorrow? I already have tons of orange juice. We're going to have to work together to keep my blood count up."

"I...I...how?"

She bit her tongue not to laugh at how flustered he looked. "It's simple, really. For as much as I'm a hopeless romantic, I'm enough of a cynic not to trust my feelings to anyone other than myself. I didn't want to lose you before we gave this a chance, and I knew enough vampire mythology to suspect you might try and hypnotize me into forgetting we ever met."

He chuckled at where this was going. "Glamour, not hypnotize."

"See? I was right. But the key ingredient in either is a willingness to relinquish control. You would have had a better chance glamouring me when I was begging for your cock than waiting until afterward."

Impressed, he flashed a grudging grin. "Now she tells me." Miguel gathered her in his arms. "Are you always so stubborn?"

"Yup, but tenacious is a better word." She nodded, resting her chin against his chest. "It's what makes me such a good lawyer. In this case it worked to my advantage. I was up for anything, except being sent away without my memories."

"I didn't take your memories. I just altered the facts...or tried to." He kissed her hair, inhaling her scent.

"In my world it's a criminal offense to alter facts," she whispered against his chest. "Promise me you won't do it again."

"In mine it is sometimes a necessary evil, but I promise. Never again."

"So, now that you know, *I know*, about you and your world, and you know I'm willing to give this a chance, doubts and all, where do we go from here?"

He kissed her quick and stepped back, taking her hand. "Why don't you show me the amazing view from your apartment? We can stop for your vitamins on the way."

She laughed, tucking herself under his arm. "And I thought this was going to be an ordinary weekend."

"Ordinary?" He gave her ass a playful slap, steering her toward the cab. "Never. That's a word we will never use again."

⸺❊⸺

...Miguel and Rose are just an introduction to whet your appetites for the world of the Red Veil and the hook ups started there. Longer, more fangaliscious stories are ahead. And don't forget the two character interviews at the back of the book just for this special edition paperback!

Just turn the page...

Marianne Morea

The Red Veil Diaries

Tempt Me

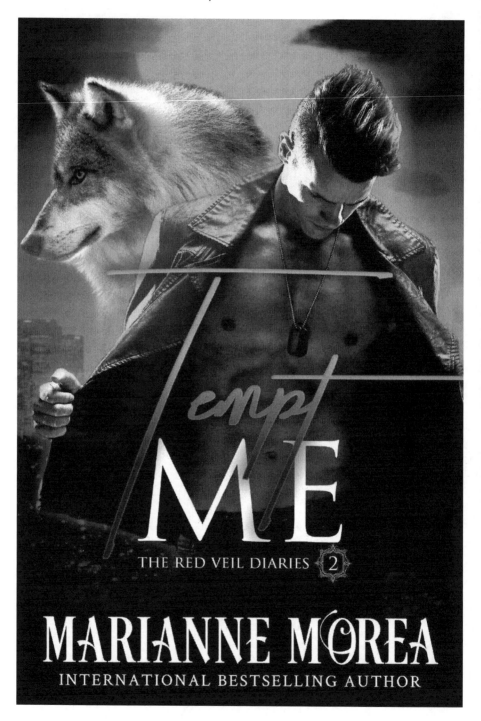

Tempt ME

THE RED VEIL DIARIES ②

MARIANNE MOREA

INTERNATIONAL BESTSELLING AUTHOR

"There is a charm about the forbidden that makes it unspeakably desirable."

~Mark Twain

Chapter One

"*S*ébastien wants to see you. He's on his way down, now."

Abigail looked up from her receipts. Her lips parted for a moment before she pressed them together instead of asking why she was summoned. The reason didn't matter.

"Thank you, Calypso. Tell Bette to have a decanter ready in the VIP lounge and make sure she knows the offering is for Sébastien. Have one of the boys keep a look out. Buzz me the minute they sense him approaching."

Abigail flicked her hand, dismissing the young woman and returned to her accounts.

Calypso stood in the doorway, fidgeting.

"What? For God's sake, stop twiddling and speak up."

"He...he..." the young Créole swallowed. "He never steps foot in the club. Should we be worried?"

Abigail put down her pen, her undead eyes fixed on the girl. "We?"

Calypso's gaze fell to her feet.

Inhaling, Abigail took in the swash of nervous color pinking the dusky hollow of the young woman's cheeks, the telltale rush of blood making the vampire's mouth water and her semi-retracted fangs, tingle.

"What the master wants is none of your concern. You will do as you're told." Abigail's blasé tone said one thing, but the staccato *tap-tap* of her pen on the desk hinted she shared the girl's misgivings, at least somewhat.

"We all have a role to play, Calypso, and it is best you remember the pecking order explained when you were given a second chance with us." Stifling her nervous drumming, Abigail clasped her hands together on the desk and studied the girl.

"Compassion is not a virtue inherent in the undead. You have Rémy to thank for us not casting you from the shadow house you helped infect with that disgusting virus." She snorted, glancing toward the pile of invoices on her desk.

"HepZ. More like Werewolf rabies," she murmured to herself before sliding her eyes back to the jumpy human. "If the decision were left to me, I would have fed you to the youngbloods."

A small grin let the tips of Abigail's fangs glint for effect. "Youngbloods are so…*enthusiastic*. But what can I say? There's something lusciously addictive about cracking open a thick-with-marrow bone once you've drained the body."

Calypso fled and a satisfied smirk ticked the corner of the vampire's mouth. With a sigh, she pushed herself from her chair and eyed the ornate mirror hanging above the credenza across from her desk.

Why Sébastien insisted on decorating The Red Veil with so much of the silvered glass was beyond her. It was the same in their private lair at *Les Sanctuaire*.

Arrogant and vain. Then again, that described their master vampire to a tee.

Nonetheless, Abigail checked her look and smoothed her strawberry blond hair and straightened her pencil skirt, giving the deep, ruffled neckline of her sleeveless shirt a brush. Matched with a pair of strappy stilettos, the classic style was her signature look.

She was sex appeal wrapped in voluptuous sophistication, taking pains to maintain a certain *je ne sais quoi,* an elegant old Hollywood style that doubled as both lure and camouflage.

Except for Sophia Loren, the iconic starlets she rivalled were all dead, but there was an undeniable timelessness about them that fascinated Abigail, and time was something a vampire had in abundance. The fact she shared the same goddess-lush curves, full hips and breasts made the fascination all the more real, letting her revel in her statuesque body.

As for the mirrors, one didn't question the head of New York's Vampire Council. Sébastien DuLac's word was law as far as she and everyone else was concerned.

A knock on the door took Abigail from her thoughts. "Yes?"

The door cracked open and Bette tilted her head in, the usual humor in the young vampire's eyes tempered by the unexpected visit. "He's coming through the doors, *now*."

"Is everything prepared?"

Bette nodded. "AB negative. Fresh and warm, with an I.V. tap in case the boss wants more."

"Perfect, thanks. I'll be right out."

Abigail noticed the spidery blue rising in conspicuous outlines across the white column of Bette's throat. "When was the last time you fed?" Serious concern laced her usually clipped tone.

The short, full-figured vampire shrugged, and her black chin-length bob swung forward to hide the trace evidence of her thirst. "I haven't had the chance. You know Sébastien refuses to drink bagged blood. I had no choice but to use outside assets."

That meant calling around to nearby shadow houses for available donors with the right blood type. Once again, Bette proved herself both quick-witted and invaluable.

Abigail exhaled. "You can't allow yourself to hunger, Bette. It's bad...both for you and for business. Since I took over the club, you've been my right hand and my best friend. I won't have you suffering. Find Calypso. Take what you need from her, but don't kill the little twit. She may prove useful at some point."

Bette's lips twitched. "Some point? You know, people are taking bets on how long it will take for you to eat her — and I don't mean opening a vein."

Abigail's lips parted, but then she pressed them together. "That's none of their business."

A snort of laughter escaped the young vampire's mouth. "You're right. It's no one's business, but for cripe's sake, Abby, you're wound so tight you're going to snap. You need release, and with something that doesn't require batteries."

Abigail's eyes snapped toward the young vampire. "You do realize I'm your boss, right? Not to mention an elder."

Bette waived a pale hand. "*Yeah, yeah.* I know who and what you are, Abigail. You've played the credentials card more times than I can count over the past century, but I'm your best friend. I want to see you happy."

Abigail's eyes dropped to a file on her desk and she opened the dull manila, pretending to scan one of the pages inside. "I *am* happy. I have the ear of the master vampire *and* his trust. What more could I want?"

Bette moved to perch on the end of one of the chairs in front of Abigail's desk. "Plenty. I'm not talking about true love here, Abs. I'm talking about taking a lover — preferably one who'll fuck you so hard, your toes will curl in an orgasm to make a century of celibacy worth the wait."

Abigail snorted. "You watch too many movies."

The young vampire stood, but crossed her arms in front of her chest. "I don't watch movies."

Tapping her pen, Abigail eyed her.

Bette grinned. "Okay, I do, but not to the extent you think. I get my freak on in the flesh and so should *you.*

Hell, Abby — blindfold a youngblood and ride him raw, or take a human and make a night of it, sex *and* dinner. Just take someone."

"Bette, please." Abigail exhaled, lacing her fingers again.

Inhaling, Bette shut up. "Okay, I get it. It's none of my business. At least promise me you'll think about it? Your cranky is reaching epic, Abs. For realz."

"Realz? What are you, a millennial? Last I checked you were ninety-something years old." A smirk tickled the corner of Abigail's mouth and she waved the young vampire out.

"Go feed, Bette. I hear what you're saying, but I'm asking you to stop or I might have to snap on *you*." She angled her head at her friend. "Calypso is probably hiding in the employee's lounge. She's A-neg. Your favorite."

Bette's nostrils flared and her eyes dilated with thirst. With a quick pivot, she turned on her heel toward the door but then looked back at her friend past her shoulder. "Not fair, Abby," she added with a wink. "Not when you know I have no willpower."

She disappeared, leaving Abigail alone. The vampire locked her office door and walked down the hall toward the club's private entrance, the subtle red paisley carpet beneath her feet muffling her already stealthy footsteps.

Anticipating her approach, a youngblood bouncer held the door open and she glided by, trailing her fingers across his muscled chest. There were perks to being in charge, and one of them was hand picking the eye candy. Male and female. Living and undead.

Her eyes traveled the length of his body, pausing at the thick bulge behind his fly. Maybe Bette was right.

"Come find me after my meeting," she said, ignoring the mix of fear and startled surprise on the man's face. " —

and don't disappoint." Her teeth grazed her full bottom lip, one fang scraping the tender flesh as a tease.

She didn't need a reply. The youngblood would come for her in more ways than one. A smug smile tugged the corner of her mouth. Control made her panties wet. She grinned to herself. Maybe a bit of fear was good and the youngblood would work even harder to please her.

She moved passed the velvet ropes and into the VIP lounge to await Sébastien, making a mental note to do something nice for Bette without her knowing. Too many people were ass kissers. It was nice to have one person to give it to her straight.

As instructed, the private meeting was set towards the back. One glance told her everything was as requested, with a crystal decanter in place flanked by two long-stemmed champagne flutes.

The red tufted couches were freshly brushed, but Abigail didn't dare sit. Years of acting as both emissary and assistant for the Head of the Vampire Council taught her that.

She caught a trace of lavender in the air and her eyes moved toward the carpeted steps. Sébastien swept passed the staff, ascending the stairs as though floating. As always, he was ageless and impeccable. From his fitted charcoal suit to his soft soled, handmade Italian leather shoes.

"*Chéri.*" His dark eyes flashed with continental charm, and he leaned in to kiss both her cheeks. "You look as lovely as ever. I hope our little meeting doesn't take you from more pressing matters."

As if she'd ever admit the imposition. Abigail greeted the man's sly smirk with a disarming smile. "Meeting with you is never an imposition."

He chuckled. "How well you've learned, my dear."
He inhaled and a full grin spread across his lips. "And you
remembered my favorite. How thoughtful."

Sébastien took a seat, and that was her cue to pour.
Abigail picked up the decanter and gave the crimson
contents a gentle swirl to gauge its clotting level.

"It looks perfect." Nostrils flaring, Sébastien held up
his glass, licking his lips as the coppery liquid filled the cut
glass.

"Please, pour a glass for yourself as well, and we will
toast the club and all you've done to make *The Red Veil* a
success," he complemented.

She did as she was told and then placed the carafe on
the table before taking a seat across from the master
vampire.

"My dear," Sébastien began. "I fully grasp the pitfalls
inherent in attaining a certain level of notoriety in a city
such as Manhattan, while at the same time maintaining the
secrecy of our kind. You are to be applauded, especially in
keeping the privacy of our backrooms unequaled
anywhere in our world."

Abigail inclined her head. "It's been my pleasure."

He raised his glass in salute and then drained it dry,
smacking his lips. "And that brings me to the purpose of
our meeting."

She cocked her head. "Privacy?"

"No, *mon petit*. Pleasure."

Confused, she raised one eyebrow. "I don't
understand."

He placed his glass on the small, round drink table
and then wiped his mouth on a napkin. "Pleasure is the
purpose of this club, is it not?"

She nodded. "I suppose—"

He shook his head at her pause. "Your hesitation is
unnecessary. The pursuit of pleasure is the primary reason

we opened our doors. That, and to provide our kind with a steady flow of fresh blood.

"The club has stocked the blood vaults of many a shadow house in this city and beyond, but sadly, those reserves have been severely diminished because of the recent viral unpleasantness. If it wasn't for certain connections, none of us would be here today."

She gave him a wary nod.

"It is those connections I wish to discuss."

Abigail refilled his glass, waiting for him to elaborate.

"We have backrooms to satisfy every desire our kind can fancy, is that not so?"

Abigail quickly bobbed her head. "It is, although we try very hard to keep certain appetites under control and within the confines of human law. Especially when mortals are the chosen plaything."

It was his turn to nod. "Yes, yes. And again, you are to be commended." He sipped from the refilled champagne flute, considering. "You are aware of the debt of gratitude we owe the Were community, are you not?"

The question was rhetorical, but she nodded anyway, ignoring her inner cringe.

"Good. The Alpha of the Brethren is sending new envoys to help us maintain the health of our shadow houses, now that we know irregularities are possible."

"Irregularities?" she asked.

The master vampire's raised eyebrow made her wince inside. The last thing she wanted was for the master vampire to think her inept.

"The new envoys are coming to sniff out those infected who slipped through the preventative measures originally put in place."

"Sébastien, I wasn't aware there were enough cases to merit additional envoys."

"Our collaboration with the Weres was done in haste. We had to stem the pandemic threatening our community here and beyond, and as with anything done in haste—" he shrugged, not offering any more of an explanation. His eyes found hers, nonetheless. "In any case, these envoys are not additional. They are replacements."

"Mitch isn't coming back?" she asked, surprised.

Sébastien shook his head. "He accepted his birthright as Alpha in his own territory. I knew this was a possibility, and to be honest, it is as it should be. He is from the northern climes and deserves to claim what is rightfully his."

She shuddered, thinking about the cold and isolation of the Canadian north. "What about Detective Martinez? He did us quite a service during the ugliest part of the epidemic. He is only half-Were, but he knows our kind and our inner workings."

"Ryan has chosen to stay in California. He will be missed."

Nonplussed, she lifted a hand. "Then who does that leave?"

"Sean and Lily are coming to introduce the two they've chosen to take over. As you know, I trust them implicitly."

Abigail exhaled harshly. "So the king and queen of the Weres are coming to deliver us a pair of pups who have no idea of our world and whom you expect me to pet sit." Her hazel eyes flashed as she looked at Sébastien, ignoring his warning glare.

"Please, Sébastien," she pressed. "Don't allow this. It wasn't that long ago Weres and Vampires were polite advisories at best. Hell, our kind is still considered a taboo in their circles!"

"Your insolence is bordering on insubordination Abigail and I will not have it. The Alpha of the Brethren and his mate are not only allies, but friends. This show of sarcastic contempt is beneath you. You will do well to treat them with the respect due their station. If not for their intervention we would have all tasted final death."

She sighed. "As you wish, Sébastien. When are they and the envoys set to arrive?"

"Tonight."

Abigail balked. "Tonight?" Aghast, she put her untouched glass on the table, its crimson contents sloshing over the rim.

"And how am I supposed to welcome these envoys?" She lifted an agitated hand and then let it drop, her voice raising an octave. "What preparations do you expect on such short notice? Are they to be given rooms in *Les Sanctuaire*? Is there a full moon element I need to be aware of? I have no idea how to provide for the fanged and furry, Sébastien. What if they start howling at the disco ball?"

It was on the tip of her tongue to add dog-walking services and regular flea baths to her rant, but Sébastien's scowl left her biting her tongue.

"Enough!" Sébastien's lips were a thin line as he waited for Abigail to compose herself.

"I am well aware of your dislike for our dual-natured allies, but you will do everything in your power to make them comfortable.

"So far they have shown themselves worthy of an alliance. They are a far cry from the ill-mannered, wild beasts we once knew. As a show of good faith, I have invited them to partake of the pleasures here at the club."

His fixed glare met her eyes. "I will leave the particulars to you and trust you to stay within our constraints. As for the new envoys and their accommodations, Sean has already provided them a place for the duration of their assignment. We are simply to welcome them to our city."

"Will Sean and the woman be here as well?"

"Why is it so hard for you to say her name? It's Lily, and Rémy's little witch is hardly a threat, Abigail."

She frowned at Sébastien's casual use of the endearment. "Perhaps. But there are still those of us who feel she has too much sway over too many of our kind, moreover, Rémy's pet name for her only adds to the perception. Hell, the woman's not even a born supernatural." She stifled a smirk. Anything four-legged and furry deserved a pet's name.

"Abigail —" Sébastien's warning tone reminded her, he missed nothing.

She wiped the amused grin from her face. "I'm sorry. Of course, I will do what I can to welcome them properly."

Sébastien stood. "*Trés bien*. They will arrive at eleven tonight. And to answer your earlier question, no, Lily and Sean won't be staying. They've invited me to accompany them as they race the moon along the beaches on Long Island." He grinned. "It should make for an interesting night."

He swept past her toward the exit, leaving her to deal with the details.

"Interesting? Try cringe-worthy," she muttered, with a frustrated exhale.

She caught Bette's eye as the young vampire poked her head in from around the side of the bar.

"Come out, come out, little mouse."

Bette chuckled, grabbing a clean glass from the bar and walked straight to the decanter. "Waste not, want not, and I certainly want."

"Please tell me you didn't kill my assistant," Abigail ground out, sitting back with her own glass.

Bette shook her head. "She's gone M.I.A. To be honest Abby, the girl's not cut out for our way of life."

Abigail looked at her halfway into pouring. "What makes you say that?"

Bette shrugged. "Gut feeling. Plus, she's been hanging around the paparazzi staked out nightly in front of the club." She took the decanter from Abigail's hand and finished pouring. "Maybe it's time to show her the backrooms. If she survives, she'll never go near the press again. If not—" she shrugged, again.

"Maybe the best thing would be to change her. Nothing coerces team spirit like thirst," Abigail suggested, but dismissed the thought.

Bette tipped the crimson liquid to her waiting lips. "Did I overhear Sébastien say the wolves are at our door?"

Abigail clicked the inside of her cheek. "That you did."

The dark haired vampire licked her lips. "Well, you certainly used the right adjective, then."

"Yup. Cringe-worthy," Abigail replied, circling the rim of her glass with her finger.

Bette smirked, laughing. "No, babe. *Interesting*."

"*Babe*?" Abigail made a face. "I hate that slang word almost as much as I hate when you call me Abs." She eyed her underling. "For a vampire created nearly a century ago, you've certainly embraced this modern culture."

Bette shrugged. "I embrace what makes me happy. Back in the day, the very definition of a flapper was a fashionable young woman intent on enjoying herself and flouting conventional standards of behavior. So why change when I've got even more reason to push the envelope?"

"You and Sébastien both seem to enjoy challenging convention."

Bette eyed her with another smirk. "You're doing it again."

"What?"

"Your face."

Instinctually, Abigail touched her cheek and then she looked into the chrome bar.

"Look harder, Abs. You look as though you sucked the juice out of a lemon instead of blood from a juicy vein."

Abigail crossed her arms in front of her chest, her vise grip on the stem of her flute threatening to snap the cut crystal. "I do not."

Bette laughed again. "Grip that glass any harder, babe, and you'll need my tweezers to pick the shards out of your fingers."

Abigail put the glass on the table. "So, I'm a little tense." She shrugged. "It's no secret how I feel about Weres."

Bette poured herself another glass of crimson gold. "You think?"

Making a face, Abigail smoothed her hair. "I don't get the allure, and you certainly won't find me drooling over them the way you do."

Bette looked at her. "You know, I'm starting to think beneath all that haute style and red carpet glamor, is the same buttoned-up puritan Sébastien turned 250 years ago."

"That's not only untrue, it's unfair." Her eyes shifted to the tall, muscular youngblood pacing by the door for her. "Smell that?" she asked her friend. "That's the scent of lust and anticipation waiting for me at *my* request."

Bette lifted a hand and smiled. "Wow, Abs. I guess you were listening. Good. I get it. Vampires. Great. We love to fuck each other and feed from each other, but there are more flavors than just vanilla."

"I like vanilla. It goes with anything on top and I like to be on top."

She scoffed. "So I've heard, Ms. Rough Rider."

"Bette!"

"Come on, Abigail. Give in. Let your wild side take you places you've never been. Immortal life gets very boring otherwise, and don't tell me you don't agree. Take advantage of what fate placed in your lap. Open your knees and let whatever happens, lap up the juice. You like control? This is *your* club, in *your* city. You call the shots."

Abigail didn't comment.

"I'm not saying you should take up howling at the moon, but don't hate on the Weres simply because they walk a different supernatural path. After all, we all like to play in the dark." A wicked grin tugged at her lips. "So go chase a little tail tonight. Literally."

"Ugh. I'm not into bestiality, thank you very much."

Bette lifted a frustrated hand. "Vampires are sex incarnate. We're all about seduction." She paused, licking a droplet of blood from her thumb. "Think about it. The lure, the hypnotic caress, the tingle in your fangs and between your legs at the scent of fear and arousal. The visceral pleasure from fangs sinking beneath fragrant skin to penetrate a pulsing vein."

She shivered with a laugh. "I'm getting myself hot and bothered. I'd better feed for real or a club-jockey is going to be missing a pint or more, tonight." Bette waggled her eyebrows. "But I always make it worth their while."

"What you just described doesn't count." Abigail sniffed. "That's for feeding purposes only. It has nothing to do with the smelly, furred and fanged. Frankly, I want my meals the same way I like my sex, without hair in my mouth."

Bette shrugged. "Have it your way, but I heard feeding from an aroused Were can quench a vampire's thirst for a month. Besides, —" She leaned in close. "I've been told when a male Were comes, his cock head swells to twice its size and won't release until every last drop is spent."

Abigail made a face. "*That's* gross."

With a snort, Bette shook her head. "Speak for yourself. I, for one, want to see if it's true or not, and these pups tonight might be just the ticket." She winked at her friend. "Interested?"

"Not a chance, but you do you. Just don't come running to me if you end up with fleas."

Chapter Two

Abigail tugged on the youngblood's hair. "More tongue, less dribble. If I wanted a spit bath, I'd take one."

With an exhale she gripped the back of his head, forcing her slick folds further into his mouth. "That's it, *Mmmm*…use your fingers."

The muscled vampire wrapped his arm around her lower back, pulling her ass toward the edge of the office couch. Her legs spread wider to accommodate his broad shoulders. The youngblood slid two digits into her wet cleft and curled his hand, rubbing her sweet spot.

She moaned again and the sound urged him deeper. He grazed her clit with his fangs. Sucking her hard nub, he ramped up his finger-fuck to supernatural speed.

Abigail's head dropped back, and she inhaled through her teeth, her breath catching in her throat. "Yeah, baby — right there."

Visions danced through her mind as he worked her. A faceless Were, his body covered in sweat as he gripped her hips, his large cock, engorged and thrusting, its swollen head ready to burst.

The youngblood licked her deep and then pulled his fingers from her dripping sex. He unbuttoned his fly, freeing his member.

Grabbing her by the legs, he plunged his hard length into her hot, wet core. With a cry, she ground her hips up, matching him thrust for thrust. Her body tensed as her inner walls convulsed.

With a snarl, red eyes flashed, and she threw her head back, her body trembling as she exploded against his shaft.

The youngblood bared his fangs and forced his cock deeper, his razor tipped teeth sinking into her bared throat.

With a vicious shove, Abigail pushed him from her, her own blood dripping from her neck to her breasts.

Flickering images of the Were tantalized and taunted her mind, and she crawled forward, predatory and ready to strike. Holding the youngblood down, she straddled his waiting cock, impaling her wet pussy. Plunging her teeth into his chest to draw heart's blood, thick and black, she rode him hard until he cried out.

In her mind's eye, the Were howled and she shivered, spent, but wanting more. Wanting the wolf.

With a frustrated scowl, she pulled the youngblood's face to her throat and he licked her wounds closed before she did the same for him, sealing the bite on his chest.

"Get dressed and get out." She climbed off his hips, giving his thigh a shove. "You're done here."

His eyes locked on hers as he used her panties to clean the blood from his skin before tossing the ruined lace back. "Glad to be of service, ma'am," he said before tonguing her scent from his fingers.

"Get out!"

Abigail slumped onto the couch, throwing her soiled panties at the closing door. She exhaled hard, dropping her head against the leather sofa back.

"Damn you and your big mouth, Bette." Memories flooded her mind unbidden, and with them came remembered hurt and shame. She pressed the heels of her hands into her eyes, smearing her makeup.

"Who's there?" A young man's voice called from the riverbank. "Show yourself."

Fear skittered down Abigail's spine. She was warned to stay away, to keep her presence hidden. Sébastien said there was much she didn't yet understand about her new existence, but she couldn't stay away. Each night she ventured close to the settlement, hoping for a glimpse of her family.

The youth pushed through the trees, ducking the hanging branches. "Show yourself!"

Abigail froze holding her breath, but a distinct growl followed the sound of heavy paws hitting the earth. Ground birds took to the sky and she screamed. Panic gripped her throat and she ran, newborn preternatural speed taking over.

Unaccustomed to the pace, she slowed, swallowing back on the blood and bile forced into her mouth. She no longer needed to breathe, but she sucked in large gulps of air regardless and steadied herself against a tree.

"Stop! Don't be frightened. I only wish to speak with you."

Silver light dappled through the trees from the full moon, its glow illuminating the dark with long shadows. The young man's voice jerked her gaze toward the dark thicket. How did he catch her?

He slipped past the low hanging branches and stood naked in the patchy light. Abigail's lips parted. He was beautiful. Radiant in ways she couldn't comprehend. And his smell— Good God!

An involuntary sigh caught in her throat. Every sense was suddenly alive and a strange tingle formed in her lower belly, a damp itch between her legs. She'd heard the young wives talk in the village, but she'd never felt it herself. This feeling had a name. One the reverend warned against from the pulpit. Lust.

Desire, hot and demanding, coursed through her body. She wanted the young man's hands and mouth on her everywhere, and the itch between her legs turned to a throb. Abigail's mouth watered and her new fangs tingled with a need of their own.

"Who are you?" His voice was soft, but his eyes burned as they traveled her length, his nostrils flaring slightly. "Where did you come from? Are you a child of the moon?"

His tone seemed lonely, with a desperate edge. Abigail understood. Since the awful night she awoke to darkness, loneliness was her constant companion as well.

She shook her head. "I…I don't know."

"Does the moon rule your life?"

She nodded. "It is my only friend." Her gaze dropped to the leaf covered ground.

"And so it is with me. My name is Nathan..." He walked closer and she tensed, until warm fingers slipped beneath her chin and he lifted her face to his —

Memories fast-forwarded lightning fast behind her lids. Their friendship. Their laughter. Their first kiss. The way their bodies twined and fit. How he left her breathless and craving more.

Her palms dug further into her eyes at the remembered feel of his hands on her body. A desire that grew urgent and pounding, until one unguarded moment changed everything.

He ripped himself from her. "Get back! Devil's spawn!"

Abigail's hand flew to her mouth, covering her bloodstained lips and teeth. "Nathan, please! I'm sorry."

"Sorry? You led me to believe you were like me, but you're an aberration! Unclean!"

"Don't say that! What I am is as much outside the realm of nature as you!" she begged.

"Nature? Vampires possess no nature except what they steal from living veins as you did from mine!"

"It was a mistake," she sobbed. "I love you!"

"Love? Your undead flesh mocks the very notion. Leave my sight before I drive a stake through your fiend's heart!"

Abigail cursed again, pushing the memories deep into the closet of her mind. Annoyed, she closed her eyes and shoved her hand between her legs to purge the residual from her body and her brain, but all she saw was the full moon and a pair of angry, lust-filled eyes.

Chapter Three

Music thumped and the very walls vibrated with the heavy bass. The concrete dance floor pulsed with their energy as people from all walks of life packed the three bars and the upstairs balcony of The Red Veil.

"Didn't I tell you? This place is off the chain!" Gehrig laughed, shoving his brother's shoulder. "Just look at all the hotties." He spread his arms and inhaled. "God, I love the scent of estrogen-soaked air."

"Estrogen? Seriously?"

Gehrig snickered. "The promise of sex, bro. Can't you taste it? The atmosphere is thick with untapped lust, like a throbbing, erotic fog."

"Ignore it. We're here to do a job, Gehrig, not hunt for pussy in heat."

"*You're* here to do a job, Dash. I'm here for the fun." He crossed his arms and eyed his older brother. "Remember fun? Excitement? The rush from an illicit night out? You used to be up for anything. That is until you started getting all political on me. Tonight I'm looking for a hook up. Preferably one whose name I don't know and won't care to remember."

"Jeez, crude much, Gehrig? I know we're wolves, but do you have to be such a dog about it?"

Gehrig howled, giving his brother a teasing shove. "Lighten up, Francis. My nocturnal prowling is practice for the real deal."

"Real deal?" Dash rolled his eyes not really wanting to know.

"Yeah." his brother winked. "When I take a mate I want her to pant for me and what better way to make sure that happens than to hone my boning skills in a sea of anonymous pussy."

"Watch it. Sean is the Alpha of the Brethren, and he's the only reason we're even in New York."

Gehrig snorted. "If it wasn't for his hot wife, our top wolf would never step foot in this city. I've heard the stories. Lily's a live wire." He clicked the inside of his cheek. "Good ole' Sean needs to lighten up even more than you do. I swear, if he reads us the riot act one more time about keeping our professional distance from the vampires, I'll snap."

Dash's brows knotted. "He's right to worry, Gehrig. Our truce is too new. It has no roots yet. Any step over the line could break the contract, not to mention get us served up as a warm lunch with our hearts in a wooden box sent back as a warning."

"Yeah, yeah."

"Gehrig, don't be a douche. You may play it cool, but keeping the peace is just as important to you as it is to the rest of us. Besides, I really need your help with the shadow houses. Leave the politics to Sean and Lily."

Gehrig flashed a wide smile. "No problem, bro. I'll do whatever you need during the day, but once the sun goes down, I intend to experience everything this city has to offer in the time we're here. Uptown, downtown and everywhere in between."

"Which won't be long if you keep eyeing the vampires like that—are you even listening to me?" Dash jerked his brother's arm, turning him back to the conversation at hand.

"What? I heard you, man—" Gehrig cut his retort short, his eyes tracking a pretty woman across the bar. "Dude, look at that one! Talk about a ringer for Marilyn Monroe!"

He slapped Dash's arm. "I bet it *is* her!" Thunderstruck, his mouth dropped. "I've heard stories about her death being some kind of cover up, but I always thought they meant the CIA. Now it makes sense. Like Elvis—*holy fuck*, she smiled at me! Marilyn Monroe. A fucking vampire!"

Gehrig gestured for Dash to head toward the crowd at the bar. "Get us a couple of beers. I'm going in. I gotta get me some of that!"

"Gehrig, no." Dash grabbed the back of his brother's shirt.

"What? Let go! Do you know how many guys still masturbate to her nude pics? I know I do. It's fucking Marilyn Monroe *and* she's a vampire. Two bucket list hits in one night."

Dash made a face. "First off. TMI, dude. Second. No. And thirdly. NO! Vampires are still taboo, regardless of the truce. Sean would never allow it, and I've got news for you, neither would Sébastien." He slid his eyes toward the 1950's blonde bombshell. "Besides, I guarantee you'll be very disappointed if you try and tap that."

"Disappointed? Not a chance. I'm going to nail that legendary sex symbol—"

"Bro, she's not a vampire. She's a guy."

Gehrig blinked. "Huh?"

"You heard me. She's a dude, as in female impersonator."

Gehrig shot his brother a doubtful look and then glanced at the starlet, again. "No way." He snorted, but then his smug grin faded when he caught a quick glimpse of her rearranging her balls in the mirrored wall. "Oh man! Talk about a boner kill."

Dash burst out laughing and clapped the young Were on the shoulder. "Like you said, there's plenty of fish here tonight. Just be careful where you cast your net, little brother. Manhattan is not Maine."

Gehrig glanced at the woman again and then looked at Dash. "Is Sean meeting us or did he and Lily leave us on our own to meet the council?" he asked, suddenly all business.

Dash chuckled at his brother's sudden about-face. "Sean's already here." He pointed toward the VIP lounge at the back behind the dance floor. "It was his idea for us to meet the vampires on their own turf. Show of trust and all."

"Excuse me. Are you Dash Collier?"

The older Were turned and his eyes locked on the pretty dark haired woman waiting for his reply. "I am. And you?"

"Sent to fetch you. If you'll follow me, please."

She was pretty and pert, with terrific curves. Her pale skin faintly lined with blue made it clear she was undead. Dash gave his brother a quick nod, and the two fell in step behind the vampire.

"Let the games begin," Gehrig muttered, earning a sharp look from Dash.

The vampire's hips swung with natural grace as she led them toward the velvet ropes prohibiting general admission. She paused, flashing a brilliant smile as white as her skin.

"Thank you, Miss?" Dash asked as she unclipped the brass hook.

"Elizabeth Mason, but everyone calls me Bette."

"Ms. Mason," Dash replied with a nod before stepping past her and heading up the stairs.

"Is he always so P.C.?" she asked with a laugh, watching the older Were smooth the front of his jacket. "I mean, who wears a suit to an underground fetish club?"

Gehrig raised an eyebrow. "One who's been entrusted to help keep you leeches happy and healthy."

Bette slid her eyes to Gehrig. "Attitude and a protective vibe." She smiled letting her fangs descend. "Yummy. The combo gives your scent a little something extra that makes my mouth water."

He let his eyes travel her fully fleshed curves, and smirked. "And I smell more than curiosity behind that fanged swagger. Makes me wonder if anything else on you is *wet*?"

She laughed giving him an appreciative nod. "Quick. I like that."

"Gehrig!" Dash motioned for him to come.

Bette's lips spread into a teasing grin. "Better go, Fido."

Gehrig raised an eyebrow and met her smirk. "I come when I feel like it, and I promise, there's nothing *quick* about it."

"Gehrig!"

The young Were winked at Bette, and then took the trio of stairs in one leap, falling into step with his brother without missing a beat.

"Seriously, bro? In less than ten minutes you went from fantasizing about nailing Marilyn Monroe to chatting up bloodsucker Bettie Boop. Pick one pussy and point your erection there. You're starting to give me whiplash."

"What's the matter, jealous?"

Dash held up his hand not bothering with a reply, and the two Weres walked side-by-side in silence toward the back table to meet Sean.

All eyes focused on them from the bar. "We're surrounded," Gehrig murmured under his breath.

Dash answered with an almost imperceptible nod. "Eyes and ears open, bro. This is not a drill."

Sean stood, leaving one hand on Lily's shoulder as he greeted the two wolves with a nod. "Sébastien, may I present Dash Collier and his younger brother, Gehrig."

The alpha eyed the two in silent communication not to be rude.

"It's an honor to be here," Dash replied, earning a close-lipped smile from Sean. He nodded to Sean and then took a step closer to Lily, seated on the low, plush couch. "Hey, gorgeous," he whispered leaning in to give her cheek a peck. "How goes the howling?"

A sound of disgust jerked Dash's attention from the alpha's mate, his eyes turning toward the unexpected grumble.

Sébastien frowned, and his hard eyes swept Abigail's face, his displeasure locked on her. "You'll have to excuse my subordinate, Sean. As you may recall from the last time we met, Abigail is not as accepting as we'd like, and she's unaccustomed to public displays of affection that aren't sustenance based."

The master vampire's words addressed Sean and Lily directly, as the alphas of their group, but Dash knew the explanation was for everyone's benefit. Neither he nor Gehrig had ever set eyes on the woman before, and he stifled an involuntary cringe at what the man meant. Sex for blood and blood for sex.

The taboo images rang through his mind, but at the same time his crotch tightened as his eyes found Abigail, again. His cock thickened at the sight of the stunning vampire.

Despite her scowl, she was a haughty cross between Grace Kelly and Jackie Kennedy, with all the beauty and mystery plus a hint of real danger. Sex incarnate with death on the side just for kicks.

Dash glanced at Sean first before addressing the beautiful vampire. "I'm sorry. It wasn't my intention to make anyone uncomfortable. Lily and I are friends, and I haven't had the pleasure of her company in a while."

Abigail exhaled again. "It's not your friendship I object to, nor your silly words. It's the need for your presence here at all—" She paused, ignoring Sébastien's warning glare. "And you reek of wet dog." She wrinkled her nose.

"Abigail!" Sébastien stood, and the motion was menace made flesh. He didn't utter another word, but his expression spoke of punishment no one wanted to think about.

She shifted her eyes from the master vampire to Dash, dipping her head slightly. "My apologies."

A tiny smirk played at the corner of Dash's mouth. "Well, you're not that far off the mark. It *is* raining out."

Gehrig burst out laughing and Sean pressed his lips together, stifling a chuckle.

Tension diffused, Lily placed her hand on Dash's arm, giving Abigail a small smile. "Pheromones. It's a male thing, Abigail. It has to do with the proximity of the moon. When its waxing is close to full, their instincts get a little wired, if you get my meaning."

She gestured to the three Were males before looking back at the vampire. "Trust me, if you were an unmated Were female, you'd be squirming in your seat, eager to roll in their scent."

"She'd want to roll around with more than just our scent, that's for sure!"

"Gehrig…" Sean warned.

Amused, Sébastien pursed his lips, sliding his eyes toward Abigail. "It's settled then."

Everyone stopped. "What's settled," Abigail asked, the pitch of her voice rising in apprehension.

"Not what, but whom. The one I choose to be my ambassador and escort the wolves to our shadow houses."

"Certainly, you can't mean me, Sébastien?"

He waved a dismissive hand at Abigail's balk. "My dear, you will spend the next few days with both Dash and his younger brother. The moon will be in full flush during that time, and in my stead you will be as accommodating to them as Sean has been to us in our time of need."

"But, Sébastien—"

He shook his head. "It is my wish, Abigail, and you will do as instructed." His unblinking stare met hers. "Or do I need to show our guests how easy it is to bend you to my will?"

At the naked threat, Bette sucked in a breath, and Abigail's white skin paled even more.

"That won't be necessary." Abigail's reply was no more than a whisper, but loud enough to earn the master vampire's nod of approval.

"Good." In a very old world gesture, he held out his arm for Lily before turning to Sean. "Shall we then? The sunrise awaits and it has been decades since I've indulged in its pink and gold splendor. I can think of no more glorious place to watch the dawn break, than over the ocean."

Lily placed her hand on Sébastien's arm and stood. "Sunrise?" she asked.

Sébastien flashed an indulgent smile. "Dearest child, when you achieve my great age, there is little left that is a threat, including the sun." He cast his eyes toward Abigail. "Even my impolite progeny is old enough to suffer the sun on cloudy days."

Gehrig looked at Bette toying with her drink, her straw submerged in a thick, red liquid and it wasn't cherry slush. "What about you? Want a playdate in the park?"

She angled her head giving him a sideways smirk. "New York has strict leash laws, Fido." At the look on his face she grinned, shaking her head. "Technically, I'm still a youngblood, so the sun is still a no-no for me. Then again, I prefer to play in the dark."

Sean laughed, picking up the keys to his Harley from the small corner table. He winked at his wife. "Whaddaya say, Lil? Feel like holding tight and riding the wind behind a Were that smells like wet dog with a hard-on?"

Lily flashed him a sexy, seductive smile. "Is there any other way?"

Eyes flashing red, Sébastien snapped his fingers and Calypso moved to his side from behind the bar. He took her arm, his long finger trailing the length of her bare skin to her chin. "Abigail, since your assistant will be seeing to my needs this weekend, I suggest you let Bette help see to your responsibilities."

The master inhaled, his eyes dilating at the nervous pulse visibly beating in Calypso's throat.

"Don't disappoint." His words were directed at Abigail, but his gaze never left the pretty Creole as he steered her toward the club's private exit. The four left, leaving the others to watch as the door to the street closed behind them.

"Is your assistant going to be okay?" Gehrig gestured toward the exit door. "Sébastien looked at the poor girl like she was a hot lunch."

Unconcerned, Abigail lifted one shoulder and let it drop. "One. I don't know, and two, what else would she be to a master vampire?"

"Okay then. On that note, what time should we get started in the morning?" Dash asked, redirecting the conversation.

Abigail shrugged. "Why wait? Shadow houses are at their busiest this time of night."

"Because I'd rather not spot check the donors when they're otherwise occupied."

At the sour look on Abigail's face he exhaled. Clearly, this was not going to be as smooth as Sébastien hoped, whatever his threat.

"How about a compromise, then? We can investigate a shadow house that's close by, tonight. Hopefully, one that doesn't have too much traffic." Dash didn't know how else to phrase it. "Then tomorrow we can start wherever you feel is best."

"Whatever," Abigail replied with an offhand wave.

He frowned. "With an answer like that, you should be snapping gum and twirling your hair, instead of negotiating with me as Sébastien's agent."

At Bette's snort, Abigail shot the younger vampire a dirty look, but didn't respond.

Dash exhaled. "Look, like it or not, we're on the same team. HepZ nearly destroyed the Weres, and we all have Lily to thank it didn't do more damage to either of our races. We need to get beyond this Vampire versus Were bullshit and do what we came to do."

"Fine," she snapped.

"Fine?"

Abigail eyed him with bored annoyance. "You heard me, dog. In my world, I say things once, and I don't plan on spending the next three days repeating myself for the benefit of two ham-fisted canines."

"You're a real piece of work, you know that?" Gehrig moved from where he leaned on a chair beside Bette.

The younger vampire put a staying hand on his arm and shook her head.

Abigail ignored the younger Were, keeping her eyes glued to Dash. "You think you know so much, but you don't know a thing about vampires."

Dash snorted. "And you think you know about Weres? Trust me, honey, you haven't a clue. If it wasn't for Were blood, you'd be a maggot magnet in some worm ridden grave, but then again, vampires are nothing more than walking corpses, anyway."

Abigail's eyes flashed red and she shot to her feet, fangs fully descended.

Dash answered with a low feral growl at the back of his throat.

"Okay. Show and tell time is over!" Bette insinuated herself between the two. "You two need to cool off, so why don't we postpone this little pow-wow for now. You can meet early in the morning and hit the shadow house on Jane Street before the sun becomes a danger. It's one of our bigger houses and has at least twenty donors in residence at a clip."

Neither Abigail nor Dash said a word.

"Good idea," Gehrig added. "And I plan to learn as much as I can about vampire culture, tonight." His eyes took a walk over Bette's lush curves. "Care to be my personal tutor?"

Abigail threw her hands in the air, her fangs retracting with a snap. "Fine. Meet me here tomorrow at eight a.m."

Dash licked his lips, trying to ignore the sexy way her anger made her chest heave, highlighting the gorgeous swell of her breasts and her trim waist. She stood and smoothed her pencil skirt over her hips and he watched her hands travel the lush curves before she straightened.

His body tightened with need he hadn't felt in ages and his senses tingled at the exotic scent of her. The sexy vampire was fire and ice and the fact that she was close enough to touch and taste, but completely taboo, made him want her even more.

As if she could read his thoughts, Abigail walked away in disgust, leaving the three of them standing at the table.

Gehrig slipped his arm around Bette's shoulders, but kept his eyes on his brother. "Go home, Dash. Get some sleep, because that one's going to put you through the paces." He gestured toward Abigail's retreating figure.

Bette went up on tiptoe and licked the pulse beating in Gehrig's carotid. "She's not the only one."

Gehrig growled low and slid his hand down to cup her rounded ass. "Bring it on, babe."

She kissed his throat, but then pulled back to look at him. "What about your taboo?"

He cupped her chin. "Rules are made to be broken, baby. Consider this a fact finding mission for us both. You show me yours and I'll show you mine." He grinned. "Just don't kill me, okay?"

She laughed. "Deal."

Arm in arm they moved toward the stairs. "Don't wait up, bro—" he called over his shoulder and the two disappeared into the crowd.

Dash watched them leave. "And then there was one," he muttered. "With a raging hard-on for the vampire queen bitch."

Chapter Four

"It's about time, wolf. You obviously have no concept of time or my constraints. We have a lot of ground to cover before the sun gets too high."

Dash pulled the plastic tab back on his coffee and blew across the narrow opening. He watched her, almost enjoying her agitation as he took a slow sip. "And good morning to you too, Abby."

"It's Abigail. Not Abby." She looked at him and then at her watch, wrinkling her nose.

He exhaled, running his thumb along the steam covered seam. "Can we please not start the day like cats and dogs? It's exactly eight a.m. as agreed." He sniffed. "I took pains this morning not to offend, and since it's no longer raining, why the sour face?"

She answered his question with a question. "Is that foul beverage portable?"

He laughed. "Who would have thought the smell of fresh brewed coffee would offend more than the scent of wet dog."

"Well?"

"Yes, Ms. Abigail, the coffee is portable. Gehrig kept me up very late last night, and I need a jolt of caffeine to get my juices flowing."

His eyes took in her long legs and her black knee length leather boots. Her leggings hugged her curves perfectly, as did the low cut of her blouse, giving his imagination plenty to work with. Clearly, she had dressed down for what was ahead, but kept the sex appeal in high gear.

"I thought Gehrig was with Bette all night?" she asked.

He took another sip of coffee, eyeing her over its white plastic rim, one eyebrow up.

Her eyes widened.

"Exactly," he replied.

A reluctant smile pushed at the corner of Abigail's lips. "Well, considering I know what vampires are capable of, I'm surprised you have any juices left this morning to get flowing."

Dash's mouth turned down. "The walls of our apartment are paper thin, sweetheart. I'm not into threesomes with the walking dead. Bette is pretty and all, but she's not my type. Besides, I prefer my partners not fall into a corpse-like state at dawn."

"Too bad." She eyed him with a jaunty angle to her head.

Dash looked at her. Was that an offhand invitation or was she just being snarky?

She kept her unnerving gaze on him. "So you were forced to be an auditory voyeur?" she asked, getting up from her chair.

"Unfortunately, yes." He didn't know where she was headed with this, but if she wanted to play, then he was game, too.

He put his coffee cup on a low table and reached for her jacket, holding it open for her. She shrugged one arm into her sleeve, the sweep of her hair brushing against his arm.

Her scent was intoxicating, and he held her collar against the nape of her neck a little longer than necessary just to breathe her in.

She was cold to the touch, but he anticipated as much, though he never expected her to smell like sunshine. The taste like chocolate and strawberries on the back of his tongue. His mouth watered and he had to stop himself from spinning her in his arms to claim her mouth and every other inch of her.

Abigail froze at the feel of his lingering fingers. "Uhm. Thank you, Dash."

It was the first time she'd spoken his name, and he smiled behind her. "No problem." He hiked her coat up a little more and gave her shoulders a gentle pat.

They stood in awkward silence for a moment until a shirtless young man in leather pants walked toward them with a chrome travel cup on a small round tray.

"Bette called before dawn. She left word for this to be ready for you when you came downstairs." He handed her the cup. "She also said not to wait for the other wolf. They'll meet you here after sundown."

Dash shook his head, fishing in his pocket for his cell phone. He scrolled through his contacts and pressed Gehrig's number.

"Unbelievable," he grumbled into a hard exhale when the call went right to voicemail.

"Don't waste your breath, Dash. If I know Bette, your brother will be out cold for hours."

He shoved his phone into his pocket again. "What now?"

"Can you handle verifying twenty donors yourself?" she asked.

He looked at her and his eyes locked with hers. "I can handle anything you give me."

Abigail licked her lips, her nostrils flaring a bit. "We'll have to see about that."

❦

"Yes? May I help you?" A tall, lanky vampire stood in the open doorway. He glanced over Dash's casual attire and sniffed. "If you're looking for a room, I'm sorry, we're full up."

Dressed like a downtown hipster, the pale vampire looked to be in his early twenties, but appearances meant nothing. The beanie wearing bloodsucker could be older than dirt, especially since it was morning.

"I bet. And I know exactly the kind of guests you have occupying those rooms," Dash replied.

The vampire raised an eyebrow and took a backward step ready to shut the door.

Dash's hand shot out, grabbing the edge of the beveled wood. "Not so fast, chief. I'm here at Sébastien's request."

The hipster's dark eyebrow hiked even further.

"Stop playing games, Dash." Abigail stepped out from the safety of the building's shadow and moved in front of the door. "You certainly took your time answering the bell, Micah. Move aside and let the wolf pass."

She took off her sunglasses, letting the full force of her red eyes stare him down. "Or would you rather trade places with me in the morning sun? It's overcast, but it'll give you a good sizzle nonetheless."

Micah dropped his gaze and stepped to one side as Abigail brushed past with Dash close behind. Micah closed the door and Abigail paused, considering the young vampire.

"Where is Finn?" she asked with a snap.

Micah looked up. "He's in with Mairé. He asked not to be disturbed."

She didn't comment, but her lips thinned at the news. "Thank you, Micah. You should go to your rest. You're far too young to man the door at this time of day."

"But—"

She shook her head. "I'll see the house is secured."

The hipster vamp nodded and then headed for the stairs. Abigail motioned for Dash to follow her down the hall, past various sitting rooms and an obvious bar until she stopped at a door marked private.

Turning the knob, she pushed the heavy oak open and stood to one side. "Wait in here. I'll be right back."

The room was clearly the manager's office. A large desk stacked with files and one large black ledger sat adjacent to a stocked wall-length bookcase. A decanter and two dirty wine glasses stood on a side table, a thick crimson residue ringing the bottom of each.

Dash opened the ledger and scanned the old fashioned scrawl. The handwriting was ornate and looping. From what he read, it was clear the pages were an account of every blood donor in the house, their age and where they came from, the length of their involvement at the shadow house and a list of their primary hookups.

Yelling in the hall jerked his attention away from the accounts and he closed the book. Abigail yanked the office door open. "Get inside. You're a disgrace!"

She shoved a half-dressed human male through the threshold, the force making him stumble. He caught the edge of the desk to stop from pitching to the floor.

"Abigail, please—"

"Shut up, Finn. I sent word myself, we were coming this morning, and yet you left the safety of the shadow house and all its residents to a youngblood not old enough to distinguish the scent of a werewolf at the door! All because you couldn't think past the end of your erection!"

She shot the man a warning look not to open his mouth. "Pull up your pants before I drain you here and now. Then sit in that chair and answer every question asked of you. Got it?"

He nodded, shoving his shirt into his pants and buckling his belt before slinking behind his desk to sit as directed. He smoothed his thinning hair back over his face, his eyes furtive.

Dash inhaled. The metallic scent of sweat laced fear was clear and it poured off the man. He was scared, and rightly so. You didn't cross a vampire, even if you had a cross in your hands.

The wolf smirked to himself at the pun and Abigail shot him a look, too.

"You find this amusing, I suppose." She exhaled an aggravated sigh.

Dash shook his head. "Not in the least, but the stupidity here is surprising, especially since this was left out for anyone with prying eyes to see." He gestured toward the ledger.

Abigail looked at the book and her gaze hardened. She lifted her flinty eyes to Finn for an explanation. "Well?"

"As you said, I knew you were coming today so I left the book out. I didn't expect you so...so...early."

Abigail threw her arm in the air. "Really! And if it was too early for me that I'm three hundred years old, didn't you think it was too early for Micah? The boy's face was riddled with blue veining from thirst and daylight exhaustion. He should have been at his rest well before dawn!"

"I...I..."

"I don't want to hear your excuses, Finn. I warned Sébastien your fetish would bring trouble."

Dash couldn't resist. "Fetish?"

Abigail made a face, and Finn cringed. "Our human friend here likes to fuck the dead. He's a necrophiliac. Sébastien thinks it funny, but I don't. Finn likes to prey on youngbloods, waiting until they fall into a deathlike sleep at dawn before he violates their cold bodies. He can't get it up any other way, can you Finny-boy?"

The man dropped his face into his hands, crying. "Stop it. Please…stop."

Abigail perched on the end of his desk, lifting a ruler from the cup holder. "I should tell Mairé what I found you doing to her ass. She's very resourceful and I'm sure she'll come up with interesting ways to deal with *your* ass." She slid the sharp end of the ruler under his chin and forced him to look up.

"I meant no harm." He sniffled.

Dash shook his head. "Deal with him however way you see fit, but do it later. We have a job to do, and it's almost ten am. I don't need to return you to The Red Veil burned and weak."

His eyes met Finn's. "If you were a Were, your testicles would be ripped from your sack and fed to pigs."

Abigail laughed. "I'll have to remember to share that tidbit with Mairé." Her eyes narrowed and she tapped the black ledger with the ruler. "Where are the donors?"

"In their berths," Finn replied. "Or still with their regulars."

"Berths? What is this, a ship?" Dash asked.

"The building is a vintage landmark. We maintain the guise of a chic downtown hotel for appearance sake." She gestured toward Finn. "It's one of the reasons we keep a human proprietor."

"And?"

"A century ago the building was a safe haven for sailors. We keep the rooms in the same fashion, with berth-like bunks for the resident donors. We also have donors who have retired from the lifestyle, but they still come when called."

"Then I suppose Micah's script when he met me at the door is the standard when humans call for reservations," Dash said, impressed.

She nodded. "Yes, but we do allow humans and other supernatural species to stay from time to time. It's good for business, and it keeps our undercurrent out on the street without raising too much suspicion."

"Other species?"

With a shrug, she waved absently toward the upstairs before picking up a small stack of unopened envelopes on Finn's desk "The Fae and of course, blood witches." She sorted through the mail. "Not the Harry Potter wannabes or those who fancy themselves mystical. I mean, real witches, the ones whose families carry true magic in their blood."

She smiled, showing more than a bit of fang, her eyes dilating with remembered pleasure. "Their kind is only accommodating when they need something from us, and their blood is a true delicacy in return."

"Unlike Were blood," he baited.

Her smile disappeared and she slipped off the desk to walk around and stand beside Finn, ignoring the little man's obvious cringe. "Enough chat." She opened the ledger with a muffled thud.

"We'll deal with the house residents first." She slid her eyes toward the sweaty little human. "Rouse them. All of them. Have everyone gather in the bar. I want every donor downstairs and ready for a spot check in ten minutes. Understood?"

He bobbed his head, pushing back on his chair with such force, it was clear he wanted to put as much distance as possible between himself and the vampire.

Abigail smirked at his obvious escape.

"Making friends and influencing people everywhere you go, huh?" Dash chuckled.

"I don't need friends. Least of all among *your* kind."

"My kind? Do I need to remind you why we're on this little venture together?" Dash raised an eyebrow at her, watching as she fidgeted with the pages in the ledger. He squelched the knowing grin itching at the corner of his mouth. He made her nervous.

Inhaling, he raised an eyebrow, surprised at the unexpected trace in her scent. Nervous, yes. But also aroused. Abigail the vampire bitch queen was turned on, despite all her bravado. His cock thickened with the knowledge.

"And for the record," he continued, "my world is just as full of the natural and unnatural as yours."

She froze, semi-distracted by the bulge at the front of his pants. "I'm sorry, what?"

"You heard me," he replied, consciously not letting on he caught her checking out the goods. "You think we're so different, but we're not. Weres and vampires, Fae and witches—we all hide our true natures in one way or another. It's what makes us the same, regardless of our differences."

He moved around the desk and took the ruler from her hand, taking a moment to push a stray lock of hair behind her ear. "It's also what should bind us together, but it doesn't." He dropped his hand, his arm brushing her breast in the process.

She pushed him away, the reaction almost kneejerk. "Don't touch me, *dog*! There is nothing about us or our worlds that is similar, and there is nothing that entices me to bind anything to you."

Dash put his hands up. "Have it your way, Abigail. Keep telling yourself that. It won't change the truth." He raised an eyebrow and looked at her. "And scents don't lie." He paused. "Still, neither Sean nor Sébastien can say I didn't try."

"Try what?"

He sighed. "Forget it."

She opened her mouth to retort, but the office door opened.

"They're all assembled," Finn interrupted, holding a bloodstained handkerchief to his throat.

"What's all that?" Dash asked, pointing to the mess at the man's neck.

"I had to disturb a few of our...our...members when gathering the donors. One was not quite finished and took the balance of his need, out on me."

Abigail burst out laughing. "Karma is a real bitch, isn't she, Finny ole' boy?"

She moved to the door with sudden speed and turned an icy glare toward Dash. "Let's get this over with, shall we?"

Chapter Five

"You're infected," Dash kept his face composed and his tone calm, but even so, he watched as confusion and then fear crossed the young woman's face.

"Infected with what? How? When?" Her voice hitched.

"You have HepZ. A form of viral hepatitis. It's a rare strain that attacks both humans and the paranormal. It's a long story, but the good news is, there's a cure."

"What do you mean Leah's infected? This shadow house was cleared early last spring." A young man complained, moving protectively to where the stunned girl stood. "A different set of wolves swept the entire place. Anyone with even a hint of disease was removed."

"That's right! We were told everything was fine and there was nothing to worry about." Another added "What are you telling us now?"

Leah's eyes flew to Abigail and then back to Dash, her words halting in her fear. "Does this mean I'll be…be…changed?"

Abigail blew out a disgusted snort. "Of course not, you silly girl. Have you learned nothing in your time here? We'd sooner end your pathetic existence."

The girl burst into tears and the first young man gathered her to his arms, shooting Dash a desperate look.

Dash raised both hands to try and diffuse the growing commotion. "There's no need to cry, and no need for worry. No one is ending anyone." He shot Abigail a dirty look before shifting his attention back to the terrified girl.

"Leah, once your body starts making antibodies on its own, you'll be as good as new. The same goes for anyone else who becomes infected, but it does mean you probably spread the virus to whoever you've been with."

Leah balked. "Been with? I haven't been with anyone."

Dash looked to Abigail who looked to Finn for explanation.

"Leah hasn't been assigned to anyone yet. She's new and still being screened," the sweaty little man answered.

Abigail snarled and the room cringed. "Screened! You call letting an infected donor through our doors, screened?"

"Abigail—" Dash tried.

Her eyes flashed red. "This is none of your business, wolf. Just use that snout of yours to point out the infected lot and I'll do the rest."

"Really!" He laughed at her. "And what is it you think you can do, besides terminate every infected member of this household?"

At his words the entire room panicked, and he shook his head, hoping they understood he was simply making a point.

He held up his hand and continued, looking to calm their fears. "If donors are infected, then it follows so are the vampires. Are you prepared to destroy your own kind or are you going to shut up and listen for a change?"

She ignored him, instead turning again to Finn. "Was she infected when she came to us?"

He shook his head. "No. Her test results are in her file."

Abigail thought for a moment. "Have they been given sample doses of our blood to see how it affects them?" She gestured toward the gathered group. "You know we have no tolerance for addictive personalities, especially not in our shadow houses."

Finn nodded. "Of course. That's protocol with any new donor. It's why Leah is still being screened." He visibly flinched using the word again.

Abigail's mouth opened, but she closed it again. She turned to Dash. "Well?"

He considered her. "Well, what? We thought we caught every case last spring, but this new outbreak means one of two things: either we missed a dormant strain or the entire virus has mutated. Based on the weak scent of disease in Leah's blood, my assessment is she has a mild case, but the entire house needs to be quarantined, regardless."

He shifted his eyes to Finn "I'm assuming the test samples fed to donors are a mixture of vampire and human blood in graduated strengths to ensure against addiction."

"Yes. That's exactly right," Finn replied.

Dash exhaled. "Then I'll need access to everything you have in storage, both the test sets and every bag of donor blood used for—" he hesitated trying to remember the term Sébastien used. "For sustenance."

Finn nodded.

"In addition," Dash continued. "I'll need access to every vampire who either donated or drank from the source."

Abigail shook her head. "This is much more than anyone anticipated. More than even Sébastien anticipated, I'm sure. I'll have to get permission from him before we can formally begin."

"Of course. I'll need to contact Sean, as well, and discuss how to proceed from here. I can't very well detect the virus through sterile plastic. It's impermeable."

A dull hum rose from the donors and Finn looked to Abigail.

"Silence!" she yelled.

When the room quieted, she looked at each donor, her eyes moving from face to face. "No one is to enter or leave the premises until the wolves have done a full assessment of everyone. If you leave, we will find you and bring you back, and whether or not you survive the return trip —" She shrugged, letting the full meaning behind her clipped words sink in.

"However, if you stay and cooperate, once this matter is cleared you will be given the choice to continue with us or move to a shadow house of your choice or leave of your own free will. No harm will come to you if you decide to return to your previous lives."

Abigail turned on her heel and stormed out of the bar, not waiting for a reaction.

"Abigail —"

She waved Dash off, turning the corner toward the office without a word.

He looked at the sets of eyes all focused on him. "Finn, I suggest you put in for supplies. I have no idea how long this assessment is going to take. Everyone needs to be evaluated and then inoculated, but I'm going to need all records, official or unofficial, of any contact anyone here has had with anyone else. Supernatural or human."

Dash let his eyes travel among the group. The donors were every color, shape and size, all young, all beautiful, and most likely all sick. "I need you to be honest with me. If you switch hit lovers or met anyone on the sly, I need to know. I promise the information will stay with me and only me."

Some were crying openly, others angry, but there was nothing left to say. It was, what it was. He left the bar and headed to the office after Abigail.

The door was ajar and from just outside he heard her on the phone. She was doubtless speaking with Sébastien. It was well past noon, and from the muffled yelling coming from the receiver, the master vampire was not a happy camper.

"No, sir… I know… Yes. I've got the situation well in hand. No, I don't want Sean to send for more wolves. Dealing with this one is enough, and the other is missing in action with… What? No, please don't, Sébastien.

"We should tell Dash and his feral brother to leave. Why? Because! I don't understand why we need them at this point. We have oral antibodies stored with the blood in the vault. Yes. He gave me some excuse about dormant strains or mutations or something or another.

"What? No, not at all…I think it's time to call these dogs on the uselessness of their so-called scenting abilities and bring in the cougars. Maybe the big cats can sense what the canines can't. No, please…don't say a word to the alpha until I get back to you. Yes, sir. I'll call you tomorrow night."

Cougars? She had to be kidding. Wolves have the keenest sense of smell of any mammal on Earth.

Dash pushed the door open and stalked in. "Are you kidding me? You couldn't wait five minutes to call dear old dad and place blame on the wolves for another of your houses falling sick?"

"Dear old dad?" her eyes narrowed.

"Come on, Abigail. I know from Sean and Lily both that Sébastien changed you and then abandoned you to your own devices. It's a pattern with most of the old ones. They don't give a flying fuck who they kill or who they change. The undead are the worst deadbeat parents in the world."

"That's none of your business and it's entirely beside the point," she countered.

"And what exactly is the point?" Dash shot back. "That I and my wolf brethren are useless? Or are my ears as inadequate as my nose?"

She met him glare for glare. "No, your ears are in perfect working order, but you and your kind *are* lacking.

What good is your alleged skill if you can't detect the virus in our stored bagged blood?" She stood, hands clenched. "Useless!"

He moved with agile strength and pinned her against the desk. "I can tell you what I'm good at or maybe I should just show you." He leaned in, his lips close. "I smell your need, Abigail. Despite your posturing, your scent is drenched with arousal. Fury too, but more because you want me, and you hate yourself for it."

Dash inhaled. "If I reached between your legs you'd come in my hand, right here, right now. For such an icy bitch, your panties are soaked just from my words. You can't help it. Just like you can't help the hunger for my hard length against your curves.

"You think my sense of smell isn't all that? Well, it's telling me your need is deeper than just physical. There's something in you that's unfulfilled. A longing that's laced with anger. Oh, yes. Deep anger."

Dash slid one hand over her hip, resting his fingers on her silent ribcage. There was no heartbeat beneath his fingers. No warmth. Just tense, coiled muscles ready to strike.

"What happened to you, Abigail? Rémy filled me in a little at Sean and Lily's wedding."

Her eyes widened slightly, but he didn't stop. "This taboo between our races wasn't always the case. In fact, we rather enjoyed each other until your kind went all superior."

With a snarl, she lashed out again, shoving against his immovable chest. "Better superior, than feral! You think you know so much, wolf? Well, you don't! Not everything that bulb in the middle of your face picks up is accurate. You think you know what makes me cream? You'll need to get a lot closer than just a sniff, but you'll have to get past my fangs first!"

Gathering all her preternatural strength, she pushed him away and stormed out. Dash let her leave, chuckling at the bang from the front door.

Like Gehrig said, let the games begin.

⛧

Abigail tightened the top lapel of her short cashmere coat. Gusts whipped across the Hudson, funneling from the choppy water down the streets off Twelfth Avenue. Rushing headlong into the street wasn't the smartest decision considering the traffic at this time of day. However, morning bright skies had turned overcast, and despite the wind, she was grateful for the reprieve from the sun.

She snorted to herself. Today sucked, and not in a good way, but at least Mother Nature was willing to play ball. She needed to walk and clear her head.

In the park across the street, autumn leaves swirled in tiny gold and crimson tornadoes. She slowed to watch the mini whirlwinds, letting the blend of color calm her churning emotions before she continued down the street.

"Hey! Watch where you're going!"

A sharp breath caught her unaware, and she stopped short of crashing into another pedestrian.

"Abigail?" the annoyed voice asked, the tone changing to surprise.

"Henry? I…I didn't see you. I'm sorry," she replied., flustered

The flamboyant vampire clicked the tips of his fangs in a smug grin. "Clearly."

She made a face at the snarky remark and his over-the-top appearance. Was he a vampire or a member of a gothic cosplay troupe? "Nice cape and cravat, dude. Is there an elder gathering in the city or are you auditioning for a part in Phantom of the Opera?"

"Amusing, as always, Abigail." He sniffed. "However, the question begs, why are you rushing around the streets at this hour of the day? Are you lost or just afraid the sun will beat you to the punch?"

"I'm in no mood for your silly, competitive digs, Henry," she shot back. "No one cares how old you are, especially not me. Not when my sire's blood trumps this sorry weather and anything else snarky you could think to say."

"Why so preoccupied, then?" He dipped his head to sniff the air close to her. "*Ah...now I understand.*"

"Understand what?"

"I heard the wolves were in town again." He shot her a knowing look. "In fact, it seems they're all over the city." He gestured toward a storefront on the corner. "Even the sex trade has caught wolf fever."

Abigail looked at him. *Fever? Did he mean the virus?* She followed his line of sight across from where they stood, and in the window of an adult novelty store was a large array of dildos. Front and center was an enormous phallus with a sign, "Let the *Wolfman* unleash your inner animal."

Henry laughed at her disgusted exhale. "Immortality is much more fun if you let it ride, Abigail." He winked.

"Whatever." She made a face at his double meaning.

He waved goodbye before crossing the street and heading toward the river. "Give my regards to Sébastien."

She watched him disappear around the corner. "Let it ride? Thank you, Captain Obvious."

Standing alone, she glanced at the window again and shook her head. "Ridiculous fetish. If they only knew."

Abigail turned on her heel to go, but stopped and looked back at the dildo. " — and the proportions are all wrong." Shoving her purse onto her shoulder, she did an about-face and went into the store.

"You've got to be kidding me," she grumbled, shaking her head at the large prototype on the display table.

Surrounding the promo sample were the actual sex toys, advertised as inspired by a fictional werewolf's erection. Abigail ran her hand over the sample. The synthetic flesh strange beneath her fingertips. Its feel was completely unlike the remembered boy in her mind, or the electric reality of Dash's arm brushing up against her breast.

She stood, chewing the inside of her lip, her fangs tingling. "What the hell," she muttered and grabbed an unopen box.

Chapter Six

Abigail locked the door to Sébastien's suite. The vampire council kept rooms behind the club, should the need arise, with easy access to any and all backroom play at The Red Veil.

It was their *Les Sanctuaire*, but with Sébastien away, it became her private haven. Bette was the only other person with a key, and she was currently holed up with Gehrig.

The elegant vampire dropped the adult novelty non-descript plastic bag on the couch and took off her coat.

Dash's scent lingered on her clothes, and his natural fragrance hit her like a punch to the gut. Not to mention his words. Hot, raw and sexy as hell. Just like him. Ugh. A hot bath and some essential oils were exactly what she needed to free herself from its hold. From his hold.

Stripping, she dropped her clothes in a line on the way to the bathroom and turned on the tap, letting the hot water gather in the deep cast iron clawed-foot tub.

An antique dressing mirror stood beside the sink and she took in her reflection. Her fingers traced the blue veins along her throat and down to her breasts. She needed to feed, the bluish lines made that evident, but something else gripped her body, making her shake with a need greater than thirst.

Naked, her hands cupped her breasts, kneading the cold flesh. Images of strong hands grasping and teasing, danced through her mind until she inhaled through her teeth, closing her eyes and letting the tingle spread down her belly.

The water was ready and so was she. She switched off the lights and lit the blood-scented candles on either side of the tub before padding out to get the adult novelty box from the other room.

Not waiting, she tore the cardboard and cellophane wrapper, her nails slicing through the wire twisty ties holding the synthetic cock in its place.

The man-made phallus was heavy in her hands and as long as her forearm, with a slanted blunt-cut tip on one end and the largest scrotum knot she'd seen on the other.

The synthetic flesh was soft to the touch, with veining that made her mouth water thinking about the rich blood that would engorge a real wolf's cock.

What if what Bette said was true and Were blood *could* sate her thirst for weeks, if not months?

Three centuries were too long past for her to remember the taste and feel of an erect wolf, and the possibilities made her shiver thinking about sinking her teeth into Dash's throat as his hard length sunk deep between her legs.

Abigail placed the dildo on the low table beside the tub. She slipped into the scalding water, a sigh on her lips as it skimmed over her skin, the steam from the heat swirling along the surface like a thin fog.

Dash.

She filled her mind with images of him. His sexy smirk, the curve of his rugged jaw. His scent gave away as much as he claimed *her* scent did, and she gauged the layered flavor, his honesty surprising in that he actually meant what he said. Including wanting her as much as she wanted him.

Not that she'd ever admit it.

From the moment he put his hands on his hips in the office, pushing his jacket back, she wanted him.

At the outline of hard muscles visible through his thin dress shirt and the way his pants glided over his thighs, hugging his ass and the package between his legs.

He'd held her pinned, and it was all she could do not to rip his pants from his body and fist his cock, sinking her fangs into his throat.

Instead she used her strength to shove him away. She exhaled. Self-protect. That was the name of the game, yet the feel of his hard lines and how immoveable his body was beneath her fingers threw her for a moment, almost costing her intended force.

Giving in was not an option. She was the one in control. She'd been there, done that and been burned, so the alternative was unthinkable.

Her hands cupped the steaming water and slipped over her arms to her shoulders, letting the cascade trail across her breasts. Her fingers followed, pausing to circle her nipples, pinching and teasing each before sliding further to her shaved mound.

Bringing her knees up, she let her legs fall open. Closing her eyes, she glided both hands into the water, one circling her clit while the other spread her pussy lips. One finger at a time working their way into her slick entrance.

She let her head fall back against the tub pillow, enjoying the feel of her own hands and the tiny waves cresting and teasing her nipples. Lifting one hand from her slit, she reached for the wolf's cock, dribbling a thin coating of lube up and down its shaft and over its head.

Spreading her knees wider, she lifted her buttocks and plunged the dildo into her pussy. She hissed and then gasped back a breath, pumping the synthetic cock deep and hard, working herself fast.

Moaning, she used her fingers on her clit, teasing and pinching until she felt the crest of her climax. Muscles tensed, and she held for the onslaught of spasms and pleasure, but it wouldn't come.

Frustrated, she ignored the unfulfilled pain and numbness and closed her eyes, letting what remained of Dash's scent fill her senses.

Images of his muscled chest and thighs rippled in her head, his bare body twined with hers, but the picture twisted and changed until she smelled loamy earth. The soft crunch of leaves beneath her, the full moon and a delicious musky scent, his skin and her fangs against his flesh.

Nathan

She squeezed her eyes tighter, focusing on Dash and the here and now. Her climax built again, but Nathan's face…his expression…his revulsion…

Eyes still closed, her head jerked up from the pillow. "Get out of my head!"

Body shaking with unspent lust, she worked her pussy deeper, faster. Feet planted against the white curve of the tub, she gripped the dildo white knuckled, clenching the base so hard the artificial flesh crumbled in her hand.

With a guttural snarl she threw the ruined cock against the mirror, smashing the glass. She screamed and every ounce of frustration and pent desire poured into the pained yell.

"What the hell is going on in here?" Bette asked, shoving the bathroom door open.

She stood in the doorway, mouth open as she looked at the shattered shards covering the tile and the squashed dildo at the center of the mess.

"Is there something you need to tell me, or do I need to call one of the youngbloods from downstairs to help release whatever caused all this?" she asked, her hand sweeping the bathroom.

Abigail slipped under the water, submerging her head and face.

Exhaling, Bette walked on the broken glass and reached into the water yanking the older vampire up by her hair, not caring if she was insubordinate.

"Enough drama queening! Abby. Answer me or I'm going to call Sébastien. What the hell has gotten into you?"

Sputtering, Abigail pushed wet hair from her eyes and face. "Nothing. Everything. That thing—" she pointed a dripping hand toward what was left of the synthetic wolf phallus.

Bette's eyes followed and shook her head. "Come on Abs...seriously? A dildo caused all this? You have access to the finest vampire cock in the city and you choose to shove a piece of fleshy plastic into your snatch? Why?"

Abigail didn't respond, just stared at the offending sex toy. Bette looked at it again as well, and her eyes widened.

"Oh my God, it's a werewolf cock." Her lips spread into a deliberate smile. "You little lying bitch. You have the hots for Dash."

Abigail stayed silent, but her eyes found Bette's amused face. She stared at her, chewing on the corner of her lip before finally sitting up in the quickly cooling water. She opened her mouth to answer, but then stopped, eyeing her friend's face instead. "Bette. Your skin."

Her friend nodded with a giggle. "I know, right!"

"What did you do? You look almost—" she bit her tongue, clipping her words when she realized why.

"Almost what?" the younger vampire asked with a chuckle. "Human?"

Abigail nodded, reaching her wet fingers out, but then pulling her hand back.

With a close-lipped grin, Bette took her friend's hand and placed it on her cheek. "It's Gehrig." A wistful sigh left the younger vampire's lips. "I told you wolf blood could sate a vampire's thirst for a long time, but what I didn't know was how it could warm an undead body from the inside out. Giving back a bit of what the darkness took, even if only for a little while."

Embarrassed and happy, Bette flushed warm and pink, so much like a human. Abigail slid her hand down to her friend's chest, half expecting to find a heartbeat inside.

"Amazing," Abigail whispered, almost awed.

Bette covered her friend's hand with hers. "You could have it too, you know. And you're right, the feeling is amazing."

Abigail pulled her hand away.

"What?" Bette's brows knotted. "You know I'm right."

Abby shook her head. "No, Bette. To use a modern turn of phrase, *been there done that* with the furred and fanged set. Thanks, but no thanks."

Bette shrugged. "Suit yourself. You always do." She straightened from the side of the tub and handed her friend a towel from the warming rack, toeing some of the broken glass aside.

"You'd better call for someone to sweep up this mess, and have a donor sent up as well. You look like shit."

Abigail stood in the now cold water and wrapped the soft terrycloth around her body. She frowned at Bette's sharp tone and the harsh expression on her friend's face.

"Bette—"

The younger vampire held up one hand. "I don't understand, right?" She shook her head. "That's your standard answer, Abs. Well, how can you expect me to understand when you never share what's behind this angst nonsense? I love you like a sister Abigail, but you are one fucked up vampire. You walk around like the Ice Queen, reveling in your bitchiness, but I know better than that."

Abigail waved her off. "Forget it. Forget all of it."

Bette exhaled with another nod. "Whatever you say, your Highness." She inhaled, shaking her head at the unspent need still hanging in the air.

"You know nothing, and no one is going to sate whatever *this* is or wherever *this* came from." Bette swept her hand past the broken glass, again. "At least not for very long."

She looked at her friend still standing in cold water. "You need to do something, or this constant craving is going to make you snap. You didn't deny it when I said you had the hots for Dash. For whatever reason, past or present, the idea of hooking up with a wolf sets your fangs on edge, and I get it. But you've exhausted all other means—" her gaze fell on the dildo. "Actual and imitation. It's up to you."

Bette bent to pick up what was left of the crushed sex toy and handed it to the older vampire. "Trust me. The real thing is *much* better. Do it, Abigail, and exorcise your damned pussy-punishing demons once and for all. Immortality is too long a time to shoulder whatever leftovers you're carrying."

Abigail didn't answer, just chewed on the inside of her cheek.

Bette's gaze softened at the new vulnerability on her friend's face. "Look, I'm meeting Gehrig in an hour. Come with us. Maybe he can help."

Abigail raised an eyebrow, a teasing half-smile replacing the uncertainty on her face. "Is that an offer to share?"

Bette laughed out loud, her eyes sparkling. "Absolutely not! Finders keepers and you can find your own."

Abigail stepped out of the tub onto the mat opposite the pile of shards. "Like you said, I have to feed first. Then we'll see. I still have to call Sébastien about what we found at the shadow house, and who knows how long that conversation will take and what he'll want me to do."

Bette eyed her, concerned. "That bad?"

Abby shrugged. "We don't know yet. That's the problem. I'm supposed to regroup with Dash tomorrow and take it from there."

Bette's lips pursed in a side grin. "And I'm sure you'll have no problem telling him how you like to take it."

Abigail smiled, but her silent heart warmed with affection for her friend. "Funny. Now get out. Go meet your wolf. I'll catch up with you later or tomorrow."

Chapter Seven

"You're late!" Abigail stood at Finn's desk, ledgers open and the computer humming. Her hands were on her hips, her long fingers accenting her curves.

Dash let his eyes travel the length of her body. "It's the dead of night and there wasn't a cab to be found. Besides, there's a full moon tonight or did you forget?"

Bitch queen or not, the pull of the moon and the edgy tension between them sent his sex drive into high gear. Even if he wanted to tell her to fuck off, his cock wouldn't let him. If she wanted to fuck off, it damn well would be on his dick.

Ignoring him, Abigail leaned over and punched a few keystrokes into the computer, glancing at him over the top edge of the monitor. "Sébastien gave me the security codes for the downtown vaults. We recently had them restored and restocked from the temporary site we were forced to use after Hurricane Sandy."

He smirked. "Viruses, hurricanes, and yet everyone thinks vampires are immune to human circumstance."

She didn't even glance up. "That's a stupid thing to say. Vampires *are* impervious to most of what would kill a human, or even a Were for that matter, but immortality isn't what it used to be."

Impressed, he nodded. "That's quite a concession coming from you. Then again, I suppose the modern world presents dangers more sophisticated than say, a stake through the heart."

Abigail straightened, crossing her arms in front of her chest. "Seriously? First off, it's cliché. Second, name one creature a stake through the heart *wouldn't* kill, and why are you so surprised to hear we take precautions?"

He shrugged. "I'm not, really. It's just nice to see you admit you're vulnerable." He grinned. "You know, vulnerability gets a bad rap, especially with you undead types. In stolen moments, it's actually an attractive quality. Makes you accessible. Don't you want to be accessible, Abigail?" Dash raised an eyebrow.

An annoyed exhale dismissed him outright. "Okay. Moving on."

"Why is the idea of vulnerability so hard for you?" he pressed.

"Sébastien wants us to head to the vaults after we've determined which blood batch was assigned to this shadow house," she said, purposefully ignoring his question. "I've accessed everything we need in the database." She gestured toward the keyboard.

"Once we're done cleaning up the mess here, we can trace the delivery route to the other houses and then you and Gehrig can take it from there." She looked at him. "Did you bring what we need?"

"You didn't answer me."

She chewed on the inside of her cheek. "And I don't plan to. Again, did you bring what we need?"

"Maybe," he replied. He slid the insulated bag from his shoulder and dropped it unceremoniously onto the chair, and then moved around the desk to stand beside her. "Now stop answering my question with another question."

"I have no intention of getting into this with you, wolf. You and your insipid questions are irrelevant and beneath me to even acknowledge. You don't interest me. I find you and the rest of your kind distasteful and lacking in every way. Some may get a cheap thrill in dabbling with the taboo, but I'm not one of them."

She uncrossed her arms and spread her hands in mock invitation. "So, if you don't mind, can we get back to the business at hand?"

"Oh, honey. You need it bad, don'tcha?"

Abigail's eyes flashed. "It?"

He met her angry stare with a grin.

"You really are a juvenile," she shot back. "Even if that were true, what makes you think you're the one to deliver?"

Knock, knock.

Both sets of eyes jerked toward the open door.

"The vampires are waiting for you in the lounge." Finn's gaze didn't move from the floor. "As requested, the last delivery of food and supplements are due this morning. The truck has been instructed to unload by the downstairs side entrance."

Abigail's eyes slid to Dash. "Very well, Finn. You may go."

The man left without another word and she continued to stare down the wolf. "No answer? Hmmm...guess we're not quite the big bad wolf we like to think we are, huh?"

"I don't need to give you an answer, Abigail. Scent doesn't lie." He tapped the side of his nose and then reached out, running a knuckle over her cool cheek. "As for being a big bad wolf, you'll have to see for yourself how big and bad I am. Care to find out?"

She shoved his hand away. "Nice try, fur ball, but I've got better things to do with my time than waste it teaching you to beg."

He looked at her, amused. "You really are beautiful when you're bitchy.""

She didn't reply, just crossed her arms in front of her chest, her eyes unblinking. "And you are like a dog with a bone. Does the fact you keep changing the subject mean you didn't bring the required serum with you?"

"Of course I brought it." He gestured to the insulated container on the chair in front of the desk. "Gehrig drove with Bette last night to our compound in Ogunquit for the vials of oral antibodies."

Abigail didn't comment, just followed his gaze to the essential package.

"In fact with this new outbreak, Sean thinks an emergency supply should be kept here with you," Dash added.

"With me?" She raised an eyebrow.

"Wow, Abby. Self-important, much? No, your majesty. Here, as in, kept with the vampire council. You already have the necessary facilities to store blood. You can house the serum, too. What Gehrig couldn't find in any decent quantity was untainted blood. On such short notice, there wasn't enough on hand. Your kind requires fresh blood infused with living antibodies. Lily is the original source, the healing font if you will, with the strongest antibodies of everyone."

He watched her face as she listened before continuing. "She will give each of the infected vampires an ampule of her blood when she and Sean return with Sébastien. There's nothing better under the circumstances, and since the virus ravages living flesh much faster than it does the undead, your donors need our help first."

Abigail couldn't argue with facts, however much she wanted to. "Shall we, then?" She indicated with a nod toward the door.

He swung his arm out for her to lead the way. Without so much as a blink, she turned and walked out of Finn's office. Neither said a word as she moved through the hall to a door marked private.

The lights snapped on automatically and he followed her down a curved set of stairs. It hit him then, they were heading toward an isolated bunker, the lair for the vampire residents of this shadow house. He was outnumbered, and his shoulders tensed at the dangerous potential for this to go badly.

Abigail stepped off the bottom stair into a spacious common room. There were no windows and no doors, or at least none he could see. As Finn had assured, the vampires were waiting. Some sat, others stood, but they all wore the same irritated expression and Dash's body went into defensive mode.

"Abigail, what's going on? Why have you dragged us from our leisure to be subjected to this inquisition, yet again?" one asked. "There is a rumor the donors are infected with HepZ. How is that possible?"

She lifted her hand to stop the hum of complaints. "Our donors were screened, but somehow a small amount of tainted blood made it through to our stored blood. Most likely from the original outbreak. We have the situation well in hand, and the wolves have supplied the antiviral to administer to the donors, but the degree of vampiric exposure must be determined and dealt with. This is Sébastien's command, not mine."

The grumbling vampire made a face. "And what are we supposed to do until the wolf cleans house? Starve?" His glare shifted to Dash. "That's providing the wolves can do it properly this time."

Annoyed, Abigail fixed the vampire with an impatient look before answering his question with a shrug. "Stop whining. You will all do what vampires have done for millennia, but I caution you to hunt with care. We no longer have an ally in the police department to cover unintentional mistakes."

"What about *intended* mistakes?" The same vampire snickered, his question more of a sneer than a joke.

A few others laughed, and the room buzzed with sudden excitement. He grinned, flashing his fangs and high-fiving the male vampire standing to his side.

"Hitting the clubs for fresh blood and young pussy, now that's a remedy I can sink my teeth into." He slid his eager gaze toward Dash. "So, wolf boy, where do you want us for the sniff test?"

Dash's jaw tightened and he turned on his heel toward the stairs, twenty sets of undead eyes following his angry stride.

"Where are you going?" Abigail called after him.

"Some place where I can breathe. The level of asshole down here stinks."

"You can't go. You have orders from your alpha," she shouted after him.

Dash stopped and pivoted around, his eyes blazing. "No one orders me to do anything, Abigail. I volunteered for this mercy mission and now I un-volunteer." One corner of his mouth curled up in annoyance. "And you have the nerve to say my kind is lacking? Take a look in the mirror, honey. This room is choked with cold-blooded disrespect for life. I'd rather let you rot than lift a finger to help any of you."

With a snarl, the same eager vampire lunged for Dash, his fangs bared and his hands clawed ready to strike.

Electricity skimmed across Dash's skin, a slick burn penetrating deep into sinew and firing through synapses and nerves. His eyes shifted from soft brown to a glowing yellow and his muscles coiled and undulated beneath his skin.

Thick, black fur rippled across his body and he flung himself upward with a snap of bone and ozone. His clothing in shreds as his body reshaped to a large black wolf.

"NO!" Abigail shouted at them.

The wolf launched himself at the vampire and the two collided in a twist of claws and fangs.

Saliva dripped from the vampire's lips. His long, sharp fingernails reaching for the wolf, digging into fur and flesh, but the beast was too strong. With a wrench of his large jaws, Dash sent the vampire crashing into the wall.

Plaster crumbled, and glass from the entertainment system shattered to the floor in shards and jagged pieces.

An audible wheeze left the vampire's lungs on impact and blood dripped from his mouth and nose. He ran an arm across, smearing the dark crimson mess and his eyes darted to the enormous wolf.

Dash advanced. His lips peeled back over his canines. He lowered his head in warning, snapping and snarling, but the vampire didn't heed. The bloodsucker sprang from his squat by the wall to attack.

Another vampire moved to circle in, but the first hissed, the sound slurring past his fully descended fangs. "He's mine!"

It was all the distraction Dash needed. He vaulted from muscular hind legs. His large paws hit the vampire square in the chest, knocking him back, only this time sharp canine's sunk deep into the vampire's cold throat, the sound of crushed cartilage and bone muffled in the wolf's ears.

The vampire gurgled, blood pouring from his wound as he tried to fight. With one violent jerk, Dash tore the undead's head from his shoulders, throwing it against the ruined wall.

A collective gasp shook the room, but no one else dared approach. Dash stepped off the vampire's headless chest, black blood pooling beneath the severed stump.

The wolf turned with a growl. His bloodstained lips pulled back over his teeth in warning to the others before his entire body quaked, reshaping to his human form.

Naked and panting, he glared at Abigail daring her to speak. When she said nothing, he walked silent but deadly to the stairs, his body tight and smeared with blood-streaked sweat.

❧

Abigail's eyes tracked Dash as he disappeared up the staircase, but she didn't follow. Instead, she whirled to face the others. "Fools! All of you! Clean up this mess."

Her gaze moved to the shattered glass and the lifeless vampire decaying rapidly in the bloody gunge on the floor and walls. "And you will NOT call the donors for help. They are sequestered until further notice. Deal with it."

Ignoring their protests, she climbed the stairs after Dash. She needed to fix this and fast. How the hell was she going to explain to Sébastien if the wolves bailed?

Finn stood in the hallway outside the entrance to the private den, his eyes furtive and blinking.

"Where is he?" Abigail demanded.

"I…I put him in the only empty suite left on the first floor." He motioned toward the staircase and then led her up, reluctantly waiting beside the closed door as she knocked.

"Dash! We need to discuss this."

No answer.

She exhaled. This did not bode well for either of them. Curving her finger over her lip, she glanced sideways to Finn. "You're the proprietor. Use the master key."

He fumbled in his pockets, excuses and apologies flying.

"Oh for heaven's sake!" She wrapped her hand around the doorknob and twisted. A quick snap of metal and the door snicked open.

She pushed on the broken lock, swinging the door just enough for her to see Dash standing by the window. The muscles in his back and arms still coiled and tight, telling her to approach with care.

His fingers curled in and out, but when she called his name again, his hands stilled, and he slanted his head to the side as though willing to listen.

Wrong time, wrong place, but the scent of him took over and her eyes swept his naked body. She licked her lips. Wide shoulders tapered in thick muscled ropes to a narrow waist and his solid buttocks fed into strong thighs and long legs. It was all she could do to keep her fangs to herself.

"Finn, find the wolf suitable clothing and then get out. There are matters to be discussed. We are not to be disturbed." She shot the man a look that said immediately if not sooner and then dismissed him outright.

The nervous proprietor bobbed his head and neither she nor Dash moved until he came back with a pair of sweatpants and a sweatshirt. Finn swung the door closed behind him, first snatching the do-not-disturb sign to hang on the broken lock.

"This is the best we could do for now," Abigail gestured to the clothing Finn laid out on the bed.

Dash didn't respond.

"No one here is as big as you, so no shoes. Sorry. I'll call a car service to take you home when we're done here."

"Don't do me any favors." Dash's tone was low, but severe.

"I'm not. You still have a job to do. This is vampiric culture, Dash. Our way of life. You don't have to like it, and quite frankly I don't care if you disapprove, but you will respect it."

At the word *respect*, he gave her his full attention, turning completely around.

Mouth dry, Abigail couldn't take her eyes from him. He was magnificent. His anger enhanced the smell of his natural musk beneath the rush of adrenaline in his blood and her mouth watered. That coupled with the lingering scent of his recent phase made her head swim. She inhaled and her body reacted. Slick wetness gathered between her legs and her nipples ached. She wanted him so badly she could taste it.

"You find my kind repulsive, yet you demand I respect you and yours. You're a cliché, Abigail. A fraud. From your glamor-goth, cosmo-chic vamp look to the bullshit defenses you surround yourself with. You don't find me distasteful, Abby."

"I told you not to call me that."

Paying no attention, he continued. "In fact, it's the complete opposite. All you can think about, is how I taste. My blood. My cock. Right now you're so preoccupied with me, you can't see straight."

Abigail smoothed the front of her fitted blouse, ignoring Dash's unwavering stare, but she couldn't keep her gaze from drifting to his groin.

Dash's cock thickened at the unconscious shift in her body language and she knew her pupils spread dark and dilated in clear arousal, the evidence of her grudging desire.

That was all the invitation he needed. The feel of his body was pumped. Every lust-driven trigger tightened its hold on the need for release as he grabbed her around the waist.

"Wait—" Her hesitation was half-hearted, and she knew it.

He didn't let her finish. Instead, he crushed his mouth to hers. He bit her lip, sucking it into his mouth before drawing his tongue along the tender ridge. "Say it, Abigail. Tell me you want me."

The taste of him filled her, sending her senses reeling. She sucked in a breath, gasping at the raw need and the visceral feel of him coating her tongue.

She licked the tender flesh beneath his jaw. The flavor of the dead vampire's blood mixed with Dash's sweat, left her head dizzy and her mouth watering for more.

Emotions tore through her. The one time she gave of herself and expected love in return, her tenderness was shoved back in her face. She'd lived the rest of her existence fighting the leftover worthless feeling, never good enough to love, so she demanded respect instead. Sex was a tool. Nothing more.

Memories tormented and harassed. *Push him away. Rip him to shreds. An eye for an eye, a head for a head.* But she didn't. Instead, she shoved her fingers through his hair, urging his kiss even deeper.

A haze of red lust covered her and she fisted Dash's hair, yanking his head to the side, exposing his throat.

Her fangs descended piercing her lip and the taste of her own blood fueled her frenzy. She drove razor tips into his jugular, gulping as his hot coppery blood filled her mouth.

Dash moaned and her lip curled in satisfaction as warm, crimson rivulets ran over her chin. Without warning he yanked himself away, the punctures on his throat raw and bleeding.

"Heal the wounds or I'll end you, permanently."

Excitement raced through her at the dangerous gold, ringing his intense stare. Abigail grabbed the sides of his head, only this time licking the torn flesh and veins, sealing them.

She let go and stepped back. Her tongue darting to lap at the bloodstained corners of her mouth. "Not bad for a wolf."

The yellow halo spread, and Dash growled low, his pupils dark and as dilated with arousal as hers. His cock jerked and he clutched her shoulders to spin her around, reaching for the long, antique letter-opener from the writing desk against the wall. He wrapped his hand around the scroll-worked handle before pushing Abigail face first onto the bed.

One tug shoved her skirt to her waist, the clingy fabric bunching at her lower back, exposing her completely.

Her ass was gorgeous. Like the finest marble, rounded smooth and firm with a tiny piece of black lace trailing the seam of her crack. Holding her down, he snapped her thong, tearing it with a single twist of his thumb and forefinger.

"Hey! That was expensive!"

Whack! The flat edge of the long, blunt letter-opener smacked her firm ass. She sucked a breath through her teeth and her body tensed.

The scent of her wet pussy made Dash's nostrils flare and he smirked. "You like it rough, don'tcha, vamp-girl?" *Slap!* The flat of the blade struck her again.

A moan left her mouth and she arched up onto her knees, her fingers curling into the bedspread as her belly and thighs flexed taut.

He took the pointed tip of the dull opener and drew it across the white globe of her bottom, tracing the rising red welts in her cold flesh. To his surprise a thin line of thick blood formed, seeping in a delicious drip down the porcelain curve toward her crack.

Already buzzed from the vampire blood swallowed in the fight, Dash's inhibitions drained, and his need intensified. With a deep rumble, he dropped the blunt tool to the floor and gripped Abigail's hips, his tongue trailing her tempting crack, lapping at her blood.

She moaned at the rasping feel, sliding her knees up to invite him to her luscious ass. His fingers dug into her cold, soft flesh and he spread her wide, dipping in to lick her wet folds.

On all fours, she threw her head back, grinding her slick pussy into his mouth. He pushed her thighs apart and ran his hand along the inside curve, slipping his fingers over her taut nub as he plunged his thumb deeper.

In a flash, he flipped her onto her back and without missing a beat, little stings from his teeth on her clit and soft pink folds sent her over the edge, her legs quivering as her orgasm crashed through her body.

Dash tore his mouth away and she snarled, ready to dig her fingers into his hair and shove his face back to her pussy. Demanding snarls turned to whimpers as his thumb took over, working her wet slit while he stroked his cock with his other hand.

A feral growl left his mouth and the untamed sound rippled over her skin. She bucked, riding his hand until he pulled away to plunge his cock deep into her hot, waiting flesh.

At the slick tight feel of her walls, his member swelled, his head bulging, stretching her until she cried out with pain and pleasure.

Abigail's body spasmed against the hard length of him. Her skin, electric beneath his hand, beneath the heat pouring off his body.

He rode her hard, thrusting against her sweat sheened skin, the sweet sting of each slap adding to the merciless tension. She wept blood tears, her body spread wide and betraying her each time she exploded in climax.

Dash reared back with a howl, his cock corded and tense with the need for release. He held her still, burying his thick shaft to his balls. Hot jets pumped deep and pleasure shuttered through his cock and into his lower belly as her inner walls milked him dry.

Abigail shuddered. Every nerve ending shivering with pleasure, every cell tingled with living warmth, the kind she hadn't felt since she was human.

Her body quivered in aftershock and then the tension ebbed, but Dash's body held her hostage.

"Get off me!" An indignant half-snarl, half-whimper left her mouth and she reached out, her fingernails scoring his face and shoulder, but his swollen head refused to let go.

Slowly he moved his hips, working his still engorged sex, emptying every last drop into her tender flesh.

She reached for him again and this time she caught his wrist and yanked him forward, sinking her teeth into the blue veins of its tender underside.

His blood coated her tongue and her clit pulsed with the copper taste laced with sex and sweat. She cried out again, her body shivering with the intensity until his cock relented and released its hold.

They fell forward together on the bed, spent. She licked his wrist sealing the wound, lapping every last drop from his skin, her shoulders shaking with unshed sobs.

Shocked at the unexpected show of emotion, Dash reached for her, but she slapped his hand away.

"Abigail?"

She shrugged him off, scuttling from beneath his weight. A ragged breath tore from her mouth and she wiped her few tears on the back of her hand.

He reached for her again and this time she turned on him.

"Don't touch me," she ground out.

"Come on, Abigail. Don't be that way."

Jaw tight, she stared at him. "I don't need or want your pity."

"I don't pity you, Abby. I'm just trying to understand you."

She climbed off the bed and pulled her skirt down, smoothing the front and sides before running a hand over her mussed hair.

"There's nothing to understand, and there's certainly no need for any conversation other than what's necessary to accomplish the task assigned us." She drew in a steadying breath and frowned at the visceral taste of him lingering at the back of her throat.

"That's cold. You can't ignore what just happened," he countered.

Her eyes narrowed as she looked at him, naked and resting on his elbow. "Are you that hard up you need to make more of this than it is?" She dabbed a finger to the corner of her mouth. "We weathered a little hate sex. So what. Sometimes you need to let the steam out of the pot before it blows."

Her eyes betrayed her again though, drifting to his still swollen member and she caught his smirk.

"Lose the smug look, wolf-boy. You made me come. Big deal. You're not the first, and you won't be the last."

"We can always go for a new record. Olympic level orgasms." He nudged her with his foot. "I'm game if you are."

His suggestion made her clit throb, and anger spiked at her body's unconscious response. "Touch me again and instead of sucking your cock for fun, I'll use it as a straw and drain you dry."

Without another word, she turned and swung the door wide, leaving him there. He called after her, but she ignored him, stalking past Finn at the bottom of the stairs, disregarding him as well.

"*Uhm*, should I—" Finn began, but one look from Abigail and he shut up.

Yanking the front door open, she stepped out onto the tall steps and sucked in a breath. The wolf's scent enveloped her, making her senses swim. It was all she could do not to turn on her high heels and ride him until he begged her to stay forever.

She sniffed. "If you want a dog, Abigail, get one from the shelter."

She was lying to herself and she knew it. Dash Collier was in her blood and there was nothing she could do about it. The question was, would she want to?

Chapter Eight

*T*he Red Veil was in full swing. The clock read well past two a.m., yet people were everywhere, making Dash grateful for the quiet corner reserved for him in the VIP lounge.

"Wait. Are you telling me, you and Bette are officially an item?" he asked, eyeing Gehrig over his beer.

His brother shrugged, stealing a glance at his new girlfriend, a huge grin spreading at her unexpected blush. "She gets that high color from me." He gestured to her rosy glow. "Literally, man. From me." He grabbed his crotch and gave it a squeeze.

"Ugh. Do you have to be so crude?" Dash made a face.

Bette giggled. "Dash is right babe, but then again, I fancy your raunchy side."

Gehrig growled, moving Bette's hand to his crotch as well.

Dash rolled his eyes. "Okay, shock junkies. Dial it down on the touchy feely. Mission accomplished. At least now I know to take cover when the shit hits the fan tomorrow night."

Bette slipped her hand from between Gehrig's legs to lace her fingers with his. "Why be negative, Dash? Gehrig and I both want to give this a chance. We're no different from any other couple, despite the odds."

Dash put his drink on the square napkin. "What about the taboo? Sébastien is coming back tomorrow to check on the progress we've made on his stored blood —" He frowned, not finishing his thought.

Gehrig took a deep sip from his beer. "If that's what you're worried about, don't," he countered. "I'm here to help with whatever you and Abigail have left to finish. Bette and I both are. We told you that yesterday."

"It's not that." Dash shook his head.

"What then? If you're concerned about the shit storm coming from Sean and Sébastien—" he spared a glance for Bette. "We're prepared for that too."

Dash exhaled. "It's not that, either." The older wolf rubbed a palm over his face. "Abigail and I will see the job through. You're my brother, and I've got your back no matter what road your love life takes. It's your choice who you hook up with."

His voice trailed off as he spotted Abigail on the other side of the dance floor walking toward her back office.

She paused for a moment, her eyes finding his through the mob of moving bodies.

Meeting the weight of her gaze, Dash moved to get up, but Bette put a staying hand on his arm.

"What is going on?" Gehrig asked, looking from his brother to his girlfriend for an explanation.

Dash didn't reply, but Bette shifted her gaze from Dash to Abigail's retreating figure and back again.

"Looks like I'm not the only one with pink cheeks tonight." Bette gave Dash a half smile.

"You can tell that from here?" Dash glanced across the dance floor and back again, doubtful.

Bette offered a small laugh, tapping on the corner of one eye. "Vampiric sight."

Gehrig's mouth dropped open when he realized what she meant. "Ha! After all your preachy bullshit you went and melted the ice queen." Grin on his face, he lifted his hand for a high-five. "Dog!"

Exhaling again, Dash shook his head before picking up his beer. "Please, I've been called that enough over the past few days, not to mention a few other choice names. And I didn't *melt* anyone. We sort of froze each other out, if you want to know the truth." He frowned. "Parts of me still have freezer burn."

"Ouch." Bette laughed. "Though, believe it or not, Abby's not the bitch everyone thinks she is."

She waited, hoping Dash would take the clickbait and comment, but when he didn't, she sighed. "In case you're too pigheaded to figure it out on your own, Abigail is all hard candy coating, but only to protect the sweet mush on the inside. It's all a front, Dash."

His eyes met Bette's nod. "I know."

She put down her drink and slid over to take his hand. Surprised at how uncommonly warm her fingers were, he didn't flinch.

"Abigail expects the worst from everyone, especially those who are different from us," she continued. "Every other race has disappointed her. Human, Fae, and especially Were. As for our own kind, we're notorious for arrogance and superiority, so Abigail hides herself in a cloak of dominance.

"She uses our natural conceit to keep lovers at bay and then discards them before there's time for feelings to develop. Sometimes even before they're done between her legs."

"Nice." Gehrig chuckled, earning a slap on the arm from her.

"It's not funny, babe." She frowned. "Abigail's nickname is Rough Rider, and not because she likes aggressive sex. It's because she flays the skin from anyone who tries to get too close."

"Is this just an observation or are you giving me fair warning to back off?" Dash asked.

Bette shook her head. "Abigail took pity on me when I had my heart broken by my sire. She witnessed what happened, and then taught me to be hard for my own self-preservation, but I never took my pain and disappointment to the lengths she has. Abby's made hate an art form, yet—"

"Yet what?" Dash prompted at her hesitation.

She looked at him. "These past few days with you—this is the closest I've seen her to cracking in almost one hundred years."

Gehrig exhaled hard. "Dude, maybe we better finish this job without Abigail. I know I jerked your chain about taking chances, but psychotic vampires are not the kind of playmates I had in mind."

He flashed Bette a quick smile. "I don't mean you, love, but your friend Abigail is a train wreck waiting to happen and I don't want my brother in any more danger than we bargained for."

Bette covered Gehrig's hand. "I understand, but Dash is under Sébastien's protection, like you. He has nothing to worry about."

Dash raked a hand through his hair, puffing out a rough breath. "I appreciate the insights, Bette, but you're not telling me anything about Abigail I didn't already suspect. Problem is, I can't get her out of my mind. It's like she's infected my blood worse than any virus. I need to know what happened to make her so hard, but she'd rather slit my throat than talk."

"You could always ask Sébastien. He would know." Bette offered. "He's her maker. It all started with him."

Dash snorted. "Now *that* speaks volumes." His smirk sobered and he looked at Bette, shaking his head. "Abby is going to tell me herself, even if it means I have to drag it out of her."

Bette's customary easy humor faded. "Dash, please don't take this the wrong way, but if this is just curiosity, then I'm asking as a friend—leave Abby alone. There's nothing to be gained if your only aim is satisfying your own morbid fascination."

He shook his head. "It's not curiosity, Bette. What I'm feeling goes way deeper than anything I've ever felt before. I can't explain it."

Bette exhaled, patting Dash's thigh. "Lots of layers to peel, then." She shifted her gaze toward the doors leading to the back offices and the private entrance to *Les Sanctuaire.*

"Dude." Gehrig eyed his brother, shaking his head. "If you're headed where I think you're headed, better take a big blade."

A small grin tugged at Bette's lips as she slid in beside Gehrig again. "From what Abigail said, he already has one of those." Chuckling, she walked her fingers toward Gehrig's crotch again. "Like older brother, like younger brother."

With a growl, Gehrig swept her up to straddle his lap. "You know it, baby."

Shaking his head, Dash drained his beer, dropped a ten dollar tip on the table for the waitress, and left them to their public display of affection.

As he walked through the crowd toward the back offices, his mind replayed the events of the past two days. Abigail cried in his arms and it wasn't just from the intensity of the sex.

Or was it?

He shook his head.

It went deeper than that. He knew it in his gut.

Her words said one thing all along, but her actions said otherwise. From her aloof, almost dismissive tone, to the way her eyes burned when she looked at him.

Nearly twenty-four hours had passed since she stormed out of the bedroom at the shadow house, and he couldn't shake the feeling there was a reason behind why Abigail had grabbed hold of his body and mind. It wasn't her blood or the lure of the taboo. It was more than that and for some reason it felt old. He nodded to himself. Something unfinished.

The bouncer posted in front of the private entrance barely nodded when he held the door open, and when the youngblood offered directions to Abigail's office with a knowing smug look, Dash didn't say a word.

He didn't care, just kept his wits about him. Especially, considering where he was and who else of the undead might be in residence tonight.

Abigail's office door was ajar. He pushed it open to find another youngblood sprawled naked on her couch.

The beefy vampire cracked one eye open at the intrusion and yawned. "She's not here."

"Any idea where I might find her?" Dash asked, trying to keep his face impassive.

The bloodsucker tucked one arm under his head giving Dash a once over. "You the new wolf?"

Dash nodded and the vampire answered with a grin. "So *you're* the one who got Frosty the Snow Bitch so hot and bothered. Man, I don't know what you did, but she was torqued and ready tonight. Her pussy was already soaked when she pulled me in here. It was good. Fast, but *Mmmm*, delicious." He licked his lips, fondling his balls.

Dash pivoted on his heel to leave.

"Don't waste your time, man. I mean it," the youngblood called after him, leaning up on one elbow as the wolf stopped, but didn't turn.

"Take my advice, one dude to another. She's not made for your kind, wolf. Hell, she's barely made for *our* kind. If she wants you, just fuck her for the hell of it and be grateful she doesn't kill you in the process."

"Where. Is. She?" Dash ground out.

"Probably feeding" the vampire said through a yawn. "After the way she rode me, she definitely needs refueling. Her rooms are upstairs toward the back, but you're not allowed above club level. You'll never make it past the guard."

Dash glanced over his shoulder at the languid bloodsucker. "Watch me."

∽

Dash walked down the corridor, careful not to call too much attention to himself. Not that it mattered. The vampires could smell him a mile away.

Abigail's suite was the one at the end of the hall to the left, according to the less than enthusiastic guard at the lair's entrance.

Dash had Sébastien to thank for his *get-out-of-jail-free card* or the sentinel would have made him a free lunch. Still, it was no picnic convincing the undead Neanderthal to check the log for approved guests while dodging a set of razor sharp fangs.

Abigail and four other elder vampires shared the building's middle floor, while Sébastien had the entire penthouse to himself, with a separate staircase leading to council chambers and the infamous backrooms of the club.

Dash heard the stories about those quarters and what went on behind closed doors. Based on the little he witnessed, there was no doubt in his mind about the depraved pleasures housed in those back rooms.

Mild curiosity would kill more than just the cat when it came to sticking one's dick where it wasn't welcome.

Besides, admission was strictly vampire and even then, only by invitation. He had no intention of switching teams, however curious he might be. Losing his place in the sun for a fuck session on a bed of sharpened nails was a deal breaker no matter how hot and tasty the vampiric lure.

He stopped in front of what he hoped was the right door and knocked.

"Abigail?"

No answer.

He made a face. Wasn't it like a woman to give the silent treatment where it wasn't warranted? He knew she could smell him as clearly as he smelled her. She was playing tit for tat, but he had good reason for not answering when she first knocked on the guestroom door at the shadow house. An adrenaline soaked Were was not one for rational conversation.

He sighed. Then again, perhaps a starving, sexually frustrated vampire wasn't either.

"I know you're in there, Abigail. I can smell you through the door. Talk to me!"

Nothing.

Dash inhaled again and the taste on his tongue was the same as what permeated her office. Sweat, blood and saliva. A confusing wash of anger and jealousy flooded his veins and heat skittered across his skin.

"Abigail!"

Still nothing.

"You're going to have to face me sooner or later." He pounded on the door, shouting, his voice echoing purposefully for everyone to hear. It was a dirty trick and he knew it. "You're afraid, Abby. You know it and I know it."

The door yanked open and Abigail stood in the threshold, her eyes blazing. "Why can't you leave me alone? What makes you think I'd have anything to say after you shout my business to everyone in the building?"

He blinked at her, taken aback. The usually elegant vampire was a mess. Her hair was a tangled nest and her mouth and throat were smeared with blood. Her once delicate silk shirt was torn down the center exposing bare breasts. It hung in long shreds to the top lace of her thigh-high stockings, but he knew she was otherwise naked underneath.

Stunned for a moment, he shook off his surprise, concentrating instead on what made him barge in on her in the first place.

A moan from inside the apartment pulled his attention from Abigail's disheveled appearance.

Behind her a young man lolled against a black leather chair, his eyes glazed in a satiated daze. His skin was ashen, and his throat, chest and arms dripped with blood from where she fed, yet he seemed almost blissful.

Dash pushed past her. "What the hell, Abby? He smells half dead!" The question didn't need an answer and the young man cried out in protest when Dash pulled him to his feet. "Can't you see he needs help, or he'll die?"

"Well, well. What have we here?" Another vamp-in-residence asked from the still open doorway. "I thought I sniffed something fresh and delicious."

With a giggle, the youth wormed his arm from Dash's grip and stumbled toward the waiting vampire, the bloodsucker's undead eyes already dilating with thirst.

"For God's sake, he needs help." Dash took a step toward the door. "Abigail took too much from him."

"I would worry more about who is going to help you, wolf." The vampire looked past Dash to Abigail. "I'll return him when I'm done, sweetie. It looks like you've got your hands full."

A vase sailed past, missing Dash by a fraction of an inch. Ceramic blue shattered against the wall, but the wolf didn't flinch.

"Are you done? Because we really need to talk." Dash asked, toeing broken glass to the side with his foot.

"I have nothing to say to you." She turned on her heel and headed toward the bathroom.

"Walking away isn't going to solve anything, Abby, and you know it."

She switched on the tap to wash her face, ignoring him as he moved to the bathroom doorway.

"You're being a baby and for someone as old as you that's pretty embarrassing." With a smirk, he crossed his arms and leaned on the door jamb.

Glancing at Dash's reflection in the mirror, Abby grabbed a towel and dried her face. "At least I don't age seven-to-one in dog years, Fido."

"Woof." He grinned, letting his eyes take in every inch of her. Bette was right. Abigail's color was plump and pink, with an air of human health and vitality.

"Abby, c'mon. The silent treatment is for weak women with nothing to say." He tried again. " —and you are *never* at a loss for words."

She shrugged out of her ruined blouse, wiping what was left of the blood from her neck and collarbone before turning to lean her lower back against the porcelain vanity, naked except for her sheer black stockings.

"Did it ever occur to you, I got what I wanted from you and now I'm done?" She met his eyes. "Why are you here, Dash? What's there to solve?"

"Us," he replied.

She dropped the soiled towel to the floor. "Us. And what does that mean, exactly?"

Dash took a step forward, moving closer until they were toe-to-toe. "Whether you want to admit it or not, there's something between us Abby, and it's buzzing like live current."

Running his knuckles over her bare arm, he grazed her bare nipple with his hand. "The thrill, the lust, but it's more than that and you know that, too."

Abigail's hand shot up, seizing his wrist. She forced his hand down, spreading her legs. "Is this what you mean? Is this the profound connection we share?"

He growled, cupping her mound and she hissed as his thumb slid into her slick slit. She rocked her hips against his palm, riding his hand and slipped her hand behind his head to urge his mouth to hers.

The tip of her tongue stroked the seam of his bottom lip and she sucked on the tender skin. Drawing blood with the edge of her fangs, her fingers dipped to free his cock from his pants.

"You're full of surprises Dash," she whispered as his thick member filled her smooth palm, a tight ring at the base of his shaft making her raise an eyebrow.

He chuckled as she squeezed his shaft, her lips spreading in a grin across his mouth. "All the better to please you with, my dear." His eyes closed as electricity skimmed over his corded flesh.

"That's my point. I never imagined you for the kind who'd settle for sloppy seconds." She shoved him back, his hand jerking from her pussy. "Did you happen to pass the youngblood in my office as you sniffed around for me?"

His eyes snapped open and his gaze flashed yellow in the mirror. Provoked, he growled low, but bit down on his urge to smash her face into the glass. He wouldn't take the bait. Instead, he pivoted her around with a rough shove toward their shared reflection.

"Look at yourself, Abigail." He gripped both wrists in one of his hands while fisting her hair in the other, forcing her to look in the mirror. "There's a flush to your skin tonight that could pass for human, but you're not, are you? You're light years removed from the tenderness of a beating heart."

"A human heart was something I left behind a long time ago." she snorted in reply. "Big deal."

Shaking his head, his lips were a thin, controlled line. "You're a—"

Her eyes flashed and she cut him off. "Go ahead, Dash. Say it. I dare you!"

His eyes met her reflected glare, but he didn't reply.

"I'm a what?" She goaded again. "Say the words so I can rip your tongue out with my teeth!" She lifted her chin, her mirrored eyes as hard as flint.

"Okay, Abigail. I'll say it. Out loud. You're a beautiful, foul-tempered wench sometimes, but behind your fanged bravado, you're still the most exciting woman I've ever met. I can't get enough of you, Abby, and if you stopped your bitchy bullshit for one moment, you might see you can't get enough of me, either."

She blinked at him, but the shadow that crossed her face didn't escape his notice. He let go of her shoulders, leaving her to watch in the mirror as he walked from the bathroom into the adjacent room.

Standing with his back to her, he finally turned and sat on the edge of her bed. "Why do you insist on baiting me? I don't appreciate whatever it is you're playing at, Abby. We had a connection. I felt it. You felt it. So, what now?"

Unapologetic, she smiled, grabbing a robe from the back of the bathroom door and shoved her arms into the sleeves. "I thought you liked playing with me."

Dash raked a hand through his hair. "Jesus, woman. Your emotional whiplash is killing me."

With the ghost of a smile, she tied the front of her robe. "If I wanted you dead, wolf, you'd be a drained pile of fur by now."

He got up from the bed and moved to stand in front of her again. "So why the attitude? I came here to talk. Not have you bite off my head." He flashed a mischievous look. "Though, you can use your teeth on my other head all you like."

Abigail's lips pushed to one corner. "You interrupted my dinner, Dash. What else would you expect from a hungry vampire?"

"First off, that wasn't dinner, Abby. That was vampiric binge eating."

She laughed out loud. "Vampire's don't have eating disorders, dude. I don't binge."

"If that wasn't binge thirst, then what was it? With the amount of my blood in your veins, you shouldn't be hungry for weeks." He angled his head her way, a slow grin spreading on his face. "Unless you're as insatiable in that department as you are in bed."

She smiled again. "You wish."

Dash hooked his fingers into her belted robe. "Are you telling me you aren't insatiable?" He tugged her against him, letting the hard bar of his cock say the rest.

Abigail lifted her chin, a denial on her lips, but before she could say a word, his mouth slanted over hers.

"Denial is a river in Egypt, your Majesty. You want my dick so bad, you tried to cock-block yourself gorging on that donor. Why is it so hard to admit you can't get enough of me?"

She snorted. "Nice try, wolf. You're fun to pet and play hide the stick with, but otherwise?" She shook her head. "Dogs may be man's best friend, but wolves are pack only. I learned that a long time ago. Your kind doesn't play well with others. Not long term, anyway."

"And vampires do?" he shot back.

"There's no need for prolonged playtime, Dash. Short, hard and sweet. Be happy with that."

Dash heard her words, but her scent told him differently. "You're lying, Abigail. You want more from me than just my dick and for longer than just a few days."

Her eyes found his. "Do you tempt me, Dash? She shrugged. "Yes."

"Then why—"

She cut him off again. "Will this ever be more than a casual fuck?" She shook her head. "No. Been there, done that, and the experience was nothing short of a fur flying shit show with a steaming side dish of betrayal. So I use you for your dick. Big deal. Why should I care when wolves use my kind for a quick high and nothing more?"

His jaw tightened. "I'm not like the rest of my kind, Abby. When you figure that out, come find me." He let go of her robe and stepped back. "Until then, I suggest you stay out of my way so I can finish the job we started."

"I can't do that."

He exhaled. "You can't have your cake and eat it too, Abigail, regardless of what your vamp code tells you."

"It's not that, Dash."

"Then whatever it is, just spit it out."

"One of the Jane Street donors is dead, and another is gravely ill. Your serum didn't work. Sébastien is on his way home," she said the words quickly.

"What?" He stared at her. "When were you planning to tell me? Is this the reason you're giving me the brush off?"

She opened her mouth but then shut it again as if not sure what to say. "No, but it's for the best."

"Why? So you can tell Sébastien this is my fault?" he shot back.

Abigail blinked at him. "Of course not, but you're as much to blame as I am."

He nodded. "You're right, I am. But I'm not the one who's guilty of burying my problems in sex and blood instead of facing them."

"Guilty?" The word was half question, half accusation and she inhaled. In that moment her eyes changed. They weren't her normal blue, nor were they vampiric red from blood or lust. They were a wild swirl of both.

"How dare you!" She flew at him, pummeling his chest. "You should die of the guilt you carry! You left me without hope! I loved you and you broke my heart, leaving me with nothing but an empty hole and a stake through my chest! You betrayed me!"

"What the fuck?" Stunned, he gripped her wrists. "Abigail! What the hell! Stop it!"

She fought, snarling, her teeth gnashing at him.

"Abigail Bigly! Stop. This. NOW!" He shook her hard, not knowing what else to do. It was as if she couldn't hear him.

At her full name, she crumpled in his arms, sobbing. "What you did, killed me more than when Sébastien took my human life."

Mystified, he didn't know what to say. "Abby, what are you talking about? I didn't do anything to you."

"Liar!" Her sobs were soft hiccups.

Dash's mind raced. Did vampires have breakdowns? "Abigail—do you know where you are?" He cautiously stroked her damp hair. "It wasn't me who hurt you. I swear it. What can I do to help you?"

She blinked and his words seemed to penetrate. Her eyes cleared and when awareness hit, she jerked back from him.

She blinked at him, just as confused. "I'm so sorry, Dash. I don't know what happened. Your scent—it—" She shook her head, her words trailing off.

His eyes searched hers, trying to understand as she mumbled to herself. "My scent, what? Abby?"

She didn't answer.

Reaching for her, he folded her in his arms and kissed her forehead. "I don't know what just happened, Abigail, and I don't think you do either, but I swear I'll help you figure it out once this serum issue is cleared up."

Embarrassed, she sucked in a ragged breath and nodded. Straightening, she took a step away from him, wiping her face on the back of her hand.

With a small smirk of a grin, he puffed out a breath. "You're a complete mess, you know that?"

She laughed looking at the red tear stains smeared on her hands and wrists. "Inside *and* out, it seems."

With a sad smile, she motioned to the crimson marks dotting his shirt and his neck. "Looks like I got you good, too."

Dash reached for her hand. "I would say so. Inside *and* out." He gave her fingers a squeeze.

Walking her backwards, he steered her into the bathroom until her butt pressed against the porcelain vanity. He untied her robe, slipping it from her shoulders. Lacing his fingers with hers, he pushed both hands to her pussy and stroked her clit with his thumb.

"You asked if this was our profound connection," he said, his lips hovering over hers. "It's part of it, Abigail." His rough pad circled her nub. "Want to help figure out the rest?"

Dash lifted her onto the vanity, and she spread her legs, her knees on either side of his hips. He reached behind and turned on the tap, letting hot water run.

Stepping back, he stripped his ruined shirt from his body, letting it drop to the floor before doing the same with his pants.

Naked, he moved between her knees again and kissed her, reaching for a washcloth from the shelf above the toilet.

His fingers slid over her lower back to the curve of her ass, his thumbs running along the soft globes before he dipped the square into the steaming water.

Dash bit her bottom lip, drawing the tender flesh through his teeth as he pulled the dripping washcloth from the basin.

Wiping her cheeks and neck, he let the mix of water and blood drip over her breasts and belly. He repeated the motion, grazing the rough terry over her nipples before squeezing fresh water over the firm mounds.

He let the clean water pool, mixing with her slick juices until he washed away every trace of the youngblood, earlier.

With a groan, he licked the trace of blood from her taut peaks, working his way to the juncture between her legs. "Your pussy is soaked, Abby. Even more than the rest of you."

She leaned back, gripping the side edges of the porcelain, spreading her knees even wider as he licked her slick folds.

He teased her clit with the rough edge of the terrycloth, and she gasped, jerking her ass closer to the end of the vanity and further into his mouth.

"You're mine, Abigail Bigly. MINE until I say otherwise, and that's never going to happen."

Dropping the cloth, he straightened before grabbing both her wrists. He held them in one hand behind her back as she arched forward. He bit her nipples, sucking the hard peaks until she begged for his cock.

He shook his head. "Not until I say. You're a control freak, Abigail. Too much so. You've baited me and tried to ride roughshod, but your nickname means nothing tonight. I call the shots."

Holding her hostage, he slid her forward, and when her feet hit the floor, he pulled her hands around toward her belly but didn't release his grip.

"On your knees, Abby." He helped her sink to the floor, keeping her hands locked above her head.

Her pink tongue darted out to moisten her lips and his cock jerked in response. He pressed his thick head to her lips. "Take every inch."

She opened her mouth and sucked him in, taking his full length. Dash growled, holding her wrists tight as he fucked her mouth.

He pushed her arms back, folding her elbows so he could grab the hair at the nape of her neck, keeping her locked, pushing her to take him deeper into her throat.

His head swelled to near bursting and he pulled his cock from her mouth. He wrapped his hand around his shaft and squeezed, running his palm over his smooth, full head.

"Show me your tongue," he growled.

Abigail parted her lips and licked the underside of his bulging head, cupping the pearl of cum at its end with the tip of her tongue.

The raspy feel sent Dash over the edge and he fisted the back of her head, urging her face up. Throwing his head back, he roared as spurts shot from his cock, hot and salty, onto her tongue and face.

Abigail squeezed his shaft, her hands milking him as she lapped every ounce, sucking his engorged head until he slumped forward, his arms around her shoulders.

Shaking, she pushed him back and climbed to her feet, her own body demanding satisfaction. Wiggling herself onto the vanity, she spread her knees, slipping a finger between her shaved folds.

"My turn," she murmured.

Cock still hard, he dipped his head and licked her clit, savoring the slick, sweet taste. His tongue laved her wet slit in short quick strokes, his hands gripping the sweet curve of her hips.

He shoved her thighs wider, letting his fingers delve inside her moist sex, her juices slick against his palm while his tongue and teeth worked her hard nub.

His mouth moved in time with his fingers, and Abigail fisted his hair, grinding her pussy farther into his hand. She cried out, her hips thrusting as she rode his palm, his mouth sucking her clit until her climax rocked her backward and her head cracked the mirror behind her.

Dash didn't blink. Instead he lifted her onto his thick cock and shoved her against the bathroom wall, burying his member hard and deep into her pussy.

She locked her legs around his waist, and he rode her hard. His hips bucking and thrusting upward until she exploded again, her fingers digging into his back as her juices dripped down his balls.

Exhausted, she slumped against his shoulder, her body shuddering with aftershocks.

With a grin, he nudged her chin up, taking her mouth again. He kissed her gently, the taste of their mingled essence teasing his tongue.

"Now you know," he whispered against her lips.

"Know what?" she replied with a gasp.

"What being a bitch will get you when you play with the big dogs."

Abigail nipped the bottom edge of his lip. "I can always bite back. Don't tempt me."

The erotic mental picture made his cock stir within her and Abigail's breath hitched in her throat.

"God help me, woman, everything about you tempts me."

Chapter Nine

"*I* cannot and will not have this in my absence, Abigail. I am most disappointed," the master vampire frowned.

They were alone in the council room. Sébastien with his back to the crackling fire, pacing before he settled into his council chair, Bette and Abigail side-by-side in front of him. Summoned.

Against Sean's better judgement, the wolves were in attendance as well, relegated to the back of the room. The Alpha of the Brethren of Weres and his mate did not look happy.

Dash watched Abigail. She stood straight with her head high while Bette fidgeted. Every muscle twitched in his body with the need to protect, to shove Abigail behind him and take whatever the master vampire dished out.

He knew it wasn't his place to interfere or interject, and reminders of where they were and who they faced loomed as large as the specter of the empty council chairs on either side of the master. What could he do? As it was, Sean barely had a say.

Four powerful vampires encompassed the New York council, and Sébastien was first among them. The others were not present, but with a snap of his fingers they would come, and Abigail and Bette would suffer, unless their master was persuaded otherwise.

Abigail would take the heat, and Dash's jaw clenched with the knowledge. The realization like vinegar in his mouth.

She dipped her chin before lifting her eyes to meet Sébastien's unwavering stare.

"There is nothing I can say in my defense. I allowed myself to become distracted, and in doing so, failed in my duties. I'm sorry, Sébastien." Abigail didn't blink, her voice surprisingly steady, considering.

He eyed her, his lips a harsh line. "*Ah,* but from the sweet glow evident in your skin and your even sweeter scent, clearly not sorry enough."

The vampire slid his eyes to where Dash and Gehrig stood, and quietly sniffed. "One need not stretch the imagination to guess what was so diverting."

Sébastien templed his fingers, shifting his attention to Sean. "I trusted you to choose emissaries that would uphold our truce, not abuse my hospitality."

Sean's eyes were flinty, but from his stance it was clear he measured his words. "I have no doubt my hunters made a foolish choice, though I wouldn't go as far as to claim your hospitality was abused. Not when the home team was so willing." His eyes turned to the two vampires standing in front of their master.

"Fraternization is strictly forbidden," the alpha continued. "Especially when on assignment, and liaisons with vampires are doubly so. I'm not thrilled with the incident, but it's done, and we have more important issues to discuss."

The master vampire raised an eyebrow. "You sound as though you forgive their indiscretion." He paused, studying Sean. "This from the same man who thought nothing of cutting a man's heart from his chest and offering it to me in a box. Has mated life rendered you so lax, Sean?"

Lily's eyes flashed at the unexpected insult. "I understand you're upset, Sébastien, but hurling passive aggressive jibes is uncalled for and completely unjustified. The four of them hooked up, that's all. It was just sex. They didn't commit murder, although it sounds as though you would have preferred that."

The master lifted one shoulder and let it drop, the exchange reeking of classic seventeenth century French *manqué d'intérêt*. Cold indifference.

The casual dismissal didn't faze Lily. "Vampire blood is a narcotic, Sébastien. It is addictive to our kind, and you know it. Vampires revel in how their blood intoxicates, leaving victims in a state of euphoria. Dash and Gehrig's lack of caution is what upsets us. Not that they bumped uglies with your girls."

The vampire made a face, but didn't argue the fact. Instead he turned to address Abigail. "It's beneath us to fraternize with animals. Bette is yet a youngblood. I left it to you to curb her appetites."

Sean glared at the master vampire, disbelief and anger dancing in his eyes. "Animals?"

Sébastien waved a dismissive hand in the air. "A manner of speaking and certainly not one for you to take offense. It is how we distinguish our kind from the dual-natured. I meant no disrespect."

"Then mind your words. I find them offensive," the alpha's voice was low, but firm.

The vampire inclined his head, but the muscle in his jaw clenched at the rebuke. His narrowed gaze swept the wolves before focusing again on Abigail and Bette.

"You will sever your attachments, immediately. Seek to further them no more. Have your needs seen to elsewhere, and if your proclivities run toward the unsavory, then pay a visit to our backrooms."

In tears, Bette glanced at Gehrig before finding Sébastien again. Her lips parted, but she dropped her gaze not saying a word.

"Is there something you wish to say, Bette?" their master asked, raising an eyebrow.

She shook her head, looking to Abigail for help.

"You'll have to excuse her, Sébastien. In the short time the wolves have been with us, she formed a romantic attachment to the young one."

Abigail glanced at Gehrig, her eyes resting on Dash before turning back to Sébastien. "They are — that is to say, both wolves are —"

Sébastien waved her off. "I was not born to darkness yesterday, Abigail. I am well aware of their intoxicating nature, but of all my fledglings, you alone should know to stay away from their poison. The lure of their blood and their pretty tongues are a curse. I forbid any further interaction."

Fists clenched, Sean moved to take a step forward, but Lily placed a hand on his arm.

The master vampire's eyes snapped to Lily. "No, my dear. Let your wolf approach. I have no fear of him or the feral anger stirring in his body, however compelling and heady the scent."

"I banned my hunters from consorting with your vampires as well, but clearly for different reasons," Sean shot back.

"Enough!" Sébastien slammed his fist down on the arm of his chair. "I refuse to let you paint this as anything other than what it is. Mixed relations are an embarrassment. I will not have it."

Sean eyed the master. "Nor I, but only because of the likelihood of addiction, and nothing else. We've chosen not to buy into the old prejudices. Like it or not, the world is changing."

"No more." Sébastien lifted a hand, bringing the argument to a halt. "My verdict is final. As you said, we have important matters to discuss and we've wasted precious time. What do you plan to do about this newest scourge? This unexpected outbreak?"

Sean blinked. Clearly Sébastien was not a fan of change, even in the abstract.

"This is not a new virus. It's most likely a new strain of the original. Viruses mutate. It's a fact that keeps scientists working round the clock. The serum our doctors developed worked perfectly in the spring, and preliminary tests pointed toward complete eradication."

"Preliminary?" Sébastien raised an eyebrow. "Are you saying you used the vampire race for clinical trials?"

"Sébastien, you know both races were treated on a wing and a prayer," Lily interrupted.

"Yes. With you as our savior." The master narrowed his eyes further. "How convenient."

Lily stalked two steps forward. "That's unfair. The wolves offered their help because it was the right thing to do. I offered *my* help because Sean asked it of me. I was under no obligation then and I'm certainly under no obligation now. I thought our races had finally found a meeting of the minds, but right now you appear as one-sided as ever."

Crimson streaks seeped into the vampire's brown eyes, his fingers curling around the carved end of his armchair in warning. "Keep your witch subdued, wolf."

Sean pressed his lips together, guarded. "Time is of the essence, Sébastien, and this is accomplishing nothing. We need to stop posturing for each other's throats."

"Which throats remain intact are yet to be decided, wolf." Abigail's words ground out.

Her glare flashed red and as though instinct kicked in, she moved to her usual spot flanking Sébastien's right.

Surprised, Dash's eyes jerked from Sean to Abigail. Unapologetic, she lifted her chin and flicked her gaze to Dash, yet when their eyes locked her face softened.

Sean ignored the outburst, concentrating his attention on the master. "You know better than to accuse us of using vampires as guinea pigs. The virus had spread to the human world. We had no choice but to use the serum as it stood. By late spring everyone tested clear. Vampire, Were, and donor. You saw the data and the results firsthand, Sébastien.

"It was you who labeled the virus, *HepZ*, congratulating yourself on your own cleverness. Z — the omega — the last letter of the Greek alphabet and the last we would see of our plague."

Sean exhaled before continuing. "Clearly more research is needed. If the current strain proves to be a retro-virus, then I'm not sure what can be done to prevent the spread other than a change in lifestyle.

"Vampires may have to alter the way they take their pleasure. This has already happened in the human world with the HIV pandemic."

Sébastien looked at Sean, aghast. "Unacceptable. Are you suggesting vampires screen their prey before they strike?"

"Prey?" Lily asked, ignoring sharp looks from both Sean and Sébastien.

"You are not one to question me, my dear." Sébastien snapped. "This is the second time you've overstepped tonight, and however fond I am of you, you *will* remember your place in my presence. Rémy is not here and cannot mitigate for you."

Lily waved her hand at him. "Sébastien, this is not a time for pomp or protocol. Anger and frustration have thrown both sides into old habits. This weekend you spoke of our races moving to the next level. That our truce should expand from a mere exchange of service to something more substantial.

"People are dying, and we can't be sure if even my blood is potent enough to wipe out this new strain. You must listen to reason, Sébastien."

Sean nodded. "Lily and I plan to head to the infected shadow house. As promised, she will give each resident vampire a dose of her blood. With your permission, we need current samples from those vamps infected for our researchers. We have the facilities to run further tests. We also want to take the body of the deceased donor—" he glanced at Dash.

"Leah. Her name was Leah," the wolf replied.

Sean nodded. "We want to take Leah's body for autopsy. We would also like permission to transport the other donor. The one who is gravely ill. I believe we can save her life."

Sébastien glanced to one of his guards and the man shook his head. With an annoyed exhale, the master vampire met Sean's waiting gaze. "No."

"No? Why not?"

"The infected donor you so gallantly hope to save has also expired. You may do with both bodies as you please, as we have no use for them, but I'm afraid this is where our association ends." The vampire spread his hands. "However amusing our connection has been, you also are no longer of use to us."

"Use?" Lily questioned. "You certainly toss that word around with ease, Sébastien. What about our truce? Our plans for the future? Don't you think you're being rash?"

The vampire's irises glowed red as he pushed his chair back. "You were warned, witch." In a flash he vaulted forward, fist raised in a backhanded strike.

Lily slid into a defensive stance and lifted her arm to block the blow, but before she could defend herself, Sean lunged for the vampire. Rage poured through his body, his muscles coiling and writhing with the need to phase, but he held back.

Sean seized the rush of fury in his veins, harnessing the power. His fingers ripped through the vampire's custom-made suit, a vise grip taking hold of the master's shoulder.

"Touch her and you die."

Eyes flashing, Sébastien hissed, but relented. He shrugged Sean off and smoothed the front of his ruined suit jacket.

Dash and Gehrig turned with Lily toward the guards, staring them down ready to phase, but Sébastien snapped his fingers and his guard pulled back. The master walked to his chair and without a word backhanded Abigail, sending her flying into the wall.

Concrete dust and bits of rock crumbled around her as she slumped to the ground. One of the guards bent to help, but straightened with a single look from Sébastien, leaving her where she fell.

Dash pushed forward to help her, but Gehrig held him back. "Leave her be. It's not our place."

Sébastien sat, his eyes sweeping Sean and the rest. "That is correct, wolf. At least one of you realizes that fact. It is NOT your place."

He shifted his sight to Sean, ignoring the alpha's still tensed muscles and hair trigger fury. "Whatever fellowship we enjoyed is over. Take yourselves from my sight. I have no desire to begin a war, but should our paths cross again do not expect the same civilities."

He let his gaze move to Lily, defying Sean's warning growl. "Rémy will be informed of our breach, though it is his choice to continue under your spell or side with his own."

"Both of you please, stop. This meeting has spiraled out of control. What about the virus?" she asked.

Sébastien spread his hands, resting his palms casually on either arm of the council chair. "We are no longer your concern. I gave my orders before one word was uttered in this unfortunate debate."

"What orders?"

"Death. You heard my guard—" He gestured to the vampire standing beside Abigail as she struggled to her knees, her hair and shoulders covered in gray concrete dust and blood. "The second donor regrettably did not survive."

Lily exchanged a glance with Sean. "But you said she succumbed to the virus."

Sébastien's grin was evil. "Exactly. The moment she took her last breath the entire shadow house was put to death. In the future, death will come to any and all infected, along with everyone they encounter. Vampire, human—" Sébastien's eyes locked on Sean. "Or Were."

"Then you do have a taste for war after all." The Alpha of the Brethren pulled himself to his full height, all six foot four inches of solid muscle supernatural glory.

The master shook his head. "*Au contraire, mon ami.* I have a taste for blood. Now get out before I choose to sample yours."

"Time and place, Sebastien. Name it and I'll be there, claws and fangs waiting."

Chapter Ten

"What is this?" Sébastien asked, looking at the stack of folders in Calypso's hand.

"Bette asked me to bring these to you. They are the reports from the Jane Street shadow house." Her gaze dropped.

He eyed the human. "Look at me, child."

Calypso lifted her eyes.

"Why did Bette give this to you instead of bringing them herself? Where is she?"

The girl chewed on her lip. "Finishing up with tonight's scheduling and staff assignments."

He took the reports from her and put them on the desk blotter, but didn't open them. "Why is Bette handling the staff? Where is Abigail?"

Calypso's eyes went wide with dread. "I...I..." she stammered. "I...don't know."

"Leave the child alone, brother. Can't you smell her fear?"

Both sets of eyes slid to the visitor at the chamber door leading from the council room.

"Rémy. I wasn't expecting you," Sébastien frowned.

The blond vampire walked in with his signature cloak draped over his arm. "The weather in Russia is foul this time of year and Jenya had a desire to see the foliage along the east coast."

He set his coat on the sofa and moved to a chair in front of Sébastien's desk. "Calm yourself, Calypso. No one is going to shoot the messenger. Tell Bette to come upstairs after she gets the staff settled."

The girl didn't need to be told twice. Between Sébastien's growing annoyance and the way the firelight highlighted the ruined half of Rémy's burned face, she disappeared as quickly as possible.

"Foliage?" the master raised an eyebrow.

A wry smirk played on Rémy's lips. "Why not?"

Sébastien's gaze narrowed. "The wolves called you."

"Just one."

"Sean?"

Rémy shook his head. "Lily."

Sébastien shoved his fountain pen back into its holder. "She's not even a true wolf."

His brother laughed. "No? I thought running with them on the beach two weeks ago proved that otherwise."

Sébastien shot him a nasty look. "That means nothing."

"Oh, it means a great deal, brother. Even more than you think, or have you forgotten she has the ability to walk between worlds, to harness the dead and sees the past as well as the future."

"What has that got to do with anything?" The master's frown pulled down even more.

"It doesn't," Remy replied. "But you seem to forget burning bridges. Especially such powerful and fateful ones, are not how you and I survived these past centuries."

Sébastien shrugged. The same indifferent shrug he gave Lily two weeks earlier.

"And imagine my surprise when I learned you severed all connection with the wolves. That you had done so alone, without as much as a nod from the rest of the council." Remy's feigned shock was more accusation than anything else.

"Last I checked, I was the supreme, and I do not require a *by your leave* from anyone." Sébastien sniffed.

Rémy tilted his head in doubt. "I wouldn't be so sure about that, brother. You may be our supreme, but not when you play fast and loose with the wellbeing of your own kind. You ordered an entire shadow house put to death rather than allow the wolves to come in."

"They crossed the line," he shot back

Remy's brow shot up. "You mean they didn't bow and scrape."

Sébastien's eyes narrowed. "Have a care, brother."

"I do care. Something it seems you are incapable of."

Sébastien shook his head. "First the Alpha of the Brethren, now you."

"What?"

The master laughed, but the sound was scornful. "You've both surrendered your manhood to what lies between a pair of shapely legs."

Remy sat back in his chair and pursed his lips. "If I didn't know you better, I would take offense to that."

Both sets of eyes looked at the beautiful dark haired vampire standing in the doorway.

Despite Sébastien's glare, Rémy's lips pulled into a genuine smile. "*Moya lyubov.*" My love.

Jenya moved to Rémy's side, the Russian endearment bringing a glow to her dark eyes. She dipped to kiss his mouth, trailing her fingers along his cheek before turning to greet his brother.

"Rather imperious these days, aren't we, Sébastien. Your Napoleon Complex is showing." She grinned. "Sounds like you need to get laid."

Remy took Jenya's hand and laughed, but Sébastien sniffed. "Neither of you have a right to judge. You're off enjoying the delights of marriage and I'm here dealing with this." He lifted the files from his desk, letting them drop from his fingers for effect.

"Dramatics, brother?" Rémy chuckled, sliding his arm around Jenya's waist and easing her onto the arm of his chair "Last I looked, there are no chains keeping you at your post. You revel in control. A trait you and your progeny, Abigail, have in common. Where is she anyway?"

Almost on cue, Bette knocked on the open door. "You sent for me?"

Sébastien waved her in. "You remember my brother in blood and his mate." He gestured to Rémy and Jenya.

Bette nodded. "It's an honor to meet you. Would you like some refreshment?"

"That can wait. Where is Abigail?" Sébastien interrupted.

Bette looked at the master vampire and squashed the urge to fidget or drop her gaze. "Abigail is ill. She hasn't left her room for three days."

Sébastien stood, pushing his chair back. "Why wasn't I informed? Has anyone thought to take her sustenance?" He reached for the phone. "Where is the closest shadow house with donors to spare? Calypso is too weak yet, but I will sacrifice her if need be."

Bette shook her head. "She won't feed."

His eyes found Bette's and slowly he put the phone back in its cradle. "What do you mean *won't* feed."

"She refuses."

"That's ludicrous! I won't have it." His hand slapped the desk. "Is this some kind of hunger strike because I sent her wolf lover away?"

"What?" Rémy asked. "My, my…look what we miss when we stay away so long. And what does the Alpha of the Brethren have to say about this, brother?"

"Shut up, Rémy. Why don't you ask Sean yourself?" Sébastien grumbled.

Remy eyed him. "I don't need to. I already know."

Ignoring the other elder, Sébastien looked at Bette for explanation. "Well?"

"It's not a hunger strike, Sébastien. You should know better than to accuse Abigail of being vindictive. I told you. She's ill."

"Ill? With what?" No sooner did the words leave his mouth than his lips parted in stunned silence. He sunk down in his chair.

HepZ.

Rémy got up from his seat, pressing a quick kiss to his wife's temple. "Get Sean on the phone. There's no time to lose."

"No." Sébastien's voice was low but firm.

They all gaped at him.

"What do you mean no?" Rémy's surprise and doubt warred on his face. "Abigail is your only remaining progeny. Would you see her die the same horrible death as Amélie? Maybe worse since this strain is unknown?"

"The animals insulted me. I will never call them."

"Then I was correct," Remy countered, anger in his soft voice. "You don't care. Not even for your own blood." He turned away from Sébastien. "Bette, have Abigail taken to the private exit. Jenya and I will drive her to the Compound in Maine. The wolves will see to her there."

Bette shook her head. "I can't. She won't go."

Sébastien's gaze shot up from his folded hands. "Why not?"

Bette licked her lips, her fingers twisting inside her pocket. "She blames herself for the deaths at the infected shadow house. The donor she fed from is already dead. She refuses to feed now because of the chance of spreading the virus. She is ready to die as you ordered. Same as the others."

He stood. "The illness is that advanced?"

Bette nodded. "She wants you to be the one to end her life since you gave her this existence."

Jenya's eyes were severe as she looked at Sébastien. "It's very easy to give a faceless death-order from behind your desk, but very hard to watch someone you love die by your command. Think carefully before you speak next, Sébastien. Immortality is a long time to carry regret."

❦

"No. He attacked you."

"He tried to attack me, Sean. You came to my rescue." She paused. "Not that I needed it. Plus, after you nearly crushed his shoulder, he'll think twice before doing it again." Lily shot back over her shoulder.

"That's not the point."

She stood in front of her closet, boots in hand, the knee length shitkickers ready with the rest of her packed clothes. "Then would you mind telling me what is the point?"

"Stop packing. We are not driving to New York." He didn't look up from his brooding in the bathroom doorway, his eyes on the low fire in the grate in the bedroom.

She put the boots by her suitcase and shoved her hands onto her hips. "They need us, Sean."

"The vampire council cannot snap their fingers and expect us to jump. What kind of precedent does that set for me as Alpha of the Brethren? Weres do not bend to vampires or any other race," he replied, but seeing the frustration and disappointment in her face, he yielded a bit.

"We tried, Lily." He shrugged. "However, a one-sided compromise will never work."

Lily sunk onto the edge of their bed. "I get that, but don't you think the more important precedent is that your hunters know they come first? Not your pride?"

He looked over at her. "That's not fair."

She flung her hand toward the bedroom door. "Dash is downstairs waiting for you to decide, as are Rémy and Jenya. Hell you're going to have to buy a new area rug with the way he's pacing if you don't get off your gorgeous ass and do something."

Sean's eyes narrowed. "When did you talk to Rémy?" He turned, lifting one hand. "You know what? I don't want to know."

Lily looked at her husband. Sean was the bravest man she'd ever met, dedicated and loyal to a fault, but once crossed he'd sooner rip your throat out as look at you.

"You're right. I should have talked to you before contacting Rémy. It's not fair, but Dash loves her."

"Who?" Sean asked, annoyed.

Lily just looked at him.

"Abigail?" the alpha scoffed. "You can't be serious. She's a vampire."

"Now you sound as pig-headed and prejudiced as Sébastien. What happened to not buying into old taboos?" she countered.

"It's not the same thing and you know it. Since Mitch left to claim his position as Alpha in the Canadian North, Dash is in line to be my second. Gehrig is too young, however talented a hunter. Dash is not going to risk himself or his position shacking up with an undead bitch queen."

"He loves her. I know it, Sean."

Sean pointed a finger at her. "Ah ha! He never said he loved her. You just assume."

She shook her head. "No. I *know.*"

Lowering his hand, he stared at his wife. "Lily, what have I said about tap dancing inside my hunters' heads? You can't trespass on people's thoughts simply because you have the psychic ability."

"Now who's not being fair? I didn't trespass." She crooked her fingers into quotation marks. "Dash is broadcasting his feelings so loudly I didn't have to. I can practically taste his ache, and let me tell you, that boy has it bad.

"Gehrig is infatuated, too. He likes the dark-haired flapper vamp, but his connection is more physical than anything else. He's the one we need to worry about when it comes to addiction. Dash is in love. Full blown, tail wagging, face-licking love. He's not going to become dependent."

Sean scrubbed his face with his palm. "I don't know, Lily." He let his hand drop to his side, his eyes finding hers. "What about Abigail? You know as well as I, she's a callous predator to the core. Loyal to Sébastien and not exactly a fan of the fanged and furry."

Pride swelled in Lily's chest. Even with his silly pun, the torn look in his blue eyes and the set to his gorgeous jaw, told her he'd do the right thing.

"It's all a front. Abigail loves Dash as much as he loves her." Heat climbed up her cheeks at his suspicious look. "Okay, so I trespassed a little. But only in Abigail's head."

"How? They've only known each other a short time."

Lily shrugged. "When it's right, it's right. Abigail fought it hard to admit, even to herself. Trust me. This is not exactly her dream scenario, but like it or not, she loves him."

Sean grumbled a low consenting growl and nodded. "All right, you win, but only for Dash's sake and I will make certain the master vampire knows that going in."

She got up from the bed and went to him standing beside the bathroom door. She dragged her hands over his arms and muscled shoulders, twining herself around his neck.

"Thank you," she murmured, going up on her toes to press her lips to his.

"You're only saying that because you got your way," he replied, circling her narrow waist.

"That's not all I'm getting." Twisting in his arms, she took him by the hand and led him toward the shower.

Chapter Eleven

"*A*bigail—" Dash pushed past the vampires at the door to her room, ignoring the argument behind him.

Stunned, he looked down at her motionless form. She was a flicker of the woman who held him entranced just weeks before.

Lush curves had wasted to a bony frame and her cheeks were hollowed and sunken. Even her luxurious strawberry blonde hair hung in dull, lifeless strands. And the smell. Like decay.

It was clear. Her body was deteriorating at an unprecedented rate.

"Lily called you weeks ago." Dash glared at Rémy. "What does it take for you vampires to act? A congressional caucus?"

Rémy eyed the wolf, but there was no resentment in his regard. "Under the circumstances, I did what I could. If the decision was mine, you would have been summoned that very day. Unfortunately, Abigail's fate is Sébastien's to decide. She is his progeny."

"His *progeny*?" Dash mimicked Rémy's French accent.

"That's enough." Sean's eyes flashed and a flicker of yellow in the alpha's natural blue was a warning to the younger wolf. "Whatever your feelings, Dash, Rémy is not to blame. If it weren't for his influence, Sébastien would never have relented and Abigail would have no chance. I suggest you channel your emotions into something constructive or I will have you removed."

Sean's words were no joke, and he stared down the angry hunter, driving his point home.

Disbelieving, Dash glanced from Abigail's wasted form to his Alpha. "Look at her, Sean. One more day —" He couldn't finish the sentence.

Rémy put a hand on Dash's shoulder ignoring the wolf's immediate reaction to jerk away.

"Your sentiment for Abigail does you credit. She is near delirium, which means she has been in and out of lucid consciousness. We must work fast and we must work together if we are to help her at all."

Heavy truth behind Rémy's words was too much and Dash's shoulders slumped. The vampire tightened his grip before steering him to the opposite side of the bed.

"Sit beside her. Take her hand in yours," Lily encouraged as she moved toward the bedside.

Rémy looked at Dash pointedly. "You will need strength, both physical and emotional, to do what needs to be done. Abigail is not herself, and though she looks weak, her body will use whatever reserves necessary to protect itself against a perceived threat. Vampires do not die easily."

The vampire turned, gesturing for Lily. "Her fate is in your hands now, *ma petite sorcière*, or more exactly, in your veins. Work your magic. Touch her mind if you can. Reassure her."

Lily moved beside Rémy, her fingers brushing the ruined side of his face. "Your anxiety is so loud in my head you're deafening my ears."

He looked at her. "The contents of my thoughts are not your concern today, little witch." He took her hand from his cheek and moved it to Abigail's arm. "Focus your talents, here. She needs you. I do not. Have no fear."

Lily gave him a soft smile. "What lies beyond, holds no fear for me. Neither should it for you."

Without a word, a dusky shadow crossed the vampire's eyes and his jaw tensed.

Clearly, her words touched a vulnerable nerve, but she didn't push the issue. Instead, she nodded to Dash. It was time.

He scooted closer on the bed to stroke her pale cheek. "Abigail? Can you hear me, love? Open your eyes."

No response.

"Abigail—wake up. Look at me." He tried again, giving her a gentle shake.

This time she moaned, turning toward the sound of his voice. Her papery lids lifted and Dash cringed.

Her once sultry eyes were sickly yellow and marbled with bloody streaks—and not the uninhibited crimson he'd seen when she was angry or aroused. Abigail was no longer Abigail.

Her blank stare met his, so he tried again. "I'm here love and I'm not going anywhere. I've brought help."

Lily tried to probe her mind, but a curtain of black and red mist blocked her vision. She glanced at Rémy and shook her head.

"She needs blood before I can reach her mind. It's a confused jumble, but a cloud of rage is brewing, same as what this virus produced last spring. We need to work fast."

Sean moved to Lily's side and slipped a hand around her waist. "Lock your mind with mine. I won't let you do this without some kind of tether."

Lily shook her head again. "I'm fine. We are a long way off from that. Body first, mind later."

He kissed her temple. "Do it anyway. For me."

She nodded, opening her mind to his and locking their intimate mind path.

Okay?

He nodded. *Go for it.*

Rémy lifted Lily's wrist to his mouth and kissed the soft underside. Watching the harsh line of Sean's lips, he bit down, careful not to pull from her veins and risk the alpha's wrath, however tempting.

Blood pooled, and Rémy reached to turn Abigail's head. Lily held her wrist a few inches above her mouth, letting her blood drip onto Abigail's parched, retreated lips. It coated her teeth, dribbling from either corner onto the pillow.

"Drink, love. Please!" Dash encouraged, squeezing her hand.

"*Oui. Mon cher. S'il vous plaît,*" Rémy added. "Please, dear one. Drink."

The vampire opened her jaw, careful of her fangs. He massaged her throat, but seconds bloomed into minutes and minutes into longer.

No one spoke, and the quiet drip, drip, of Lily's blood was the only sound for what seemed like ages.

"Try her mind again. Maybe some of your blood got through," Dash suggested. Eager hope palpable in his voice.

Lily closed her eyes.

Abigail? I know you're in here. Talk to me. Yell at me for old times' sake. Tell me to go to hell.

A voice muffled back, the response far away and unintelligible, but an answer, nonetheless.

"She's in there," Lily said with a nod, "but she seems lost, muddled. Distant."

"Let me link with you. She might not answer if you call," Dash pointed out. "You're not exactly her favorite person. No offense."

Rémy looked at Sean. "The wolf cub has a point."

Dash exhaled. "For the last time, Rémy. I'm not a cub, I'm a full grown Were, and one of Sean's elite hunters. What is it with you vampires? You demand respect but feel it unnecessary to give any in return."

Rémy opened his mouth to reply, but Lily shushed them, lifting one finger. "Wait. I saw something."

All eyes focused on Abigail. Her stare was still blank, but then she blinked and for a split second the blood cleared, and her eyes were a lucid brown before sinking back into a yellow haze.

"She's in there. I know it. Maybe Dash is right, and he should merge with me as well." Lily looked between her husband and the elder vampire.

She locked her eyes with Sean's, and when she nodded, he released his mindlock, allowing Dash's mind to merge with Lily.

Ready?

The younger wolf's chuckle feathered across her mind. *This is trippy, but yeah.*

Call to her. Taunt her if you have to. Sean and Rémy will keep her from harming us on the outside, but it will be up to us to stop her from fucking with our minds in here.

He nodded, surprised to find he could see Lily in the mist surrounding them.

Abigail! Where are you?

Scuffling echoed in the distance and Lily nodded, gesturing toward the thicker fog.

She knows you're here, Dash. Try again.

Abigail!

Abigail walked through the miasma, but it wasn't the confident, elegant vampire he knew.

Who's there? Show yourself.

It's me. Dash…Remember?

She seemed smaller and almost fragile. Her hair hung long, to her waist and her manner of dress seemed colonial, almost puritan. She was dirt smeared and her skirts were torn and muddied a good twelve inches from the hem as though she had waded through a bog.

Her lips and mouth were stained red, as was her linen shirt and rough corset. It was clear she was alone and had been for a while, fending for herself.

I know no one by that name! Trickster! Who are you?

Anger welled in Dash's chest at Sébastien. The master vampire had taken Abigail's human life, that much he knew, but from the fear in her eyes and her disheveled appearance, it was clear he left her to live or die without a second thought. Not even a crash course in vampire survival 101.

Dash's body shuddered with black rage. His mind churned with the need to avenge Abigail for what she endured. Sébastien forced this on her, and that she could still give him centuries of loyalty pushed him over the edge.

Feeling the young hunter's fury and the silent twist of coiled muscles ready to strike, Lily's eyes flew to his in the mist.

No! Dash. Look at me! You CANNOT phase. You'll kill us both! Control yourself!

Every muscle in his body ached, fighting his restraint. He clenched his jaw, biting back on the urge to kill.

Dash...Sébastien can wait. Abigail can't. Remember why we're here. She needs us. Needs YOU!

Lily's words reached him, and he calmed, letting his need to save Abigail cleanse his mind of his hunger for payback.

Soft, muffled crying reached them, and Lily motioned for him to go.

It's you she needs, not me. I'm here as a conduit and an anchor. What she needs from me her body is already taking. Like Rémy said, vampires don't die easily. I can feel her pull on my veins even now. Sean is making sure she doesn't take too much, and that means we don't have a lot of time before I have to break the mind link. Go...now!

Dash walked through the swirling fog.

Abigail. Come back. Where are you?

Stay away from me!

I'm not going to hurt you. I want to help.

Lies! That's all I've been told. Lies!

Dash stopped. The Abigail here in this psychological no man's land was not his Abigail. She was the trigger — the same memory that caught Abigail back in her room the night she went ape shit.

He turned, looking back toward Lily.

She's caught in some kind of memory loop. I'm not sure what happened after Sébastien left her, but it has something to do with a Were. He hurt her somehow, and she thinks I'm him.

Tell her you're not.

He shot her a cynical scowl.

Gee. What a great idea, Lil.

Lose the sarcasm, fur ball. We have no time for drama. I'm already feeling light-headed, and I know Sean is going to pull the plug on this any second.

I tried rationalizing with her weeks ago when her mind went AWOL in a fit of anger. Got any other suggestions?

Lily chewed on her lip.

If she won't believe you aren't this mystery Were, then BE him.

No! Are you nuts?

Listen to me, Dash. You said he hurt her. Well, it must have been very traumatic for the memory to have such a grip on her psyche. Maybe it happened shortly after Sébastien changed her. Use that, only this time apologize for whatever. Grovel.

I don't know any of the details or even the dude's name.

It doesn't matter. Just go with it. Improvise. We're running out of time.

Dash sucked in a deep breath.

Abigail! I've been searching for you all over. Near the fort, in the woods —

He looked at Lily, lifting his hands at the futile attempt.

—by the homesteads, but you were gone. I...I'm so ashamed.

Lily nodded, waving him on, and a hiccup sounded not far from where he stood in the mist and he turned.

See—it's working. Keep going.

I can hear you, Abigail, but I can't find you. Please. I need you. I'm so sorry. I'm so filled with shame at what I said and how I hurt you. I can't sleep. Forgive me, please. Abigail—

Abigail walked toward him, blood tears mixing with the dirt on her cheeks. Her head was tilted at an odd angle, almost as though listening with a broken neck.

Nathan?

Dash nodded.

She blinked, studying him.

How can I trust your words after all you said, all your hate? You hurt me.

Because I was a fool.

And now?

Now I know my own heart and I'm no longer afraid. No longer bound by the chains of suspicion and prejudice that infect both our worlds. I love you, Abigail. I'll fight for you and walk by your side as long as fate allows.

Lily cried out, and both Dash and Abigail jerked toward the sound.

Dash's body went rigid and then he stumbled back. Abigail reached for him, but something drew him, pulling through the mist, his image waning as he faded from her.

⁓

"NO!" Abigail lunged from the bed, pinning Lily to the ground, her teeth sunk deep in Lily's wrist.

She snarled, gulping down blood, tearing at Lily's arm.

"Rémy!" Lily screamed.

He and Sean scrambled, pulling Abigail's flailing body from Lily. Sean held her, pushing her face down into the bloody sheets while Rémy healed Lily's wounds.

"She's too far gone, Abigail will have to be destroyed," Rémy shouted over his shoulder as he lifted Lily from the floor.

"No! Give it a little time. Lily's blood has got to work. Please!" Dash stood at the side of the bed, anger and worry clashing in his chest.

Sean looked at his hunter's harried face. "If she doesn't show improvement within the next couple of hours, then I'm with Rémy. I'm sorry, Dash. There's not anything else we can do. In the meantime, we have to restrain her."

Dash looked at Lily's weak body resting in the chair where Rémy placed her, away from Abigail's reach.

"Lily isn't a full Were…*uhm*…I mean, not by birth," he quickly added, avoiding Sean's warning glare. "What if we combine my blood with hers? Maybe that's the key."

Sean shook his head. "I won't risk you to this infection. Lily has antibodies enough to weather this, plus the doctors gave her a booster before we left Maine. You have neither, and in this case, love is not enough."

Dash rolled up his sleeve, his eyes still on the Alpha of the Brethren. "With all due respect, I don't agree." Before Sean or Remy could stop him, Dash shoved his wrist into Abigail's waiting mouth.

With two hands she clutched his wrist, pulling long, deep draughts from his veins. Dash's eyes glazed over as her bite sent his body into pleasure spasms. Visions of Abigail's body, her mouth, her wet pussy and the taste of her coating his tongue danced through his mind.

His lids closed and behind them images of her smiling, laughing, even her eyes flashing in anger played for him. He sent every ounce of feeling he had for her coursing through his body.

Abigail froze and pulled her fangs from his wrist. She blinked, and her eyes cleared.

"Oh. My. God." She looked at the bed and the sheets covered in blood. She glanced down at the state she was in and at Dash, her fingers shredding his skin and arms.

Without another breath, she licked his wounds, sealing them completely and let go of his arm as though it burned to the touch.

She backed away from the wolves, her eyes unsure, but completely lucid. Her gaze swept the rest of the room and the havoc, until she settled on Rémy.

"What happened? What have I done? Where is Sébastien?"

"Sébastien? After all this, after everything he's done. Leaving you to die not once, but twice, you still want to crawl back to your master?" The look on Dash's face was incredulous and hurt.

Dash scrambled from the bed, rolling his bloodstained sleeve over his wounded arm and wrist.

"I should have known better." He exhaled, angry. "They warned me. All of them said the same thing, including your own kind. Tap her undead ass if you want, but don't get involved."

He stalked around the bed to Lily's chair. He stood beside Sean, his hands on his hips and his eyes narrowed at Abigail. "You're healed enough now with the correct HepZ antibodies for this new strain to be the font of all health for the vampires of the world. I guess that makes it a win-win for you and *your* master. As soon as Lily is strong enough to move, we're outta here."

Dash turned to move toward the door.

"Wait! Dash! Please! That's not what I meant—" Abigail struggled to sit up.

Ignoring her plea, he stormed out, growling deep and loud at the vampires gathered outside the room.

Sean watched him go and then turned away from the open door. He gently picked Lily up in his arms and looked at Rémy.

"Come see us when you have everything sorted here." He glanced to the door. "A male Were that angry should never be left to his own devices. Whatever else, my duty is to my wife, my hunters and to my pack. I gotta go."

Rémy nodded. "Of course, but please, stay in the city tonight. I have a feeling my brother will want you to join him as he eats crow for the first time in centuries."

He looked from Sean to Abigail's stricken face and back again. "And if we're lucky, we just might mend more than just a single broken body."

Chapter Twelve

"She was disoriented, Dash. Like when you wake from heavy anesthesia. Your brain is in a freefall, almost on autopilot. Abigail's mind went where it was most familiar, and like it or not, that means Sébastien. He's her past and her present. You may be her future, but right now you're too new," Sean stated, his eyes watching the brooding hunter.

"Sean's right, Dash." Lily added. "You overreacted, and understandably so. The stress of the situation and being linked with her mind while she took a vacation from reality would be a lot for anyone to process. Unfortunately, your kneejerk reaction might be something we can't fix."

The living room of their rented apartment was cozy, but tonight the atmosphere was almost claustrophobic.

Lily lay on the couch recuperating. Even with her quick-healing Were abilities, she needed an old fashioned kick-start. A half empty glass of orange juice sat on the coffee table beside a bottle of vitamin B complex.

"I agree with Lily." Gehrig nodded. "After what everyone said, it doesn't seem as though Abigail slighted you on purpose."

Dash looked at his brother. "What do you know? You just got here."

"Yeah, and I'm glad I wasn't around for a stroll down Abigail's psychotic memory lane. Then again, I was busy with my own trip back in time."

Dash perked up. "You found the connection?"

Gehrig nodded. "I think so. The information is incomplete, but it fits the timeline and the geography you said to check."

Sean looked from one hunter to the other. "What are you two babbling about?"

"After Sébastien threw us out, Dash couldn't let go of what happened. Especially the things Abigail said when she lost it on him. He obsessed about it."

"I did not," Dash grumbled.

Sean chuckled. "Which time? From what I heard, she spent the entire weekend losing it on him, in more ways than one."

Gehrig laughed at his brother. "Dude, you were almost Rain Man about it."

Lily snorted, nearly choking on the last of her orange juice. "Rain Man? Seriously?"

"You have no idea. He drove me crazy for a week, so I shut him up by doing a little sleuthing into our family's history."

"And?" Dash asked.

"Impatient fucker, ain't he? From what you all said happened during Lily's *Amazing Kreskin* moment in Abby's mind, this shit with her fucked up past has been brewing for a long time."

"Gehrig!"

He laughed again. "Okay…jeez." Gehrig reached for his backpack and pulled out a folder. He drew out a large folded piece of paper.

"This is a photocopy of a map and notes I found in the great room archive at the Compound. Most of it is bullshit. Surveys and land allotments, but there was a whole section of notes on legal jurisdiction and civil and criminal complaints."

Gehrig unfolded the map, and on top he placed a photocopy of a piece of parchment with looping script. He tapped the top sheet. "This is the smoking gun. It's cited April 1767."

Dash took the copy, his eyes scanning the document while his lips sounded out the strange old English cursive. Finally, he looked up.

"Well?" Sean asked.

"It's hard to read and even harder to understand, but the gist of the complaint is that a juvenile by the name of Nathan Aloysius Fawkes broke the church imposed curfew to engage in 'wicked and impure' relations. They use the terms 'conjuration' and 'consorting' with evil."

He paused, scanning more. "It goes on about how he was shunned and made to help church elders track down what they called 'devil's spawn'."

Sean nodded. "Considering Fawkes is your ancestors' name, this raises an eyebrow. Pack records show they migrated north to Maine after the Revolutionary War." He grinned. "*Wicked and impure relations.* I guess you two come from a long line of horny hound dogs."

Lily waved Sean off. "Could the Nathan in Abigail's mind be one and the same? Maybe Abigail's subconscious was triggered because she recognized you as the same lineage."

Gehrig shrugged looking to Dash. "Possibly, but who the hell knows?"

Dash stood and walked around, pacing. "This conversation is completely academic. Besides, it really doesn't matter, anyway. It's over."

"Oh, I wouldn't be too hasty, *mon ami.*"

All eyes turned as three vampires stood inside the open doorway.

"I thought you couldn't enter without permission," Sean joked, getting up to greet Rémy. He gripped the vampire's forearm brotherhood style. "Thank you for coming."

Rémy smirked. "Thank you for leaving the door unlocked."

Jenya moved to Lily's side and before she could object, the vampire bit down her own wrist. "You cannot refuse. Your mate needs you at full strength, so drink."

Sean nodded. "Do it, babe. I hate seeing you look like the walking dead."

"Gee, thanks." Lily looked at the blood pooling on the vampire's wrist and shook her head. "In the glass, if you don't mind."

Jenya raised an eyebrow, but did as asked, and no sooner did Lily drain the cup than her coloring improved almost immediately.

"I'm sorry, Lily." Abigail moved ahead of Rémy, a small bouquet of flowers in her hand. She laid the flowers on the coffee table. "For what it's worth, thank you."

Dash stood, his eyes riveted to the once again elegant vampire. She was still somewhat gaunt, but at least her face and eyes were no longer sunken, and her hair had regained its sheen.

"Abigail—"

He took a step toward her, but stopped when she raised one hand. "Before you do or say anything, let me say what I came here to say."

She waited for him to say something, but when he didn't reply, she looked to the others. "Perhaps it's best if we speak in private."

Dash's eyes never left her face, but he motioned toward the narrow hall.

Abigail nodded and turned to follow him. She looked at Gehrig as she passed. "Bette is at the club. She said to text her if you want to meet up later."

Gehrig grinned, but his face sobered at the dual warning glares from both Sean and Rémy.

"What? It's okay for Dash to have a private chat with his vampire—" he crooked his fingers into bunny ears. "but I can't meet mine for a drink, later?"

Lily sat up, holding onto Jenya's arm. "It's who'll be drinking from whom that worries us. So the answer is no. Not until we figure out how to keep you from selling your soul to the devil for your next fix."

Gehrig's mouth dropped and he stood, eyeing Rémy. "And you have no problem with this stereotyping?"

The vampire fixed the young hunter with an ice cold stare, and Gehrig immediately sat his butt back in the chair.

"My little witch isn't wrong. I've seen addiction up close. It is not something to be trifled with. I understand your feelings for Bette. She is most alluring." He winked at Jenya. "Nevertheless, there is much to be said for caution. If your alpha and his mate want you to abstain, then I suggest you do so until further notice. Bette has nothing but time to kill. If it is meant to be, she will wait."

⚜

Dash crossed his arms and sat on the edge of the mattress in the small bedroom. "So, you wanted private. You got private. Say what you feel you need to say. I'm all ears."

Abigail clasped her hands and rubbed them together, almost as though she had a chill. Ridiculous, really. Vampires were already cold.

"I don't know why I feel so vulnerable," she began. "Maybe it's the residual effects from being so close to truly dying."

"You don't have to feel vulnerable around me. I'm not going to judge you, Abigail, and I'm sorry I lost my cool when you were still so sick. I understand now."

She angled her head. "What do you understand?"

"That Sébastien is your world. That he's all you really know." He shrugged. "I could call it Stockholm syndrome, but I'm guessing it's more a vampire thing. Progeny and sire and all that vamp jazz."

"I suppose that's true, or at least it was. I'm still a vampire, and like it or not, Sébastien is my maker and my master."

"I don't have to like anything, Abby. It's not my business what you do. But I do understand. More than you think."

"How so?" she asked.

"Gehrig found the connection between us. It took two weeks of digging, but he found the answer to why my scent and my presence have been the trigger for all your flashbacks and anger."

"You make it sound like I have PTSD."

He shrugged. "In a way, you do, but we can get into that another time. As long as you realize it wasn't me, regardless of the past. Maybe in some small way, Lily and I helped put all that to rest."

"I think so. Something else happened tonight. Something unheard of in my world," she said.

"What?"

"Sébastien set me free."

"Free?"

She nodded.

"I don't understand. Weren't you free before? You seemed to run the show regardless of council approval." He couldn't help it, he smirked.

"Sébastien's word was law in most things, but he overstepped his bounds. Tonight the council was called. Sébastien is gone from us."

Dash's lips parted, stunned. "Gone? How?"

She spread her hands, almost at a loss. "One of the worst crimes a vampire can commit is final death. Killing another vampire without sanction. Sébastien broke that rule in spades when he slaughtered the entire shadow house on Jane Street."

"But he made it sound as if he had the right to act."

She nodded. "Yes, but he acted on his *own* instead of calling for the other adjudicators. He might have been the master vampire, but there are some laws that even a master can't disregard. They would never have gone against him. As you said, there was cause, but he didn't follow the rules. He went rogue, plus he broke a truce that was hard won and long in the making with the Weres."

Dash blinked, trying to process everything. "So Sébastien is dead?"

Abigail shook her head. "No, not dead. Just gone. He's been forced to take a sabbatical. He left for Rome. Perhaps time in the Eternal City will give him a new perspective. He's been ordered to stay with Dominic De'Lessep, one of the oldest known vampires in Europe. Dominic knows how to deal with a vampire with too much ego."

"But that doesn't answer my question. How does that free you?"

She sat beside him on the edge of the bed, her skirt hiking up her thighs. "Before Sébastien left, he released me from my blood bond. I'm no longer tied to him."

"And this is a good thing, why?" Dash's eyes skimmed her legs before moving to her face.

She slipped her hand in his. "I still have to obey the laws of my kind, just like you have to obey the laws governing the Weres, but I no longer have to follow what Sébastien says or risk physical pain."

Dash angled his head. "So if he goes to backhand you again?"

"I can smack him right back. Not that I would." She chuckled. "He's still got centuries on me."

"I had no idea that disobeying your master meant physical pain for you. Is it like that for all vampire progeny?"

She nodded. "Sometimes it sucks to be a vampire."

He cracked a wry smile at her pun. "So again, what does all this mean, exactly?"

"It means if I want to spend every minute of every day in bed with you, I can. It means if I want to explore every inch of your amazing body, taste every part of you, learn all there is to know about you inside and out, I can—" Abigail paused, almost as though weighing her next words. "And if I want to take these vulnerable new feelings I have for you and see where they lead, I can do that too."

She slipped her hand from his and reached to unbutton his pants, but he caught her wrist.

"And I don't have any say in this?" He raised an eyebrow.

She froze before lifting her eyes to his. "Of course, you do.

"Tell me, then. What new feelings are you talking about?"

"The same ones I think you have for me, or at least, I hope you do," she answered, softly.

He watched her face. "Hope. That's kind of a four letter word for you."

She gave him a soft smile. "It used to be, but I'm learning a whole new vocabulary with a new set of four letter words."

"Such as?"

She shook her head. "Let's just work on *happily* for now. *Ever After* is a long time. Trust me. If nothing else, immortals *know* time."

Dash laughed. "The lady's got a new vocabulary, but still likes to be the boss."

Shadows crossed her face, and the uncertain look spoke volumes. He squeezed her hand. "Okay, Abby. Let's go for it. Happily-for-Now with an option for Ever After."

She grinned and both his heart and his cock jumped. The same protective vibe he felt before crashed over him in waves. She was his, for now at least.

Dash trailed his knuckles across the soft skin above her knee. "So, anything else you want to say?"

He swept his thumb higher up her leg, the rough pad trailing her inner thigh.

Sucking a breath through her teeth, she leaned closer, spreading her knees so his fingers had full access. "How about thank you, sir. May I have another?"

With a chuckle, Dash took her mouth. His fingers found her pussy and he stroked her soft folds through the panty lace. "Only if you promise to bend over."

Marianne Morea

The Red Veil Diaries

Tease Me

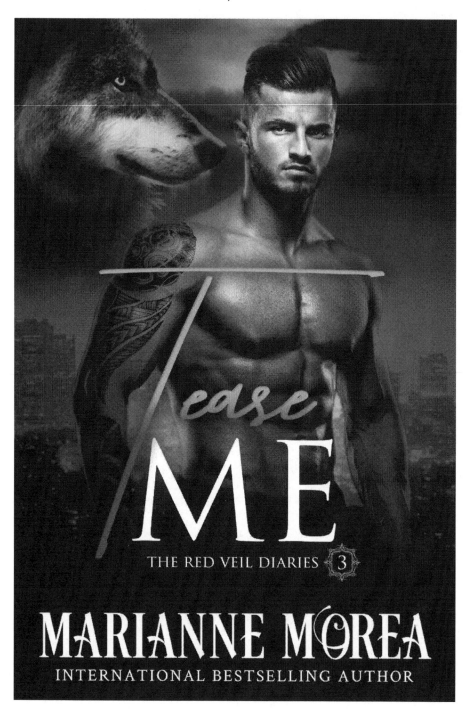

Tease
ME

THE RED VEIL DIARIES 3

MARIANNE MOREA

INTERNATIONAL BESTSELLING AUTHOR

"What do I wear in bed?
Why, Chanel No. 5, of course."

~Marilyn Monroe

Chapter One

"Nika! Telephone!"

From her perch on a cypress branch, the sleek black panther ignored her mother's summons, one tufted ear barely flicking in reply. Instead, the cat kept her wide green eyes on the small boat bobbing in the marshy water near the far shore.

Her gaze fixed on the sweaty man struggling with a telephoto lens. His eyes darting between watching the house and watching the gators cruising beneath the murky surface near his bow.

The big cat chuffed. Maybe the alligators would get lucky today.

"Nika!" her mother called again.

The elegant animal stretched behind the cover of thick Spanish moss, her long, sinuous body shifting to the size of a house cat before jumping soundlessly to the high grass.

Green eyes spared another glance for the river and the photographer swatting at the mosquitos feasting on the man's exposed skin.

Swamp, one. Paparazzi, zip.

The cat padded on silent paws toward a stilted bayou house, climbing the steps to the wrap around porch. The screen door opened and shut, and Nika stole across the kitchen, tail swishing as she circled her mother's legs.

"Annika Lee," she chuckled, "that's enough sass out of you, *cher*. Ariel's on the phone from Los Angeles."

At her agent's name, Annika stopped mid-purr. Her body tensed, fur rippling along her long, horizontal spine as she phased to human.

Her mother smiled, a soft hand reaching for her daughter's cheek. "The cordless phone is on the dining room table." She handed Nika a knee-length sweater from the back of a kitchen chair, gesturing toward the other room. "I put her on hold."

Annika slipped the soft cable knit over her head, the supple cotton falling over naked curves to mid-thigh. "Did Ari say what she wanted?"

Mom shrugged, moving back to the stove. "Ask her yourself."

Walking through to the dining room, Nika's lip caught between her teeth. It was Jesse. Her gut clenched knowing it couldn't be anything else.

A year and a half had passed since that boy sent her life up in flames. And not in a good way.

She shivered, realizing the paparazzo bobbing around in the marsh meant one thing. It was showtime.

With a breath, she clicked the hold button. "Ariel, it's good of you to call."

"I'm not sure you'll feel the same once I tell you why."

Nika braced for the worst. "That bad?"

"A jury has been selected and Jesse's trial is set to start in less than a week. The motion to have the venue moved to Louisiana was denied."

Nika didn't reply.

"Annika? Did you hear what I said?"

She exhaled. "Yeah. I...I can't believe it's really happening."

"It's been a year and a half, sweetheart. You had to know it was bound to be sometime soon."

"I know," Nika sighed. "Some days it seems like forever ago, and others like it was yesterday."

Ariel exhaled a breath on the other side of the phone. "Media stories never go away. They get archived until they crop up again and start trending on twitter."

Nika rolled her eyes. "Don't get cute. Still, it's not as bad as I thought."

"What's not, honey?"

Moving toward the dining room window, Nika peered through the gauzy sheers at the backyard and the water beyond. "Being a has-been at twenty-six."

"Nonsense," Ariel shot back, annoyance clipping her tone. "We've gone over this, Annika. You need to get back to the land of the living. The band is gone. Jesse is finished. YOU are not."

"Ari, please."

"No, lovey. You were the driving force behind Dracone Noir, and the only band member with brains *and* talent. Not Ki, not Jean, and certainly not Jesse."

"Ari, c'mon."

"Look, at one time or another we all fall for the bad boy. Believe it or not, me included. Especially when all that defiant charm is wrapped in a dreamy James Dean package."

"James Dean?" Nika chuckled. "Dating yourself much, Ari?"

"Hey, I may be old, but I'm not blind. Jesse may be hot-headed, violent and irrational, but he is definitely easy on the eyes, so who can blame you for waiting to see if his brains would catch up to his biceps?"

"Me," Nika replied. "I blame myself for being so stupid."

"You need to stop that, *bubalah*. You're not the first girl to have her common sense ambushed by her private parts. Been there, done that. Hell, men think with their dicks most of the time, so what's good for the goose is good for the gander, right? What's important is you got out before you ended up on a stainless steel slab next to Ki."

Annika's throat tightened. Ariel wasn't the warm and fuzzy type, but she also wasn't devoid of emotion. Her offhand comment was nothing more than ice cold fact. She may not have meant to stun, but her words did so just the same. Ki Palmer wasn't just Dracone Noir's drummer. He was Nika's best friend.

"I'm sorry sweetie, but the truth is what it is. It could have been you on the receiving end of Jessie's blade that night."

"I got lucky," Annika replied.

"No, you were smart to stay out of it. It's time you opened your eyes to what really happened, love. Yes, Dracone Noir was the hottest sensation to hit the Goth rock scene in a while. You had millions of YouTube followers, and yes, that made my job a hell of a lot easier when it came to landing you a recording contract with all the perks, but it wasn't a cake walk, Nika. You worked hard to get where you were, yet Jesse carried on as if the band's success was all on him. And his antics? He acted as if you were still a bayou garage band with no responsibilities."

Nika exhaled. "I know."

"Still, anyone who knows anything in this business realizes you're not to blame for what happened. We had such high hopes, especially for you." Ari added.

"And?"

Ariel chuckled. "And nothing. Those hopes are what I'm banking on now."

Nika's eyes widened. "You don't mean—"

"I always knew you were a smart cookie, bubbie. I pulled the proverbial rabbit out of the hat once already. Given half a chance, I can do it again."

Annika snorted. "Thanks, but no thanks, Ari. This time I think I'll pass on the fame and fortune." She gazed at the softly swaying cypress, trying to ignore the photographer still manning his post.

Exhaling hard, she ran a hand across her forehead. The man was a blunt reminder of the dark side of fame and how ill prepared she and her friends had been when it struck.

Easy money and drugs quickly turned into missed recording sessions, jealous fights and eventually an unfinished album, but nothing compared to what happened on the beach that fateful night. When the sun came up, Ki was dead, and Jesse jailed for his murder.

Overnight, the paparazzi swarmed thick as flies as record company attorneys dragged remaining band members into an ugly breach of contract suit.

Endless police questioning sent Annika's life into a spiral, so she retreated. With no peace and nowhere else to turn, she went home, bringing the media storm with her. Now it was back for round two.

"You're being emotional, Annika," Ariel replied, clearly not taking no for an answer.

A rough grumble left Nika's mouth. "After everything that happened, how else do you suppose I be?"

"Professional."

The agent's reply was curt, and Annika winced at the single admonishment "Ari—"

"No, honey. You're setting your jaw because Jesse's trial is about to start. His situation has nothing to do with you. Not anymore. Did you know he was so drugged at the end, he claimed he could turn into some kind of tiger? With the way Ki's throat was slashed, Jesse's claims gave the defense a real shot at an insanity plea."

Annika cringed. For a bayou shifter, being outed to the world was a tangible fear, but being outed by one of their own was inexcusable. What made it worse, their elders predicted Jesse would betray them.

"Will I be called as a witness?" Nika deflected, changing the subject.

"Most likely, but my guess is not initially, so you have time to prepare."

"Prepare? Ariel, there's no way to prepare for the grilling the prosecution has in store. The press is still painting this as a love triangle with me as the prize."

"Don't worry about that." She answered with a sniff. "I've dug up so much on Jesse, there's no way that claim will stick."

The room was suddenly claustrophobic, and Nika sank to the floor by the window. "I've gotta get out of here, Ari. I can't go through another social media execution. Can't you arrange for me to go somewhere?"

"You know that's impossible, love."

"Why? I'm not a suspect. Even the media stopped implying that."

Ariel exhaled a soft chuckle. "It's amazing what a court-sanctioned gag order and the threat of a libel suit can accomplish."

"I'm serious, Ari." Nika's voice cracked. "I won't be a sitting duck this time. You've got to know somebody with a house I can borrow. Maybe somewhere secluded and tropical?"

"Sorry, honey. No can do," Ariel replied. "The judge ordered everyone involved not to leave the lower forty-eight."

An exasperated exhale slipped from Annika's mouth. "Then book me a flight to Los Angeles."

"Nika, do you really want to go straight into the teeth of this? Think about it. If just the idea of media coverage is giving you hives, how will you manage the horde of photographers waiting to greet you at LAX?"

Nika threw a hand in the air. "What do you suggest I do, then?"

Arguing outside drew Annika's attention and she got to her feet pushed the dining room sheers aside to look.

"Crap, there's another one," she mumbled.

"Another what?"

"Paparazzo," Nika replied.

"Already?"

"Yes. Now do you get why I want out of here? I spotted the first parasite watching the house this morning and another one just showed up. Sounds like they're fighting over turf."

Nika let the sheers fall back into place. "I can't stay here, Ari. It's only a matter of time before the bayou is crawling with vermin, and not the kind native to the swamp. I won't do this to my family. Not again."

Her agent didn't answer.

"Ariel? Are you listening to me?"

"I'm here. I'm just thinking. The only way the media won't pester you or your mother is if they think you've left the area."

"That's what I said."

Ariel ignored her. "What if we plan it so the paparazzi see you leave for the west coast? I'll have my office put out a press release saying you're taking a house in an undisclosed location until the trial starts. The paparazzi will beat a path to Los Angeles faster than you can blink. They'll scour the city looking for any sign of you."

"Okay, then what?"

"I'll make arrangements for you to leave L.A., but under the radar," Ariel replied.

"And go where?" Nika's voice raised half an octave. "I can't come home. It's the first place they'll look."

"You'll go to New York."

"New York?" Nika balked. "Those insects will find me there as quickly as they can in L.A."

"Not necessarily, lovey," Ari countered. "New Yorkers are notoriously disinterested in celebrities. Why do you think so many A-listers live in Manhattan? New Yorkers don't give a crap. They're more interested in getting where *they* have to go than rubbernecking the latest celeb-du-jour. It's the perfect place to hide in plain sight."

"And?" Nika prompted.

"And what?"

Annika leaned on the wall beside her mother's china cabinet, her fingers twisting one sweater cuff. "Ariel, you never do anything without an ulterior motive, especially when you pick up the phone yourself."

"Not nice, bubalah."

She snorted. "Yeah, yeah. Cut the crap. Why the sudden push for Northeast?"

Ariel paused. "I booked you a gig."

"What!" Nika's voice rose. "I already told you no."

"It's time, Nika."

Annika shook her head, mild panic mounting in her chest. "No, Ari. I'm not ready."

"Yes, Nika. You are. Besides, you've been living like a nun for way too long. I know you love your family, but baby, you need to spread more than just your wings." Ariel clicked the inside of her cheek. "This venue is very intimate, and it's just the ticket to get you back in the saddle—in more ways than one."

"Let's leave my non-existent love life out of the equation, thank you. Finding a hook up is the last thing I need right now." Nika paused, chewing on her lip. "How intimate is intimate?"

Ari laughed. "The venue or its possibilities?"

"Ugh, Ariel…will you stop trying to set me up? I'm not looking to date anyone anywhere. Period. I meant the venue."

"Who said anything about dating? You need a nasty roll between the sheets to take your mind off what's happening in Los Angeles."

"Ariel, seriously."

"Okay, okay. The club is a trendy underground hotspot, but still very private."

"Trendy and hotspot are the total opposite of private." Nika shook her head. "No, Ari. I meant what I said. It's too soon."

"No, it's not, Lovey, and the timing couldn't be more perfect."

"Why? Because Jesse's trial is set to start?"

Ariel paused. "Yes."

"That's cold. Even for you." Nika exhaled a breath.

"No, it's business, Bubbie. When it comes to the entertainment industry there's no such thing as bad PR. The trial will put you front and center on every media outlet. YOU. I've always said you were better off as a solo. I told you a thousand times before Dracone Noir went up in smoke, but you refused to leave that tweaked out hothead."

"Ari—"

"No, Nika. I'm your agent and your attorney, not to mention your friend. I know you felt responsible for everyone in the band, especially Jesse. When you finally saw him for what he was, you still wanted to make things work for the sake of the band. It's done, love, and now it's time you did something for yourself. Listen to me for once, okay?"

"And it's about time you listened to your mama as well, *cher*," A third voice added.

"Mother!" Annika yanked open the dining room door and stared at her mother. "Get off the phone!"

"No, *bebe*. Ariel's right. It's your time to shine."

Ariel chuckled, despite Nika's hard exhale. "Thank you, Jolene. Between the two of us, maybe we can get your girl to see reason. Jesse LaFont had his shot. He made his bed and frankly I'm grateful it's not one Annika has to lie in as well."

"In more ways than one." Jolene snorted. "So, amen to that."

"Mama!"

"We all need to be on the same page here," Ariel interrupted. "As for you, Nika, it's about time the world knew how special you are. I've been urging you to get back to the land of the living for months now, and this is the perfect opportunity.

"We'll set up under the radar," she continued. "Like when a headliner does an impromptu set at a neighborhood bar, although this place is far from local."

Nika spared a glance for her mother, still listening on the line. "Yeah, but afterwards It'll be all over social media. So much for lasting peace and quiet."

"Annika, you'll have to face the press at some point. By the time you're done with this one night gig, Jesse's trial will have started, and chances are you'll have to head to L.A. anyway." Ariel exclaimed. "At least this way the press will be on your terms. Besides, New York is better for your solo debut, especially now that you've—" she hesitated. "Sampled your mother's cooking again."

Both Jolene and Nika exchanged a look. "And what's that supposed to mean?" Nika asked.

"You've spent enough time in Los Angeles to know exactly what that means. Hollywood is obsessed with appearance. Look at the problems other celebrities have endured under that kind of scrutiny. Who can forget how the media crucified Jessica Simpson when she tipped the scales."

"Ari—"

"I'm sorry, love, but our industry is cold. You're curvy now, and whether we agree with it or not, Los Angeles is an unforgiving place. Better to be in New York where the public isn't as superficial."

Annika chewed her lip. "I'm telling you now," she paused, "I won't starve myself to fit some industry mold. My talent has nothing to do with my dress size and if they don't like it, too fucking bad."

"Amen again, *cher*." Her mother nodded.

Nika puffed out a resigned breath. "Okay, Ari. You win. What's the name of this perfect venue?"

"The Red Veil."

Chapter Two

*A*nnika hung up and walked into the kitchen. Her mother's not-so-quiet inhale at the club's name, not something she imagined.

Jolene's face said it all. Her mother needed no explanation as to what The Red Veil was or who ran the place.

Avoiding her mother's eyes, Nika took an apple from a bowl on the kitchen table and rubbed the red skin on her sweater before taking a bite.

"You know," she said, chewing slowly. "It wasn't easy growing up with a mother who could hear a pin drop in the swamp, let alone deal with her uncanny premonitions, but now I'm glad. What do you think, Mama? Do I go to New York or not?"

Jolene Lee put the phone receiver back in its cradle and then moved to stir the fragrant gumbo simmering on the stove. "My extraordinary talents kept you from plenty of trouble when you were little, not that you ever listened."

"Mama, you didn't answer my question."

Her mother covered the cast iron pot before turning with the roux-stained wooden spoon in her hand.

"I don't like it, Nika. Not one bit. Ariel Fischer has no clue about our kind or the supernatural in general, so she has no idea this Red Veil is a blood club. Vampires. For God's sake!" She shook her head. "Plus, something else feels off about this and I can't put my finger on it."

Jolene lifted her forearm, holding it out to show her daughter. "Look at the hair on my arm. It's all electric and standing tall. I'm never wrong when my body reacts like this. Something is brewing and it's not the weather."

She pointed her wooden spoon at her daughter. "Ariel's jaw is hinged in the middle sometimes, and you know it. Her entire living is made off the talent of others and my gut tells me she has her own reasons for sending you to New York."

"Of course she does, Mama. Ariel's my agent. She's doing this for me. For us."

Jolene crossed her arms in front of her chest. "On the surface, yes, but Ariel is an opportunist. She's not going out of her way if there's no payoff. You heard her yourself. She planned this to coincide with that good-for-nothing LaFont boy's trial. She's had this up her sleeve just waiting for the right time. You better read the fine print on this one, *cher*." Her mother looked at her. "Besides that, I'm not happy about this plan for other reasons. Reasons closer to home."

Annika wiped her mouth on a napkin and then tossed it and the apple core into the trash. "Let me guess."

"Don't get fresh with me, *bebe*. Shifters and vampires do not belong together, and I forbid you to go."

"Amen to that," a deep voice interjected.

Both women turned.

"Guy, what a nice surprise," Jolene's lips spread into a genuine grin and she smoothed her hair back from her face.

"Sheriff." Annika nodded.

He took off his hat and walked to her mother's side giving Jolene's cheek an awkward peck. "Something smells amazing."

Jolene blushed. "Go on with you." She gave the man a playful shove, but her eyes sparkled at his double meaning. "Gumbo's just about done. You know where the bowls are."

"Who said I was talking about the stew?" He winked at Nika and opened the cupboard to the right of the sink and took out three bowls.

"So what brings you out our way, Sheriff?" Annika asked, putting spoons and napkins on the table. The man was smitten with her mother and she stifled a knowing grin.

"You mean besides your mother's famous gumbo?" He grinned. "I came to check up on you, now that you ask. A little bird put a bug in my ear those pesky photographers were setting up house again, but I see you're okay."

He pursed his lips, his eyes soft and appreciative. "You look good, Nika. In fact, I haven't seen you look this good in a long time. Healthy. I guess your mama's cooking is doing the trick bringing you the rest of the way back from la-la land. I'm glad to see it. You're as pretty as ever. Not that nervous skeleton that came home exhausted and terrified."

Annika smirked. "You didn't come all the way out to the swamp just to compliment me, Sheriff, much as I appreciate it. Have you heard something about Jesse's case?"

"Nah." He shook his head. "The Los Angeles prosecutor's office can have that miscreant. I've got trouble enough with the rest of his pack."

"More camp break-ins, Guy?" Jolene asked.

"No. Some of the LaFont boys partied in the cemetery last night, and while I usually don't bother with minor criminal mischief, this time graves were damaged. Some desecrated, and I won't have that."

Jolene made a face. "That family has been nothing but trouble for generations, right up to this nasty business with Jesse." Jolene eyed Annika, shaking her head. "How many times did I warn you about that boy?" she sighed, letting her words trail off.

Nika looked away. Her mother was right. Guilt slashed at her chest for being so stupid and naïve. Jesse LaFont was the bad boy all her friends fantasized about.

From the cool, rebuilt motorcycle he rode with his cousins, to his tattoos, and of course his electric guitar, Jessie was drool worthy from one end of Terrebonne Parish to the other. The fact he could body double for Jax from *Sons of Anarchy* only added to the allure.

The memory stung and Nika winced.

"I hear you're thinking about starting a band," Nika's voice cracked a little as she approached, but she played it cool.

Jesse nodded, his eyes giving her a quick once over. "Yeah, so?"

"Maybe I could sing for you sometime. I'm pretty good."

He laughed, swinging his leg over the side of his Harley. "Drop some poundage, little cow. Then you can show me how 'good' you are. I might even let you sing, too."

She cringed at how she'd starved herself for two months, anticipating the moment when he'd notice her for real. That time came quickly enough. He was sitting on his bike outside the Dairy Queen. It was a full moon, and every shifter in the parish was on the prowl. It didn't take long for Jesse to spot her sleek new curves.

Things moved quickly from there, but his bad boy act got old, fast. Especially since the sex, like everything else, was always on his terms, and when he was done, that's all she wrote. Problem was Jesse wasn't done with her. Not by a long shot.

The boy wasn't as dumb as everyone thought. Nika was his ticket out of the bayou, and he had staked his claim. Not in a formal shifter claiming and Annika exhaled knowing full well she dodged a bullet in that respect. No, Jesse's claim was more proprietary. Nika was his, same as his guitar, and the two together were his path to success.

By the time the record company came sniffing around, Jesse was needy and jealous. He made it clear he'd see to it no one would want her if she ever left. He was never specific, but the veiled threat was real enough to scare.

Annika sighed, closing her eyes, and a pang of guilt bit into her gut. Everyone said no, but she knew Ki was dead because he tried to help.

As if reading the emotion on her face, Guy patted her hand, bringing her back from her memories. "Spilled milk, *cher*. Don't let what happened buy real estate in your head. You're home now. No more carrying on with that lot."

"Why does everyone hate the LaFont pack so much?" Annika asked putting sliced French bread on the table. "Jesse is one thing. What he did is unforgiveable, but why the whole pack?"

Her mother put her wooden spoon on a damp dishcloth and leaned against the sink.

"It's a long story, love. With roots that go back farther than anyone can remember, but most recently it has to do with Old Marie Bergeron."

Nika's brow knotted, confused. "The voodoo priestess? I thought she died years ago."

Guy nodded. "She did. It's got to be going on ten years now. She passed not long after her daughter committed suicide and her grandson ran off. That boy couldn't have been more than seventeen."

"You were only four or five at the time, Nika, so it's no wonder you don't recall," her mother added.

Annika looked at them. "What has any of this got to do with Jesse?"

Jolene shrugged. "It doesn't. Not directly, anyway. It has more to do with his people. You see, Old Marie was a formidable woman in these parts. Respected and feared. She knew the swamp as though its ebb and flow coursed through her veins. She was powerful. Much as she was admired, folks kept their distance."

"And?" Nika prompted.

"Fabienne, Marie's daughter, didn't want to be associated with anything that had to do with her mother. In fact, she did everything she could to separate herself from her Créole roots and her mama's voodoo. She wanted to be somebody else. Anyone other than what she was. Sad really."

Guy nodded in agreement. "If she lived, Fabienne would have been about your mama's age. Back in the day, the girl ran around something fierce, and she had a particular fondness for the LaFont boys. No one could talk sense to her, though she was barely sixteen.

"You see, *cher*, Fabienne Bergeron was beautiful. Exotic. She had long black hair and eyes so dark they could pierce the soul. Tall and statuesque with smooth ivory skin.

"She turned heads wherever she went. Sadly, she ended up pregnant, and when Marie confronted old man LaFont, he refused to acknowledge the child as his blood.

"They never did figure which one of the LaFonts was the father, but even if the guilty party came forward, their grandfather would never permit the child to carry the family name."

A disgusted sound left Jolene's mouth. "They're a bigoted bunch. In their eyes, Créole blood is slave blood. Same as if the last hundred fifty years of progress never occurred."

"So what happened?" Nika asked.

Her mother shrugged. "Marie raised the boy as best she could. His mama was useless. Drunk most of the time. He learned everything he could from Marie. He took to the swamps and cypress forests like he was part of them, same as his grand-mére.

"He grew up wild, running with the deer and crawling with the gators. He was the best tracker in these parts, until the day he found his mother floating in one of the canals.

"Fabienne heard old man LaFont was dying, so she went to try and get him to acknowledge her son before it was too late, but he refused. She was laughed out of their camp. Humiliated. The boy found her drowned not too long afterward."

Jolene paused. "His grand-mére went crazy. She swore vengeance, conjuring a dark, evil magic only hate and pain can summon. Marie Bergeron cursed the LaFonts with a powerful gris that robbed them of any peace, leaving their children to suffer loss and shame generation after generation."

Nika looked at her mother. "What happened to the boy?"

"No one knows," she replied with a shrug. "He hasn't been back since, but rumors swirl each time something unexplained happens in the swamp. It's said Marie gave him the key to dark magic."

"Dark magic?"

Jolene nodded. "They say the voodoo priestess made him Rougarou."

"Oh, come on. Seriously?" Nika's mouth wore a dubious sneer. "A shifter with a human body and the head of a wolf? Please. That's an insult to our kind."

Her mother shook her head, annoyed. "That's beneath you, Annika. The dual-natured are a part of the natural world, but to be Rougarou is black magic, a dark burden placed on someone's soul.

"The beast craves blood and that means a constant struggle between light and dark for whoever bears the curse. Marie gave her grandson the dark power as vengeance on his father's bloodline."

Annika inhaled and let her breath out slowly. "Well, it doesn't sound like much of a curse if he's never been back, and considering the LaFonts were partying in the cemetery last night, it doesn't sound like her curse is working on them either."

"Oh, it's working." Her mother nodded. "Most of the adult LaFont men are either dead or in jail. Swaggering, puffed up pretty boys."

"Pretty boys?" Nika questioned. "And why didn't anyone tell me this before I went halfway across the country with Jesse?"

Jolene snorted. "As if you would have listened. That boy had you so bewitched I could have sprouted horns and played the blues and you wouldn't have noticed. No surprise, though. What the LaFont's didn't get in character, they made up for in good looks. As mouthwatering as a juicy apple, that is until you take a bite and get a mouthful of brown mush and worms."

"On that note, I think I'll hit the road," the Sherriff pushed his chair back, but her mother laughed, waving him back.

"Sit yourself back in that chair, Guy Fortinet." She winked, lifting her hand to his cheek. "You have your own brand of charm and you know it."

He cleared his throat, glancing toward the window and the arguing that started up again in the usually quiet marsh.

"Those photographers are multiplying like insects out there," he redirected, craning to pinpoint their location in the tall cypress. "Want me to run them out of the parish like I did the last time? I have no problem bending the law when it comes to protecting my own."

Annika shook her head. "That won't be necessary, Sherriff. They'll leave as soon as I do."

He turned his gaze to her. "The last time you left home you ended up in a heap of trouble and worried the pack sick, yet here you are planning to pack up again. Since I couldn't help but hear the word vampire tossed around this kitchen, let's just say my curiosity is more than a little piqued."

"Curiosity killed the cat, Sheriff. Remember?"

"Don't get fresh, young lady. Or have you forgotten it was Guy who saved our behinds the last time those pizzarrazos set up in the swamp."

"Paparazzi," Annika corrected.

Jolene raised one eyebrow.

"Sorry, Mama." Her eyes flashed downward before looking up again. "And I'm sorry you had to hear Ariel's suggestions on improving my love life. I'm surprised your ears aren't bleeding."

Her mother wiped her hands on a dishtowel, considering. "*Bebe*, do you think you're the only one to feel the pull of the opposite sex? I may be older, but I still like the feel of an appreciative eye checking out more than my gumbo."

"And trust me. Your mama has enough spice to turn any man's head, especially mine." Guy winked.

Jolene's cheeks flushed, despite the small grin tugging at her lips. She cleared her throat, turning back toward the stove to give the gumbo one last stir. "That's quite enough of that. We're discussing Nika. You're a pretty girl, *cher*. You *should* be sowing your wild oats." She looked past her shoulder at her daughter. "Within reason."

"Even at a vampire club in New York?" Nika's teasing smile faded the moment she saw the look on her mother's face.

"Running wild with your own kind is one thing, but mixing with the undead or even joking about it —" Jolene shook her head and hung the dishcloth neatly on the stove. When she looked up again, her jaw was set.

"That's it," she continued. "You'll stay here where you belong. I won't have you traipsing around a godless city where the undead are celebrated front and center.

"The pack will rally and keep the reporters away until this business with Jesse LaFont blows over like a temporary squall. You'll settle into the bayou life you were born to and that's that."

Annika shook her head, knowing she was about to break her mother's heart. "I can't, Mama."

"For heaven's sake, why not?" she argued.

Nika looked at her mother's worried face. "Because Ariel is right. I need to start over."

"Why can't you stay here and start over?" Jolene's voice hitched.

Ready to reply, Annika set her jaw, but Guy got up from his seat with a chuckle, slipping his arm around Jolene's waist.

"It's no use, love. She's pigheaded, just like her mama." He took Jolene's fingers and laced them with his own. "Nika's made up her mind and nothing is going to change it."

He tightened his grip, giving her a squeeze. "You raised a smart girl. After her dealings with the LaFont boy, Annika won't forget who she is again. She'll find her way home, even if it's from New York."

"But the vampires, Guy—"

He kissed Jolene's temple, sparing a wink for Annika. "Nika can handle herself. Vampires aren't the only ones with sharp fangs. My money is on our bayou shifter to show them what's what."

Nika blew him a kiss, offering up a silent prayer he was right.

Chapter Three

"What'll it be, miss?"

Annika looked at the handwritten menu tacked to the side of the coffee truck. "I'm not sure. What's good?"

"Lady, it's all good. We got people waiting. What'll it be?"

She shot the guy a peeved look, but before she could say anything else, another man pushed the rude one aside.

"Beat it, Sal. Find some other place to loaf — and stop annoying my customers"

This man was older, with eyes that shined with quick laughter. He gave Nika a swift once over and then gestured to the black and gold logo on her tee-shirt. "Where you from, sweetheart?" he asked, wiping his hands on a stained dishtowel.

"New Orleans," she replied, and in her full drawl it sounded like *'Nawlins.*

He nodded. "Nice. I'm a fan of the Saints, too. Well, when the Giants aren't playing, anyway." With an easy laugh, he gave her a chin pop. "Now what can I get you?"

"Just coffee and a donut." She pointed to a glazed cruller.

"In the Big Apple it's never just coffee. It's coffee regular. That means milk and two sugars."

"Then coffee regular sounds perfect," she met his smile with one of her own.

"Good, and to make up for my buddy's lack of manners, I'll throw in a buttered bialy just to say welcome to the Big Apple."

"A bialy?" she raised an eyebrow.

"A New York tradition right up there with bagels and cream cheese," he explained while wrapping her food.

"No charge, sweetheart." He handed her a grease-splotched paper bag. "Welcome to the *City that Never Sleeps.*"

The small crowd waiting in line behind her applauded, and Annika thanked the man before scooting out toward the street. Had they recognized her? She shook her head. Not likely. Not with her back to the queue the whole time.

Breaking off a piece of the cruller she walked toward the famed New York City Library munching on its buttery goodness.

Midtown Manhattan was a crawling mass of humanity, and at this time of day they seemed to all congregate on the steps of the library with its giant lions guarding the steps to enlightenment.

An array of diverse scents set her Were senses on fire. Annika wandered into Bryant Park and sat at a small wrought iron table, sipping her coffee.

Lifting her face to the warm spring air, she inhaled, trying to enjoy the small slice of nature as people rushed back and forth. She ignored their frenetic pace until a riot of scents hit her. Her eyes flew wide, turning to stare at a particular man as he tossed a paper bag into the trash.

He was ultra-thin and geeky, complete with bowtie and dandruff, and Annika snorted out a laugh from the scent of raw sex clinging to the man. Literally.

Holy fuck! The nerdy dude clearly had hot, nasty, monkey sex with more than one partner. In the last hour or so! The sticky musky scent tickled the back of Nika's throat, and she coughed.

"God bless," he replied automatically.

Biting the inside of her cheek, she muttered a quick thank you trying not to giggle.

He nodded absently. "Have a good day."

"Not as good as yours, I'm sure," she mumbled back with a giggle.

He gave her a curious look and she couldn't help it. She burst out laughing and watched as he headed in the opposite direction toward the library.

Annika shook her head. If the music didn't pan out, she could always make a living as a private investigator sniffing out cheating spouses.

She finished her food and headed out of the park to the street. Lifting her hand, she tried hailing a cab like she'd seen others do, surprised one pulled over almost immediately. She opened the rear passenger door and slid onto the backseat.

"Where to, lady?" the cabbie asked, glancing at her in the rearview.

The newspaper on his dashboard showed a front page picture of her with the band, but even with her face splashed across every tabloid in town, no one recognized her. Or if they did, they didn't care.

Annika grinned, and for the first time in ages she felt free.

"Sweetheart, the meter's ticking. Where to?"

She met his eyes in the mirror.

"The Red Veil."

❧

"Oh my God! You're here! You're really here! Annika Lee is in the house!" A perky brunette with a short, 1920s bob came forward, her pace almost a giddy skip. "I'm Bette Mason. Welcome!"

Annika bit the inside of her cheek as she took the enthusiastic woman's hand. It was cold and marble-white, and when the girl smiled, a definite hint of fang peeked from beneath her red lipstick.

"I'm pleased to meet you. Are you the club's manager?" Nika replied.

The brunette vampire's short, chin-length hair brushed both cheeks as she shook her head. "No, that would be Abigail Bigly. She'll be here later tonight."

Youthful appearance wasn't always what it seemed when it came to the undead. Bette might look to be in her early twenties, but the vampire could have been around since God was a boy.

"Does that mean you're my personal assistant for the time being?" Nika hoped she didn't sound like a diva. Some celebs liked the term handler instead, but for the dual-natured it reeked too much of zookeeper.

She shook her head, clearly disappointed. "Unfortunately no, although I did ask to greet you when you arrived. The late afternoon still zaps my strength, but I'll feed after I get you settled and be right as rain before this evening. The Red Veil is our playground, and tonight it's yours, too."

"I'm trying to keep a low profile, Bette, so I hope that doesn't mean you've planned something elaborate."

The woman turned, wrapping Annika's arm in hers. "I am such a huge fan! It's too bad what happened with the band, but I'm thrilled you're trying for a solo career. Ariel Fischer didn't have to work very hard to sell us on the idea."

The vampire had evaded her question, and doubt crept across the back of Annika's mind.

"Come, let me show you around." Bette gestured toward an inside door with a smile.

A labyrinth of office hallways wound until they reached the entrance to the main club. Bette motioned for the bouncer to open the door and then practically skipped through its threshold.

"This is it. The place that can boast Annika Lee's solo debut!"

"I'd hardly call it a debut, but I appreciate the vote of confidence. Please, call me Nika."

The vampire fangirled a silent squeal and squeezed Annika's arm. "Our setup isn't what you're used to, but we have an amazing FX Manager who will help design your lighting and special effects."

She pointed toward a corner off the back of the stage. "His name is Derick. He's a shifter. Or at least, I think so. I've been around a lot of Weres, especially of late, and Derick's scent screams dual-natured, though I can't quite place the species. Still, he's a yummy slice of heaven on earth."

Yummy?

Bette burst out laughing and Nika knew it was from the stunned look on her face.

"Oh my God! I meant yummy as in eye-candy! My boyfriend would freak if I fed from another guy."

Nika didn't know what to react to first. The fact she was even here in the first place or that she was face to face with the reality of vampire life.

Good luck with that, home girl. Too late for a crash course in vampire 101.

She gave her head a mental shake and concentrated on the club itself instead.

Garage grunge and acid punk set the tone for the place, and Annika glanced around unfazed by the raw feel emanating from all sides.

Shadowed nooks peeked from everywhere she turned, and she wondered if that was by design. If the rumors were true, dark corners made it easier for concealed feeding. She exhaled hard.

Stop thinking about it already! You knew what you signed up for when you accepted the gig.

"Is Derick my daytime contact, then?" Nika asked, redirecting her own thoughts.

Bette nodded. "We figured you'd be more comfortable with one of your own. He doesn't say much and keeps mostly to himself. You know, the strong silent type."

Derick had his back to them, and Annika looked at the man's broad expanse and inhaled. A trace scent tickled her nose along with the man's natural musk. Bette was right.

There was something at the core of his scent that conjured a sense of cool moss and loamy earth, a rawness that made her mouth water.

He was dark haired and chiseled and Annika couldn't drag her eyes from his muscled shoulders as he lifted boxes of equipment and heavy speakers from a forklift.

"He's been getting the place ready for your show for days, now. We wanted nothing left to chance," Bette added.

Derick peeled his shirt from his back and wiped his brow with the white cotton. He turned tossing the garment onto a speaker box, giving them a sideways view of his sculpted chest.

His torso gleamed with a fine sweat, and Annika's eyes followed the line of stacked muscles toward the sexy V at his hips, until it disappeared beneath his low-rider jeans.

Oh my God.

Sex and maleness incarnate. Those were the two words that came directly to mind. Not just from the sheer beauty of his sculpted arms and broad back, but how he moved. His profile was strong, with a carved jaw and the sexy scruff of a day old beard.

Annika closed her eyes and inhaled again, only this time expanding her senses. The air around her was ripe with the scent of the secret and forbidden.

Heaviness, thick with the essence of concentrated sex crowded her mind, and she gasped at the hungry feel. Urgency pulsed through her body, stronger than she'd ever felt and her panties dampened at the unexpected throb in her nether regions.

Her body tingled with immediate need and she swallowed hard against the effect, curling her fingers into her palms. Ariel was right, again. It had been too long.

She opened her eyes as Derick turned, only this time her breath caught for a different reason. A tattoo as clear as day on his left bicep. Three crowned lions.

Annika had seen that exact ink on Jesse's arm. It was the LaFont crest. Their mark. A rite of passage branded into their skin when they first phased.

No fucking way.

Her eyes narrowed and she unconsciously took a step closer. It had to be a coincidence. LaFont features were distinctive, light-haired and blue-eyed. Nothing like this tall, dark, delicious man standing thirty yards away.

Bette dipped her chin, her lips curling in a close-mouthed grin. "You're feeling him, aren't you? She chuckled. "Say the word, honey, and it's a done deal."

Annika ignored the question along with Bette's undead eyes dilating at the scent of her knee-jerk arousal.

Yeah, I'd like to feel him and then some.

She squashed the thought. She was here to do a job and nothing more.

The pretty vampire didn't push the issue, instead pointed toward a short set of stairs leading to a private bar.

"The VIP section." Bette swung one hand wide as they stepped onto the bar's carpeted floor. The club was empty with only scattered wait-staff stocking the bar and cleaning the concrete dance floor.

"This is where you'll be between sets. We don't want you overwhelmed. Beyond the ropes are our backrooms, but whether you visit them or not and with whom, is entirely at your discretion." She paused as if waiting for a reaction.

"In the past, entrance to the backrooms was by invitation only. Vampire invitation. However, Weres and shifters were recently granted an all access pass, although there are a few rooms still too raw for daylighters."

Nika blinked, angling her head. "I'm sorry, did you say daylighters?"

"A daylighter is what vampires call any supernatural not confined to the night," Bette replied, "but it mostly refers to shifters and Weres. My boyfriend hates the term."

Annika gawked at her. "Your boyfriend is a shifter?"

"A Were, actually." Bette nodded. "Mixed relationships aren't exactly mainstream, but old taboos are lifting. In fact, it's how I got them to approve your performance."

Annika rubbed her arms. There was something about this place that made her shiver, and it wasn't the pretty vampire standing beside her. She glanced past her shoulder to Derick.

The vampire grinned, giving Nika a knowing nudge. "The moon's pull is strong in the city. Don't fight it, Annika. I can smell its effect on your body already, and lingering scents from our backrooms don't help. This place reeks of sex for those of us with hyped senses. If you're not planning to hook up, I'd take a hard run in the park or you'll be in knots by the time you take the stage."

Annika swallowing hard again, her eyes darting back from Derick.

"My boyfriend says a hard run is what shifters do to help take the edge off when sex is off the table." Bette shrugged. "Personally, I like it on the table or the floor or anywhere I can sink my teeth into that wolf of mine."

Nika's eyes widened. If Derick was a LaFont, then he had to be a wolf. Did that mean Bette and he were—?

"Are you...I mean...Derick and you...is he..." she stuttered, feeling her cheeks burn.

Bette burst out laughing. "Me and Mr. Talks-To-No-One? Not a chance, babe. I like my men hard, but that one is too hard, and I don't mean in the way I like. He's complicated. Moody and dark. Like he's running from something, and to be honest, I get enough of that brooding crap from my own kind."

The vampire paused, sparing a glance at Derick, too. "Then again, if that's what turns you on, go for it, girl. No questions asked."

Annika didn't say a word, and Bette laughed it off with a quick wave. "Okay, back to business, then. Your agent wants us to keep you under wraps until the show, so maybe it's best for you to stay here."

"Here? In the club?" Nika asked.

"No. At *Les Sanctuaire*. Ariel has you booked into The Benjamin Hotel on 33rd Street, but personally, I think you'd be happier here. I had accommodations readied for you, just in case. Of course, you're totally free to come and go as you please."

"*Les Sanctuaire?*" Nika repeated in perfect Cajun French.

Bette grinned. "Our lair, and where visiting vampires rest during the day."

"I don't know, Bette. Taboos might be lifting, but not fast enough. You're a fan, but I'm not so sure the other residents will share your enthusiasm. No offense, but I wouldn't want to unknowingly cross paths with someone whose more interested in my blood than my music."

Bette shook her head, adamant. "I would never put you anywhere near the residents. You'll have the entire east wing to yourself. The only other person who shares that side of the building is Derick. Since the sun rises on that side of the building, I guarantee no one will bother you."

"I don't know." Nika hesitated, but she couldn't say no to the hopeful look on Bette's face. "Okay, I'll give it a try. Once the house lights come up I'm going to need a fortress to keep the paparazzi at bay, and something tells me this place is exactly what the doctor ordered."

Bette grinned, nodding. "No one gets into our lair without permission, and our bouncers know the consequences for breaking the rules."

Movement across the staging area caught her eye and she turned watching Derick shrug back into his shirt. "I'll have to get my things from the...*uhm*...the hotel."

"No need," Bette's eyes followed hers. "I can arrange whatever you need." She nudged Nika's elbow. "And I do mean *whatever*."

Nika nodded absently, her eyes still on Derick's broad back. "Will I see you later, then?"

"Absolutely." Bette beamed not knowing if the question was directed at her or the gorgeous man's fine ass.

Chapter Four

The rest of the afternoon flew by with meet and greets as the club arose from its slumber. It was well past eight p.m. when she finally collapsed on her bed in the east wing.

Her accommodations were fit for a queen. She spent the better part of an hour soaking in a giant claw foot tub in a bathroom bigger than her mama's house. She took extra pains getting ready. Tonight wasn't an official appearance, but it was still her first in the public eye in ages.

It was near midnight when Annika walked toward the VIP section dressed to kill. A black ruched skirt with blood red trim fell to mid-calf. Its rustle a soft whisper against her thighs as she climbed the stairs. A Victorian bustle cinched tight under a plunging leather over-bust corset. The perfect counterpoint for the club's ambiance.

The outfit hugged her full curves and a feeling of freedom washed over her as she trailed her fingers along the brass railing.

She was back.

Nika took her seat at the reserved table overlooking the lower bars. The music pounded, and the rasping, almost incoherent vocals reverberated with heavy bass across the concrete floor. Tonight, every version of Goth culture in the house.

"Compliments of The Red Veil." The waiter appeared from nowhere carrying a small silver tray. He placed a stemmed glass on a coaster and then turned the wine bottle in his hand, presenting its distinctive label.

"Vampire wine," Nika replied with a nod. "Now that's appropriate."

He smiled, flashing sharp teeth. "Bette picked this especially for you."

With an audible pop, he pulled the cork from the bottle's slim neck and poured. "It's a proprietary blend. Enjoy."

The server placed the bottle in a bucket stand beside the table and then turned for the bar. Proprietary blend of what? Annika picked up the glass and sniffed.

"It's just wine. Don't worry."

Stemmed glass in hand, Annika turned toward the tinkling voice. An exquisitely dressed woman in a black vintage gown, approached. She had an air of style and confidence, and if there was such a thing as Haute Goth, she would be it.

"We don't lace the wine unless asked, and then only for very special customers." The elegant woman held out her hand, perfectly polished fingernails gleaming red. "Abigail Bigly, manager of The Red Veil."

"I...I... didn't mean..." Nika stuttered.

She pressed her lips together to stop from rambling. What was it about these vampires that made her so unglued?

"Annika Lee." She steeled herself and took the woman's hand. "It's a pleasure to meet you."

Amused, the classy vampire smiled. Formidable as she was graceful, Abigail looked at Nika with eyes that seemed to pierce and detect.

It didn't take long for Annika to guess the woman's role in their veiled subculture. Abigail was vampire elite, and only one degree from the famed New York Vampire Council.

"I was told you decided to stay with us after all," she said. "I trust you've found everything to your liking?" The vampire tilted her head, clearly curious.

Nika nodded, meeting the vampire's unnerving gaze. "Yes, thank you. Everyone has been more than accommodating."

Yeah, like I would complain.

"Good." Abigail inclined her head. "Then I'll let you get back to your evening. Please don't hesitate to ask if there's anything you want."

She walked away, yet her gait made it seem as if she floated toward the bar. Bette gave a small wave from the corner and Annika let out the breath she'd been holding.

She raised her wine glass to her new friend, sniffing again before bringing it to her lips. The wine hit her tongue and Nika held it to the roof of her mouth, opening her senses.

The individual scents separated much the same way they had when she tried to place Derick's heredity. Funny, both he and the wine held something she couldn't place.

She couldn't stop thinking about him since she left for the east wing with Bette. Inhaling, she scanned the lower club. He was somewhere in the crowd. She sensed it.

Closing her eyes, Nika concentrated on his remembered scent. The uniqueness of it. She smiled to herself and then lifted her lids, focusing on a shadowed silhouette in the far corner.

Derick leaned against the wall with one knee bent, his foot against the concrete wall. A longneck bottle dangled from his fingers, and somehow she knew his eyes were closed.

A lone woman approached from the opposite end of the dance floor aiming straight for him, only stopping when they were practically toe-to-toe.

Interest piqued, Annika focused her hearing as well as her nose. Bette called him *Mr. Talk-to-No-One*. Would he brush off a quick piece of ass?

211

"I've been watching you," the woman murmured, her eyes taking in Derick's broad chest and chiseled face.

He dropped his chin, his gaze meeting hers with indifference. "There are way more interesting people to watch here than me."

A slow, seductive smile graced her lips. "Not from where I'm standing."

No shit, sweetheart.

Derick didn't blink. "Then maybe you should take another look around. Get a better feel for the place."

Annika sat up straighter. Derick's stance shifted in that moment and she caught the distinct scent of aroused interest.

"I'd rather get a feel for you. Or better yet, let *you* get a feel for *me*." The woman practically purred.

Derick reached for the woman's waist, running his knuckles over her belly before stoking her pussy through her tight leggings on the way back up to her midriff.

"Like this?" he asked.

His voice was a low husky growl and the woman sucked in a breath, but when she opened her mouth to comment, he pressed the cold tip of his beer to her lips. "I've no use for a Chatty Cathy."

A smirk spread on her lips and she dragged her tongue over the bottle's wet glass. She took the beer from his fingers, stopping to lick his palm from the base of his hand to the tip of his thumb, circling the rough pad with her tongue.

"I can think of a much better use for my mouth and my time." She nipped at his skin.

Annika's grip on her wine glass tightened. "Fuck!" She scrambled back as the thin stem snapped in her fingers.

Red wine dripped from the edge of the table where the glass fell. She cursed again, mopping up the mess with her napkins.

A strange edginess gripped her chest and envy pinged from nowhere. What did she care who Derick Bergeron fucked?

"Eavesdropping are we?"

Nika jumped, nearly knocking over what was left of her wine glass. "Bette — I didn't hear you walk over."

"Obviously." The young vampire laughed. "Let me give you a hand with that." She turned to signal the waiter and he appeared again out of nowhere with a bar towel.

"At least you didn't ruin your dress with all that snooping." Bette giggled.

"I wasn't snooping!" Embarrassment flamed in her cheeks and Annika knew she was beet red beneath her careful makeup. "I was — people watching."

Bette chuckled. "Right...and I'm the ghost of Christmas present." The vampire's gaze tracked Derick as he disappeared with his bimbo through a door to the backrooms.

Nika watched as well, and made a face. "Are you sure there's nothing in this wine but grapes? Your boss said you sometimes lace the drinks."

Bette ignored the question. "Come with me, babe. I've got just the thing."

Annika got up from her seat and followed Bette from the VIP lounge. They headed in the opposite direction from where Derick disappeared, stepping through yet another reserved exit.

"What've you got hidden behind all these private doors? Secret passages?" she asked.

Bette laughed. "Kind of. They lead to our underground."

"Underground," Nika repeated. "I'm guessing you don't mean the London subways."

Bette smirked, placing a thumb on a small biometric scanner. "There's people watching, and then there's people watching, Nika. Trust me."

"Bette—" she tried, but the young vampire shook her head.

"We can't have you wrapped so tight you can't perform tomorrow night. I have the perfect place for you to continue your sport in private."

"Sport?" she asked. "I don't understand."

Bette flashed a hint of fang. "Oh, you will."

She took Nika's hand and led her down a corridor to what looked like a private viewing room.

Low, tufted couches sat back-to-back facing large ornate mirrors on either wall. The set up was very turn of the century brothel.

"What is this place?" Nika asked.

"*Le Miroir.*"

"The looking glass?"

Bette nodded, impressed she understood the French name.

"This is one of our famed backrooms. As I said, they are by invitation only, so tonight I thought I'd invite you. Maybe even help take the edge off before your big night." Giggling, she pressed a button on the side of the wall.

The lights dimmed and a waiter came in carrying a tray with a wine decanter and matching glass, a small crystal jar with a silvered top and a warm towel.

He placed the items on a narrow table against the wall and left without a word.

Bette lifted a hand toward a row of buttons in a recessed control panel beside the couch. "These control everything, and experimenting is half the fun. Enjoy the show."

"Wait! What show?" Nika asked, turning to catch Bette before she left. "I don't understand."

The brunette vampire glanced back with her hand on the door. "Trust me. You will, soon enough."

Annika shook her head, confused. "I'm not sure I like this, Bette."

Bette smirked, angling her head slightly. "I may be undead, but I'm still female, Nika, and I can tell when one of my kind has the hots for someone."

"But I'm not a vampire."

Trying not to laugh, Bette nodded. "No, honey, you're a panther, which makes it even worse. When you're in heat there's no hiding it, honey. You're wound so tight you're going to snap like that wine glass if you don't get some relief." She swung her arm wide. "You're welcome."

"Welcome? For what?"

"For how bad you want to wrap your legs around something hot and hard. I heard your thoughts, Annika. Loud and clear. Especially while you watched the seduction scene in the corner earlier."

Annika's mouth fell open. "You heard my thoughts? I didn't know that was even a thing."

"You haven't been around vampires much, have you?" Bette asked.

Nika shook her head. "Is it that obvious?"

"Yes, but don't worry." Bette answered. "What happens at The Red Veil, stays at The Red veil. What's that human saying? Be careful what you wish for, because you just might get it?"

She took Annika's hand and placed the small crystal jar in her palm. "This is what you wished for Nika — well, almost, but it's a start. Who knows where it might lead?"

Nika looked at the jar in her hand. "I'm guessing this isn't moisturizer."

"Bingo!" Bette laughed. "Even now the blood is flushed beneath the surface of your skin." She picked up the decanter and poured a glass of the red wine. "Agitation, yes, but also anticipation. Let yourself go, Annika." She held the glass out. "You just might surprise yourself."

Nika took the glass from Bette's hand. She opened her mouth to reply, but stopped. Voices muffled in the distance and she caught Derick's scent. Unmistakable.

Annika's eyes jerked toward the dark mirror. She lifted a hand to stop Bette from leaving, but it was too late. She was already at the door.

The lights dimmed even further, and silhouettes formed behind the glass. A man and a woman.

He gathered her to him, his fingers clutching her hair, while his other hand roamed her thin body. He kissed her hard, bending her backward until she fell onto what appeared to be a bed. The girl clamored to her knees and licked her lips and Derick unbuckled his pants.

"Do you still want to leave?" Bette asked.

Annika ignored the question and lifted the wine glass to her lips, draining it.

"The top button will change the aspect from silhouette to full view. The middle button will let them see you as well, though it's up to them to give you access for full participation — if you know what I mean.

"Pull the red velvet cord when you're done, and someone will escort you back to the club or your room. Your choice."

Annika couldn't tear her gaze from the glass. The door snicked shut and her eyes jerked toward the exit.

"Bette — wait!"

The woman behind the glass gasped, her moan pulling Annika's eyes back to the erotic scene unfolding in front of her. She tossed back the wine in one shot and poured a second glass, shooting it back the same way.

Warmth spread through her body and her senses heightened. A slow burn started in her lower belly, same as when she first saw Derick, the same tingle along her skin.

Her hands mimicked his as he cupped the girl's breasts, and she ran her fingers along the boned sides of her corset. She reached behind and loosened the stays. Tugging the stiff garment down, she freed her breasts enough for her nipples to graze the rough edge of the crisscross laces and metal topped leather.

Nika reclined on the couch, her back against the arm. Derick stroked his cock and Annika moaned wishing she could taste him. She pulled the hem of her skirt up and pushed her underwear aside, running her fingers along the wet seam of her pussy.

Moaning, her fingers worked her slick folds as his hand jerked his stiff member, and when he slid his hard cock between the girl's lips, Nika shoved her fingers, palm deep, into her own sex in frustration. She needed more. Wanted more.

She wanted him.

Their hips bucked in time as she watched, one hand clasped to her breast, squeezing and pinching her stiff peaked nipple while the other moved in and out of her sex, her thumb grazing her clit until she cried out.

At that moment Derick's head turned toward the dim glass and it was as though their eyes met. His hips worked the girl, fucking her mouth, but his eyes fucked Annika.

He snarled, fisting the girl's hair and driving his cock further into her throat. His gaze never left Nika. It was as though he could see her body, her hands, and smell her sex as clearly as she smelled his.

"You want it. You know you do. Take it. Cum for me." His words were for Annika, and when he reached down and gripped the girl's pussy, Nika cried out, riding her own palm as she came, hard.

Her body spasmed, clenching against nothing and she whimpered. The release came in a violent crash, but slumped against the back of the couch, the satisfaction hollow and incomplete.

Derick snarled again, pumping his hips. The girl gagged as he came, his head thrown back in a frustrated howl.

He shoved her away from him, jerking what was left of his climax into his hand as he stared at Annika.

The glass went black and she lay in the darkness. Panting. Wanting. Did he want her, too, or was it just a tease?

Chapter Five

Annika's lids fluttered open. Chilled, she rolled to her side barely registering her surroundings. One hand hunted for blankets, but found nothing but velvet upholstery.

Her eyes snapped open and she sat up. She was still in the viewing room. Still half-dressed from the night before.

"Good afternoon."

The voice was deep and husky. The same voice that haunted her dreams all night, urging her to cum, to let go.

But it was just a dream, right?

"Much as I admire your bold look, you might want to change if you plan to get anything accomplished today," the voice said.

Still fuzzy, she glanced down at her state and the night before flooded back in a heady rush.

Oh God. Derick.

Ignoring his appreciative stare, she covered her bare breasts with her arm. "What are you doing here? *Ugh.* I must have slept the day away. Fuck!"

She twisted around, eyes still on the couch. "I need to get to my room and change. God, it's late! Where's my phone?"

"That's a ramble if I ever heard one. You need to calm down and take a breath, *cher.*"

At the familiar endearment, she exhaled in resignation and looked at the man, truly seeing him for the first time.

Derick's tan skin held golden undertones that complimented his pale green eyes. He was a beautiful mix of races, more gorgeous than she originally thought, and the cadence of his voice was pure Créole.

Too embarrassed to say anything or God forbid ask the questions burning to be asked, she hiked her corset over her breasts and randomly knotted the ties to keep it in place for the time being.

"Now that's a crying shame. I bet those sweet parts don't see enough daylight, pale as they are," Derick replied, clicking his cheek.

He leaned against the doorjamb, his white tee tucked into a pair of jeans that molded to strong thighs, showcasing all six feet two inches of lean body. With his arms crossed against his hard chest, his eyes danced with humor at her expense.

"You can lose the smirk. I need a hot shower and a cup of coffee," she shot back.

He tilted his head, flashing a sexy sideways grin. "If coffee is what you're looking for, you're not going to find it close by. At least not the kind I think you want. There isn't a taste of *'Nawlins* chicory to be found anywhere in this city."

She stood, straightening her skirt. "Coffee regular will do me fine, so if you'll excuse me."

With a dismissive wave she brushed past him, but he caught her arm and pulled her close against his chest. So close, she had to look up into his dark eyes.

"I think I already know what'll do you fine." He slid his free hand behind her head and leaned in, kissing her hard.

Annika froze. His scent overwhelmed her, sending heat coursing through her body and her unsated hunger from the night before into overdrive.

The taste of his mouth was a drug, and her body screamed for more. She wanted every inch of him for real, not secondhand like some sad backstreet peepshow.

Her self-reproach rebelled. The last time she gave in to raw desire, it ended with one friend dead and another paying for the sin.

She pulled back, straining against his grip.

Her refusal was silent but obvious, and Derick released her. He stared at her for a moment, his dark eyes unreadable.

"Go on. Take your shower and make your important calls. I've got work to finish, too." He shoved her away like he did the girl last night.

He strode down the hall at a fast clip and Annika didn't know whether to call him back or chase after him. "Wait!"

Derick stopped, but didn't turn. His fingers stretched and then curled into his palm.

"How do I get out of here?" she asked, knowing her question was not the reason he stopped.

He gave her his profile, and it was as perfect as the rest of him. She swallowed the urge to rush ahead and wrap her arms around his waist and climb his hard body.

Derick didn't look at her, almost as if weighing his response. It was a perfect set up for a crude comeback or a snarky remark, but to his credit he stayed quiet.

"Follow me, if you can keep up."

Annika took two steps to his every one until she caught up with him. No one likes to be rejected, but at least he wasn't being an asshole. He didn't say a word, and he didn't make eye contact.

"Look, I'm sorry. You took me by surprise. I didn't know where I was, let alone that I would have company," she tried.

He slowed his pace and he glanced past his shoulder at her. "You're pretty full of surprises yourself."

Heat rushed up her cheeks to her ears. "How do you mean?"

Derick turned, giving her a slow, southern smile. He didn't answer, instead he pointed to a nondescript door. "Go through there and you'll come to an elevator bank. Press the button on the left. It'll take you to the east wing. I'm sure you can find your room from there."

Without another word, he continued down the hall in the opposite direction.

Annika watched him go, her eyes taking in every inch of him. She should have kissed him when she had the chance.

≼

Annika got out of the shower and dried off, toweling her hair before twisting the dark mass into a loose bun on the top of her head.

She shrugged into a terrycloth robe and dropped the damp towel on the floor near the bed. From the window overlooking the Hudson River she watched the shadows and dim orange light dance on the water and the horizon. Dusk.

"A few more days and my internal clock will be permanently on vampire time."

Glancing at the clock on the nightstand, she noticed a bulky envelope sitting beside the lamp. She padded over to see what it was.

Thought you might need this since you mentioned it earlier. It's been ringing off the hook in the coat check all day.

Derick

She tore open the top flap. He found her cellphone and thought enough to return it.

Annika's finger curled over her lip. The man was a contradiction. Controlling and dominant sexually, yet considerate.

With only ten percent battery left, she plugged the phone into its charger and scrolled down the list of recent calls twenty-seven missed calls. Most from Ariel and her mother plus five unidentified calls with a Los Angeles area code. She frowned. There was only one person who'd call from there.

Jesse.

Annika sank onto the end of the bed and pressed Ari's number for callback.

"So, the prodigal client returns," Ari joked. "I only left umpteen messages. Where have you been?"

"Don't ask."

She laughed. "Taking New York by storm, no doubt." With a pause, Ariel sighed. "Listen, I know you're enjoying your anonymity, but your show is tomorrow night. I need you to focus and rest."

"Shouldn't you be nagging me in person?" Nika chuckled, tucking a stray hair behind her ear.

Ari exhaled. "I'm not sure if I'm coming, yet. I don't think I have the stamina."

"Stamina? It's just me and my acoustic guitar. The Red Veil did what you asked and hired a studio drummer and backup rhythm guitarist to help with chord harmony and pulse, but that's it. Exactly what I want.

"I don't know what everyone thinks this is supposed to be," she sighed. "The house manager slipped stage directions under my door with a note asking what kind of pyrotechnics I want. The club has some kind of FX specialist. It's crazy, Ari. I have a strong suspicion everyone is going to be disappointed."

"Nonsense. You did an acoustic album with Dracone Noir and it went platinum. Just tell them you want a clean sound and you'll be fine. You wrote half those songs, you know how best to stage them," Ariel replied.

"I wrote those songs with Jesse."

Ari was quiet. "He's been asking for you."

Annika's gut clenched. "I know. I have missed calls I'm assuming are from him. He must be using his attorney's cell phone."

"Don't call him back. There's no legal reason for you to keep that line of communication open."

"I don't know, Ari." She shook her head, pressing the phone closer to her ear. "My guess is he probably feels like I've abandoned him, but my gut tells me to stay away until I absolutely have to be in L.A."

Ari let out a breath. "Good girl. My source at the D.A.'s office says you might not be called. Don't aggravate the situation. Jesse is an attention junkie along with everything else. Allowing yourself to be dragged into a media circus only feeds his obsession."

"I suppose. Look, I gotta go. I'm supposed to meet with the sound manager," she murmured.

"Sound manager? Why are you doing your sound check today?"

"I'm not. He's got questions that need answering or something like that."

"Go, then. I'll see you, when I see you. Break a leg, Nika."

"Hey, Ari…"

"Hmmm?"

"For what it's worth. Thanks."

"Yeah, yeah. Call your mother. She's been calling me, too. Something's got her spooked."

"Will do."

Annika pressed end on her phone and tossed it on the bed. Everything was happening so fast. Or at least that's how it felt. She hadn't sung outside the shower or to herself in a year and a half, and the prospect of singing in public tied her stomach in knots.

Ari would say she was being ridiculous. Once a professional, always a professional. But she wasn't there when Ki took his last breath.

She glanced at the desk and the stage plans waiting for her comments and revisions. Whatever her fears, whatever her guilt, Ki would have hated her throwing her career away. If she shrank from what was hers, then Jesse still called the shots.

Anger squeezed her heart at the thought. No more. Ki would have wanted her to take this chance, so Jesse be damned. Annika picked up a pen and sat at the desk.

It was time.

She would do this. For herself and for Ki.

∽

For so late in the day, the stage was a buzz of activity. It was almost dark, but the venue had finally taken shape for the show.

"Derick?" she called softly.

He turned, lifting one hand and motioning for her to wait.

"Take those black PVC brackets to the back and put them with the rest of the cables. I'll sort them later. After that, go home. All of you. Tomorrow's a long day."

"Derick. I don't mean to interrupt, but I need a minute," she tried again.

"Not right now, Annika. I have a lot to do or the show is not going to be what Abigail expects. No offense, but she signs my paycheck, not you," he replied, adjusting a large speaker at stage right.

Hmmph. "If you're so busy, then why are you sending everyone home?"

He raised an eyebrow, shooting her a look. "Because tomorrow they work set up, clean up, and break down. Eighteen hours at least."

"I didn't realize. Sorry." She winced in apology.

Derick blew out a breath. "Artists rarely do."

"You wouldn't happen to know where I can find the sound manager, then." She looked around. "Someone left me a note saying I need to meet with him. What about the house manager? I need to go over the stage directions with him."

"You're looking at him," Derick said with an exhale.

She blinked. "You're the house manager?"

"House manager, stage manager—" he nodded. "Sound, lighting and special effects."

Eyebrows hiked, she chuckled. "You're kidding, right?"

"I wish."

Flabbergasted, she looked at him. "What if I had come with a full band complete with entourage? A one man roadie crew would cave."

"We'd hire out if that was the case, just like we did for this show." He shrugged. "You've got studio artists working with you, remember? Plus, not every club is owned and operated by vampires and Weres. We have abilities humans only dream about."

Derick straightened to his full height. "Talents my nose tells me you share." His voice dropped and he cocked his head, eyeing her.

Annika ignored the probe. "This is not what I expected," she said, shifting the focus from her to the stage. She swung a hand toward the two hundred foot stage and the set dressers already designing the eerie feel for the night.

"Life is never what you expect, *cher*, and hardly what you want. Haven't you figured that out yet?" he flashed a soft smile.

She crossed her arms in front of her chest. "It should be, though."

He lifted one speaker and adjusted it, moving it to the front right of the stage, doing the same with the left. "If you want something different, talk to Bette. I just work here. I don't get involved."

"That's not what it looked like last night," she said and no sooner had the words left her mouth then she clapped a hand over her lips.

Derick stopped what he was doing and looked at her. "That's exactly what it was last night. Uninvolved."

"Not from where I stood," she lifted her chin.

He grinned, ducking under the mounted DSR system. "Stood? Last I looked darlin', you were flat on your back with your hand shoved between your legs, your own juices running down your fingers as you watched me mouth fuck that girl."

Circling past the speaker, he stood close enough for his scent to make her mouth water.

"I'm pretty good at reading people, Annika. I think you are, too. We sense things others don't. Secret things." He ran his knuckles over the bare skin of her upper arm.

"We use those talents to our advantage. You seduce your audience the same way I used that girl to seduce you through the mirror."

"It's not the same thing," she replied.

"Sure it is, even if you won't admit it." He considered her. "Your voice, your body. As the music takes you, your audience feels it. The intensity is as real as physical foreplay, even stronger because the sex is between their ears as well as between the legs. Your fans crave it. They crave you."

Derick leaned in as he spoke, his lips hovered above the hollow at the base of her ear. The rough stubble on his chin teased the tender flesh, and his low husky voice vibrated against her skin. "I know how they feel."

She swallowed. "Derick—"

He walked her backwards until the back of her legs hit the hard, flat side of a low amplifier. She lost her balance and he caught her before she landed on its soft, mesh cover.

His eyes searched hers. "You feel it as well. The pull between us."

She pushed at him. "I don't want this."

"Yes, you do. You wanted it when I woke you, you wanted me, but something held you back. Even now you're so wet the air is thick with need. I can already taste you on the back of my tongue."

"Stop teasing me, Derick. It's a full moon. Nothing more."

Even she heard how lame that sounded. Her lips parted to argue again, but Derick kissed her, running his tongue along the seam of her bottom lip.

He took her mouth, and this time she gave in to the seduction, breathless at the feel of his body and the taste of his lips.

Derick ran his hand over her thigh to the full curve of her hip, sliding the cotton of her skirt upward, inch by inch. He swept his arm beneath her one leg and spread her wide.

"You're right," he agreed, grinding his full hard length against her damp panties. "It is a full moon, which makes this even more necessary."

She froze mid-groan.

He reached down to move the lacey edge of her underwear aside, but she grabbed his wrist.

"What do you mean *necessary*?" Her eyes met his, angry and full of sudden fire. "Did the vampires put you up to this? Did Bette? She mentioned the moon and something about taking the edge off when I first arrived. Is this her plan to ensure a better show?"

Derick blinked. "What?"

"You heard me." Annika pushed him back, forcing him to release her leg.

"Annika, don't—"

Her body rushed with heat, and not the kind he expected. "No, *you* don't." She'd been manipulated enough for a lifetime. With Jesse, the record company, but no more.

Stunned, he stared at her. "Look, I may work for the vampires, but they don't own me and they certainly don't own my cock. I fuck who I want, when I want."

"How nice for you."

He threw one arm up. "Stop it. You're twisting my words. You really think this is some kind of orchestrated seduction?"

When she didn't reply, Derick exhaled shaking his head. He turned to leave, but then stopped. "I'm not for hire, Annika. I want you and I know you want me. Like it or not, full moon or not—"

Her phone rang cutting him off.

"Don't answer that."

She shook her head and reached for her cell in her skirt pocket. Glancing at the screen, she made a face. "I have to take this."

Derick slid his knuckles over her forearm inching toward her hand, but she jerked the cellphone out of reach.

"You don't understand. It's a member of my band. I have been avoiding him for days."

His hand froze on her wrist. "Jesse LaFont?"

She nodded, surprised. "Jesse was our guitarist."

"I know who he is. He's a jealous liar and a con artist, not to mention a bigot. I'm not surprised he killed your friend."

"That's quite a statement, even if you are from the bayou," she shot back

One of the stagehands interrupted, poking his head in from the outside loading dock.

"Annika, I was heading for the subway when this came up in my feed. I doubled back to show you. Check it out." He handed her his phone.

She glanced at the screen. The TMZ clip showed Jesse surrounded by paparazzi and reporters as he headed into the courthouse, with a headshot of her plastered at the bottom right of the screen. A voiceover questioned her whereabouts, wondering if she'd show for the proceedings.

The news clip shifted to a tape of her and Jesse walking with Ki on Sunset Strip a week before his murder. As always, Jesse mugged for the paparazzi.

Nika remembered that day like it was yesterday. Without warning, Jesse grabbed her around the waist as they walked the strip.

He bent her back, cupping her crotch. She pushed him away and Ki intervened, getting between them. A shoving match ensued, and the incident was all over social media.

Annika held the man's phone, staring at the screen. Finally, she looked up with an aggravated exhale.

The stagehand shook his head. "That dude is either a first class douche or a genius at working publicity."

Derick snorted. "Trust me. He's no genius."

The man blew out a breath. "If I wasn't afraid Bette would rip my heart out and eat it, I'd call TMZ myself. They're offering big money for anyone who knows Annika Lee's whereabouts, but I'd like to continue breathing, so no thanks. Vampires always find out."

Derick slipped the phone from Annika's hand and gave it back to his guy. "No more of these, okay? Now, go home. We need everyone's A-game tomorrow."

"Hey, man. I didn't mean to upset her." He looked at Annika. "I'm sorry, really. I didn't think."

Derick gestured with his head for the guy to leave, and the stagehand ducked out without another word.

"I'm sorry about that, *cher*, but it only proves my point," he commiserated.

Annika sucked in a ragged breath. "You may know of Jesse, but you don't know him. You can't make assumptions based on what the media reports. There's more than one side to every story."

His eyes burned as he looked at her, and his intensity scared her. "I know more than you ever will."

Unshed tears pricked Nika's eyes. So much for peace and freedom. She walked away with the weight of Derick's eyes on her back.

Chapter Six

"Knock. Knock." The door was ajar and Bette pushed it open. "Nika? You decent?"

"In here."

"You said you didn't want to go out, so I brought you dinner. I hope that's okay," the vampire called from the other side of the door.

Annika opened the door to her bedroom. A tall vampire holding a tray full of food stood next to Bette in the sitting area. The look on his face was comical, as though the smell of the food made him want to vomit.

"Wow, I didn't think vampires could go green around the gills." She chuckled. "Why don't you put the tray down on the coffee table before you yak?"

The vampire did exactly that and then moved back to the door, releasing a hard exhale.

Nika laughed out loud. "If it's any consolation, dude, I gag thinking about what *you* eat."

Bette snorted, dismissing the vampire with a quick wave. "Sorry about that. I forget how sensitive youngbloods are around anything human. He's just gotten over his uncontrollable cravings, so I thought I'd start breaking him in for the club. You may have noticed most of our staff are supernaturals."

"I did. Daylighters for daily work and vampires for the club. Smart and practical."

Bette smiled and the tips of her fangs glinted in the light. Her gaze softened as she looked at Nika already in her pajamas.

"Look, I get you need to rest and prep for the show, but are you sure you don't want to join me for a little while? It's only nine p.m., and I've been so busy, I feel like we haven't had a chance to hang out."

Annika shook her head. "I want one more night of relative calm. One of the stagehands showed me a TMZ clip, and speculation on my whereabouts is trending hard. After tomorrow, the entire world will know I'm here. It's going to be a nightmare."

"I told you this place is a fortress. Vampires and Weres may be on opposite sides most of the time, but not when it comes to protecting our combined secrecy. No one gets in without clearance."

Annika laughed again. "You make The Red Veil sound like a compound."

"Ha! How ironic. The Alpha of the Brethren of Weres will be tickled you used his word. It's what he calls their center of operations in Maine."

Nika nodded. "How could I forget?"

Eyeing her, Bette leaned over and snagged a dinner roll and handed it to Nika. "It's my job to keep you happy until you have to leave us, so eat."

She took a bite out of the roll. "Then I might have to stay forever."

Bette laughed, flashing her fangs, again. "That can be arranged. One little bite and you and I could be sisters of the night." She giggled. "Hey, cool name for a band, right? Whaddaya think?"

"No, thanks." Nika shook her head. "I have a hard enough time finding time to properly shift, but you were right about a full moon and the city. My skin is crawling with the need to get out and run."

"From what I hear, the moon isn't the only reason." Bette winked, flashing even more fang. "The backrooms are still an option, but if you really need wide open spaces, the only place that comes close is Central Park. Wait until after midnight, though. Too many joggers otherwise for you to shift in secret.

⋛

Annika pushed her food around on her plate. She had no appetite. Right now she was too tired and too confused for anything other than a night of channel surfing and her pillow. Maybe an old movie with no interruptions would coax sleep.

She toed the tray to the end of the bed and slumped against the headboard. Her phone buzzed, and she glanced at the blue lighted screen.

"Hey, Mama."

"*Bebe*... Are you okay?"

"I'm fine, Mama. Ari said you've been calling. What's going on?"

Jolene blew out a breath. "I can't shake this feeling something is going to happen. Something bad. I keep seeing Jesse's face in my dreams. He's taunting me to get to you."

Nika chewed on her lip. "It's just your imagination. I know you're the local premonition queen, but Jesse has been behind bars for eighteen months. He's not going anywhere. Not for the rest of his life."

"That may be, but I know what I know. That boy is cunning *and* he's a shifter. The LaFonts stop at nothing when they want something. When they lay claim, they never let go no matter what the cost, and Jesse is no different."

Annika shook her head, holding the phone between her chin and her shoulder. "I'm not a boat or a fishing spot. Jesse can't lay claim to me."

"Don't sass me, *cher*. You know what I mean."

"I do, Mama, and I appreciate the concern, but Jesse can't have me. Not anymore. It doesn't matter he's a

234

shifter and from one of our clans. He's a bad seed and I finally realize that."

"I just hope it's not too late, *bebe*. That clan is mercenary and has been known to use their abilities to get what they want."

"What's Jesse going to do? Shift into a panther in the middle of a prison yard? The roof guards will shoot him dead."

"How do you know he can't shift into the rat he is?"

Annika's heart clenched at her mother's anxious tone. "Because he can't. For fun we'd sneak into the Los Angeles zoo at night—me, Jesse, and Ki. We'd take turns shifting into different animals. Jesse couldn't do it. He called us mongrels."

Jolene was silent.

"Mama?"

She exhaled a ragged breath. "If you say so, *cher*, but I want you to call me every day until that boy is behind bars forever. You hear?"

"I will, Mama. In the meantime, why don't you stay with Tante Louise? You know how much you love to whip her butt at *Bourré*."

Jolene chuckled. "I'll talk to you tomorrow before the show, right?"

"I love you, Mama."

"I love you too, *bebe*. Try to get some rest."

～

The phone rang and Nika groped on the nightstand, disoriented.

Knocking over a glass and the remote control, she shielded her eyes from the flickering light from the television and found the phone. Squinting at the screen, she went to press ignore call, but pressed accept instead.

Shit

"Annika? You there?"

Shit. Shit. Shit.

"Jesse?"

"Finally. I thought I'd never get you."

Fully awake, she sat up. "How are you calling me? You can't have a cellphone in prison."

"I have my ways, Nika. Don't you know that by now?"

"Are you crazy? Don't you care about the trial? Can't you play by the rules for once in your life?" She dragged a hand through her hair.

"Oh, baby, I had to talk to you. I started thinking you ran out on me, but you wouldn't be so upset if you didn't care, right?"

She didn't reply.

"So when are you coming out? I need you here," he asked.

"I'm not. Not unless I have to."

He balked. "What do you mean? You have to. I'm telling you."

"No."

"Annika. No joke. Get your fat ass out here. I mean it."

She laughed at him. "Or what? You gonna hit me again? Jesse, you killed Ki. How am I supposed to forgive that?"

"It was self-defense."

A snort left her mouth even as a frown tugged at her lips. "Bullshit! You killed him because he had the guts to tell you what a piece of shit you were to me. He was my friend, Jesse. Just my friend, but you couldn't handle that."

"Like I said, it was self-defense. He was trying to take what was mine and I was defending my claim."

Annika closed her eyes as her mother's words raced through her head. "Claim?"

"Cut it out, Nika. You know what I mean. I'll never lay a hand on you again. That's all in the past."

"No, Jesse. It's not in the past. It's now. It's always. I can't forget it. Any of it. Ever."

"You will. Give it time. You'll see I did this for us."

His voice was low and like silk, but it no longer worked on her. "Us? You must be crazy. There is *no* us. Not anymore. I'm not coming to L.A. unless subpoenaed. If that happens, I swear I'll tell them everything."

"You owe me!"

She snorted. "I owe you nothing. Dracone Noir wouldn't have an album if it wasn't for me finishing it with Ari's help. You're lucky I pushed for you to collect royalties or your legal team would be court appointed."

"Don't do this, Annika. I'm warning you," he ground out.

A harsh exhale left her mouth. "Do you even hear yourself, Jesse? How can you say you need me with one breath, and then threaten me with the next? You're all about you and only you, Jesse, and I want no part of *you* anymore. See you in twenty-five to life."

She hung up and slumped back against the pillows, quiet tears threatening.

⋘

Annika tossed in bed for the hundredth time since Jesse called, finally shoving the covers from her body. Heat skimmed across her skin and she moaned, turning into her pillow.

Mist surrounded her, but she wasn't alone. The swirling fog caressed her, and she gasped at the feel of invisible fingers through the filmy dress highlighting her curves.

"Annika..."

A voice called, hidden in the miasma. She struggled to see, but couldn't.

"Close your eyes. Find me —"

Her lids slid closed and she followed the sound of the deep voice. Derick's voice. He was aroused, that much she knew. With her sight gone, her other senses heightened, and she smelled his urgency, his need.

"Annika — you're close, so close."

Her nipples hardened as her body reacted to his voice, his scent. An unseen hand skimmed her breasts and she gasped as they grazed the puckered tips.

The mist parted and she saw the stage, empty except for Derick. He was naked, and his light bronze skin gleamed in the dim light. Shadows rippled and played along his carved physique, highlighting the muscles in his chest and thighs. His cock was thick and corded, and he stroked his member, holding his other hand out for her.

"Why are we here?" she asked, taking his hand.

He pulled her close, pushing her hand down to clasp his cock. She caressed his hard length as he kissed her mouth.

"You wished this. That's why," he murmured against her lips.

With his free hand he untied the knot holding her dress, and the fabric puddled to the floor. He dipped his head and tasted her breasts, sucking and nipping their hard peaks.

"What do you want, Annika?" he asked.

"To be free."

He lifted his head from her and turned her in his arms. With one arm around her waist, he walked her toward a large speaker. He ran his fingers over her inner thighs, skimming her wet folds. She gasped, bending over to give him full access. Annika gripped the amplifier, straddling its width to spread her legs farther for him.

His fingers delved deep, her juices coating her sex until he pulled back and drove his cock, balls deep, into her pussy.

Another man laughed in the distance and an electric guitar pierced the silence. Heavy chords vibrated through the amplifier, the power-driven pulse driving deep into her sex along with Derick's cock.

Her full breasts swung back and forth, her nipples scraped raw against the speakers' mesh as pleasure and pain crowded her *senses. Neither would let up as the cadence from both men grew to a frenzied pace.*

"You will never be free — "

With a gasp, she sat bolt up in bed, sweat covering her body. What the fuck?

Annika scrubbed her face and looked at the digital clock on the nightstand. Twelve forty-five a.m.

She had to get out. She needed air and she needed speed. Her skin itched and she couldn't shake the dream. What the hell was her subconscious trying to tell her?

She wanted Derick. That much she would admit. Wanted him badly. But Jesse? What role could he possibly play other than past regret?

Maybe that was it. Until she let him go and forgave herself for her own stupidity, he'd have a hold on her in some weird way.

She shook her head and got out of bed. Enough with the psycho-babble.

She rinsed her face and threw on leggings and a tee-shirt. No bra, no panties. The less she wore the better when shifting. She grabbed her phone and some money and threw them into a drawstring pack and headed out of her room for the elevators.

Bette said Central Park after midnight.

Perfect.

Chapter Seven

"How does anyone breathe in this city?" Annika mumbled. "At least in L.A. I could run on the beach, but here it's all concrete and grit." Her nose wrinkled at the pungent scent of old urine.

"Honey, you get used to it, but for us, the city that never sleeps is a twenty-four hour buffet of predators preying on predators."

The vampire snapped his fingers, and Nika had to laugh at his fanged and fabulous air.

"Dion, you kill me." Bette laughed, keeping pace with the two.

"Never has the crime rate been kept in check in such a delicious way." Dion pursed his perfectly lined lips. "Now pay attention, Nika-baby, because Bette and I have a date with a crack den that needs a lesson in manners."

"*Uhm*, okay?" Annika laughed, unsure of what she was supposed to say.

Bette grinned, slipping her arm through Dion's elbow. "It's all part of Rémy's *Robin Hood* plan."

"Who?" she asked.

"Rémy du Lac. He's our supreme for the time being. Since New York's current mayor shackled the city's police department, we've decided to intervene. We clean up the criminal element where we can, especially when it benefits us."

"That's right, boo. I located the one crack den responsible for polluting an entire supply of donated blood. They were warned, but —"

Bette patted his arm. "No matter. We'll deal with them as needed, but enough civics for one night. Duty calls."

"Miss thing is one hundred percent right, and we really can't get into details," Dion said as they slowed to a stop by a crossroads path. "This is Eagle Vale Arch. Just find your way back here and you can easily get to the West Side and then hop a cab or a train downtown to The Red Veil."

Annika looked around and then inhaled trying to mark the scent. "Thanks."

Bette smiled. "No problem, sweetie."

Nika's eyes went wide and she couldn't help but stare. Bette's fangs were razor sharp and fully descended.

"If you follow the scent of horse you'll find the Ramble. The vampires hunting there won't bother you. They're too busy keeping the riffraff from menacing the homeless."

"Ramble?" Nika questioned.

Bette nodded. "The Ramble is a wooded preserve within Central Park adjacent to the lake. It's dense with trees and perfect for you."

"Thanks."

Dion's eyes darkened and he took on a predatory gleam, inhaling. "Wish we could stay and play, darlin', but it's dinner time."

Bette took off with him, barely sparing Annika a backward glance. "Remember, keep off the streets or you'll end up in the pound!"

Bette's tinkling laugh faded into the darkness as the two vampires disappeared without a trace.

Nika sniffed the air again and refocused, this time she caught a trace of thick trees and brush riding just below the scent of horse.

Close enough.

She followed the scent past a castle like structure until she spotted a heavily wooded area with rocky outcroppings.

Bingo.

She followed a dirt path deep into the darkened thicket. The air was still tinged with the grit from the city, but the trees and wildflowers no less an unexpected treasure in the middle of this concrete jungle.

The moon had crested to its height and Annika lifted her face to its silvery light, closing her eyes.

She drew a breath through her teeth, remembering home. The bonfires, the smell of loamy earth as crickets and cicadas sang.

Spirit bottles swaying, clinking in the humid breeze, and the chants churning the life force surrounding them while drums called her animal forth. She opened her mouth, a roar called to the moon.

Annika's eyes snapped open. Her human brown had shifted emerald green, and sensitive night vision pupils already tracked body heat in the thicket.

She froze, sniffing the air.

Derick

He was half dressed and gorgeous. His face was toward the moon as well, and every muscle seemed tense, rippled and pronounced as though ready to phase.

She took a step toward him but stopped. Maybe he didn't want company.

"I know you're here, Annika."

She sucked in a breath and silenced her inner panther, cringing against the pain of burying the animal she had just awoken.

"It's okay, *cher*." He turned, lifting his left arm to beckon her over and there on his bicep was the LaFont tattoo.

She'd forgotten about it.

"Bette said this was a safe place to phase," she explained walking into the small clearing to join him.

He nodded. "Most nights, yes. As long as you can ignore the vampires."

She inhaled. He was nowhere near phasing, but his body smelled amazing.

"I interrupted you. I'm sorry," he offered.

Annika shook her head. "Not at all. I sensed you, first. Actually, I saw the outline of your body heat. You're hot." She coughed realizing how that came out.

A tiny smile played around the edges of his mouth. "Good to know you think so."

Her eyes dipped to his chest and then again to his tattoo. This time he noticed.

"We've been going in circles around each other for days, Annika. Don't you think it's time we stopped?"

She nodded.

"You have questions and doubts. I don't blame you. It's one thing to hook up for nameless sex, but it's something else when you realize you may have ties. Ties that go deeper than you imagined."

"Ties?"

"Affiliations, then."

With an internal sigh, she plunged ahead. "I know that tattoo. I've seen it before."

The words blurted from her mouth and she waited for him to shut her down or walk away, but he didn't.

"I know."

"So it's not just a coincidence?"

"No." A frown puckered his forehead.

"How?"

"Because Gerard LaFont is my father."

Annika searched her memories but came up blank. She'd known Jesse her whole life. She sank to a nearby boulder, her mind spinning. He was an only child. If he wasn't, that meant…

Derick looked away, and she followed his gaze. In that instant, she knew. Annika studied his profile. His face, his cheekbones and the shape of his mouth. Even the small cleft in his chin.

LaFont.

"You might not remember me, but I remember you. I know who you are Annika, and not just your media persona. I know your pack, your people, too."

"Bergeron. You're Old Marie's grandson."

Derick's lips parted but then he pressed them together, giving her a curt nod.

"People say your grandmother cursed you to get even with the LaFonts. Is that why you're out here tonight?" she asked.

He laughed, and the sound was genuine. "That's ridiculous. Nothing but bayou superstition. My gran-mère was a lot of things to a lot of people, but she couldn't conjure what wasn't already in the blood regardless of what people choose to believe."

"So you're not a *Rougarou*."

"No." He laughed again, eyeing her. "You look almost disappointed."

She waited, glancing up from her feet. "Do you shift?"

"No."

Annika lifted her hand in confusion. "But what about all that talk about our talents and things only humans dream of?"

"I didn't say I can't phase. I just don't." He shrugged.

"Then why are you here?"

He didn't hesitate. "Because you are."

"Phase with me, Derick. My skin is crawling the higher the moon rises, and yours has to be, too."

He shook his head. "I don't shift. Ever."

Her hopeful expression melted. "That's impossible. How?"

"I found other ways to channel my needs." The husky tone of his voice changed, and the sound made her breath lock in her throat.

"You're trembling." His eyes found hers and he licked his lips.

She took an involuntary step forward, drawn to him the same way the moonlight pulled her into the park tonight.

"How did you know I'd be here?"

"Lucky guess."

She shook her head, moving closer. "So you were prepared to loiter in the park after dark on the off chance I'd show up."

"I may have hedged my bets a little."

Eyes burning, the full moon highlighted his smooth tan skin, and Annika's fingers itched to touch him again.

"Is that so?"

"There's a connection between us neither of us understand, Annika. But it's also one neither of us can deny. It's primal. I dream about you. I can't rest. I can't even fuck another woman because it's your face I see, your body I want."

"I've been dreaming, too."

A sexy smirk took his lips. "Tell me."

She shook her head.

"Then I'll tell you mine."

She shook her head, again. "Show me."

Those two words were all it took.

He pulled her into his arms and the warmth of his hands made her skin burn with anticipation. Nika wet her lips.

The tip of her pink tongue made Derick's cock harden. "Keep that up and I'll have no choice but to put that pretty mouth of yours to good use," he murmured.

His lips crushed against hers, hot and rough. Every ounce of patient frustration chased through his veins. He licked her mouth, teasing her lips with his tongue.

Annika moaned, running her hands along his bare chest. Derick fisted the back of her T-shirt and pulled it up, breaking their kiss only long enough to yank it over her head.

She shivered, not from the cool air, but from the feel of her nipples against his skin.

"Is the rest of you commando, too?" His fingers dipped low, sliding beneath the seamed waistband of her leggings. His hand gripped her bare ass, cupping the full flesh and pressing her against his hard length.

"What about you?" she asked, sliding her hands forward along his lower belly.

One by one, she unbuttoned his fly. Dark fuzz tickled the tops of her fingers and she grinned, reaching all the way in to grip his swollen member.

Derick sucked in a soft breath as she freed his sex, shoving his jeans over his hips.

"What was that you said about my pink lips?"

With a groan, he pushed Annika to her knees and fisted the back of her hair. "Say *ahhh.*"

She wrapped her mouth around Derick's cock and sucked halfway, using her hand to grip his shaft. Her fingers worked him, moving in time with the pressure from her tongue.

Derick let his head drop back, and Annika curled her tongue around his head, skimming the rigid flesh and the underside of his bulging tip.

"I'm going to cum all over your face if you don't stop soon."

She flicked her tongue, lapping at a pearl of pre-cum before sitting back on her heels. She cupped her breasts and lifted them, working her nipples between her thumb and forefinger.

"If that's what you want you can cum in my mouth or on my face or right here." She squeezed her tits, leaning forward to rub his hard length between the soft mounds. "Your choice."

He slid two fingers under her chin, lifting her gaze to his. "I haven't waited this long to fuck you only to settle for jerking myself off."

He helped her up onto the boulder she sat on earlier and gently rolled down her leggings, helping her slide them off.

She leaned back on the wide flat rock and Derick spread her legs. He knelt between her pale thighs and kissed her belly, running his tongue in circles upward, cupping her breasts.

She had offered them, teasing him as she worked her own body, but now he sucked and nipped, drawing her hardened peaks between his teeth. He rolled her nipples between his fingers, and she gasped.

Annika grabbed his hair and yanked his face up, taking his mouth. She kissed him hard and fast and then pushed his head and shoulders back, lifting her hips for him to take her with his mouth.

Her lower body shook with need, soaked and dripping. Derick licked her pussy, spreading her legs wide.

"Is this what you want?" He bit her clit, dragging the hard nub along his teeth before sucking it deep. "Or is this what you want?" His tongue delved deep into her wet folds.

Annika could barely breathe. "I want you."

"Me? *Hmmm*. But which part? My mouth?" He kissed her inner thigh. "What about my tongue? I know you like that." He dipped his head lower and swiped his tongue along her swollen sex.

"Or my fingers?" Derick trailed his hand down her leg to palm her pussy before sliding two fingers deep into her wet cleft. "What, Annika? Tell me what you want."

"Stop teasing me! Fuck me, Derick. I want your dick deep and hard. I need it. I want it." Her voice was barely a whisper, but when he stood over her and waited, she snarled, her eyes shifting to panther green.

"Derick! Now!"

The scent of her hunger and her feral eyes forced a low roar from the back of his throat.

The feral feel coursed through his body jerking his cock. He held her ankles wide and drove hard into her pussy, lifting her back off the flat rock.

His body reeled. She was so hot and tight, he groaned as her walls stretched to take all of him.

Annika's body rocked with spasms, her walls gripping his shaft as he rode her, her clit throbbing for more.

Flushed and pink, her pussy gleamed swollen and wet in the moonlight and Derick's mouth watered to taste her again.

"I want to cum deep and hard inside you, Annika. But I want you on all fours, spread wide and feral."

Her eyes found his and she pushed him back, scrambling to her feet. She bent over lifting her hips, and reached behind to spread her ass.

Derick slipped two fingers into her slick wetness. "Nice and wet." He fisted her hair and pulled her head back, bringing his fingers to her lips. "Suck."

Annika opened her mouth and took his fingers in one by one, licking them clean. He let go of her hair and she put her arms down, moving her legs apart, waiting.

He smacked her bottom and shoved her cheeks apart, sliding his thumb from her wet folds to her tight little ring. "I want all of you Annika. This too…" He rubbed the tip of his cock in small circles, nudging the snug opening. Nika moaned pushing back against his cock. "But I want your pussy first, *cher*."

He pulled back, swiping his hand down to her slit again, grazing her swollen bud. Derick slid his hands back and grabbed her hips, driving his cock deep, again. He rode her hard, his fingertips digging into her flesh.

Annika threw her head back and snarled as he reached around to cup her sex, shoving her body up with each thrust. She met him pound for pound, his balls slapping against her ass.

His thumb ringed her nub, pressing and rubbing in time with his hips. Annika cried out as she came, her muscles clenching as spasms took her again.

Balls tight, his head swelled to bursting and he threw his head back and roared, the primal sound wild and echoing off the trees as he emptied himself inside her.

Panting, they both slumped forward, Derick's arms shooting forward not to smack into the rock.

"You okay?"

Annika exhaled a soft sigh. "Absolutely. What about you?"

With his cock still inside, he tightened his arm around her waist and he pulled her against his chest. He held her close as the aftershocks of their climax ebbed.

He kissed her neck and her cheek at the base of her ear, nestling his face in her hair. "I'm good, *cher*. Real good."

She laughed softly, settling back into his arms. "That's an understatement."

Derick nuzzled her neck and slid his hands up to caress her breasts. He pinched a sensitive nipple and she drew in a quick breath.

"You really like to tease me, don't you," she sighed.

"Only if it gets me round two."

Annika turned her face and pulled his lips to hers, smiling as she felt him harden inside her. "Showtime."

Chapter Eight

"*Vampirul este cu ochii pe noi!*"

Bette threw up one hand. "Why do they always do that?"

"Do what?" Nika asked, amused.

The vampire exhaled hard. "Refer to me with that mumbo jumbo and then scurry like scared rabbits."

Annika shrugged. "You're the boss. Plus, they know it's not coffee you're keeping warm in that travel mug."

"Funny," Bette snorted.

Nika shrugged, peeling back the tab on her coffee regular. "Taboos may be lifting, but the idea of blood for breakfast still gives most Weres the willies."

A rude sound left Bette's lips. "I still don't get why they have to refer to me as *the vampire*? And always in Romanian. Like I'm supposed to understand simply because I'm undead." She glared at the remaining crew. "I'm *American*, people. An American vampire in New York," she shouted in general.

Nika chuckled, taking a sip. "Sounds like a movie title."

"Ha! It should be."

"Maybe they're afraid of you, Bette."

She threw a hand up. "Why? I'm not some creepy Nosferatu. I'm cute and perky, with a soft spot for humans. Hell, if I sparkled, people would orgasm as I walk by."

Annika choked, nearly spewing her coffee. "Not to mention modest. You sure you're not buying your own hype?"

"Ha, ha." The vampire's pink lips slid into a smirk. "But seriously, when Abigail insisted we bring in a work crew from Transylvania, I thought she had slipped a cog. 'A taste of the old world, Bette. Just what the club needs.'" She mimicked her boss, wrinkling her nose.

"The old world?" Nika asked. "I thought Abigail was turned on the Mayflower?"

Bette snorted. "Not quite, but close."

"Then why the fascination with Eastern Europe?" she questioned.

Bette shook her head. "Who knows? Maybe it makes her feel connected. The vampiric version of ancestry.com."

Derick's voice carried from somewhere backstage and Annika turned. Bette followed with a smug expression.

"From the look of anticipation on your face, my guess is you blew a little more than just steam last night in the park," she laughed, and Nika's answering blush left the pert vampire with a grin.

"Good for you." Bette swirled what was left in her cup. "As much as I'd love to stay for the juicy details, the sun has set, and this isn't going to cut it." She lifted the empty travel mug.

Annika wrinkled her nose. "Do what you gotta do, just don't tell me."

With construction chaos behind her, she watched her friend walk toward the residences. "Hey, vamp girl—" she called after her.

Bette stopped, turning halfway around.

"Come by my room around nine and help me get ready for the show. It's a bitch lacing a corset alone."

Undead eyes brightened and Bette squealed like she did that first day. "Deal!"

She winked, giving Annika a quick salute before heading down the stage steps.

"So what do you think so far?" a deep voice asked from behind.

A soft smile tickled Annika's mouth, but she didn't turn. "That depends."

"On what?" The question fanned across the back of her neck like velvet fingers.

"They say you're only as good as your last performance—" she murmured.

Derick whirled her around and she wrapped her arms around his neck.

"Is that so?" he replied.

"Yup." She licked her bottom lip, grazing it with her teeth.

"What do they say about teasing your lover with a luscious mouth?" he asked, sliding his hand behind her head.

"Practice required."

He kissed her softly. "Something to keep in mind, then." Lingering with his lips on hers, Derick stroked the sensitive skin at the nape of her neck before stepping back.

"So, what do you think about the set so far?" he asked getting back to business.

Annika gave the area a proper look. Dark brocade drapes marked both stage left and stage right, while gray-white sheers hung mortuary style in a sweeping drape on either side of a huge, backlit, floor-to-ceiling screen.

"What's the screen for?"

He moved toward center stage and stood on the circle spot marked for her grand piano. "I've done a design of eerie trees and mist for a backdrop and put it on an LED loop. Sort of a dark thicket surrounding the stage. I think it will add a taste of magic and mastery to the show since you said no to the pyrotechnics."

"A wooded thicket?"

Derick's eyes found hers and held. "Apropos, considering."

Her heart squeezed at the romance behind the idea. Either their night in the Ramble meant as much to him as it did to her or he was very good at setting the stage for repeat performances. "I love it, Derick. Truly."

"I'm glad."

She broke eye contact and glanced at the stage plot marked along the floor. "The configuration for the instruments looks good. I'm glad you listened."

"I always listen, even when you think I'm not," he replied softly.

Nika met his eyes with a smile. "Now that's a scary thought."

He walked to a circular mark at center stage. "Your piano will be the focal point of the performance and I designed the lighting based on that. I want all eyes on you." He looked at her from the mark. "I know mine will be."

Heat flushed across her throat and up her neck. "What about mics?"

"You'll have the boom above the piano, but there are also standalone mics. Their placement is marked on the stage floor with single dots. They can be moved around at will."

She curved her finger over her lip. "When does the crew break for dinner?"

He looked at her. "The instruments have yet to be set up, and there's your final sound check. Why?"

Annika walked toward one of the amplifiers still to be positioned and turned it on its side. She straddled the base, sitting on the hard, molded edge.

"Because—" she replied, dropping her chin, locking her eyes on his. With a slow smile she hiked her skirt inch by inch above her knees to mid-thigh.

"Do you like my boots? They're new," she asked, letting her fingers caress the pale, smooth skin above the thigh-high leather.

Derick's mouth parted and a sly grin spread across his lips. He grabbed the closest working mic and tapped its steel mesh grille. "Everyone out! Dinner is on me tonight. One hour."

At the crew's startled looks he nodded, shooing them out. "NOW! Get out. One hour."

He dropped the mic.

Annika had one leg up on the base of another speaker, stroking the thin lacey strip of her thong riding between her ass and her pussy.

His entire body pulsed with need. Never had his skin pricked with this kind of want. Annika was a drug and he was hopelessly addicted after one taste.

Neither one cared if the crew had left or not. No one else mattered. She was all he could see. All he wanted.

Sticky and slick, he peeled her panties from her legs, over her boots and spread her knees wide. Her sex glistened wet and ready and he cupped her pussy, his fingers curling in, teasing her G-spot as his thumb worked her hard bud. He pulled her blouse down from her shoulder, ripping the stitching to get to her breasts.

The garment hung in shreds, dangling over her exposed flesh. He molded one breast with his free hand, teasing and twisting its nipple while he lapped at the other, drawing the hardening peak in with a sharp, violent suck.

Annika gasped and dropped her head back between her shoulders, her arms braced, shuddering on either side of the amplifier as she edged toward climax.

He pulled his hand back and stood, freeing his cock from his jeans. Positioned between her knees he pressed his engorged tip to her willing lips and she licked the rigid flesh, running her tongue the length of his corded girth and then back again.

She circled, curling around the bulging end, wetting him completely before sucking him in, taking him fully into her mouth.

Derick growled, forcing himself to ignore the urge for release. He eased himself back from her and lifted her legs.

With his eyes locked on hers he plunged his cock deep, letting her tight folds engulf him. He plunged again, thrust after thrust, tremors building until Annika cried out, her flesh squeezing his cock as her inner muscles convulsed.

Derick's body shuddered, every muscle tense as hot jets spilled into her.

He slumped forward, gathering her into his arms, her legs tangled around his hips. He lifted her back, cradling her against his chest, her dark hair a silken curtain around them.

"Maybe we should get up and move somewhere more private," she mumbled against his neck.

"I think we're past that, babe. Do you want your panties?"

She smiled against his skin. "I'd better or else I'll be a drippy mess in the elevator."

He pulled back and grinned at her. "I'm game if you are?"

"Repeat performance?"

He nodded. "Love in an elevator."

"Hey, isn't that a song somewhere?"

Disentangling himself, he tossed her panties onto her lap. "Cute."

"Look at me, doing the walk of shame with my torn shirt and my panties in a wet wad," she teased scrunching the limp lace into a ball.

"When I'm done with you, *cher*, you'll be lucky if you can walk at all."

◆

Annika stood off stage right watching the club floor. It appeared as though tonight would be standing room only. Which was a surprise considering no one knew she was to perform, and as far as she knew, nobody had leaked a word to the press.

Outside, it was business as usual, with the crowd lined along the alley for admission.

Until Dracone Noir, she never understood the philosophy behind the velvet holding ropes. Now she got it. It was elegant crowd control. Did certain clubs play fast and loose with elitism? Sure, but there were assholes everywhere.

At least tonight everyone would have a chance to see her perform. The Red Veil usually charged for live shows, advertising the upcoming event with posters and flyers and in the local paper, but this was special. They truly showed solidarity with her as a fellow supernatural and kept the entire gig under the radar.

With the stage prepped and in clear view, there was already a speculative buzz humming through the club. Now all Nika could do was hope her solo gig was a well-received surprise.

The instruments were in place. She and the studio musicians had warmed up, and Derick was satisfied with the sound check.

She smiled to herself. He was satisfied in more ways than that. And so was she.

An eerie calm settled over her, though she knew in a matter of minutes her bubble of anonymous peace and freedom would burst.

The minute she took the stage, camera phones and Instagram posts would light up the Internet.

So be it.

She'd never felt stronger or more alive. For the longest time, Jesse dictated so much in her life, including how she defined herself and her self-worth.

Derick had given her the chance to let go, to feel what it was like to be truly wanted. No strings attached. Whatever their path, alone or together, she would never forget that, and a small part of her heart would always belong to him.

Pride swelled as she looked at the stage. It was dark, but the keys on the grand piano made her fingers itch to play. The first song in her set was for Ki.

A lump formed in her chest every time she thought of him, but this was the night to exorcise that and replace it with warmth. He deserved that much.

Tall candelabras in graduated heights formed a semi-circle on either side of the LED screen framing the instruments. The décor was just enough. The music would do the rest.

She hoped.

"You look beautiful!" Abigail said, walking beside Bette who wore an ear-to-ear fanged grin.

"I told you," her vampire friend said with a short squeal.

Annika fluffed the layers of light gray chiffon in her full ballroom-style skirt. "I feel like a Goth marshmallow."

"Stop that! You look gorgeous, and there's just enough black in the underskirt to give you that graveyard panache."

"Graveyard panache?" Nika laughed. "I guess it fits considering the lace on my corset looks like widow's web."

"Your corset is perfect," Bette replied with a sigh. "I didn't cinch it too tightly, did I? We don't need you passing out on stage. The media will go off the rails, and tomorrow it'll be all over that you're checking into Betty Ford."

"Okay, that's enough. Leave Annika to meditate or whatever it is she does to banish pre-show jitters." Abigail pulled Bette away, leading her by the arm toward their front row seats.

Bette was right, though. She felt beautiful.

The corset was just enough to give her that needed edge, and her hair was loose with soft curls, pinned up for a gentle cascade.

She did her own makeup, giving herself the Goth glam look she loved, even adding a little sparkle to her white skin to make it shimmer in the spotlight.

The house lights dimmed.

"Ladies and gentlemen. The Red Veil proudly presents a surprise performance. In a one night only solo debut, please welcome, Annika Lee!"

The crowd was silent for a stunned moment and then went crazy. Frenzied cheers and whistles carried through the air as she took center stage.

She glanced stage right, and Derick was where he said he would be. He winked and kissed his finger before giving her a thumbs up.

Annika curtsied, waving to the crowd as the studio musicians took their places. Without a word, she slid onto the piano bench and laid her fingers over the keys.

Breathe. One. Two. Three. Breathe.

She inhaled and held it for a second.

"This one is for Ki," she murmured.

Her words were soft, and in her ears they seemed barely audible above the sound of her heart pounding in her chest, but the crowd exploded.

Her fingers caressed the keys and the strains of the last song she wrote with her friend filled the club.

I hear the ticking of the clock
My time has come, the night has called.

Half a lie told, half a life lived,
Do angels pray?
Do angels pray?
I feel the darkness in my soul
At heaven's gate, will you be there?
Half a lie told, half a life lived
Do angels pray?
Do angels pray?
Can I fight the obscene?
Can I cleanse the unclean?
Drowning in my darkness,
Now you're not with me.
At heaven's gate, will you be there?
If angels pray.
If angels pray.

Power flowed through her and Derick's words replayed in her head. *Seduce them, Nika. Let them love you.*

She poured every ounce of her soul into the song, and when the last chord faded, she looked up from the keys and took a breath before facing the crowd.

Fans sobbed and the applause went wild. Annika stood and took a bow.

"Thank you all. Thank you so very much. Not just for me, but for Ki. The world lost a talented artist and I lost a treasured friend, but we learn to live and honor their memory, and if we're lucky, we find peace and friendship in unexpected places."

She glanced off stage to the right and kissed her fingers, placing her hand on her heart for Derick, and then she found Bette's sob-swollen face in the front row and blew her a kiss, too.

Annika laughed, and hugged her middle. This was the way it was supposed to be and never was. She shielded her eyes from the footlights and looked into the crowd.

"So, who wants another song?"

Chapter Nine

"*H*ow amazing was that!" Bette threw her arms around Annika's neck, nearly knocking her to the ground. "We need to celebrate!"

"Hold on there, cowgirl. Maybe you'd better ask if Nika's up for it, first," Derick interjected, giving the cute brunette a warning eye.

"*My my*, have we grown a protective boner, lately, Derick?" Bette grinned, flashing a little fang.

Annika choked, snorting beer out her nose.

"Snaps, girl! I'm glad no fans were allowed backstage or you'd never live that one down!" Dion laughed, handing her a wad of napkins from the backstage spread. "And don't worry about Ms. Snarky Pants. I'd have a protective boner, too, if I had a chance with anyone as tall, dark and furry as that one."

Dion pointed a long, pink-sparkled fingernail at Derick, and at the look on his face, Annika laughed so hard she had to cross her legs.

"Stop! I can't," she coughed, trying to catch her breath.

Her phone rang.

"Saved by the bell," Derick muttered, eyeing the undead group.

Nika hiccupped. "Nope, more likely saved by my agent, Ari. She said she would call when the show was over."

Bette handed her the cellphone, but when Annika looked at the screen she sobered.

"What?" Derick got up immediately and moved to her side.

Annika held up two fingers. "Hello?"

"What? Slow down, I can barely understand you."

Annika stood, her eyes widening with each passing second.

"I need paper and a pen! NOW!" she yelled, not caring if she sounded hysterical.

Bette handed her a small notepad and a pen from her purse.

She scribbled down a telephone number and then picked up the paper, staring at it. "You're sure this is the correct number? What? No! Tante Louise, don't do anything or call anybody until I get there. I mean it. You have to listen to me. I know what I'm talking about."

She listened for a moment and then shook her head. "No, if he knows that much then leave it at that, but *do not* tell him about the message. Not until I get there and figure out what to do."

"No—" Nika exhaled. "I'll leave tonight, now, even if it means I get in a car and drive until I can get on a plane. Please, Tante Louise, promise me. Call no one."

She nodded. "Okay, I love you, too."

Annika pressed end on the phone and then sank onto her chair, all levity gone.

"What happened?" Derick asked.

"My mother—"

"What?"

She turned to him, eyes burning with tears and fear. "He took her."

"Who?" Derick asked.

"Jesse."

Bette looked at her, stunned. "Oh my God, how? I thought he was in jail."

Annika shook her head. "He escaped. Right from his jail cell. They have no idea how, but they suspect it was an inside job."

"Inside job." Derick grunted "More likely his cousins helped him."

She watched Derick get up to pace. "I don't care how he did it. All I know, is I have to get home. He won't hurt her as long as I do what he says."

Nika looked at the vampire entourage surrounding her. There was no one present who wasn't a supernatural of some kind.

"I'm sorry to sing and run—" her voice broke and she dropped her head into her hands, her shoulders shaking as she sobbed.

Derick stopped pacing and wrapped her in his arms.

"Nika, we have to call the police. This is human jurisdiction," Bette said trying to be helpful.

Annika picked her head up from Derick's chest and sniffed, wiping her eyes and face on the back of her hand.

"No. I know Jesse. This might be human jurisdiction on the outside, but Jesse is a Were. A shifter with a superiority complex and the temperament of a spoiled toddler. Except when he throws a tantrum, people die. He killed Ki in a fit of temper, and he won't think twice about killing my mother. I have to handle this alone."

Derick stood, pulling Nika to her feet. "No you don't."

"No, Derick." She shook her head. "I can't ask you to do this."

He stared at her. "You're kidding, right? You forget, my last name may be Bergeron, but I'm a LaFont by blood, much as I loathe to admit it. I know Jesse. I know how he thinks, how that entire pack thinks. You think because I've been gone for ten years, that anything has changed?"

She didn't reply.

"If he took your mother, that means he's in the swamp. I grew up roaming the backwoods bayou. I know every inch of that swamp and every camp along the canals. If anyone can find him, I can."

Nika glanced down at her phone lying on the chair beside her. "It's three a.m. The earliest flight we can grab has got to be nine a.m. this morning."

"Then we'll drive and catch a flight out of D.C.," he said.

"That won't be necessary." All eyes turned, and Abigail stood. "You can use our plane. It's at JFK in the executive hangar. I'll make the call."

Annika rose, her eyes misty as she took a step toward the elegant vampire. "Thank you, Abigail."

She waved her off. "*Pffft*. With the paparazzi on your scent, you wouldn't get two feet from the curb come the morning, and you can forget trying to board a commercial flight. The concert is all over social media, and late as it is, I've already had requests for interviews with you on the premises.

"By morning the club will be surrounded by every kind of parasite looking to score a picture or a few words. I'll send a few youngbloods to get rid of any who've decided to stake out the exits."

Abigail smiled, and the effect was calculating and eager, yet frightening. "Youngbloods can be very persuasive, and if they encounter any resistance...." She shrugged. "Well, birds gotta fly, fish gotta swim, and vampires gotta eat."

Annika looked at Derick, who shot her a look that said it was best not to question.

"Thank you again, Abigail. I don't know how I will ever repay you," Nika said.

The elegant vampire blinked, lifting one delicate shoulder. "Come back and do another concert now that you're officially a solo. One where we can charge full admission price." She actually smiled. "I have a reserved fondness for certain Weres, and you just made the list."

Annika smiled back. "I'm honored, I think."

Bette laughed. "You should be. You wouldn't want to know what the cost of admittance was for the others."

Derick picked up Nika's cell phone and the note with the telephone number and gestured for the door. "Come on. I'll help you pack."

Abigail laid a cold hand on Nika's arm. "I'll have a car waiting to take you to the airport, but hurry." Her usually unnerving gaze, softened. "Whether you believe it or not, most of the undead remember their human mothers with wistful nostalgia. I'm doing this for all of us, so whenever you're ready, I'll be in the VIP lounge."

Annika covered the woman's hand with her own. "I appreciate that."

Derick took Nika's elbow and steered her toward the private doors backstage.

"Whose phone number is that?" he asked, pushing the elevator button to the east wing.

The elevator pinged and the doors slid open. Derick put his arm out, letting Nika go ahead. He pressed E and the doors slid shut.

"I don't recognize the number. It's not the same one Jesse used when he called me this week. I'm assuming it's stolen, but for all I know it could belong to one of his cousins or even his—" she stopped short, biting her lip.

"His father's." Derick looked at her. "It's okay, Nika. His name means nothing to me. I got over that a long time ago. He never acknowledged me, and I gave up acknowledging him. If Jesse is the kind of son he raised, then I'm better off.

"My mother paid a dear enough price trying to get that man to accept us. I'm lucky. I had Marie Bergeron for a grandmother, and that old woman was no joke."

"I know, and you're right. I'm sorry," she said.

He shrugged. "Don't be." He looked down at the phone number. "Are you supposed to call?"

The elevator stopped and they got off, turning toward her room.

She nodded. "The instructions were to call when I get home. He's given me forty-eight hours."

"When we land, we're going to have to find a way to get to your family's camp without anyone knowing. If he knows you're not alone it won't bode well."

"My aunt said detectives from Los Angeles called the sheriff's office to let them know Jesse was a fugitive. They've got a national APB out for him and a bi-coastal manhunt is in full swing.

"Guy Fortinet is the local sheriff now, and he has men posted at every point possible in our neck of the woods, but you know as well as I do if Jesse wants to disappear, there's no better place to do so than the swamp. Even the sheriff's office said there's not much to count on, not if Jesse doesn't want to be found."

The little muscle in Derick's cheek worked overtime. "That may be, *cher*, but then again, Jesse didn't count on me."

᠊ᠥ᠊

The plane landed in New Orleans and good to her word, Abigail had a car waiting to drive them into Terrebonne parish.

"This is taking forever." Annika exhaled, fidgeting with the adjustable strap attached to her carry-on. She ran the leather through her fingers, flipping the flat end into her palm with short, sharp snaps.

"It's an hour and a half ride from the airport. You know there is no way round it."

Jaw tight, she squirmed, crossing and uncrossing her legs. "I know."

Derick watched her nervous energy twist. "If you don't calm down, I'm going to bend you over and spank

266

you with that strap." Catching her eye, he smirked. "Then again, knowing you, you'd probably enjoy it."

She tucked the bag on the floor between her legs. "I'm not a big fan of pain."

He slipped his arm around her shoulder and reached around to pinch her nipple through her tank-top. She sucked in a breath through her teeth, but didn't push his hand away.

"Somebody's telling a fib, Pinocchio."

She didn't reply, but shifted enough in her seat to give him better access. Her eyes dipping to the bulge behind his fly. "If I'm the one who's fibbing, then why are you the one sporting a woodie?"

He leaned down and kissed her mouth, letting his fingers gently stroke her full breast. "Your stress levels are through the roof, *cher*. I smell the anxiety coming off your body, and if I can, it's certain every living creature in the bayou will, too."

"So?"

"We've got an hour's ride left in this limousine before we reach the parish. I think it's time I helped rid your excess tension."

"Just my tension?"

"Adrenaline gives me hyper focus, but you..." He shook his head. "It'll make you emotional, unreasonable and lead to mistakes. Mistakes in the swamp lead to death." He ran a thumb over her bottom lip. "Let's just say I like my woman better alive and kicking."

His gaze was so intense it made her breath catch in her throat. Without a word, he raised the privacy screen and reached for a small drawstring backpack on the floor. He moved it to the seat opposite Annika and sat the bag beside him.

"Take off your shirt and your pants, Nika."

"You're kidding. What about the driver?"

Derick shook his head. "The screen is only operable from the backseat and is completely impenetrable. The backseat is also soundproof. The vampires designed it that way for obvious reasons."

Annika licked her lips and glanced toward the black partition. "You're sure?"

He nodded.

With her eyes on Derick, Nika lifted her tank top over her head and dropped it to the seat next to her. She unhooked her bra and did the same before wiggling out of her shorts and underwear. She sat on the cool, black leather seats completely naked.

Derick knelt in front of her and reached above her head to dim the interior to just the floor lights. He dropped his hands to her shoulders and cupped her face, kissing her, his lips soft. Her mouth parted and he swiped his tongue along hers and deepened their kiss.

She sighed and he slid his hands lower to cup her breasts, grazing each nipple with either thumb. Hard peaks formed and he dipped his head to suckle each one until Annika arched her back, pushing her breasts higher, urging him on for more.

He stopped and sat back on his heels, reaching for the draw string bag. "I brought a couple of surprises in case of emergency."

"In case of what emergency?"

Swiping his thumb across her hard nub, she gasped, her clit jerking at the rough feel. He brought the glistening digit to his mouth, licked the pad. "This."

From the drawstring bag he took out what looked to be a triple chain attached to a circular ring. At the end of each chain was a clamp.

"What in the world is that?"

Derick held it up by the first set of clamps, squeezing the close-pin action on each, while the third dangled down, swinging back and forth with the motion of the limo.

"It's called a triple treasure." He clicked the end moving the rubber tips up and down. "Are you game?"

It didn't take much to figure out where Derick would put them, and heat ignited across her skin at the thought of how they would feel attached to hard, sensitive buds.

She nodded, not trusting her voice to squeak in such an erotic moment.

Derick's lips slid into a sexy grin. His mouth claimed her breasts again, teasing and biting, squeezing her flesh until she coasted close to climax. He pulled back and fastened the first two clamps to her nipples. Giving them a quick tug, she gasped arching her back again.

"More?" he asked

She nodded again and he adjusted the screws even tighter.

Holding the central ring he slid his thumb through the hole and splayed his hand across her stomach, keeping the chain taut on her stiff peaks.

Derick dipped his head and worked her clit the same way, teasing and biting until the nub hardened, swelling past its fleshy hood.

"Ready for the next one?" he asked, using his thumb to circle her nub and slide up and down her wet slit.

Annika lifted her hips, her hands pushing his thumb into her pussy, she cried out in frustration as he curled the thick digit up and flexed. He pulled his hand from her folds.

"Sit on your hands, Nika."

Her eyes opened. "What?"

"No touching. Sit on your hands."

She eyed him, but did as he said.

"Good girl. If you move your hands again, I'll tie them above your head."

Nika's eyes went wide and her pussy puddled at the sound of his command. She nodded and he attached the third clamp, testing its pull with the center ring.

Annika cried out, digging her bare heels into the car floor. Her hips came up and she hissed as pain and pleasure flooded her body in an intense bliss.

"Do you want to come?"

She stared at him. "Derick!"

He chuckled, reaching for his fly. He unbuttoned his pants and pushed his jeans to the floor, tossing them to the side.

"Sit up," he ordered. "No hands until I say."

He released the ring chain and fisted the back of her hair, kissing her hard. He devoured her mouth before wrapping his other hand around his swollen shaft.

He rubbed precum on her lips. "Open your mouth, Annika."

She took him in, swirling her tongue around his hard ridge, sucking the salty taste from his head. She drew him in fully and he growled.

"Spread your legs."

She slid her knees apart and he pulled his cock from her mouth and picked up the ring again, giving it a series of short yanks, tantalizing her with each pinch. She hissed, squirming against the seat looking for release.

He pulled her to her feet and clipped a fourth chain to the ring. This one was split, like the reins on a horse.

"Turn around." She faced the leather seat and he pressed her forward, so her knees butted against the seat.

Derick eased the chain over Annika's hips and held it in one hand. He tugged again and she sucked in a breath, and as she did he grabbed her shoulder with his free hand and drove himself deep between her folds.

He thrust deeper and harder, and each time he pulled back, he tugged on the chain.

Little pained, pleasure shocks intermingled, and a scorching need spread from her clit, deep into her pussy and she pushed back on Derick's engorged cock.

He let go of the chain and wrapped his arm around her waist. She lifted one leg onto the seat, and he thrust up, sliding his hands up to cup her breasts.

They dropped forward and he grabbed her hips driving hard and fast until they both cried out, her body spasming, her walls convulsing, milking every drop as he spilled deep inside her.

Together they collapsed in a sated, sweaty mess on the limo floor, his arm still around her waist.

Chapter Ten

Derick let Annika sleep. The two arrived at the dock a little after nine a.m. They had both been up for almost twenty-four hours.

The house was bigger than he expected. Thank God no paparazzi were camped out, and he had the feeling it was all Guy Fortinet's doing. He was the last word when it came to the law in these parts, and the fact he was also a shifter made protecting his own even more part of his blood.

Derick sat on the porch watching Annika dream. Curled up on the couch just inside the screened porch, she looked like a child. *Peaceful.*

He smiled and his cock jerked thinking about their limo ride. She was most definitely not a child. He pursed his lips. Problem was, he didn't know what she was to him. He enjoyed her, that's for sure. He shook his head. Now was not the time to dwell on the, *what ifs.*

The here and now. That was what mattered. What he always counted on. That and himself. The, *what ifs,* caused pain because they brought hope.

"Penny for your thoughts, boy."

Derick turned to see Guy Fortinet walking silently up the back steps from the yard.

"Sheriff."

"Long time no see, son. How you been?"

Derick nodded, wary. His usual when it came to any male from the Terrebonne packs. "Been good."

He laughed. "Until now."

Derick exhaled, picking up his beer to take a swig. "That's for sure."

"You got a plan?"

"Yes, sir, I do."

"You gonna share it with me?"

Derick shook his head. "No, sir."

The sheriff whistled low. "Still protecting those good for nothings? When you gonna learn they don't want you and they never will. You're better off without them, son. Don't you know that by now?"

"Sheriff!" Annika's voice was sharp. "Kindly refrain from insulting *my* guest in *my* home."

The older man looked from one to the other and pushed his hat back on his head. "Lordy, I should've known. You've always had a soft spot for the LaFont boys, don't you, *cher*?"

"My last name is Bergeron, Sheriff. I'm not protecting anyone except Nika and her mother, and would hope it was the same with you. As for my personal history with the LaFont pack, my father was nothing more than a sperm donor. I owe them nothing."

The sheriff nodded. "Glad to hear it, son." He eyed the boy. "Look, we got off on the wrong foot, again. I want Jolene back safe and sound as much as ya'll do. Let me help. Hell, I love that woman."

He looked at Annika. "Louise tell you I proposed to your mother?"

Eyes wide and a smile tugging at her lips, she shook her head. "No, she didn't. Not that I gave her a chance."

Guy nodded. "Yeah. The day she went to stay with your aunt. I drove her out there and we went for a walk. It was time. I should've done so when you were younger, but she wasn't ready."

He kicked at the loose paint on the porch floor before looking up at Nika, his eyes pained. "I should've taken her worries more seriously, *cher*. It's my fault Jesse got to her. I thought she was overreacting because of you and the trial and such." He paused. "I'm sorry, *bebe*."

Nika's heart squeezed at the very personal endearment. Only her mama called her *bebe*, and that he did, made her realize how much he did love her.

Annika opened the screen door and stepped out into the heat and into Guy's waiting arms. He stroked the back of her hair. "We'll find her, honey. Don't you worry."

"Sheriff?"

Annika stepped back and Guy cleared his throat before looking over at Derick.

"I plan to set out as soon as it's dark. I think it's best if you came, too. Jolene doesn't know me, and it's clear Nika needs us to work together." He offered the man a small smile. "Plus, it stacks the odds in our favor for a successful hunt."

He nodded. "For sure, boy. For sure."

Annika crossed her arms in front of her chest. "Then I'm coming, too." She eyed them both, daring them to argue.

∽

The three pushed the outboard from the dock as quietly as they could. Crickets and cicadas deafened the swamp with chirping. The water was black, and the submerged plants looked like fingers reaching out of the murky dark.

When they made it through to the cypress forest, they cut the engine and used poles to push forward, trying to stay as quiet as possible.

The marshy ground made sucking sounds as they moved along, telling Derick the swamp floor was boggy and dangerous. Like slush or quicksand, and if they abandoned the boat they might sink and not come out.

"Careful. In case being away has stunted your memory, a gator can strike faster than you can snap your fingers."

Derick sneered. "I remember."

274

"Well, the terrain has changed a lot since you were a boy."

"It's not that different, Sheriff. Even then, the land changed every hundred feet or so, and with storms blowing through it was even more so. My gran-mere used to say the land isn't rooted to the earth. It was rooted to the spirits and that's why it had to be free to float."

The sheriff grinned. "I respected your gran-mere, but lord, her hocus pocus scared the bejesus outta everyone around here and you know it.

"Some say this swamp is the Bermuda Triangle of the south, as dangerous as the predators lurking beneath the surface. You can get in, but you ain't getting out."

Annika looked at the two. Both had taken strategic positions in the boat, and though they chatted like they were out fishing on a Sunday afternoon, neither missed a thing going on around them. Eyes and ears and every Were sense they possessed, was in high gear.

"Are you sure this is the way?"

Derick nodded. "I tracked him this far this afternoon, but now I'm positive."

"How?"

"You called him as instructed, right?"

She nodded.

"And he demanded you come alone, so you could talk things out."

"I already told you this."

Derick nodded. "You also said, he had a fit when you refused. Like a toddler throwing a tantrum."

"Jesse is melodramatic. That's no surprise."

"No, it's not. At least not to me. While you took a nap, I went out and did some tracking in the swamp. One thing that never changes about Cajuns is how much they love to talk, especially when the story is juicy.

"Word on the canals is Jesse's family abandoned him when the record company put a lien on their shrimping boats to cover what he owed on the unfinished record."

Annika shook her head, confused. "That doesn't make any sense. I finished the album with Ari, and I even made sure Jesse got his royalties from the album same as me. He didn't owe the record company anything."

"People around here don't like big companies messing with folk and their livelihoods. The LaFonts aren't anyone's favorite by a long shot, but they're still townies."

The sheriff agreed and Annika crossed her arms in front of her chest. "So they're protecting him, even after what he's done to my mother."

"Noooo, *cher*. You got that wrong. Folks just want it to be me who deals with him...or Derick, since he's one of our own as well."

"Seems Jesse made his family silent partners in his share trying to be a big man in the pack, but he also made them responsible for his debt."

The sheriff coughed.

"What?" Do you know something we don't?"

He nodded. "After Jesse was arrested, he gave his father power of attorney. They spent every dime of his royalties. It seems Jesse took large advances against those royalties without letting anyone know. It's how he kept up with the Hollywood set."

Annika shook her head. "I can't believe it."

"When Jesse skipped town, prosecutors put pressure on the record company to lien the shrimping boats. They were hoping Jesse's family would give him up to avoid ruin. They didn't. The prosecutors also told us Jesse killed Ki not just because of you, but because Ki planned to tell the rest of the band and get him kicked out."

"Jesse is a coward and he's desperate. When he was a kid, any time he'd get into trouble or couldn't get his way, he'd hide out in one place. And right now I'd bet my last dollar he's there. But we have to be quiet and stealthy. The place is warded and booby-trapped."

"Booby-trapped? You mean like with trip wire and rabbit-snares?"

He shook his head. "With IEDs"

Annika looked at the sheriff.

"An improvised explosive device. That means a simple bomb made from household items. What they lack in sophistication they make up for in deadly force."

She clamored up onto the very back bow as if to get as far away from the idea as possible.

"You can't be serious. How the hell are we supposed to navigate around that? We need to call in special services."

"Calm down, cher, we have something they don't." He pointed to his nose. "We can smell them."

The sheriff nodded. "The Weres on the force go through very strict swat team training and we use any and *all* talents. I'd put our swat team up against any other in the country."

"That's great, Guy. But your swat team isn't here."

He grinned. "Yes, they are." He glanced toward the shore and there they were in wolf form running along the marshy ground alongside them. "I've got their gear in the boat with us."

Derick signaled, telling everyone to be quiet. He pointed ahead to a hollowed out cypress trunk at the edge of a part of the forest hit by lightning. The lack of foliage made it easier to see, and the full moon gave them enough light that their own dual-natured night vision sufficed.

The ground cover was an obstacle course of ferns, brush, and overgrown roots along with fallen branches.

Heat and humidity drenched them as they geared up and fanned out. Up ahead was an abandoned camp. Rundown with broken windows and a ramshackle porch. Smoke rose from a pipe poking through a makeshift hole in the roof that looked seconds from collapse.

Annika closed her eyes and inhaled. Her mother was here. Her natural scent underlined by her favorite perfume filled Nika's nose. She smelled blood and pain as well, and her eyes burned with anger at what her mother had endured.

"She's here. I can smell her. What do I do?"

"You, *cher*, are our bait. I want you to strip down to whatever you feel comfortable in so if you need to phase you can. Your mother is too injured to phase, that much is clear from her scent," the sheriff replied, loading his hand cannon.

Annika glanced at the gun and then up at the sheriff again. "Are you planning to use that?"

He nodded. "When I shoot darlin', I shoot to kill. If Jesse phased to escape once, he'll do it again. I'm sorry."

She shook her head. "Don't be. In my gut, I knew his cousins didn't break him out. When the news said his escape was an inside job, I had my suspicions. You just confirmed what I already knew. Somehow he taught himself to shift to a small, insignificant creature."

Derick frowned. "A rat. It certainly fits. He probably crawled through the sewers and blames you for it."

Her mouth dropped. "I didn't tell you that part."

He shrugged. "You didn't have to. I told you I know him."

The men covered their bodies with mud from the swamp to cover their scent and Guy gave the signal and they closed in.

The four swat members broke into pairs and circled either side of the dwelling. Guy took the rear and Derick stayed by the front entrance with Nika.

"Go, I've got you covered. It's been far too long for him to remember *my* scent, but he's not stupid. He's got to know people are around.

She nodded and stripped out of her leggings and tank top, handing them to Derick to stow in his pack. In a pair of black boy-short underwear and matching sports bra, she walked through the soft leaves and mulch to stand ten feet from the front of the house.

"Jesse!"

No sound. No answer.

Derick motioned for her to call him again.

"Jesse Andrew LaFont! You wanted me here, so I came."

The door creaked open and he stood in the doorway, a jug of moonshine dangling from his thumb and forefinger.

"If it isn't the slut."

"Jesse, please. You said you wanted to talk, so I'm here to talk."

"You're here for your mama." He pointed his finger, stumbling two steps forward.

"You're drunk."

He nodded. "How very observant, Nika." He licked his lips and gave her an appreciative once over. He grabbed his crotch and rubbed, pursing his lips. "You're certainly dressed for negotiations. How'd you know I'd be horny enough to fuck a fat bitch like you?" He laughed, putting the jug on a broken lawn chair.

Jesse unzipped his fly and dug out his flaccid member, jerking the limp flesh with his tongue shoved out the corner of his mouth.

"Where's my mother?"

He jerked his head toward the door. "Inside. You come up here and get on your knees and I'll let you have her. You can beg while you suck me off."

She snarled, eyes turning green as the anger sent the need to phase tingling across her skin. "You'd need an erection first, Jesse. But you can't get it up anymore. Just look at that limp piece of meat. Like a shriveled cocktail wiener."

He threw his head back and roared, leaping for her over the railing. Bone and muscle reshaped on the fly as sleek brown fur rippled over his skin.

Shock tore a scream from her throat. She turned to run, to give herself time to shift but his paws hit her in the back knocking her to the ground.

The impact forced the air from her lungs in a painful rush and she struggled to suck in a breath before she passed out.

Jesse threw his head back, his sharp canines descended, ready to strike when he flew off her body with a loud screech.

She struggled to her knees scrambling away from whatever it was that attacked.

The animal was majestic, and she blinked, thinking the impact from Jesse's blow had caused hallucinations. *Dire Wolf.*

The name formed on her lips, but she shook her head. Impossible. They were a myth. Yet there it stood, dwarfing Jesse's panther.

A mane of fur surrounded its head and chest, flowing along the line of its spine and top flanks. Two fangs curved upward from its lower jaw, each razor sharp and the size of a man's forearm.

The cat twisted away, leaping to the branches of a dead cypress. The large feline launched at the creature, its scythe like claws swiping the animal's jaw.

The Dire Wolf howled, blood pouring from the wound. It reared up on hind legs, knocking the cat to the ground with a bone-crunching thud. The feline tried to stand, but slumped to the moist earth, blood dripping from its ears.

"Nika!" The sheriff rounded the side of the property, gun drawn. He pulled her out of the line of attack, propping her against the side of an old rowboat. "You okay? Can you move?"

"My mother?" she croaked, ignoring his questions.

"The swat team has her in the police boat and they're already in transit to the hospital."

Annika exhaled the breath she'd been holding and winced in pain.

"I gotta get you out of here, too. My guess is you've got broken ribs, maybe a punctured lung."

She shook her head. "Derick…" she ground out, flinching. Biting back a wave of dizziness, she lifted a hand toward the animal.

"Holy Mother of God." The sheriff slumped back, stunned. "Is that what I think it is?"

Annika nodded, wincing again.

The creature stalked toward the cat and stared down at the twitching animal. He threw his head back and roared, the sound ominous and echoing in the dark swamp. He picked the feline up by its neck and stretched the cat length wise before snapping its spine with a sickening crunch. Snorting, he threw the animal to the ground, the cat's body bent and unnatural.

Both forest and swamp were eerily quiet as the cat's prone body sputtered and reshaped to a twisted human form until Jesse's broken body lay in the muck and debris, dead.

The Dire Wolf dropped to all fours and lifted its head. The howl echoed off the trees and the night creatures answered. He swerved his enormous body with unanticipated stealth and grace, moving toward where Annika lay.

Snorting, its lips pulled back over its sharp teeth to show black gums, but it didn't growl or snap. Its great feet padded with soft steps as it neared.

"You have that hip cannon loaded, Sheriff?"

Guy nodded, cocking the trigger. He kept the gun flush with his thigh, hidden but at the ready.

To their amazement the animal lowered its chest, crawling suppliant the closer he came. A soft whine rose as he approached and when he got to Annika's feet, he rested his large head on both paws.

"Derick?" she murmured, and the animal whined again.

The creature picked up his head and crept closer, laying his big head on her lap.

"We need to get you cleaned up or that's going to scar," she wheezed, looking at his wounds caked and dirty from the fight.

He snorted, with an almost purposeful nod and moved away. With a low rumble, he curled into himself as the magic took him, the process painful to watch as he howled and writhed, his body reshaping with violent spasms.

Eyes wide, neither she nor Guy could do anything as he flung himself to all fours again. The sound of bones snapping and muscles ripping echoed in the night.

Finally Derick lay human again, panting in the dirt, and Guy approached with caution, moving him gently beside Annika. He slumped back, resting his head on her shoulder.

"I killed him," he said, his voice expressionless.

Annika stroked his hair, not knowing what to say.

"You saved Nika, son. That's all anyone cares about. If you didn't jump in when you did, that son of a bitch would have killed her. You did yourself and this pack proud."

Guy rubbed the stubble on his chin, considering. "As for Jesse, he was going to die tonight one way or the other. Either by your hand or mine. From where I sit, it was the law of nature that prevailed."

Derick sucked in a deep breath, wincing as he delicately probed the inside of his slashed cheek with his tongue.

"You'll be fine," Guy said, slapping Derick on the knee. "A few stitches and a couple of shots of bourbon and you'll be right as rain. It's Nika I'm worried about. I think we need to get her to the hospital. Her color ain't right."

Derick looked at Nika, at the pale set to her skin. He inhaled and his eyes flew to the sheriff. "She's bleeding inside. Take her. Don't worry about me. I'll be fine, here."

"No! I won't go without you."

The sheriff slipped his gun back into its holster and used the boat to help himself up with a grunt. "Derick's right. I'll send the police boat back for him and he'll meet us later."

Annika let the sheriff help her up, but her eyes were on Derick.

He waved her on. "Go, *cher*. I'll see you when I see you."

She limped out of the burnt cypress grove on the sheriff's arm, but as they turned toward the water she looked back. Derick was gone.

Chapter Eleven

"Looks like you're going to be a huge solo success, sweetheart," Ari's tinny voice said over the phone. "When do you think you'll be able to come out to the coast to record?"

Annika rolled her eyes. "Not anytime soon, and I don't want to hear a word about how short people's memories are. If they lived through what I just did, they'd have nightmares."

"I get it, honey. You're holding all the cards, so not to worry. How's your mom feeling?"

Annika peered into the living room from the screened porch. Jolene and Guy were sitting on the couch talking with Tante Louise. They were in full wedding mode.

"She's terrific. She's been talking to someone a couple of times a week to help her deal with the aftermath of the abduction, but I think knowing Jesse can't hurt her or me anymore helps a lot."

"Of course, it does. He was a psycho and never going to leave you alone. I hate to say it because it's not politically correct, but the world is better off without him. I'm glad he's dead."

"That makes two of us."

"Hey, they ever find the animal that attacked him in the swamp?" She whistled low. "If that's not a story for the Bigfoot crazies, then I don't know what is."

Annika didn't reply.

"Okay, sweetheart. I'll call you next week just to check in. Give my love to your mom."

"I will."

Ari hung up and Annika chewed on her lip. *Did they ever find the animal that killed Jesse?*

No. And neither did she—

An ache so deep sluiced through her gut, she had to wrap her arms around her middle.

No one at The Red Veil had seen Derick either. Bette had Abigail put feelers out among the vampires along the eastern seaboard, and Guy had his men scour the swamp. They even questioned the LaFonts, but there was no sign of him.

Derick was a Dire Wolf. No one knew that but her and the sheriff. They agreed not to say a word to anyone.

From the porch she looked out at the brown water lightly lapping at the shore and the swamp grasses swaying in the humid breeze. She thought back to that night in the Ramble, and how his words haunted her.

"Do you shift?"

"No."

"But what about all that talk about our talents…"

"I didn't say I can't phase. I just don't."

"Ever?"

"Never."

Is that why he refused to phase, then? Were there consequences and yet he shifted anyway to save her?

She wished she could ask him or ask someone who might know.

Her mother slid a quiet hand over her shoulder. *"Bebe?"*

"I wish I could talk to him, Mama."

Her mother hugged her close. "I know, *cher.*"

"If for no other reason than to thank him." Nika rested her head, tucked under her mother's arm.

"I'm sure he knows."

Annika shrugged. "I know we've exhausted every power on earth to find him, but—"

"That's true," her mother said cutting her off. "Every power on earth. But we haven't tried a power beyond that."

Annika jerked around to look at her mother.

"Mama, what are you talking about?"

"His gran-mere was a voodoo priestess, yes?"

Nika nodded. "Yes, but she's dead."

Jolene smiled wide. "Ah, well, as it turns out there's dead, and then there's *dead*."

Annika shook her head. "No, Mama. I'm not playing with black magic just to find someone who doesn't want to be found."

Jolene stared at her daughter. "Who said anything about magic?" She took her daughter by the hand. "We're simply going to ask Old Marie where he's at."

"Mama, no. This is silly." She followed her mother into the kitchen, and there, sitting at the table was the oldest woman she'd ever seen.

Her skin was like brown leather, barely hanging on her bones, and her eyes, two glints visible through the folds and wrinkles.

She wore a white headdress and a matching cotton shift, perfect for the humidity that hung in the air night and day.

"So you the girl who captured my boy's heart," the old woman rasped.

Annika looked from her mother to the old lady and back again. "I don't understand. Mama, who is this? I'm sorry, I mean no disrespect, ma'am, but who are you?"

The old lady laughed, and the sound was like sandpaper, croaky and dry, ending in a fit of coughing.

Jolene poured her a glass of water and she drank deeply before looking at Annika again. "*Je suis Marie Bergeron.*"

Nika's eyes flew to her mother and the woman nodded.

"Wait," she said blinking. "You're Old Marie? How? You're dead! Oh my God! Derick thinks you're dead. *Jesus!*"

Annika stared at the old woman. The wrinkled face was passive, as if Nika's words were *ouais enfin – yeah, well*, what can I say?

"How could you let him suffer?" Nika balked. "He's been alone all this time. Do you know what he's been through? How this has affected him?"

Annika paced, throwing out questions and accusations at the speed of light.

"I know I want to find him, but this? How the hell will I explain this? How will you?" she muttered, half to herself.

"*Ma cher enfant*, there's nothing to explain," the old woman began. "Derick has known where to find me his entire life."

She turned, open-mouthed. "Why, then, would you let everyone think you had died?"

"Because I wanted to be left alone, I wanted Derick to have a chance at peace. I lost my only child to a broken heart at the hands of the LaFonts, and my only grandchild lived with hurt every day afterward.

"The only way I knew to keep them from tormenting my boy, was for them to think I had died giving Derick a great evil to use against them. Voodoo is a quiet religion, but it has a dark, powerful effect on the weak-minded. Now the only other people who know my secret are you, your wonderful mother, and her man."

Annika sunk into a kitchen chair beside the old lady. "So where is Derick?"

The old woman looked past Nika as though looking into the future and her face lit up, her eyes crinkling with delight.

"Someone looking for me?" a deep voice asked from the doorway.

Annika spun around in her chair. Derick stood on the screened porch, his face healed and the rest of him as gorgeous as ever.

Nika stood slowly, her eyes taking in every inch of him before heat flashed across her chest and up into her throat.

"I see you're fine," she muttered nearly choking on the words she couldn't say.

He nodded.

"I'm glad." She nodded. "I just wanted to thank you for what you did for my mother and me."

With a shrug, he smiled. "No worries, *cher*. I did what had to be done."

Now it was her turn to shrug. "I suppose so." She sucked in a breath and folded her arms across her chest. "Okay, then. That's the last loose end in this mess to be tucked away."

She brushed past him and let the screened door slam as she went down the stairs toward the water's edge.

She followed the path that lead to a private cove. This was her place, her sanctuary, where reeds danced in the evening breeze. She stood in the middle of this serenity, but all she wanted to do was scream.

"I haven't been far, you know," he said coming up behind her.

She stopped her fidgeting but didn't turn around. A million replies flew through her mind, but each one sounded childish and sour, so she kept her mouth shut.

"I needed space, Nika. I needed to think."

She turned. "Think? About what? No one put pressure on you, Derick."

"I know, Nika. I'm the one with the heavy questions that needed answers."

Her gaze softened. "Because of Jesse?"

"You would think that, considering, but to be honest, no. It was you." He shrugged.

"Me? Why? I just wanted to know what happened, why you suddenly disappeared. After all we said. After all we did—" She had to look away.

It was bad enough sex dreams about him haunted her every night. She didn't need him to see it in her eyes.

"I know, and I'm sorry," he replied. "If it's any consolation, I came to visit you in the hospital. Your mom, too."

"When?"

He shrugged again. "While you were sleeping."

"You said you weren't far? Where have you been, then? The whole of our world has been looking for you for weeks," she lifted a frustrated hand.

"I've been with gran-mere. Guy knew, but I asked him not to say anything to you or Jolene, or anyone for that matter."

Annika looked toward the path that lead back to the house and gave it a dirty look.

"Don't be angry with Guy." Derick said. "He understood."

She snorted. "It's a man thing, right?"

"Kind of, *cher*."

"What about The Red Veil? Your friends there? Your job?" she asked.

"I quit the night we left. Abigail wasn't happy about it, but she understood. I knew the most likely outcome of finding Jesse would be a shit show. Plus, I knew I had some real soul searching to do in regard to you."

"Me? Why?" Her eyes locked with his and she could barely breathe.

"Because I think it's time."

She couldn't look away. "Time for what?"

"To tell you how I feel. I knew it the moment I thought Jesse killed you. I've spent my life keeping the wolf inside at bay. It's why I left. Anger is a trigger, and I spent so much of my life angry—at my father, my brother—at my mother for being too weak to put me first, instead of the LaFont lowlifes who used and abused her.

"I had to leave the bayou so I wouldn't put my life or the lives of those I love in danger. Gran-mere knew what I was from the time I hit puberty. It was she who warned my power would only be controlled when I had something to ground me."

Nika was almost afraid to ask. "Have you found that something?"

Derick nodded.

"What?"

"Love." He slid his arms around her waist and pulled her close. "You."

A soft smile spread across her lips. "Does that mean you'll be sticking around, then?"

He nodded again. "I'm in uncharted territory, now." He nipped at her bottom lip. "There's so much left for me to explore."

She walked him backwards to the bench overlooking the water. Pushing him down onto the slatted seat, she flashed a teasing smirk, unbuttoning her thin blouse.

"Good. You can start by sitting on your hands."

Marianne Morea

The Red Veil Diaries

Taste Me

Taste
ME

THE RED VEIL DIARIES ❪4❫

MARIANNE MOREA

INTERNATIONAL BESTSELLING AUTHOR

*"...we have tasted the forbidden fruit, there
is no such thing as checking our appetites,
whatever the consequences may be."*

*~George Washington
In a letter to Mrs. Richard Stockton,
September 2, 1783*

Chapter One

"What'll it be, ladies?" the bartender asked, flashing a hint of fang.

Eyes wide, a purple-haired girl leaned across the bar, her tits practically in the man's face. "Oh my God! Are those real?" She gawked at his teeth.

The bartender's eyes glowed, and he flicked his gaze to her ample cleavage stuffed in a leather halter above a tartan miniskirt. "I could ask you the same question."

Her jaw dropped and she looked from him to her friend. "I've heard stories about this place and the fetish backrooms, but I never—"

"Well—" He cut her off, dragging a swizzle stick in a seductive path across the soft underside of her forearm. "There's a first time for everything."

The tartan girl giggled, and Daisy Cochran made a face, watching from a seat at a VIP table.

Ugh. "This place is crawling with stupid," she mumbled, shooting the woman a dirty look. "I can't believe I let you talk me into coming here. You know how I feel about vampires and their human chew toys."

"Chew toys?" Aimee chuckled at her friend. "Coming from you, that's funny."

"Why?"

"Because you're a Were, Daisy. A wolf. Remember? Four-legged, furred and fabulous? Weres are on the A-list now. It's how I got these primo tables."

Annoyed, she shot her friend a hard look. "Why don't you shout our supernatural status from the bar, Coyote

Ugly style? People on the other side of the Hudson River didn't quite hear you."

At Aimee's raised eyebrow, Daisy sat back with a huff. "You know what I mean."

"Yes, I do, and that's the problem."

Daisy pressed her lips together. "I have no problem. Besides, you're a shifter, too. Or doesn't that count?"

"Of course, it counts. But I'm an avian with talons, so the analogy doesn't apply." Aimee winked trying to lighten her friend's mood, but Daisy's expression didn't budge.

"Come on, Dais. New York City is the great equalizer. No one cares who you are or where you're from, and this place is worth the price of admission in people watching alone. With the truce between vampires and Weres, I guarantee I'm not the only one with an interest in the undead at the top of their bucket list."

"Bucket list? I thought we'd see a Broadway show or walk around Times Square on our last night in Manhattan, not hit an overpriced tourist trap trending on twitter."

"Wow, you thought of that all by yourself or just practicing your skills in alliteration?"

"Ha. Ha."

"You said you wanted a true taste of New York." Aimee spread her hands. "Well, we've got the best seats in the house for watching clueless humans pant unawares over supernaturals." She inhaled, feigning a shiver. "Smell those pheromones, and I don't mean the mortal variety. Every Were in this place is revved and ready to howl."

Daisy took a sip of her drink, ignoring Aimee's comments. She glanced at the same purple-haired girl still flirting with the vampire behind the bar. "That twit has no clue. She's hoping for a hookup, and he's sizing her up for a midnight snack."

"Don't be ridiculous, Dais."

"Okay, so maybe he's the one vampire in undead history not looking for a hot lunch, but my guess is given half a chance, he'll nibble more than just her ear."

Aimee put her drink down and eyed her friend. "Why do you care?"

"I don't. Not really," she shrugged.

"Then why let it bother you so much? Look around, Dais. She's not alone. This place is sex and the forbidden wrapped in red velvet and concrete."

Daisy lifted a hand and let it drop. "And we're back to my original question."

"What?"

"Why we came here," Daisy replied with a huff.

Aimee laughed. "Because it's fun. Remember fun?"

"Vaguely." She scoffed, draining her martini.

"At least that's a start."

At Aimee's satisfied grin, Daisy shot her a cautious look. "What do you mean *start*?"

"Nothing, really." She angled her head. "It's a healthy sign you remember what it was like to let your guard down and relax."

"Aimee...no."

She nodded. "It's time you got back in the game, Daisy. It's been way too long."

"I'm not interested. NOT." Daisy shook her head.

"You mean you're afraid you'll get hurt again." Aimee signaled a passing waitress for another round. "You may not care if you miss out on life, but I do. You're my best friend and way too young to be old and pinch-faced."

"Hey!"

"Whether you admit it or not, we're not in Texas anymore Toto. That means no more bending over the back fence unless it's to grind your ass against a hot cowboy. You've spent too much time otherwise, and that's no way to live. Especially when that time involves the town church ladies."

"That's not fair, Aims. I have a daughter to raise. I can't run around in full moon heat just because I'm young and have a wild itch to scratch."

Aimee looked at her. "I know you have a daughter. I'm her godmother, remember? And it's completely unfair to compare you to a dried up old gossip, but like it or not, that is exactly where you're headed if you don't shake things up, pronto."

Daisy blinked at the wetness stinging her eyes. "You didn't get left at the altar, Aimee. You don't know what it's like to be that humiliated in front of everyone you know, and then find out you're pregnant on top of everything else."

Daisy watched the bodies on the dance floor, their frenetic pace keeping time with the sexual thump, thump of the bass.

She sighed. "I know you're right, Aims, but I still feel people staring and whispering behind my back every time I go into town. I hate their pity, and for Jenny's sake, I have to keep myself above reproach."

"Bullshit." Aimee slapped her hand on the table. "Let 'em talk. You're a terrific mother, and everyone knows you've had the devil's own time. It's been five years and Jace hasn't shown his face once. Even his parents haven't seen or heard from him. For all anyone knows, he could be dead."

"Don't say that." Daisy's voice caught.

Aimee's lips parted as she stared at the emotional battle in Daisy's eyes. "Oh my God! You still love him."

Daisy's jaw tightened as a practiced mask fell over her expression.

"Oh no you don't, missy. It's written all over your face, Dais. After all's said and done. You do. Ghost or not."

Daisy opened her mouth then snapped it shut when the waitress approached with their drinks.

"Here you go. Two lemon drop martinis." The server put the drinks on the table.

"Thank you." Daisy smiled at the woman, watching her walk far enough away before glaring at her friend.

"Don't psychoanalyze me, Aimee Dunne. You may be a big deal doctor back home, but you're supposed to be my best friend. I do *not* love Jace Matthews."

Aimee opened her mouth to argue, but Daisy shook her head putting her off.

"I'll block every 'but' you've got stacked and ready to argue if you don't drop this, Aimee. Jace may be ancient history, but he's *my* history. Did he handle what happened between us in a shit-ass, infantile way? Absolutely. Do I wish I could give him a piece of my mind? Sometimes.

"But I would never wish him dead. He's Jenny's father, plus it would crush his parents and they've been nothing but loving and supportive ever since he left me standing alone in my wedding dress."

"Okay, but what about the ranch?" Aimee asked.

Confused, Daisy looked at her friend. "What about it?"

"Excuse me, but aren't your father and his schemes the reason we escaped on this excursion north?" she prompted.

Daisy exhaled. "I'm trying not to think about it."

"I gotta say, Dais, in my practice I've seen people with control issues, but demanding you marry Seth is the most manipulative thing I've heard in a long time. You really believe this dude is some long lost cousin? It's creepy, not to mention shadily convenient. You wouldn't even have to change your last name."

Daisy sighed. "My dad believes Seth's legit. He's not a Were, though. It's strange, because as far as I know, everyone on the Cochran side is dual natured. It was obvious on our first date. There was no concentrated musk, no jitters skittering across the skin when we were together and the moon crested.

"Then again, his connection to us is so far removed I ignored his single nature, chalking it up to diluted genetics. The Matthews' side is usually the one with random Were traits. It's part of the reason they're so possessive about Jenny. She's a pure blood."

"Still."

Daisy sighed in acknowledgment. "My dad can't get past my brother's death. In his eyes, this is the only way to keep the bloodline and the Cochran name intact."

"If you ask me, it's more like he can't get past your brother being a traitor," Aimee said over the rim of her martini glass.

Daisy shook her head. "I won't believe that."

"Dais, your brother sold his own for a promise of power. You and your father are lucky the Alpha of the Brethren didn't sanction your entire pack. If you ask me, forcing this marriage is a coping mechanism, and in his eyes it expunges the stain your brother put on the family."

"I know." She exhaled.

"Life is too short to go on living in the past. Your dad needs to move on from your brother, and you need to move on from Jace. It's as simple as that."

Daisy fidgeted with the damp napkin under her drink. "If only it were that easy." She looked at her friend. "Jace's family will inherit the ranch if there's no male Cochran heir. My brother really screwed us when he went on his misguided power trip. The day he was accepted into the Alpha's core of Hunters, we were so proud, but as always, it wasn't enough."

"I know, honey, and I'm sorry, but I still don't understand what this has to do with you and Jace," Aimee pressed.

"If I don't marry a Cochran male, then the bloodline is broken and the ranch and all the property transfers to the Matthews pack."

Aimee shook her head. "Why? That makes no sense. Your dad was over the moon about you and Jace, and he's not a Cochran by blood."

Daisy met Aimee's questioning gaze, and Aimee froze with her drink halfway to her mouth. She put the glass down and stared at her friend.

"Are you telling me you and Jace were related? I've heard of kissing cousins, but this is getting ridiculous, and with your father forcing your current situation with Seth, it's sounding a lot like back country incest."

Daisy threw her crumpled napkin at her. "Oh my God, Aims! Get a grip. Jace was a distant cousin. Even more distant than Seth claims. Seriously distant. As in generations ago, but enough of a recorded connection to satisfy the pact."

"Pact? What pact?"

Daisy exhaled, putting her glass down. "The entitlement clause bound to our deed that keeps the ranch and all the land intact."

"Wait." Aimee puffed out a breath, waving her hands in disbelief. "Are you telling me your family abides by the laws of primogeniture? I never heard of anything so archaic."

Daisy fidgeted with the crumpled napkin. "If you mean an inheritance passing to the first born male, then yes, otherwise the property is entitled away."

"Entitled away?" Aimee slammed her hand on the table. "What? Are we suddenly living in a Jane Austen novel? Daisy, I can't believe you agreed to this. You have an heir. Jenny is half Cochran and half Matthews. Done. You need to hire a good forensic attorney to look at this so called pact."

"Wow, Aims, what a novel idea." She blew out a breath. "Don't you think I already tried that? No one disputes the contract is unusual, but they all agree it's binding."

Stunned, Aimee looked at her friend. "I'm so sorry, Daisy." She lifted a hand and let it drop. "What now?"

Daisy shrugged and then straightened her shoulders. "We finish our drinks and then head back to the hotel to pack for our flight home."

"Daisy—"

"What do you want me to say, Aims? If I don't marry someone with a drop of Cochran blood, we lose everything. At least with Jace, I was happy. I loved him and I thought he loved me."

Aimee stared at her drink flabbergasted, before lifting her eyes to her friend. "This makes no sense to me. Your families are linked. You have common ancestry."

"You don't understand. We're the Hatfields and McCoys of the Shifter world, but Jace's disappearing act blew a hole in the barn door on any kind of truce."

Aimee leaned forward in her chair. "It doesn't matter. Not enough to make the price of poker go up. Your life is too high a price to pay for a piece of real estate. Do you even love Seth?"

"He's good to me, and Jenny needs a father."

Aims pressed her lips together. "Jenny doesn't like him."

"Jenny is four." Daisy shrugged. "She'll like who I like. It's enough for now."

"Enough?" Aimee's voice rose. "That's your father talking, not you. As for Jenny being four years old, children are more perceptive than most adults and rarely given credit for seeing what we either miss or refuse to see. Hence the phrase, out of the mouths of babes. Besides, I don't care for him either, so that's saying something."

Daisy nodded. "You're right, but you're forgetting I haven't agreed to anything yet. The price attached to this fix is not just real estate, as you put it. It's my heritage. We settled the land over a hundred fifty years ago. The Cochrans and the Matthews.

"My great-grandfather, Noah, his wife, Sarah, and Jace's great-grandfather, Micah Matthews and his wife, Eva. It's how Jace and I are related."

"I don't follow." Aimee shook her head, confused.

"Jace's great-grandmother Eva and my great-grandfather Noah were brother and sister."

"So what happened?"

Daisy frowned and glanced at the undead bartender. "Vampires happened. One vampire in particular." She lifted her martini and took a sip. "It's a long story."

"I like long stories. Spill."

"This isn't the time Aimee, and if you knew the whole story you'd agree this isn't the place to discuss the details. Trust me, you don't want to know."

Aimee put down her drink and folded her arms in front of her chest, giving Daisy a fixed stare.

Daisy met her gaze and blew out a hard breath. "If we get sharp fangs aimed our way, I'm shoving you first."

Aimee smirked. "Nice, now out with it."

Daisy spared another glance at the bartender, discreetly noting any other members of the undead too close for comfort.

She looked at Aimee and leaned in, lowering her voice. "A female vampire showed up looking for shelter one winter. Noah wanted her to leave from the get go, but Micah didn't.

"He gave my great-grandfather an excuse about supernatural species needing to be more Christian when dealing with one another, but Noah didn't buy it. He didn't trust the woman or Micah's fascination with her. It didn't make sense.

"Within a month, the vampire had seduced Micah, turning him dark, and then leaving him with nothing but a thirst for blood and a lust for flesh. Noah threw Micah off the land. Ashamed, Micah wandered for a bit, but as he was half-owner of the property, he didn't need an invitation to return.

"He came back one night, but Eva wouldn't let him in. When Noah found out, he begged his sister to stay with him and Sarah, but she refused. In the end, Micah raped and killed her, murdering two of their three kids before the morning sun fried his sorry undead ass.

"Noah blamed himself for not saving his sister and the children. He took in her surviving child, a baby girl, and raised her as his own until she ran off at sixteen. He spent years tracking her down, but the damage was done. As much as he blamed himself, she blamed him as well."

Stunned, Aimee stared slack jawed at her friend. "Why didn't you ever tell me this?"

Daisy shrugged. "I don't know. I suppose I thought everyone already knew."

"So what happened next?"

"Guilt ate at Noah for the rest of his life. He set the inheritance provisos as a result. It was his hope the lure of land and security would reunite the family for his sister's sake. That it would be enough."

Daisy shrugged again. "So now you know why this is more than a simple matter of land ownership." She paused, meeting Aimee's attentive gaze. "And why I didn't want to come tonight. Vampires ruined my family."

Aimee covered her hand with hers. "No, Daisy. One vampire did. Not all. Times have changed."

Daisy shook her head. "Times may change, but vampires never will. They are predators. Selfish and superior. To them you're either prey or a servant species." She lifted her hand in a hollow gesture. "I don't expect you to understand, and I get that. Old taboos, new pacts, new tolerances—whatever. I'm tired, Aims. I'm going to the ladies' room and then catching a cab back to the hotel. Being this close to so many bloodsuckers is making me ill."

"Daisy, don't be that way. It's barely midnight. Stay."

She leaned over to give her friend a quick peck and then pushed her chair away from the table.

"Dais, we came together, we leave together, right?"

She nodded, grabbing her purse. "Of course. I'll be right back."

Chapter Two

Daisy turned toward a side alcove and froze halfway through the entrance. A tall, lanky vampire stepped from the shadows, his hollow cheeks and yellow fangs making him more graveyard than Goth.

"You don't belong here, daylighter." The man's gravelly voice was as forbidding as his appearance.

He stopped beneath the neon exit sign only steps from her, blocking a door marked private and the turn for the restrooms on the opposite side.

"I am looking for the ladies' room," Daisy replied, keeping her tone steady and her eyes trained on the vampire.

She ignored the trickle of nervous sweat between her breasts. "I didn't mean to trespass," she added, quietly slipping two fingers into the side pocket of her purse for her UV flashlight. This was exactly what she wanted to avoid tonight.

"No one enters without an invitation." The pallid-skinned man took another step closer, his thin greasy hair, limp and stringy against the white of his scalp.

Whipping her hand up, Daisy flashed a beam of bright ultraviolet light into the bloodsucker's red eyes.

Hissing, he threw his arm up to shield his face, but Daisy didn't stay to watch the fallout. She ran, not looking back until she collapsed onto the edge of a plush couch in the crowded safety of the closest bar. She gulped down air, trying to collect herself.

"Are you okay?" a female voice asked.

Daisy nodded, pressing her wrists against the railing, hoping the cold chrome would stop her from retching.

"Are you sure? You don't look so good."

She turned to give the concerned girl a halfhearted smile, but stiffened at what she saw past the woman's shoulder.

She'd recognize his profile anywhere. The curve of his strong jaw and the way his blue-black hair skimmed the back of his neck above broad shoulders.

Jace.

He sat across the bar at a small table near the steps. People milled back and forth, laughing and talking, complicating her line of sight. She excused herself and moved her seat to be sure. It couldn't be a coincidence.

Or could it?

Jace was as gorgeous as ever. His black T-shirt clung to his chest, and his flat muscular torso was just as she remembered. He sat the same way, too, with one long leg crossed flat over his knee, the edge of his favorite silver-toed boots gleaming in the light.

Stunned, her breath locked in her throat. She wasn't dreaming. Resting on his thigh was the cowboy hat she'd given him at their engagement party. A black suede Stetson with the ranch's crest on the matching leather band—a sterling silver wolf's head carved into a full moon—a symbol marking the end of a century of bad blood.

"Jace." His name left her lips in a desperate hush. Familiar emotions surged and she stood, itching to run her palms along the hard, flat planes of his chest and through his hair. She took an instinctive step forward, but the expression on his face stopped her cold.

He wasn't looking her way, but the muscles in his cheek clenched, almost menacing. She'd never seen him look that predatory, even when they raced the blood moon at its zenith.

Daisy followed the storm in his gaze to a woman sitting at the bar. She had a clear view, watching Jace's scowl deepen the closer the woman pressed her body to the man standing beside her.

A wash of jealousy tightened Daisy's chest, making it hard to breathe. Was this woman the reason he left her standing alone in the church?

She glanced at her reflection in the smoky glass behind the bar, smoothing her hands over full curves and the dress that clung to her hips and thighs.

Her body was solid from riding and working the ranch. Delicate was not a word she'd use to describe herself, but Jace loved her genuine, full bodied beauty, with her creamy skin and cascade of dark, Black Irish curls to complete the package. Or at least she thought he did.

The woman at the bar was the exact opposite. Lean and blond with barely a hint of feminine curves to fill her tiny camisole.

Daisy saw the woman's eyes flutter to half-mast, her pink lips parting in a sigh as the man at the bar brushed her long hair from her bare shoulders.

He kissed the hollow at the base of her ear, running his tongue along the column of her throat toward her collarbone, his fingers slipping beneath the lace edge of her top.

If Jace truly left her for this woman, then fate had come full circle as they both watched her straddle the man's lap at the bar with no care who saw, including Jace.

Daisy closed her eyes. There was no satisfaction in watching the karmic bitch-slap. Jace was alive. At least she knew that much, if not why he left. Perhaps she didn't want to know. Besides, Aimee was waiting for her at the main bar across the club, and her friend was right. It was time to let go.

She stole one last look at Jace, fixing him in her mind before sparing a glance for the woman at the bar. What she witnessed left her staring in disbelief, as small, sharp fangs pierced the woman's tender skin at the base of her throat. Right there at the bar. In front of God and everyone else.

Daisy blinked at the blatant display. Her eyes flew to Jace and then back to the woman.

No one noticed the girl's soft hiss of pain or how the vampire ran his fingers through her hair, allowing her blond mass to fall in an obscuring curtain. Or maybe they did and this was business as usual at The Red Veil.

The vampire licked the woman's blood from the corner of his mouth before closing her wound, whispering something that made her gasp and reach for his cock.

With a knowing smirk, the vampire took the woman by the hand and lifted her to her feet, guiding her almost trance like toward another back alcove.

Daisy swallowed, watching Jace's jaw clench. He shot back the double whiskey in his hand and got up to follow, leaving his cowboy hat on the chair.

A flood of emotion raced through Daisy's mind, leaving her body in a sweat of disbelief and anger. Like her, Jace was raised to despise vampires. Had he left her to chase after some blood whore all this time? Or was he on some kind of crusade to save every bimbo on the planet stupid enough to be glamoured into a feed and fuck?

Nausea bit into Daisy's gut at the thought. Maybe that wasn't it at all. Maybe Jace had gone rogue, and had spent the last five years hunting undead predators playing outside the rules. But why leave her for that? She'd have joined him. Gladly.

Her mind whirled with motives, possibilities and justifications. The same as it had five years earlier. Every bitter emotion fed on the one before, compelling her to follow.

Screw the karmic bitch-slap.

Jace owed her more than an apology. He owed her an explanation.

Scrambling from where she stood, she spared a quick thought for Aimee still waiting at the VIP bar and dug for her phone to send her a quick text. There was no time for anything else.

She scooted around people at the bar to grab Jace's hat. She caught a glimpse of him as he turned toward the same alcove as the vampire and his prey, but when she rounded the corner, he disappeared through a non-descript door that closed as quickly as it opened.

Damn.

"What have we here?" a male voice asked from behind.

Daisy whirled on her heel, her fingers tightening on the base of the UV flashlight still in her hand. It was another vampire, only this one was elegant and beautiful.

Sandy haired with green eyes that flashed with humor, and a charming smile to match his equally charming British accent.

"My apologies, love. I hope I didn't alarm you." He gestured toward the door. "Are you waiting for someone in particular or are you simply one of the—curious?"

He stressed the last word, letting his eyes travel the length of her curves as he inhaled.

"Intriguing. There's a distinct hint of the frontier in your scent, rather than the usual jaded cynicism we get from Manhattan locals. They only venture toward the back rooms when either drunk or trying to prove their bravery. Sometimes both."

Daisy didn't reply.

At her reserve, a smile tugged at his lips. "In view of your quiet bravado, I gather you to be a daughter of the Lone Star State." he chuckled, gesturing to her boots. "Ironic really, considering the beautifully stitched leather covering your foot is fittingly called, *the vamp*."

"Yes, well." Daisy flicked her eyes toward the door.

"Would you like to go through, love?" The red hue deepened in his eyes as he inhaled again, but he didn't come near. Instead he pressed his thumb to a small biometric scanner hidden by the door frame.

Within seconds the lock snicked open. "Entry is by invitation only, so if anyone asks, tell them you are Julian Trevelyan's guest. No one will bother you after that," he paused, flashing another amazing smile. "Unless, of course, you want to be bothered."

"Thank you," Daisy mumbled, her eyes meeting his for a moment and it stunned to see kindness in their red depths.

He inclined his head. "Take care, love. Be careful what you wish for. You just might find it inside."

Not wanting to think too hard what the vampire meant, she scooted past without a word. Was it a warning or reassurance?

The door closed and she found herself facing the center of a round antechamber. The room was empty, but the sound of people engaged in what she could only imagine, vibrated in a muffled hum from various rooms.

The antechamber was white marble with a floor inlaid with gold mosaic tiles depicting different sex acts, each pointing to a corresponding archway along the room's perimeter.

"Just follow the yellow brick road," she thought, wondering what the hell Jace was doing here and why.

The air was thick with sex and a trace of blood. Daisy held her breath waiting for her gag reflex to kick in, but her senses tingled with anticipation instead. Excitement brewed, quickening her pulse.

Jaw clenched against the seductive vibe, she closed her eyes and summoned her inner wolf. The beast rode just beneath the surface, and she inhaled, focusing solely on Jace's remembered scent.

Nothing.

Frustrated, she exhaled hard, trying to purge the teasing scents from her palate and the distraction of sex from her brain. Aimee was right. It had been too long.

She tried again, deeper. Her skin tingled as she raised her wolf again, bringing the beast even closer to the surface. Her muscles tensed and heat skittered along every nerve ending as she focused on Jace.

Still nothing.

If she didn't pull back, she'd phase and that would be very bad. With a quick breath, she let her wolf recede and her pulse calmed. She opened her eyes and scanned the room.

Was this place warded or spelled?

Daisy chewed her lip. "You're a wolf. So is Jace. Think like a wolf."

She dropped her gaze to the floor and stared at the mosaic depiction beneath her feet, opening both her eyes and her senses.

"You've got to be kidding me," she huffed. The spot on the floor that drew her attention showed rear-entry doggie style sex.

She stared at the image, remembering the muscled feel of Jace's body, the strength of his thighs and the pressure of his hands on her hips. How he teased each full moon about her craving the wild side on all fours.

"You're such a wolf whore. The moon crests and your ass is in the air, begging for my cock." His whisper tickled her ear from behind as he teased her moist folds with his large, swollen tip. "You like it hard and deep, don'tcha, Dais?"

Her panties dampened at the memory of his dirty talk and how he'd kiss the back of her throat, nipping her skin as he punished her pussy, inch by hard inch until he drove his cock deep, biting down on her shoulder to claim her twice over.

She closed her eyes, squelching the recollection. It served no purpose except to rehash old pain.

Daisy sucked in a breath to get a grip. "You came here to find Jace and make him own up to how he hurt you, not to play name that memory."

She squared her shoulders and headed down the closest corridor. Moans grew louder as did the scent of blood, the scents concentrated and intoxicating. She stopped and listened, looking for any sign of Jace.

A series of four doors lined the wide corridor on either side. Jace could be behind any one of them. She tried each, systematically. So far they were all locked but the one on the end was left ajar. Hands shaking, she pushed the door open.

The room was dim, with a large plush area rug beneath a high, four-poster bed draped with sheer crimson veils.

The skinny blonde from the bar knelt on the mattress. Her long hair sliding over her bent back in a bright curtain and her fingers fisted into the black coverlet. Her wrists and ankles were bound with leather cuffs chained to the corners of the bed and her eyes were taped shut with electrical tape.

Two men flanked her front and back, each working her body. She moaned lapping at the base of the ridged shaft shoved in her mouth, while the other man buried his face between her legs from behind.

The man at the rear lifted his head, his mouth and teeth covered in blood. It was the guy from the bar. He turned, giving Daisy a grin.

"Want to join in, sweetheart?" he asked, wiping his mouth on his arm. "Four's always a good number."

He ran his fingers over the woman's crack, spreading the coppery liquid before licking her from clit to anus. The woman gasped as he bit down, hard.

The other sucked a breath through his fangs and threw his head back. "I'm going to blow my load."

He shoved his cock deeper into her throat and the woman gagged. "That's right, honey. Take it all."

He snarled as he came, pulling back to let hot spurts jet into her mouth and onto her lips.

She groaned in pleasure, tonguing his sticky swollen head. She let go of the other's cock to scrape what was left of him from her chin and bottom lip, licking her finger clean.

The vampire leaned down and kissed her, licking and nipping at her mouth, dragging his lips over her jaw until he plunged his fangs into her throat.

The other spread her ass cheeks wide, and drove into her bloodied folds, slapping her hard with each thrust, the woman whimpering for more.

Daisy's gaze locked on the scene and she couldn't move, her body betraying her with each moan and thrust. She was spellbound and seduced, repulsed and yet drawn to what she loathed. Her own body ached as she watched the ebb and flow of the dominant and submissive sex.

She shivered at the forbidden scene before her, and when the vampire fucking the woman from behind turned his red eyes to her, she gasped at the visceral intensity of his stare.

Daisy tore her eyes from them and backed out of the room, slamming the door. She pressed her back against the outside wall, gulping in air. Her hands shook as she shoved her fingers through her hair, trying to ignore the weakness in her knees and the throbbing between her legs.

She squeezed her eyes closed trying to focus. She dismissed the countless scents assaulting her nose, concentrating instead on sifting through the layers of sex and her own unspent need to find what she looked for.

"Daisy?"

Her eyes snapped open and she froze.

"What are you doing here?" Jace asked, stunned.

She licked her lips, pressing her back even farther into the wall to stop her knees from buckling. Jace was gorgeous. Even more than she remembered, and his nearness was a gut punch.

"I could ask you the same question," she countered, her voice cracking.

He didn't answer. Instead he took in her face and her body as though starved for the sight of her.

"You look good, Dais," he said, finally.

Heart racing, she swallowed past the lump in her throat and took an unsteady step away from the wall. "After five years, that's all you have to say to me?"

"What would you have me say?" His voice was soft.

Her jaw tightened. "If you can't figure that out on your own, forget it. I'm not throwing you a lifeline, Jace Matthews. There's no phone a friend or ask the audience on this one."

"I'm sorry, Dais. You caught me by surprise. I'm not good with words. You know that."

She exhaled, glancing at the cowboy hat still in her hand. "Well, that's one thing that hasn't changed. If memory serves, the only time you weren't at a loss for words were when we were between the sheets."

No sooner had the words left her mouth than she winced inwardly. She was as bad as he. Jace couldn't think of what to say, and all she did was hurl back how fucking good he was in the sack.

Daisy toyed with his hat's wide brim, before looking up at him. "This is the last place I'd think to see you again."

"You thought to see me?" Jace held out his hand for his hat, his fingers brushing hers in the process.

Her breath hitched at the mere touch, her body betraying her again. She wanted more than a simple brush of skin.

She wanted his hands on her body, his mouth on hers, his voice whispering in her ear 'this was all a bad dream.' She closed her eyes. Stop it! It was not a dream. It was real.

With a hard exhale she fought the overwhelming urge to crawl into his arms and snapped her eyes open, pulling back her hand to squelch the feeling.

"What do you think?" She forced herself to meet his eyes. "I thought of you all right, and how you left me waiting alone in the church. No call, no note, nothing. Not even an 'I'm sorry.' You just disappeared. Why?"

The muscle in his cheek clenched as he set his cowboy hat low on his forehead.

"I deserve an explanation, Jace. I think you owe me that much," she pressed.

"How did you get back here, anyway? This part of The Red Veil is by invitation only," he evaded.

She lifted her chin. "Julian Trevelyan invited me."

Jace's jaw tightened even farther. "Trevelyan. How do you know him?"

Daisy shrugged.

He took a step closer and grabbed her arm. "Don't play games, Daisy. You shouldn't be here. Tell me how you know him."

Daisy jerked her arm back. "Don't take that possessive tone with me, Jace Matthews! Your claim expired the day you didn't show up to say I do. Who I know and what games I play is none of your business."

Jace inhaled and his eyes dilated. "Why are you here? Don't lie to me, Daisy. I can smell your need. The air is choked with it."

"Stop it, Jace. I don't *need* anything. What I want is an explanation. Don't you care how much you hurt me?" She blinked at the pathetic tears burning her eyes

"Daisy —"

Yearning warred in his eyes along with doubt, and he stared at her as though she were both a dream and a nightmare.

He took another step closer and let his chin drop to his chest. The wide brim of his hat hid his face, and when he lifted his eyes to hers, she gasped in disbelief.

Shaking her head, Daisy backed away. A silent denial filled with numbness and revulsion on her lips.

Fangs.

Jace had fangs.

"This is why I didn't show up to marry you, Daisy," he said.

Piercing red-hued eyes held hers for a moment, and she screamed, her mind rebelling before she turned on her heel and ran.

Chapter Three

"*I*t's about time, sleepy head," Aimee joked, throwing a dishtowel at Daisy as she shuffled into the ranch house kitchen.

She yawned and sank into a chair at the table. "What are you doing here so early?"

"Early? It's nearly three p.m. We have a date to see Jace's parents for dinner tonight, remember?" Aimee set a mug of coffee in front of her friend. "We agreed. You need to tell them you saw him."

Daisy picked up the mug and blew across the rim. "I can't do it, Aims. I can't watch their hopes crumble once the truth sinks in." She took a sip and winced. "How old is this coffee? It's bitter."

Aimee pulled a chair out and sat as well. "Forget the coffee. Don't you think Carson and Elinor have a right to be told?"

"It's not my secret to tell."

"That's a cop-out, Daisy and you know it. It's not like you're telling tales. You saw him."

Daisy eyed her through the steam rising from the brim of her cup. "And what happens when they ask questions I can't answer? They're going to want the how and the why of it and I refuse to lie. They've been my support system since before Jenny was born, even more than my own father."

"No one's telling you to lie."

Daisy shook her head. "I don't have the whole story, so why make them hurt even more than they already do wondering? I can't Aimee, and I won't."

"I suppose you're right. You don't have the entire story, which still irritates the hell out of me, by the way."

"Why?"

"Daisy, you managed to slip into the holy of holies when it comes to fetish fantasy, and I wasn't with you."

She snorted. "You can't be serious."

"It bites, literally." Aimee exhaled with a shrug. "Pun totally intended."

"I don't get it, Aims. What's with you and this fascination with vampires?"

Aimee shrugged. "They interest me."

"Interest you?" Daisy raised an eyebrow.

Her friend blushed to the tips of her ears. "They more than interest me. I fantasize about how they feel, what they taste like to kiss, if their cocks are as hard and cold as ice when aroused. So when you got to enter the mecca of it all, I was jealous." She shrugged again. "I still am."

Talk about being knocked over with a feather. Aimee was sophisticated and classy. Even her auburn pixie cut and spray of freckles couldn't diminish her professional air.

Daisy lifted her coffee mug. "And they say the freaks come out at night."

"What were they like?" Aimee leaned in, keeping her voice low.

"Who?"

Aimee pulled a face. "Who do you think? The vampires? The backrooms?"

"I didn't see all that much," Daisy replied with a shrug. "Based on the sheer size of the place, I imagine the backrooms are more like a labyrinth. There was a sexual map of sorts, a mosaic inlaid into the floor that directs you to different corridors, or at least that's what I assume. Kind of like the frescoed sex menus on the brothel walls in ancient Pompeii. Anyway, I only glimpsed one room and that was by mistake."

"There are no mistakes. Only lessons. So spill."

Embarrassed heat spread across Daisy's chest at the thought of the ménage. She glanced at her hands, avoiding Aimee's eyes and potential questions.

"Yeah, well, I wasn't in the mood for an education on anything other than why Jace left." Daisy sidestepped further.

"Which you didn't get."

"Don't remind me."

"Even so, he sounds exactly the same, Daisy. Chivalrous and hot as hell. Why else would he be concerned with your reasons for being there? He must know the danger involved in fetish play. People get hurt when they don't know what they're getting into." She nodded. "Yup. Definitely chivalrous and hot."

"And undead."

Aimee lifted a hand. "What has that got to do with anything?"

"Aims, why don't you go home? I'm sorry I dragged you out to hell's half acre for nothing. It's a long drive from Houston and I'm not really up for much of anything other than crawling back into bed."

"Oh no you don't, Daisy Lou Cochran. You are not dismissing me that easily."

"Don't call me Daisy Lou. You know I hate that."

"It's your middle name, so deal with it. You can also deal with the subject at hand. This isn't some random vampire we're talking about. It's Jace. The man you were set to marry. The father of your child. The man you loved, and if my guess is correct and it usually is when it comes to you, the man you still love."

Daisy tapped her nails on the side of her mug. "He's a vampire now. Enough said."

Aimee shook her head. "You're going to have to do better than that."

"What mother in their right mind would let a vampire anywhere near her child? Besides, you know my family history. There is no way I can double slap my father or my pack in the face. I won't do it."

"Double slap? I don't understand?"

"You know, for someone so smart, you're pretty thick, Dr. Aimee Dunne. My father would never forgive me if I allowed the ranch to revert to the Matthews pack, even if they are technically family, and I would never forgive myself if something happened to Jenny because I let Jace back into our lives. It's too dangerous. Vampires are selfish and unpredictable."

"Based on what you told me, that's not how Jace presented himself. You were in his territory, Daisy. He could have done anything he wanted or left you as prey for some other vampire. He didn't. Sounds to me as though your views are slightly slanted."

Daisy shook her head. "Guilt and grudges are woven into the fabric of my life. Neither the Cochrans nor the Matthews forgive easily. Even if Jace's parents wanted to bring him home, their pack would never accept him as one of their own again. Not for them and especially not for Jenny."

"So you've decided to let your family's prejudice and an outdated taboo dictate your fate?"

Daisy inhaled and let the breath out slowly. "No, not quite."

"Have you given your so-called cousin an answer yet?"

"Who? Seth?"

Aimee nodded.

"He hasn't asked me to marry him, yet, but it's coming. My father hinted at it before you and I left for New York."

"And you're planning to say yes?"

Daisy shrugged. "I guess. I'll wait and see how I feel."

Aimee laughed. "You mean you're waiting until dear old dad knocks on your bedroom door with a wedding gown in one hand and a rifle in the other."

Daisy snorted. "You know, I really hate how well you know me, sometimes."

A child's laughter caught their attention and Daisy looked out the back sliding doors to the backyard. "Looks like Dad and Jenny are home from their errands."

Aimee covered Daisy's hand. "She looks so much like Jace, it's scary."

With a sigh, Daisy smiled as she watched out the window. "I know. Do you know how hard it is to love someone who looks so much like the one person you want, but can't have?"

"No, but I can imagine." Aimee squeezed her hand. "You've got it wrong, though, Dais. You can have him. You know where he is and how to find him. It's your choice."

Another car pulled up and Aimee made a face. "Looks like Seth is here, too. Is he joining us for dinner at Carson and Ellie's?"

Daisy shook her head. "I wasn't expecting him."

Aimee gave Daisy's a gentle shake. "I think I'll get going after all. I assume you two have things to discuss, and I don't want to be around for that conversation."

"Some friend, deserting me in my hour of need." Daisy laughed. "Can't you stay? Seth won't get too comfortable if you're here. He knows you don't like him."

"At least he's perceptive." She grinned. "Drive in tomorrow, and I'll take you out in Houston. Give you a chance to weigh your options."

"Oh, no. The last time you treated me to a city slicker outing, I ended up in a room with a vampire ménage!"

Aimee's mouth dropped. "You little liar! You said you didn't see much!"

"Sue me." Daisy shrugged with a laugh.

Aimee pointed her spoon in Daisy's direction. "I'm a trained psychiatrist. I can always hypnotize you into talking, so don't push me."

"Ha."

She considered her friend. "Or maybe I'll hypnotize you into accepting you still love Jace regardless of what he's become or what both packs say."

"Not everyone is as free thinking as you, Aims. Or as accepting. Like I said, times may be changing everywhere else, but not out here."

Aimee inhaled and then pushed her chair back from the table to get up. "Perhaps, but change has to start somewhere and like I said, it's your choice."

"What's Daisy's choice?" Seth asked coming in from the yard.

Aimee eyed the man. Seth Cochran was the poster child for trying too hard. A cowboy Casanova wannabe in a rented Stetson.

"Daisy has many choices, Seth. You'd do well to remember that," she replied and then laid a hand on Daisy's shoulder. "Promise me you'll think about what I said. I know there's a lot at stake, but then again, you'll never know how much you could gain until you think outside the box."

She pressed her cheek to the side of her friend's head. "I mean it. Call me tomorrow."

Daisy blew her a kiss, but didn't say a word. Aimee left through the sliders and she watched her hug both her dad and Jenny before driving off.

"What was that all about?" Seth asked, eyeing Aimee's taillights.

Daisy got up from the table and walked to pour her cold coffee down the drain. "Nothing that concerns you."

He stepped behind her and slipped his hands around her waist. "Everything that concerns you, concerns me. You should know that by now."

She twisted out of his arms and moved to open the dishwasher to empty the clean contents, purposely avoiding Seth's eyes as much as his hands.

"I'm glad Aimee left. It will give us a chance to talk," he offered.

She looked up, glancing at her daughter skipping rope in the yard. "I can't tonight, Seth. Jenny and I are going to her grandparents' house for dinner."

He reached out and ran a knuckle over her bare skin from her elbow to her shoulder.

"Why don't you drop Jenny there for dinner and then let her stay the night? I'm sure they would be happy to have her and that way we can have dinner alone, maybe spend the night somewhere nice. Just the two of us."

Dish in hand, she used it as a convenient prop to shift her arm away from his touch and open the cabinet.

"I don't think so, Seth. Jenny was just there for the weekend while I was in New York."

He eyed her. "So? I thought you wanted her to have a relationship with *his* parents."

She straightened, taking in the sour set to his mouth. "His parents? Really, Seth. He has a name. It's Jace. And yes, I want Jenny to know his family."

"They've fed her nothing but bullshit about the man, so much so she idolizes him. A man who ran out on her mother. A father she's never met!" he argued.

Daisy crossed her arms. "You know nothing about Jace or why he chose to leave. None of us do. Until we find out, I choose to give him the benefit of the doubt. For our daughter's sake, mine and Jace's." She stressed the words, staring him down.

"Fine, but three is a hard number to navigate, Daisy, and I've been juggling my place in this relationship for a year now. I deserve more."

"Deserve?" she balked. "None of us knew anything about you until a year ago, Seth. No connection, no knowledge of family ties. Nothing. Just an ancestry.com genealogy and the right last name.

"I like you, Seth, but for the kind of commitment you're asking, it's going to take a lot more than that. It's going to take time."

He snorted. "Why are you questioning me now? After all this time? My credentials were good enough for your father. I have plans for this place and for us. Big plans. What happened in New York to make you come home like this?"

She closed the dishwasher door. "Nothing. Like I said, I need time. Besides, even if I decide to make you a permanent part of my future, this ranch and all its land aren't part of the deal."

Seth stormed out and got in his car. He pulled up the dirt drive with a spray of gravel making Jenny run in through the sliding doors, worry on her dirt-streaked face.

"Hey, Jenny-bean. You ready for a snack?" Daisy asked.

She nodded, her dark pigtails shining in the late afternoon sun. "Mommy, is Seth mad at us?"

"It's nothing for you to worry about, honeybun. How about some chocolate pudding?" Daisy asked, turning for the fridge.

Jenny slid her eyes to the gravel drive. "I don't want him to come back,"

"Jenny, that's not very nice. Mr. Cochran has been a good friend to us."

She sniffed. "He's not nice. He's mean and says bad things when you and Grandpa aren't here."

"What kind of bad things?" Daisy froze in front of the fridge, pudding cups in hand.

The four year old's lip quivered. "He said I was flea-bitten and should be put down. I don't have fleas, Mommy. I promise. Just mosquito bites."

Daisy put the pudding cups on the counter and gathered her daughter in her arms. She picked her up, careful not to let her see the rage seething in her face.

"I know, sweetheart. Don't listen to him. I promise he will never say anything like that to you again. Okay?"

Jenny nodded, wiping her nose on the back of her hand.

"Eew! You know better than that, Miss Jenny-germ bug! Go wash your face and hands and I'll get your snack." She kissed the tip of her nose and put her down.

"Can I have whip cream?"

Daisy laughed. "Of course, you can."

"Lots, okay? A whip cream mountain!" Jenny yelled running for the bathroom.

Daisy frowned. It seemed Aimee was right. She sighed, flipping a dishtowel over her shoulder, wondering if maybe her best friend was right about everything else, too.

Chapter Four

"Seth just phoned," Daisy's father said, walking into the kitchen, wiping black axle grease from his hands. "Seems you two had words."

"You could say that." She turned from straightening the stovetop to look at him.

"Where's the doodle bug?" he asked.

"Jenny's already in bed. You missed dinner. I put a plate for you in the oven if you're hungry."

He stuffed his sweat-streaked work cloth into his back pocket. "I thought y'all were going to Carson and Elinor's tonight?" He paused at the look on his daughter's face. "You know what, don't tell me. What I will hear is why you and Seth argued."

Daisy leaned back against the kitchen counter, folding her arms at her chest. "Let me think. Oh, yeah, how about he's a liar and a phony."

"Daisy—"

"No, Dad. Jenny's afraid of him. She broke down in tears this afternoon. She told me how mean-spirited and foul he is the minute you or I are out of earshot."

Her father shook his head. "I can't believe that. It doesn't make sense."

"So you're saying your granddaughter is a liar?"

"No. I'm saying there's more than one side to every story. Jenny is a sweet child, but she's only four, and you've given her license to run wild. I think you owe it to Seth to let him explain. It might be a case of simple misunderstanding."

"Dad, how is telling a four-year-old she should be put down, a misunderstanding? It took all my strength not to drive after the bastard and put him down with a load of buck shot."

She puffed out a frustrated breath. "Thank God Jenny doesn't know what putting something down means."

Her father smirked, washing his hands. "Now I know where our little spitfire gets her vivid way of talking."

"Stop, okay. Jenny may be a lot of things, but she doesn't tell tales. Besides, there are other things as well. Did you know about his big plans for the ranch and the surrounding land?"

Her father's head jerked up at that. "What plans?"

Daisy made a face. "See? He told me point blank he had big plans for the property, and it looks like he didn't bother discussing it with either of us."

She blew out a breath. "He's a phony, Dad, and I won't have him around Jenny. I trust him less now than when he first showed up at our door."

Her father lifted a hand. "Now, don't go flying off the handle like your mother, God rest her soul. Seth is out of line with Jenny, I agree, but it's hard for a man to welcome another man's child into his heart. Especially when her father is, well, let's not rehash that.

"I know the Matthews pack has welcomed you with open arms and I'm grateful for that. My guess is they did so for Carson and Ellie's sake, but the situation is what it is. If Jenny had been born a boy we wouldn't be having this conversation and Seth would be out on his ear, but that's not the case and you know it."

Daisy's lips parted but no words formed as she stared at her father. Her mind ran with disbelief and she counted her breaths not to scream.

"I'm going to ignore what you said, because I can't believe you actually thought the words, let alone spoke them. From the moment Jace disappeared, I knew my happiness and wellbeing were bargaining chips when it came to the ranch, but Jenny? No, Dad. That's where I draw the line. I won't have it. Not now, not ever. Seth Cochran is no longer welcome in this house."

Daisy stalked up the stairs and closed her bedroom door. Jenny was telling the truth, and her stomach roiled with the knowledge she let her own needs lead her blind, and at the expense of her daughter's wellbeing.

Aimee would have a field day with this. With a tired sigh, she leaned against her bedroom door. Well, there was time enough for Aims to say 'I told you so,' not that she would, but she'd definitely think it.

Daisy unbuttoned her blouse and shrugged the sleeveless cotton from her shoulders. Outside, the crickets began their nightly serenade and the first stars winked in the dark sky.

Jenny had been asleep for two hours and by now Dad was most likely settled into his chair with his plate of leftovers and the remote control. He'd be asleep in no time, which meant the house would be at peace, giving her time to think.

She finished stripping and padded naked into the bathroom, snapping on the light. A tired reflection stared back at her from the mirror. Jace said she looked good. She frowned. Not as good as he did, though.

Five years had left no trace on Jace's face or his body. He was still tall and broad muscled, dark and as handsome as ever.

"He's a vampire now, stupid. They don't age," she muttered.

She shook her head and turned on the shower. Stepping into the hot spray, she lifted her face to the welcoming stream, letting its soothing warmth soak into her muscles.

Her shoulders relaxed and she dipped her head back. The water cascaded over her face and chest, teasing her nipples. She palmed the soap and lathered her hands, skimming the whip cream bubbles over her breasts and torso.

She'd given birth four years ago, but her body still carried the gentle curves of motherhood. The soft swell of her belly and full breasts. Working the ranch left her fit, but she wasn't the same girl Jace left at the altar. In more ways than just physical.

Daisy pictured him in the club's backrooms. Lonely. Angry. Surprised. But one word nagged more than any other. Hungry.

Did she actually see desire in his eyes or was it just a projection of her own want? Jace said he smelled her arousal. He wasn't wrong, but it wasn't the carnality of the ménage that sent her over the edge. It was him.

She leaned against the warm tile, her hands skimming her breasts, her palms cupping their full weight. With her thumb, she grazed her nipples, picturing Jace's hands on her waist, sliding upward to tease and taunt.

For five years, she craved him. Not just his body, but his scent, the feel of his touch, the soft, low rumble of his laughter.

She pictured him standing in front of her, the water sheeting over her back as he knelt between her spread legs, his tongue and fingers working her wet, slick slit and hard nub until she came hard, grinding herself farther into his mouth.

How he would lift her onto his waiting cock, driving her back against the tile, his member hard and deep in her already quivering flesh, pushing her climax higher.

Daisy dropped the soap, plunging her hand between her legs. Eyes closed, she pushed her own fingers into her wetness, working her body in time with the image of Jace behind her lids. She cried out, crouching into herself before she tossed her head back riding the crest of release.

She slid down the wall to the water pooled at the base of the tub, the shower jets pelting her shoulders. God help her. Aimee was right again. She still loved him.

Chapter Five

"Where are you going?" her father asked in a rough whisper, closing Jenny's door behind him.

"Out," Daisy replied, heading down the stairs from the center landing. After their argument the night before and everything else swirling in her mind, she needed open space to think.

"I see that. Where to?"

She shrugged. "Nowhere, really. I just need to get out and clear my head. I might drive up to the north pasture to think."

Her father came down the steps, motioning for her to wait. "Listen, honey. The last couple of days you've been wound tighter than a girdle on a minister's wife, and I haven't made it any easier. I guess what I'm trying to say is, about last night—" he began, stopping her at the front door.

Daisy went up on her tiptoes and pecked his cheek, shutting him up. "Apology accepted."

He looked at her half smirk. "You know your old man too well."

She met his sideways grin with one of her own. "Like father, like daughter, but why the sudden change of heart? I was set to buck heads with you on Seth, so I'm curious."

He took off his cowboy hat and ran a hand through his flattened hair. "I did some checking, and it looks like you were right. The boy made inquiries. Not only at the surveyor's, but at the bank, as well. Seems he told everyone he was as good as my partner since he was fixing to marry you come fall."

"I'm sorry, Dad. I take no pleasure in being right."

"I think we both owe a debt to a certain four-year-old. It seems she not only inherited your fire, but your grandmother's intuition." He gave her a soft smile, but the small grin was short lived. "Do me and everyone else a favor and stop worrying about the ranch. When it comes time, we'll figure something out."

Daisy went up on her toes again. "Thanks for saying we, Dad. It means the world."

He cleared his throat, setting his hat back on his head. "Don't be too late, you hear?"

She nodded and closed the door behind her. The gravel crunched under her feet as she got into the pickup and headed toward the north edge of the ranch.

It was a half hour drive, and even with a nearly full moon to light the dark dirt road, Daisy took it slow.

The pale orb hadn't reached its full zenith in the sky, but its pull skimmed electricity across her skin. Two more days and she'd race the miles of flat stretches across the ranch, chasing birds and deer and whatever else crossed her path.

Complete freedom carried her with nothing but joy in her heart while in wolf form. The only time she could let go and breathe.

Daisy neared the top marker where their cattle grazed in the late spring, and pulled the truck close to the gate. Climbing out, she grabbed a blanket and a thermos of hot coffee and hopped the fence, not caring how unladylike it was to do so in a spring dress.

She headed toward the giant oak where she and Jace had carved their initials as teens. No one knew about their crush back then.

Their families were even more at odds then, and would never have approved. They waited until they both turned eighteen before they made their relationship public.

Headstrong and idealistic, they each swore to throw everything to the wind if the families didn't let them be. Of course, neither knew it was what everyone secretly hoped. An end to the bad blood.

They almost got their wish.

Almost.

The tree was still magnificent. Set on a grassy knoll overlooking the lower grazing fields. Daisy spread the blanket on the soft ground and settled in the middle, lying back to look at the stars.

There was nothing like a Texas night. A twinkling sky and a soft breeze to lull the senses.

She inhaled, closing her eyes.

"There's only one thing missing from this picture, otherwise it's perfect."

Daisy sucked in a breath, afraid to lift her lids. Jace uttered those same words years before, the first time they met beneath their tree. It was déjà vu. Down to the same blanket, in the same place.

There's only one thing missing from this picture, otherwise it's perfect.

Oh? What's that?

Me, kissing you.

"Jace," she whispered, dismissing the memory.

"Look at me, Daisy," he said. "I'm not going to hurt you."

She opened her eyes and had to bite the side of her tongue not to cry. "What are you doing here?"

He flashed that same crooked smile she loved. This time it was full of the same warmth and humor she remembered, not the anger she saw that night at The Red Veil.

"We seem to be asking each other that same question a lot these days," he replied. "May I sit with you?"

"Jace, I don't think—"

He didn't let her finish. "Did you tell my folks you saw me?"

She watched the tide of emotions cross his eyes and slowly shook her head. "No. It's not my story to tell."

His relief was palpable. "Thank you for that. I don't want to hurt them any more than I already have."

"But hurting me over and over again is just fine and dandy, right?" she shot back.

"That's why I'm here."

Her forehead creased. "To break my heart again? Sorry, buckaroo. There's nothing left of the organ for your fangs to get at."

"Daisy, please—"

She went poker-faced "No. I don't want to hear it."

"Goddamn it, Daisy! You're just as pig-headed and stubborn as always. Four days ago all you wanted was an explanation, and now I'm here and you won't hear me out. What was it you said? I owe you? Well, now you owe me the same consideration."

She scrambled to her feet. "Owe you? You left me at the altar. I think that cancels all debt past, present, and future."

"You don't understand."

Five years of hurt and anger bubbled to the surface, tightening her chest, making it hard to breathe. Jaw clenched, she blinked back the hot tears pricking her eyes and curled her fingers into her palms, squeezing against the pain.

"You bastard!" She flew at him flailing, wild, pummeling his chest with punches and slaps. "How could you? And now you show up and want to make nice! Fuck you, Jace!"

He grabbed her arms, locking her wrists in his, as she struggled. "Daisy, stop! You'll hurt yourself!"

She bit his hand drawing blood, and the moment the coppery liquid hit her mouth she froze. "Oh God, what have I done?"

She licked the taste from her bottom lip and her breath hitched in her throat. Her shoulders shook and sobs took her.

"Damn you, Jace! Damn you to Hell!"

He pulled her against his chest, folding her in his arms. "My life is hell, Daisy. I'm already there." He buried his face in her hair.

His body was warm, not the icy cold she expected, and his breath fragrant, not the grave rot she'd heard in the stories people told.

"I've missed you, Daisy. So much." He kissed her hair, pushing the heavy mass back to kiss her ear and her cheek.

She sucked in a small breath. Everything about him felt the same. "Jace —"

His name was a yielding sigh on her lips and Jace groaned at the surrender, crushing his mouth to hers, kissing her hard and hungrily.

Breathless, she clutched at his shoulders, pressing her body closer. "I've missed you, too."

He slid his hand past her waist to the round curve of her bottom, curling the fabric into his palm. His fingers slipped beneath the lace edge of her panties, trailing over her soft skin. He caressed her full curves, kneaded her flesh in slow circles, his thumb grazing her low cleft.

With a moan, Daisy lifted one leg and wrapped it around his, giving him complete access. Jace slid his hand around to the front and cupped her wet sex, ringing her sensitive bud with his thumb.

Daisy cried out and he pushed his palm against her mound. "Do you want me, Daisy? Do you want this?" With his other hand, he pressed hers to the full hard length bulging behind his fly.

She nodded, not trusting her voice.

Jace unzipped the back of her dress, letting it puddle to the ground. Her breasts spilled free, unbound and he lifted a hand to caress the full flesh before stepping back to drag his shirt from his shoulders and tossed it to the grass.

Unbuttoning his fly, his eyes devoured Daisy's body, watching as she slipped her panties over her legs, kicking them to the side.

She stepped closer and rested her hands on his chest the way she had itched to do, letting her palms slide downward to his open waistband.

The tips of her fingers trailed over the dark nest of hair peeking from the tease of open denim, and a private smile crossed her lips at the fact he was commando.

Jace took her hands in his and together they pushed his jeans over his hips, freeing the corded length of his cock. Daisy's fingers brushed the silken flesh and his member jerked as she wrapped her fingers around the thick shaft.

"It's been so long, Dais. I want to see you. Lock the sight of you in my memory."

Daisy stepped back and he pushed his jeans the rest of the way down, toeing them to the edge of the blanket with his shirt. His eyes never left Daisy as she stood in the moonlight.

He took in the fullness of her body, the gentle curves and the faint silvery striations along the soft swell of her lower belly.

His eyes found hers, questioning.

Daisy nodded. "They're exactly what they look like, Jace. Stretchmarks from pregnancy."

Stunned, his gaze held. He opened his mouth to speak, but then closed it.

"It's okay." She gave him a soft smile. "Ask me. If anyone has a right to, it's you."

The cryptic comment left him staring at her even more intently. "Are you saying what I think you're saying?"

She nodded. "I had our child, Jace. A girl. Her name is Jenny. She's four years old."

They both stood in the soft Texas breeze, neither saying a word, but neither looking away, either. It was as if time stood still until Jace took a step forward and cupped Daisy's cheeks in his hands, kissing her.

"I'm sorry you found out like this," she said against his mouth.

He broke their kiss and pulled back to look at her. "Sorry you told me you're the mother of my child? Something I thought I'd never have, considering my hopeless existence? Sorry you told me when I want you so badly, I can't see straight?"

He laughed, kissing her again, hard, sliding his hand over her chest to cup her breast, grazing her nipple with his thumb.

There was a new urgency now, a frenzy of passion almost as though sealing their entwined fates with entwined bodies.

Daisy slipped to her knees, gliding her palms over his chest to his muscled pelvis and the sexy v-shaped cut above his sex. Her fingers splayed across his skin as her tongue teased its way to his thick, corded member.

She held his base, lifting the hard length to her mouth. Daisy's tongue ringed the hard ridge before sucking the full length of him into her throat.

Jace threw his head back and groaned. Muscles taut as she worked his cock with her tongue and her hand. He pumped his hips, pulling back from her mouth and then watching her take every inch, sucking him deep again.

"Daisy —" he ground out. "Stop or I'm going to cum."

She eased her mouth from his head and then leaned back on the blanket, knees bent and legs spread. Jace licked his lips, a hint of fang visible. His vampiric eyes shined muted red in the moonlight, but there was still a definite trace of Were about his scent, and the combination made Daisy's clit throb.

Propped on her elbows, she reached between her legs and spread her pussy lips, running a finger through the glistening wetness.

Jace groaned and climbed between her legs. He lapped at her juice, tonguing her clit before sliding his fingers deep, curling them to hit her spot.

"Jace!" Daisy arched, pushing her hips up and farther into his hand.

He ripped his face from her, turning away.

"What happened? What's the matter?" Her pulse pounded in her ears, demanding he finish.

He turned back and her eyes widened at his fully descended fangs. "I tried to keep them retracted, but I can't." His voice was rough and slightly uncertain. "Blood is part of sex for me now."

She stared at the way they glistened in the silver white light. Repulsed—it's what she should have felt, but she didn't. Instead, the glint of fang made her pussy drip with want, a dark fantasy come to life.

She spread her legs wider and took his hand, guiding his fingers over her wetness toward the pulse in her femoral artery. "Just don't kill me, okay? Our daughter needs her mama."

His eyes held hers as he dropped his mouth to her sex, licking and sucking. He moaned, tweaking her clit hard enough to force a breath from her mouth.

"That's it, babe. I want you soaked and dripping, begging for my cock." Working her pussy he plunged three fingers deep into her slick entrance, and then drew her hard nub between his teeth and into his mouth.

"You taste as luscious as I remember, Dais, and your scent is even more intoxicating."

She came hard, drunk on the feel of him. Her walls clenched and convulsed, her muscles tense and tight as waves took her, unyielding until she slumped light-headed from the force of her climax.

"Always, ladies first," Jace teased, stroking her again.

Daisy closed her eyes, the night air raising goose bumps on her sweat-sheened skin. He stroked her again, and sucked in a breath, her lower belly jolting in aftershocks.

Her body craved more. Craved him. Jace held her gaze, circling his thumb over her already sensitive nub. Swollen and ready, she neared climax again and as she crested, his fangs pierced her flesh.

Pain and pleasure mingled, ebbing ang flowing as he drew from her vein. She was hungry for him, all of him. Her head dropped back between her shoulder, and she tensed, afraid to move.

Jace curled his fingers deep, pushing hard at her spot, drawing deeply from her vein and Daisy's breath locked, her body ready for release, but she stayed on the verge.

"Jace! Please!"

He groaned at her plea and let go, sealing the wound with his tongue. His eyes were dark and unfathomable, as he knelt between her legs. Jace lifted her hips and drove his cock deep with a single thrust.

Daisy hooked her legs around his back, and he rode her hard, plunging his dick, balls deep, filling her over and over until every muscle tensed and he threw his head back and howled, emptying himself inside her.

Panting he held her close as he finished, finally rolling with her to one side, their bodies still entwined in the aftershocks.

"Are you okay?" he asked, feeling her shiver.

"I'm fine. Good, actually. Just a little cold."

Jace laid her back and then stretched out next to her, lifting either side of the blanket over them, burrito-style.

"We used to call this our hot pocket." He chuckled, tucking one edge over her back. "Remember?"

She nodded, giving him a small smile that didn't quite reach her eyes.

"I know I have a lot to account for, Daisy, and I'm sorry. In my defense, much of what happened wasn't brought on by me. If you're willing to listen, I'd like to explain."

Her eyes dipped to the top of his chest and she nodded. "Considering I'm a captive audience right now, I suppose so."

"I didn't show for our wedding not because I didn't want to, and certainly not because I didn't love you. Our wedding night was the night I woke to darkness."

"We didn't have a wedding night, Jace."

He exhaled, scrubbing his face with one hand. "I know, Daisy. It has haunted me for five years, but I wish you'd stop going on about it and let me finish. I'm trying to tell you I was already undead. It happened after the bachelor party."

She stared at him, slowly shaking her head. "All this time and you never thought to get word to me somehow? We had the police and the FBI looking for you for over a year. The only trace we found was your old pickup. Your dad still drives it, you know. It's rusted and ready for the junkyard, but he won't let anyone scrap it."

He exhaled. "I couldn't let you know. The first year or so was terrible. All I wanted was blood. I didn't care from where or whom. I would have killed you and half the town, and not blinked twice."

"And now?" she asked.

The question was a slap in the face, and she regretted asking the minute the words left her mouth. They had just made love and Jace took her blood, and she didn't think twice about letting him.

"Oh, God, Jace. I'm sorry."

He shrugged. "Don't be. It's an honest question. I am what I am. There's no going back, but the one thing I learned I can change, is how I cope with my thirst.

"I learned to appreciate my place on this earth from an elder vampire named Carlos Salazar. He's running The Red Veil for the time being." Jace looked at her with a question. "You said Julian Trevelyan invited you into the backrooms. He's related, sort of. Carlos is his maker. You never said how you knew him."

She shook her head. "I don't know Julian at all. He didn't actually invite me into the backrooms. He found me loitering around the doorway looking for you. He let me in and told me to name drop him if I ran into trouble."

Jace nodded. "I talked to him afterward."

"Julian wasn't what I expected. Then again, neither are you," she added.

"Julian comes from a coven of vampires who foster coexistence with humans. They revere their humanity or what's left of it, and taught me to do the same. I can feed without killing, and now that Weres and vampires are on good terms, it's even better."

"How?" Daisy asked warily.

"Because Were blood can slake a vampire's thirst for a month at least, and the longer we partake, the longer we can go between feeding. For some reason Were blood warms us to almost human temperature."

She nodded. "I admit I expected you to be as cold as ice. In fact, Aimee wondered if sex with you, would feel like having sex with an ice pop."

"Aimee Dunne? Wondered about sex with me?"

"No, not you specifically, silly. Sex with vampires in general." Daisy smirked. "For a well-heeled, well-respected doctor, she's got quite a fetish fascination going on." She paused. "She's team Jace, you know. Has been since New York."

"I always liked Aimee." He grinned. "You should listen to her."

Daisy rolled her eyes. "Anyway, I'm glad you're not marble cold, but I don't want to know the details." She angled her head, looking at Jace's skin in the moonlight. It was luminous.

"In New York, Julian said something that struck me odd, but now not so much," she murmured. "He told me to take care, and to be cautious of what I wished for because I just might get it."

Jace lifted a hand and brushed her dark hair from her cheek. "What did you wish for, Daisy?"

"So," she said, evading his question. "This happened to you at the bachelor party?"

He wiggled his leg over hers under the blanket. "After the party."

"If memory serves, you drove to New Orleans with my brother and some of his friends, right?"

Jace nodded. "We bar hopped on Bourbon Street and ended up in the Barely Legal club. Typical. The more money spent, the more lap dances and free shots provided, but at one point your brother thought it funny to slip me a ruffie."

"My brother gave you a date-rape drug?" She stared at him open mouthed.

"I must have lost consciousness at some point, because the next thing I remember, was being curled up next to a tombstone in Lafayette Cemetery No. 1 with a woman.

"It was an hour or so before dawn, and she dragged me into a stinking crypt where she finished the job of turning me. She seduced me, drained me and then made me drink from her until I vomited blood."

Daisy knew the color drained from her face. "Who was it? Do you know?"

Jace exhaled, scrubbing his face. "Unfortunately, yes. Her name is Violet. She's the same vampire that turned my great-grandfather Micah."

"Oh my God." Daisy looked at him, unbelieving.

Jace's face was full of regret. "Hard to believe, I know. History truly repeated itself this time."

Daisy sat up and glanced to the dark sky. "This wasn't a coincidence, Jace. I feel it in my bones." A hoot owl cooed in the distance as though agreeing.

"It's not a coincidence. Violet reveled in telling me how she planned this with one of her blood whores. He befriended your brother to get to me."

Daisy blinked. "He?"

"Not all blood whores are female, Dais."

She shivered, and nausea bit into her gut. "So my own brother played a part in this?"

"Your brother, Jack, was guilty of a lot of things, but not this. Not intentionally. He didn't know his friend was a vampire's pawn."

The muscle in Jace's jaw tightened. "Didn't it strike you weird there are no direct male descents of Micah and Eva? Except me, of course."

Daisy nodded. "Now that you mention it."

"It's because Violet has been systematically murdering the males in my line for over a century. She kills them at different ages, under different circumstances to keep things interesting, and while pack elders attribute the tragedies to a curse, it was Violet all along.

"She's solely responsible for hundreds of deaths. She's the King Herod of the vampire world. Vampire council adjudicators placed a price on her head, but still she manages to skate under their radar.

"She told me point blank I was slotted to die much earlier, but when she saw my face, she claimed she couldn't take my life, so she turned me instead."

Daisy twisted the end of the blanket in her hands. "Is she your lover? Is that why?"

He shook his head. "No. It's because I resemble Micah. Violet was supposed to marry him, but he passed her over for money and position.

"He knew Eva had land, and with that came the possibility of power. Violet was ruined. It was the mid-nineteenth century. Micah had taken her virginity, leaving her with no prospects and no position. She eventually took to the streets.

"She became a blood whore in a vampire brothel, vowing revenge on my entire line, and when the opportunity presented itself, she grabbed it. Violet is warped, and taking Micah wasn't enough. After I was turned, I stayed away to protect you.

"The crazy bitch swore she'd kill you and your family if I didn't listen. When she heard how your brother Jack died, she laughed, saying the Alpha of the Brethren and the Vampire Council of New York saved her the trouble of killing him herself. Violet is consumed by hate. She even swore to wipe out my entire family, not just the men."

"Oh my God! Jenny! I've got to go —" Daisy scrambled to her feet, pushing the tight blanket from her body. "This was a huge mistake," she mumbled, scooping up her dress.

Jace sat up, questioning. "Go? Why?"

Daisy's eyes searched his and she laid her hand on his cheek. "Because you put our daughter in danger by coming here. You have to leave."

"Leave? No—" He held her wrist. "Doesn't this say anything to you?" He swept his free hand toward the rumpled blanket and their strewn clothing.

Daisy looked at the aftermath of their lovemaking. "It says goodbye, Jace." Shaking her head, she gently pulled her hand from his grasp.

"Goddamn it! Don't do this, Daisy. You forget I have a right to see Jenny. I'm her father."

She swallowed the tears tightening her throat. "No, Jace. It'll confuse her and she's so little, she's bound to talk. You could be seen, and there's no telling what the packs will do. Jenny is both Cochran and Matthews. Both sides would rally to protect her. Father or not, you're undead."

Jaw tight, he exhaled hard. "You're right, but I don't care."

"Maybe you don't, but I do." She locked eyes with him, but they were at a stalemate, with nothing left to say. "It'll be dawn in a few hours, Jace. There's no shelter up here, so unless you can withstand the strong Texas sun, you'll need to find cover."

He didn't take his eyes from hers. "I'm not leaving, Daisy. I'll be here waiting every night until I convince you."

Chapter Six

"Mommy?" Jenny peeked through the door, her dark eyes and little nose visible through the crack despite the darkness.

Daisy rolled over, tossing her arm over her forehead. "Hey, peanut. What's the matter?"

The little girl pushed the door all the way open and climbed onto the bed with her mother.

"Can I sleep in your bed tonight?" she asked with eyes like saucers.

Daisy held open the covers and let her scoot in beside her. She wrapped her arm around her daughter's waist and snuggled in tightly.

"Bad dream, sweetheart?"

Jenny nodded. Her silky hair tickling Daisy's neck. "I dreamed there was a man in my room."

Daisy's eyes snapped open wide. "Was it Grandpa?"

"Nope." The little girl shook her head.

"You sure it wasn't a dream, honey?"

She nodded. "I'm sure—Mommy?"

"Hmmm."

"You remember how Grandpa Carson taught me how to see things with my nose?"

"Mmhmm," Daisy replied, trying to hide her sudden annoyance at Jace's father. Jenny was too young to learn about shifting.

"The man in my room didn't smell like nothin'."

Daisy's chest tightened along with her grip.

"Mommy! You're holding me too hard!"

Daisy relaxed her grip even as her mind raced. "Everything on Earth has a smell, peanut. You must have dreamed it."

Jenny didn't say anything at first. "Promise?"

Daisy kissed the back of her head and snuggled in. "Pinky promise. Now, go to sleep."

She glanced at the clock on the nightstand. Dawn was too close for it to be Jace. She chewed on her lip. Seth wouldn't dare, and besides, Jenny would recognize him. Maybe it was just a bad dream.

She listened to the soft rise and fall of her daughter's sleep. At least one of them would get some rest tonight.

∽

"You look awful," Aimee said, pouring herself a cup of coffee with a shot of Jameson Irish. "Want one?" She chuckled holding up the green glass bottle. "Maybe the better question is, need one?"

"Need, definitely, and hold the coffee," Daisy replied.

Aimee poured two fingers high into a cut-glass tumbler and dropped in a few ice cubes. "Must be pretty bad for you to drive all this way. What did Seth do now?"

"This isn't about Seth. I really need to talk to you, Aims."

Aimee handed her the whiskey. "Well, I cancelled my afternoon appointments. I'm all yours, darlin'."

Daisy got up from the off-white couch and walked to the high-rise window overlooking the Houston cityscape.

"How do you breathe up here with no windows?" she muttered.

Aimee turned her green eyes toward her friend, watching as she fidgeted, moving from the desk to the end table, to the window. "Daisy, for God's sake, settle somewhere and talk to me. You didn't drive two hours to talk about the air quality of my apartment."

"I kicked Seth to the curb."

Aimee exhaled, nodding. "I'm glad to hear it, Dais, but you could have told me that over the phone."

"My father agrees with the decision, as well. It turns out your gut feeling about him was right. He was more interested in the ranch and what he could gain, than me or Jenny."

Aimee studied her friend. "I'm sorry, Daisy."

She shook her head and sat on the loveseat with her whiskey still untouched. "Don't be. Anyone who tells my daughter she should be put down, deserves his balls in a pair of gelding sheers, and that's exactly what'll happen if he shows his face again."

"You okay?" Aimee smirked. "I mean short of contemplating a felony with the intent to injure."

Daisy burst out laughing. "I miss having you around, Aims. Really."

Aimee put her coffee mug on the glass end table and regarded Daisy, the dark smudges under her eyes and the way she chewed on her lip.

"What's the real reason you needed to see me today, Dais? Don't lie to me, now."

Daisy scrubbed her face with one palm, before circling her temples with the tips of her fingers. "Jace showed up at the ranch last night."

Aimee smacked her thigh with her hand "I knew it!" She got up and walked back and forth in front of her coffee table. "This is exactly what I hoped would happen."

"I'm not so sure I share your enthusiasm, Aims. It's complicated."

"What's so complicated? You love him, and he obviously still loves you. Wolves aren't the only shifter species with keen senses, and mine tell me, you not only want him, but *had* him in spades last night. I can smell the sex on you from here, so don't even bother denying it."

Daisy put her whiskey on the coffee table. "I don't deny it, but sex doesn't change anything. There's a lot more to consider than mutual attraction."

"Okay, but being from different supernatural species doesn't make you mutually exclusive," Aimee countered.

"Aims, you forget the part where he lives on blood and can't survive sunlight."

She shrugged. "No relationship comes without compromise."

"I came to terms with Jace being a vampire last night." Heat crawled up her cheeks as images flashed into memory.

Aimee gave her friend a wicked smile. "That good, huh? You'll have to give me the juicy details to add to my fetish list."

"That is *so* not happening."

"You can't blame me for trying. Still, you two can make a life together, Daisy. I'm not saying it'll be easy, but you're a fool not to take what you want simply because Jace is undead. Vampires are a part of our shrouded world. It's that simple."

Daisy's face sobered. "I won't lie. I'm afraid, Aimee. The situation with Jace has put Jenny's life in danger. I'm not sure how to handle it."

"In danger how? From Jace?" Aimee shook her head. "I don't see that. Especially since you admitted you two had hot monkey sex last night. You don't have to show me the faint puncture wounds for me to know he fed from you last night. It's understood. He didn't hurt you, or worse, take your life. It's clear he's not a common youngblood in the way most are, aggressive, reckless. My guess is Jace has had guidance in controlling his baser impulses."

"*Jesus*, Aimee. When did clairvoyance become an avian trait?"

"It's not clairvoyance, Daisy. Research and common sense. Sex and blood are linked for vampires. It's part of their circle of life, if you can call their existence, life."

Daisy tipped the edge of her whiskey glass toward her friend. "You amaze me, Aims, truly. But that's not it at all. I have no worries about Jace and Jenny. In fact, I think given the chance, he'd be a good father. There's an outside threat."

She patted the loveseat for Aimee to sit and told her the story about Violet.

"Holy crap!" Aimee's jaw hung slack.

Daisy slumped against the back of the small couch. "So you see. It's not quite as simple as you think."

Aimee got up and went around her desk to her laptop and started typing.

"What are you doing?"

"I'm calling in a favor. Someone I think might be able to help with this."

"Who?" Daisy sat up straight.

Aimee glanced up from her screen. "Don't worry about that, yet. I can't do or say anything until I hear back."

She closed her laptop, and then walked around her desk to the narrow credenza against the wall. "In the meantime, let's go shopping and get you a sexy little number to wear for your icy hot vampire tonight."

"What's the use?" Daisy shrugged. "I told Jace to leave."

Aimee stopped with her purse halfway to her shoulder. "When?"

"After he told me Violet promised to kill his whole family."

She angled her head, her brows knotted. "So after you reconnected, then?"

"If that's a fancy way of asking if it was after we hooked up, then yes."

She grinned, shoving her purse the rest of the way up. "He'll be back. If not tonight, then tomorrow."

Daisy opened her mouth, but then closed it again, and the self-censorship wasn't lost on Aimee.

"What?" she asked.

Daisy shook her head. "I'm sure it's nothing, but Jenny crawled into my bed at half past four this morning. She claimed there was someone in her room. Someone with no scent. She thought it was a man, but whoever it was frightened her."

Aimee hesitated. "And you think it was Jace?"

"No, that's just it. It was too close to dawn for it to be him. I left him by the big oak in the north pasture. He didn't have much time to find decent shelter. Impulse control or not, the sun is still deadly for him."

"Then who could it be?"

Daisy lifted a hand. "That's just it, I don't know."

"Seth?"

She shook her head again. "He's too much of a pussy. Maybe it was nothing, and Jenny dreamed it."

Aimee inhaled, pressing her lips together. "Perhaps. Perhaps not. Keep a close eye on her. Just in case."

✑

"I'm back!" Daisy put her keys and purse on the hall table. "Anybody home?"

Nothing.

She walked into the kitchen and snapped on the light. Leaning against the cookie jar in the center of the table was a note. She picked it up and tore open the top.

Daisy,

I took Jenny to the Matthews's. She insisted. They're going to keep her for the night.

Dad.

Damn. What was she supposed to do now? Call and tell them their granddaughter can't stay because a psychotic vampire was using death threats to manipulate Jace?

She dug her cell out of her purse and dialed Aimee.

"Daisy? Is everything okay?"

"Dad took Jenny to Carson and Elinor's place. Should I worry?"

"I don't know. Maybe you should find Jace and discuss this with him. He's her father."

Daisy exhaled into the phone. "You're no help, you know that."

"Yes, I am, and you love me. Go find your man and put him on the case."

"Ugh"

"Love you, too."

Daisy hit end and shoved her phone into her bag. Where the hell could he be holed up? She glanced out the window at the sky. Heavy clouds and drizzle, and the sun hadn't quite set.

The Weather Channel warned of a storm brewing, which meant it would be a thousand times worse the closer she got to the north edge along the mesa. Hail, flooding, and tornados. It was that time of year.

Damn. She wasn't going to risk driving when the weather could change on a dime.

Digging her phone out again, she dialed her almost-in-laws to check on Jenny.

"Hi, Ellie! It's me. How's the peanut?"

"She's fine, sweetheart."

"The weather says there's a squall coming. You know what a handful she can be during a storm. Are you sure you want her for the night?"

"Your father helped Carson set a cot in our room for Jenny, so she will be close to us all night, and she can always curl up with me if it comes to that. It's no problem. We'll drive her home tomorrow."

Daisy hung up after talking to Jenny. It was all good. She hoped.

The clock struck seven thirty p.m. She took her bags from shopping with Aimee and headed upstairs to get cleaned up and relax.

Dropping the bags on the bed, she opened the pink striped lingerie bag and took out the tissue wrapped teddy and matching lace thigh highs.

The garment was silk and black lace, with open cup breasts and a crotch-less bottom. She rolled it up and stuck it back in the bag. Aimee was nuts. She'd never dare wear anything like this.

Still —

She bit her lip. She could always wear her fuzzy pink robe over it.

Grabbing the bag, she headed into the bathroom to shower. She turned on the spray, stripped and stepped into the water. Washing quickly, she shampooed, rinsed and repeated as directed and then got out to shave her legs and moisturize, adding a dab of scent between her breasts and behind each ear.

She wiggled the teddy up her smooth legs and straightened the straps and the crotch.

Ugh. Talk about uncomfortable.

Slipping her robe on, she opened the bathroom door and padded over to the bed.

Who was she fooling? Jace was a vampire, and without an invitation it was impossible for him to cross any threshold into the house.

She towel-dried her hair and ran her fingers through the curling mass, dropping the damp terrycloth on the floor. Picking up the remote she turned on Pandora for music, and then lay back closing her eyes.

Exhausted, sleep found her easily and her eyes drooped. She curled into her pillow, the taste of Jace's lips on her mind as she fell into misty slumber

Chapter Seven

She sighed in her sleep, inhaling as her back arched up into delicious tingles skimming across her skin. Feathery kisses tickled the sensitive underside of her breasts and soft breath puckered her nipples.

Her eyes flew open to a smirk and a pair of teasing eyes, and she scrambled up toward the headboard.

"Good evening." Jace winked, mimicking Bella Lugosi's famous vampire accent.

Her shoulders slumped and she shoved at his shoulder. "Jace! I almost had a heart attack."

He shook his head, lifting the underside of her wrist to his lips. "Your heart is fine, and its tempo is a country love song."

Inhaling, he ran his tongue along the soft flesh and blue veins just beneath.

"Okay, Romeo," she said pulling her hand back. "How did you get in the house?"

He laughed, rolling onto his elbow beside her. "This is some getup. Open access crotch-less black lace and a pink grandma fleece robe." He lifted a fuzzy sleeve, letting it drop. "Now that's hot!"

"I didn't invite you in, Jace. Just the opposite. I told you it wasn't a good idea for you to stick around."

He sat up, taking her hand in his. "You made that speech on the north edge. Technically, you never rescinded your invitation to the house."

"I don't understand."

"That means my original welcome still stands. Consider it grandfathered in. Of course, you could always throw me out and that would be the end of that," he said with a shrug.

Her eyes took in his clean clothes and freshly washed hair curling against the crew neck collar of his T-shirt. He even shaved.

"You look good, Jace. Where've you been holed up?"

"The empty riders' cabin on the far ridge."

"Also grandfathered in, I suppose." Daisy watched him watching her. "We spent a lot of time in there, as well."

His eyes took on a faraway look, and he smiled. "My first time."

She smiled back, giving his hand a small squeeze. "Mine, too."

"Talk about a comedy of errors." He laughed. "I don't think two teenagers were ever more awkward."

"We broke the lamp."

He laughed out loud. "Hell, we broke the bed. Your dad had the sheriff up thinking it was poachers."

"I couldn't find my panties from that night and was scared stiff the sheriff would find them and send them off for forensic testing." Daisy snorted a laugh.

"You watch too much television. We live in Texas, not New York and certainly not Hollywood."

Her gaze dropped to their entwined hands. "Speaking of New York. Why were you so angry at the bar?"

"I sensed you were there. Your scent is tattooed on my brain, and knowing you were so close but so far —" He let his words trail off.

"And anger was your first choice emotion?" she asked, lifting her eyes.

He shook his head. "No. I wasn't angry at you. I was angry at the vampire stalking that girl at the bar. Sensing you just added a layer of frustration to everything else.

"The girl had too much to drink and that made her easy prey. Vampires are predators, but I've got my own code of ethics. I don't glamor, and I don't take advantage of people who don't have their senses about them."

"Like what Violet did with you."

He nodded.

"So you followed to make sure the drunken twit was okay?"

Jace's eyes found hers. "That's unkind, Daisy, but in a nutshell, yeah."

"But you weren't around when I saw those two in a bondage room with another vampire, and your damsel in distress seemed to enjoy herself, in spades."

Stunned, he eyed her. "What were you doing in a bondage room?"

"I stumbled in by mistake looking for you."

"What makes you think I would be in a bondage room?" His voice rising in disbelief.

She sat up. "I didn't. I was checking random rooms."

Jace got up and walked from the end of the bed, wheeling on his heel to face her. "Of all the stupid reckless things you've done, this one takes the cake. The Red Veil is a vampire club. You knew that, and you also knew the backrooms were for fetish and fantasy with blood play.

"Knowing all that, you still decided it was a good idea to go looking for me in random playrooms where vampires are fucking and feeding. *Jesus*, God, woman!"

Daisy's chin dropped to her chest. "I didn't think. I just reacted. I was so hell bent on getting answers from you, it sort of just happened."

He sat on the edge of the bed again and reached to lift her chin. "Come on. Let's get out of here. We both need some fresh air."

She glanced at her exposed breasts and the satin straps crisscrossing her belly toward the open crotch. "I need to change."

He shook his head. "Leave it. Just throw on a pair of jeans and a T-shirt over that and let's go."

"Go where?"

"For a drive, like we used to."

"It's storming out, Jace. We can't drive in that."

"This, from a woman brave enough to barge in on a vampire bondage feast." He held out his hand to help her off the bed.

She grinned. "Okay, but we have a little girl to think about, remember?"

His eyes found hers and held. "We?"

She nodded. "You said it last night. She's your daughter, too."

He pulled her into his arms and kissed her, his hand in her hair at the nape of her neck.

When he broke their kiss, Daisy rested her head on his chest. It was warm, but silent and she squeezed her eyes closed against the reminder of what he was now and what he had endured.

"*Ssh*…don't, Daisy. I smell your worry and fear. We'll figure it out. I'm just happy you're willing to give me the chance."

She nodded beneath the hollow of his throat. "I have a question."

"Shoot."

"Last night when you—climaxed," she paused, embarrassed.

"Go on."

"Well, you howled. And there was a trace of Were in your scent. Can you still shift? Even though you're a vampire, are you still Were? The moon is nearly full. Do you feel its pull?"

"I don't really know. I still feel the pull of the moon, but the urge to shift is dulled to the point of being nil." He shrugged. "I've never met another Were who was turned, so I have no one to guide me. I guess I'll figure that one out as time passes."

She nodded again. "One more thing. Were you in Jenny's room last night?"

He stepped back, his eyes searching hers. "No. Why?"

She held both his hands. "I'm not sure. She crawled into my bed claiming there was someone in her room that had no scent. She thinks it was a man."

He glanced away, thinking before looking back at her. "And it wasn't a bad dream?"

"I thought so myself, but with what you told me about Violet, I'm not sure."

Jace let go of her hands and stalked toward her closed bedroom door.

"She's not here, Jace. She's with your parents."

He turned and looked at her, stunned. "They know she's mine?"

Daisy nodded. "Of course. I found out I was pregnant the week after you disappeared. I went to the doctor thinking I missed my period because of the stress, but the rabbit done died."

She smiled softly. "Your mom and dad have been wonderful to me and Jenny. Your mother even insisted for a while I call her mom, but I couldn't. It didn't seem right."

In two steps he had her in his arms again. "I'll make this right. I swear it, Dais."

She shook her head. "We'll make it right, together." She inhaled and took a step back. "Come on, cowboy. I suddenly feel like dancing in the rain."

⌇

Jace pulled up to the riders' cabin and parked Daisy's truck, out back. The rain pelted the dirt and grass surrounding the small log structure, gathering in large puddles ringed with hail.

"Still feel like dancing?"

Daisy flinched as the frozen mix bounced off the windshield. "Maybe later. I'm not into getting pounded by sky rocks."

Jace leaned in, tweaking her braless nipple beneath the thin fabric of her tee. "What are you into being pounded by?"

He took her mouth, his hands roaming the soft curves of her body. "Ready to make a run for it?" he asked against her lips.

She slid his hand down to the loose waistband of her jeans and he slipped his fingers inside, her wetness clear on his fingertips. "I'd say I'm ready for whatever you have to give."

He groaned, taking his hand from her jeans and licked the slickness. "God bless crotch-less."

She laughed and opened the door, glancing at him once more before sprinting for the cabin's backdoor and the cover of the roof's pitched overhang.

"It's unlocked," Jace called from behind. He followed her inside, shaking the rain from the brim of his Stetson.

Taking the hat from his head, he tossed it onto the knotty pine kitchen table and walked toward the fireplace.

The cabin was nothing more than a studio sized living room with a small adjoining bunk house to accommodate ranch hands and riders.

Jace knelt at the hearth and started a fire. "There's no bed in here, if you recall. But the couch is comfy."

Daisy shook her head and instead toyed with the frayed fabric of one of the rustic armchairs in front of the fireplace.

"The fire feels good. Warm," she replied, and walked to where Jace still knelt.

She lifted her T-shirt over her head and tossed it onto the couch, slipping her jeans from her hips, as well. She bent for the crumpled denim, letting the teddy's bare cups showcase her full breasts.

"You're killing me, Dais," Jace croaked, licking his lips.

She pitched her jeans onto the couch as well and stood in front of him in her teddy and her cowboy boots, her legs a little more than shoulder width apart.

"Does that mean you don't want this," she asked coyly, dragging a finger between her pussy lips.

Jace reached for her hips, sliding his palms around the full curve of her ass. He pulled her sex to his mouth and licked her from anus to clit, swirling his tongue over her hard bud.

Daisy fisted his hair and spread her legs farther, urging his mouth for more.

With a sideways grin he obliged, pulling her hard nub through his teeth. She hissed, and he reached for the base of the couch not missing a beat.

Jace pulled his face away and licked her slick juice from his lips. "I have a surprise for you." Opening the bag, he took out two silver silicone covered balls and dangled them from his fingers.

"What are they?"

"They're called Venus balls and they go inside," he slipped two fingers into her slit and curled them up making her gasp.

"As you move, they vibrate, and when you come, it's supposed to be amazing." He curled his fingers more, swirling her spot. "Wanna give them a try?"

"Where did you get them? How?"

He chuckled. "Vampires are very ingenious and sneaky when we want to be. Don't ask."

She leaned down and kissed his mouth, grinning against his lips. "I'm game, if you are."

Jace squeezed a drop of lube on his fingers and spread it over the balls and the silken cord connecting them. He leaned up and licked Daisy's pussy, groaning as he slipped one and then the other inside her swollen entrance.

"You said they vibrate when I move. What should I do?" she asked, heat flushing her skin at the illicit feel.

"Bend over." Jace guided her to the armchair and bent her over the cushions. Her tits hung, swinging and he stepped behind her cupping each one, the rough feel of his jeans against the sheer fabric of the teddy making her pussy drip.

He rolled her nipples between his thumb and index finger, pulling and pinching the hard peaks, squeezing the full flesh of each breast.

She moaned and let go with one hand, sliding his fingers over her belly to her mound.

"Hang on, darlin'," he whispered behind her ear.

Jace swirled his fingers over her wet sex, his thumb pressed against her clit. She gasped as he moved the pad of his thumb, the rhythm and pressure faster and harder until she cried out. He ground his thick denim bulge into her ass, the two together rocketing Daisy to near climax.

"I want you, Jace," she cried.

"You want the balls out?"

She shook her head. "No, I want both at the same time."

Stunned he pulled his hand away to free his dick and then hooked one finger into the teddy's crotch-less opening, ripping the sheer fabric up her back. With his palm, he spread lube from her pussy to her ass, gliding the rest over his thick cock.

"Are you sure?" he growled, his hand fisting his hard shaft, waiting.

With a gasp, Daisy nodded and that was all the invitation Jace needed. He spread her cheeks and plunged his cock into her ass.

Daisy whimpered, pitching forward onto the chair's cushion with the force and Jace curled his arm around her waist, steadying her.

He pulled back, moving slowly, letting her body adjust to his girth. The exacting motion and the pressure left her gasping for more. He thrusted deeper, harder, letting her feel his corded thickness against the thin membrane separating him from the silicone balls.

With each plunge, the balls rotated, rolling along the length of him along Daisy's inner walls. She cried out and he swirled her clit with his fingers, working her as he drove his cock in and out. Her tight hole squeezed him, and he threw his head back, ready to cum.

Daisy reached down and covered his hand, working her body along with him. She shuddered, crying out as she crested climax, letting go with a howl as she ground her ass back, taking Jace's full cock.

He snarled, grasping her hips, pulling back and then driving deeply, jets spurting in spasms as he came.

Daisy slumped forward and Jace held her as the last of her orgasm shook her lower body.

He held her close, riding the aftershocks with her. He pulled his member from her body, and then reached to slip the balls from her still sensitive entrance, wrapping them in a hand towel from the bag.

"I need a shower, but I doubt I can stand," Daisy teased.

"No problem." Jace scooped her into his arms and carried her to the bathroom. He set her on the closed toilet and ran the shower spray until the small bath filled with steam.

"After you," he said holding the shower curtain for her.

Daisy stepped into the spray, taking Jace's hand to lead him in after.

She let the water cascade over her body, sighing in the warm feeling.

Jace worked the bar of soap in his hand to a lather, spreading the frothy bubbles over Daisy's body, washing her gently everywhere and in between.

She moaned at the feel of his hands skimming over her skin, her body hypersensitive and ready to burst. She continued their foamy foreplay, washing him and caressing his cock to stiffness in her soapy hand.

"Round two?" he asked, not waiting for her to reply as he lifted her to the wall, driving his member into her soft folds.

He plunged into her hard and fast and Daisy clutched to his neck, locking her legs around his back against the slippery suds.

He groaned, burying his head in her shoulder as he pumped his hips. Daisy's breath came short and fast and her heart raced as she neared climax again.

Jace tightened his grip, cupping her ass against the tile as he ground his cock deeper. Her body reacted, convulsing around his thick shaft and he roared, his fangs finding the thick vein in her throat and piercing the flesh as she came.

Daisy cried out holding his head to her, blood, soap and water raining over her chest as he fed. He swiped the wound with his tongue sealing the puncture and threw his head back, his cock jerking inside her as he emptied himself into her again.

He let her down easy and the two rested against the warm tile, letting clean water wash away what was left of their play.

Chapter Eight

The fire crackled in the grate and the two snuggled naked on the couch, wrapped in a Native American style blanket, Daisy dozing in Jace's arms.

"You're staring at me," she said with a teasing half grin.

He leaned down to kiss the tip of her nose. "There's no better view as far as I'm concerned."

She swung her legs over the cushion and sat up, rubbing her eyes. "What time is it?"

"Nearly two. Are you hungry? I'm not sure what I can offer, but I saw a storeroom. I'm sure there are provisions."

She shook her head. "I feel fine, actually. Considering you've fed from me twice, I'm a little surprised I haven't keeled over."

He chuckled. "I didn't take that much. You're a Were. I don't have to. Plus, it's part of sex play, not really for feeding, but if you're concerned, I won't do it again."

"No, it's part of our play. As long as it's safe for me as well as for you, I'm okay."

"You're more than okay. Weres produce red blood cells thousands of times faster than humans. What I take out is replenished within hours."

He considered her. "There's another component I should tell you about as well."

"What?"

"Now that I've taken your blood, you wear my mark, at least temporarily."

"Your mark?" She lifted her hand to her throat. "Can people see it?"

He shook his head. "Only other vampires. But don't worry. You're a Were, so the mark wears off quickly. It has to do with blood replenishment and the waxing of the moon. On humans it lasts for a very long time."

"Does it work in reverse?

"Reverse?"

Daisy nodded. "Will you wear my mark if I took your blood?"

He laughed out loud. "No, that's a completely different thing, but what wearing my mark will do is allow me to locate you at any time, if necessary."

"Hmmm." Daisy didn't really comment, just looked toward the door and the window. "It looks like the storm passed. I should check my phone."

"What for?"

She looked at him, cocking a brow. "Jenny. She might have called looking for me."

"I thought you said she was with my folks. What are you worried about?" he asked, puzzled.

"Already a typical daddy." She laughed getting up to get her purse from the table. "They never sweat the small stuff."

Padding naked into the kitchen area, she stood by the door, the moonlight spilling in behind her.

"You're beautiful, Dais. Truly."

She turned to him and smiled. "So are you."

Taking her phone, she dropped her bag on the table and walked to the couch with a frown.

"What's the matter? What happened?"

She shook her head. "Nothing, it's just Aimee texted me a half hour ago. It's not like her to text so late."

"Maybe the storm had something to do with it. Service interruption."

She nodded, scrolling through the message. "Probably."

"What does she want?"

"Hmmm..." Daisy replied non-committedly as she read.

"Dais—what does Aimee want. She's the only other person who knows I'm back."

"What? Oh, sorry, Jace. Yes, it has to do with you. Or us, I should say."

"Daisy, you're not making any sense."

She exhaled putting the phone down. "Aimee thinks she might have someone who can help us with our situation with Violet. She had to call in a favor, so the individual must be a heavy hitter. I don't know who it is, so don't ask, but she set up a meeting for tomorrow afternoon."

She paused, looking at him. "Where is Violet now? Whoever Aimee has lined up, is going to want as much info as I can provide."

Jace inhaled, lifting one shoulder and letting it drop. "I haven't seen or spoken to Violet in over a year. She thinks she's got me under her thumb, believing the distractions at The Red Veil are enough to keep me in line. She doesn't put much stock in fate, though karma has a strange way of having its way, regardless."

He leaned in to kiss Daisy's cheek. "So, you're driving to Houston again tomorrow?"

Daisy nodded. "I have to meet Aimee's surprise guest myself, though I can't imagine it's one of your adjudicators. The meeting is in the afternoon. I'm guessing this person is a high-powered Were."

Jace shook his head. "That's not necessarily true. Very old vampires, especially elders, can day-walk like humans. Aimee is a pretty renowned psychoanalyst. I even knew that before you and I reconnected. She's helped field some of the worst cases of abuse known to the supernatural world." He paused at the look on Daisy's face. "I can't believe you didn't know that."

"I did. I mean, I do. She travels so much, that when she comes home, we just hang out as friends. She doesn't talk shop."

"Maybe coming home is a way for her to separate herself from the sick shit she hears from her patients. It's got to be hard."

"What do you mean?"

"We share the supernatural world, but while Weres and shifters have rites of passage into the fullness of their dual natures, vampires do not. No one has been born into the race of the undead in centuries. Most vampires are made, that's why we refer to whoever turned us as our makers, not parents."

"You're not telling me anything I don't already know."

"It's not the process, Daisy. It's the way the turning was executed. Pardon the death pun. In my world, if a vampire is created in cruelty, with lust and violence, when they first wake to darkness those are the only emotions they recall.

"These vampires are dangerous. They are without conscience and the most predatory of our kind. But if a human is turned with kindness and compassion, then they retain the full spectrum of human emotion. Good and bad. Like regular people. This is where Aimee is renowned. She's worked with vampires and Weres alike who have lost their humanity and suffer for it."

Daisy considered him, the fire crackling in the background throwing golden light and shadow onto Jace's handsome face.

"What about vampires who have no recollection of being turned?" she asked.

He gave her a soft, knowing smile. "You mean me, don't you?"

She nodded.

"I'm an anomaly. I've never met another Were turned vampire, and I've never heard of anyone being changed while under the influence of a memory-altering drug. So, I don't know how to answer except to say, apart from obvious differences, I feel exactly the same as before I was changed."

Daisy understood what he meant by obvious differences, and she didn't miss the shadow across his eyes as he owned the fact.

He moved his gaze to the fire, watching the flames dance. "That first year and a half was a nightmare. I had a hard time getting a handle on my thirst, but not once did I forget what it felt to love. I wouldn't have ached for so long if I didn't have a strong link to my left over humanity."

Daisy lifted a hand to his cheek forcing him to look at her. His eyes were melancholy and full of regret, and it broke her heart.

"Jace, none of what happened to you is your fault. You were dealt a horrible hand. We both were. We're strong and we found each other again. Doesn't that say something?"

He turned his face to her palm and kissed the soft skin before meeting her eyes again. "It does, but I can't help but blame myself. If I hadn't been so hellfire determined to have an all-out bachelor party, this might not have happened. Had I been more reserved, more mature—"

"Stop it," she replied cutting him off. "Violet would have found you one way or another and you know it. A different time, perhaps, but nothing would've postponed the inevitable. Talk like this only serves to fester on something you couldn't control."

She jerked his chin to make a point. "Now we need to focus on finding help to protect you and Jenny, and that's where Aimee comes in."

He took her hand from his face and kissed the underside of her wrist, resting it back in her lap. "If anyone has the contacts to help us, it's her."

"Did she help this Carlos person you mentioned?" Daisy asked.

Jace shook his head. "Not directly. She worked with his mate. She was human and near death at the hands of one of Carlos's adversaries. He changed her and she had a hard time because of the torture she was put through beforehand. Aimee worked together with Carlos to heal Trina. Aimee has helped a lot of vampires in similar situations."

Daisy inhaled turning her gaze to the fire. "No wonder she wanted to go to New York for the weekend. I wonder if it was because she needed to check up on patients. I told you, she's got a real fascination with the undead. In fact, she's been nagging me to tell her about the bondage ménage I witnessed."

Jace ran a finger down Daisy's bare arm, letting his knuckle graze the side of her breast. "If memory serves, you were completely aroused when I ran into you in the backrooms."

He cupped her breast, running a thumb over her nipple, watching her face as the bud puckered at his touch. "Seems to me you've got a fascination with fetish and sex outside the box, too."

She swallowed, leaning back to let him claim her nipple with his mouth, arching up with a gasp. He released the furrowed flesh with a pop and rolled the nub, pinching it between his fingers.

Daisy cried out and moved her hand between her legs to touch herself.

He tweaked her nipple again. "How about we take a trip back to The Red Veil once we settle everything with Jenny. I have something in mind I think you're going to want."

"Maybe, but I know something I definitely want right now," she murmured.

Daisy moved to straddle Jace's lap, looking at him over her shoulder as she lowered her swollen, wet pussy onto his waiting cock, reverse cowboy style.

He leaned up, cupping both breasts as she rotated her hips back and up, milking his member. "Ride'em, cowgirl," he groaned, sinking his fangs into her throat again.

Chapter Nine

"*D*aisy, this is Francisco César. He might be able to help you and Jace."

That was Aimee's cue for Daisy to introduce herself.

"I don't know what to say, Mr. César," Daisy replied, holding out her hand to the gentleman. "Any help you could provide with keeping this vampire in check would be appreciated."

The man raised one eyebrow at Daisy's disapproving tone attached to the title vampire, but he didn't comment.

Aimee caught his quizzical stare and placed a drink tray on the coffee table with a little less finesse than usual.

"Coffee?" she asked, lifting a delicate cup and saucer, purposely turning her head from Francisco to give Daisy a pointed look.

Daisy noted the decanter on the tray beside Aimee's porcelain coffee pot, its red contents too dark for even the boldest burgundy and her eyes widened, realizing her gaffe.

"Can I tempt you with a libation, Francisco?"

"How kind." The vampire's clipped response left Daisy inwardly cringing. She'd let years of instilled prejudice ruin their meeting before it even began.

Aimee lifted the carafe and swirled the red liquid, the viscous quality coating the inside of the glass as she poured.

"Still warm." Francisco gave Daisy a small smile as though acknowledging her slight was unintended. "But what else should I expect from one as lovely and thoughtful as Dr. Aimee Dunne." He lifted the glass in salute, draining the contents.

The man's slightly accented voice carried a faint lisp. Handsome despite the trails of blue veining beneath his pale skin. He held himself with an old world demeanor.

It was not quite noon and the sun beat hard through the apartment's floor to ceiling windows.

"Excuse me, Francisco, but wouldn't you be more comfortable in a room less bright?" Daisy offered in amends.

He spared a glance for Aimee before answering. "You need not concern yourself, my dear. I am of an age where the sun no longer poses a threat."

He waved a dismissive hand toward the windows. "On extremely robust days, perhaps a mere inconvenience of warmth, but no more."

He flashed a bright smile, the points of his fangs discreetly retracted. Clearly the man had learned to assimilate and camouflage when necessary.

Aimee poured Daisy a cup of coffee and handed her a creamer full of whiskey. "I think you need the strong stuff, Dais."

The elder vampire chuckled. "This is actually a delight. It's been over a century since I've unsettled a young woman. My life as an adjudicator general is both repetitive and dull. He lifted his empty glass in salute. "Thank you, my dears. Truly."

"Francisco was a conquistador." Aimee nodded, impressed. "He was part of Cabot's expeditions in South America."

"Yes, yes—but that was a long time ago, and unfortunately where my human life ended. Not many know the dark magic found in the jungle or the terrors that lurk."

He paused remembering. "I didn't have the expertise of Dr. Dunne to help me recover my human equilibrium.

It was difficult, but now I do what I can with the adjudicators across the country."

"Adjudicators? Are you familiar with Carlos…*uhm*…" Daisy snapped her fingers trying to recall the name Jace mentioned. "Salazar, yes…Carlos Salazar of New York?"

Both sets of eyes turned to her in surprise.

"Jace told me how his new wife had her troubles assimilating to her new existence."

Francisco momentarily glanced at Aimee. "Yes, well—I know them, both. Not that they have anything to do with the situation you now face."

Daisy blinked at the clipped answer and put her coffee cup on the table. "Forgive me, Francisco. I didn't mean to overstep again."

"No one thinks that." Aimee patted Daisy's hand but shot her another pointed look.

Francisco burst out laughing. "Oh, if stares were daggers!" With an amused grin, he held his glass for Aimee to refill.

"So, down to business." He cleared his throat. "Aimee told me of your plight."

Daisy nodded. "Yes. This woman Violet is a bad piece of work."

He swirled the stem of his glass. "Violet Beaumont has not been an easy fix. Sanctions have been leveled by every adjudicator council in the country, yet she flouts us still."

He paused, regarding Daisy. "Has she threatened you or your child? Jenny is the natural child of an existing vampire, regardless of conception, and entitled to protection, as are you as his chosen mate."

Daisy bobbed her head. "She hasn't threatened us directly, only intimidated through Jace, promising murder if he doesn't abide by her demands." She paused. "Violet is Jace's maker."

The vampire curled his finger over his upper lip. "That complicates things." He looked at both women sitting across from him on the loveseat. "Has Jace renounced Violet in front of a council, officially rejecting her for her abuse?"

Daisy spread her hands. "I don't know, but I doubt it. I don't believe he realizes that's an option."

"Traditionally, it isn't. Your maker is your maker and that is that, but in recent cases, judgements were found in favor of severing the bond between maker and progeny if the maker is found to be unfit."

Daisy snorted. "Unfit? Try psychotic. She's been systematically killing the male children in Jace's family for over a century. The woman is completely off the reservation."

Francisco put his glass down and looked at Aimee. "Is this true? Is there a way to document these claims?"

Aimee shrugged. "If we had time to dig through pack archives, we might find a link to the original incident with Jace's great-grandfather, Micah."

He put his wineglass on the tray and stood with fluid grace. "I will need those documents if I am to approach the national council for an order of execution."

"Execution?" Daisy asked shocked.

Francisco turned his unblinking eyes to her. "What did you think, my dear? You cannot order a life sentence for an immortal being. It's impractical and leaves too much variable to time."

His gaze softened and he lifted a hand in a gesture of accord. "One family cannot be made to suffer such a scourge. It isn't fair or right. Repeated, unrelenting attacks on a single bloodline is something we will not tolerate, especially when the family in question is guiltless of harm."

With a nod, Aimee thanked the man and showed him out, promising to be in touch. She walked back and flopped onto the couch with an exhale. "I think it's time you let Jace's parents in on what's been happening."

Daisy nodded. "His father is on the council for the Matthews pack. It's the only way we'll get access to those records." She picked up the whiskey, pouring the rest into her cup, shooting it back with a wince. "I'll tell Jace tonight."

"Will he go for it?"

She shrugged. "He doesn't have a choice."

⤴

Daisy pulled up the gravel dirt drive, frowning since there were no cars in front of the house. Her phone battery died halfway back from Houston and she forgot her charger.

She parked and went inside, letting the screen door slam behind her. "Hello! I'm home," she called.

No answer.

Jace's father was set to pick up Jenny today from preschool and stay with her while Dad was out repairing sections of fence along the south pasture.

"Carson? Jenny?"

Still nothing.

The landline phone rang.

"Hello?"

"Daisy! Where the hell have you been? We've been calling you for hours," her father said, his voice shaking.

"My phone died, and I didn't have my charger. Why? What happened?"

"Carson's in the hospital. He's had a heart attack. You'd better come now."

"Oh my God! What happened?"

"Never mind that now. We'll tell you when you get here."

She gripped the phone, white knuckled. "Where's Jenny?"

"She's here with us. She's fine."

Daisy exhaled. "I'm on my way."

She hung up the phone. Jeb Cochran was never one to mince words. Something bad happened and her stomach flip-flopped at the thought it might be Violet.

She drove like a bat out of hell and screeched into the visitor's parking lot. If Carson died before Jace had a chance to reconcile with his parents, he'd spend the rest of his existence soaked in regret.

Daisy parked the car and didn't bother with the elevator. She took the stairs to the cardiac care wing and blew past the nurse's station, only hesitating at the door to Carson's room.

Sucking in a steadying breath, she turned the knob. Elinor was at Carson's side along with Sam Fisher, a Matthews pack elder and Carson's best friend.

Carson had an oxygen plug in his nose and was hooked up to a portable ECG monitor and IV drip. Elinor was in a chair beside the bed, holding his hand.

He nodded and tried to speak, but Elinor shushed him. "No exertion. Doctor's orders."

"Over here, Daisy," her father whispered from the couch where Jenny slept with her head on his lap.

She went to them, leaning over to smooth Jenny's hair from her forehead. "Why is she asleep? It's only four in the afternoon?"

Jeb raked a hand through his hair. "She's sedated."

"What? Why?" She looked from her dad to Elinor and Carson and back again. "Somebody better tell me what happened."

Carson waved his hand to get her attention, hushing his wife in the process.

"Stop fussing, Ellie. I had a minor infarction. Doc said I'll be fine." He spared a smile for his wife and then called Daisy over.

"I went to pick up Jenny as planned, but when I got there, she wasn't in her classroom. Those idiot teachers at the school let Seth take her out of the parent pickup line."

"Oh my God." Daisy sank onto the end of Carson's bed, knees weak.

"I flew around to the parking lot to catch him before he left with her." Carson gestured toward Jeb on the couch. "Your dad told me what happened with him. My guess is he was trying to use Jenny to get to you. But I stopped him. He put up quite a fight, but I chased him."

He coughed out a wheezy chuckle. "Took a nice chunk out of his leg, too." He pointed his thumb inward at his chest. "Not bad for an old wolf, even if I say so myself."

"Wait, are you telling me you phased on the fly in broad daylight?" she asked incredulous.

He nodded, sucking in a breath. "He got away, but I doubt he'll show his face again anytime soon. Of course, I had to improvise for clothes once I got back to Jenny.

"One of the other moms kept her while I went after that deadbeat. It was only afterward that I felt the pain in my arm and chest. The school called an ambulance and Ellie met me here with Sam. Your dad picked up Jenny."

Elinor turned her tearstained face to Daisy. "Jenny was hysterical. She was terrified. She saw her grandfather collapse. She kept going on and on about a man in her room with no scent."

Carson looked from his wife to Jeb and back. "The bastard Seth had no scent. What the hell is going on we don't know about?"

Daisy blinked. "Why do you say he had no scent? He's been around us plenty and he smells like any other human."

Carson shook his head. "Darlin', I had the man's leg in my jaws. He had no scent and his blood was strange. I can't put my finger on it."

She exhaled, patting Carson's leg. "I wouldn't stress over Seth. Jenny woke up afraid the other night claiming there was a man in her room.

"She told me you've been teaching her to *see* with her nose, and it's what she tried to do that night, only the person in her room had no scent. I thought it was just a bad dream. Now I know it was Seth. Goddamned creep."

"Doesn't matter now. Seth Cochran isn't going to get very far. Not with his calf muscle torn out. He's not Were, so he can't phase and heal. I got the sheriff to put out an all-points bulletin on him for attempted kidnapping."

"Who is this man?" Sam questioned.

Daisy looked at the elder and his puckered frown. "Seth is a friend. Was a friend. He's some kind of long lost cousin who showed up a year ago or so. He wanted more than friendship, but I didn't."

Sam frowned. "You mean he and your father wanted more than friendship for you."

"You watch your mouth, Fisher! What I do with my pack is none of your concern," Jeb Cochran huffed.

"It becomes my concern when your harebrained schemes to keep your land affect Matthews blood," Sam shot back.

"Enough! Everyone, please. We've got bigger problems than Seth Cochran," Daisy blasted.

All eyes turned, waiting. "What do you mean bigger problems?" her father asked.

She looked at the four sets of questioning eyes and finally blurted the words she'd been holding. "I saw Jace."

Elinor's eyes went wide. "When? Where? Where's he been for the last five years?"

Daisy shook her head. "It's a long story."

She told them everything and watched her father and Sam shut down, jaws clenched. Elinor dissolved into sobs and Carson was speechless, his eyes closed in pain.

"He's here now. At the ranch."

"What!" Her father stood, letting Jenny's head loll on the faded hospital couch cushions. "You let a bloodsucker on our land? Daisy, how could you?"

"It's Jace." She shrugged, but didn't back down or offer excuses.

"I don't care what he was to you, Daisy, he's not welcome. Not now, not ever," Sam interjected. "And now you tell us he's brought a rogue vampire into our midst? Don't you care at all for your daughter? Because if you don't, the Matthews pack certainly will!"

Jeb stalked forward, grabbing Sam by the collar. "You can say what you want about that bloodsucker, but my daughter is a good mother, and no one is taking Jenny."

Sam shoved Jeb from him. "She's such a good mother that she'd consider being a blood whore?"

Jeb swung cracking Sam in the face drawing blood. "Say another word, motherfucker, and they'll be tossing lilies over your dead body."

"Stop it!" Elinor yelled.

Sam pulled a wad of paper towels from the bathroom dispenser and held them to his nose. "Jace brought this to our doorstep, Ellie. He has to go."

Carson opened his eyes. "Jace didn't bring this to our doorstep, Sam. It's been with us for generations. I've known it, and if you're honest, you'd realize every other elder knows it, too. There's no curse. It's this Violet."

"Maybe Jace can get rid of her. If he does, it will be a service to his pack and worth a note or two in his favor, right?" Elinor's eyes pleaded.

"He's a vampire, Ellie! Nothing is going to change that," Sam shot back.

"Actually, Aimee has someone who can help, but we need pack records from the Matthews archive to prove what Violet has been doing all these years. I should warn you, the help I mentioned is the vampire adjudicator general."

Sam balked. "No. I refuse to let a bloodsucker anywhere near our records." He tossed the bloody paper towels into the trash and wiped the end of his nose on his sleeve.

"What the hell is an adjudicator general, anyway?" he asked. "Fucking vamps and their protocols. A silver stake and a good old fashioned bonfire to burn the pieces once we behead the sucker is what this calls for. Not a damn judiciary."

"Why?" Elinor stood, her eyes flashing. "We have a council of elders who debate the laws of our pack. What's the difference? Or have you appointed yourself judge and jury, Sam?"

"Frontier law, that's the difference, Ellie. At the end of a loaded shotgun, if need be. You can't be expected to be rational about this. Jace was your son."

She lifted her chin. "Jace is still my son."

"Stop it, everyone. We can deal with all that later. Right now we need to think about Jenny and how to keep her safe. We need to get her away from here and I think you're the one to take her, Dad," Daisy said.

"Me?" Jeb reiterated.

She nodded. "Until Carson is better, Elinor needs to be here with him, so you're the next best thing."

"What about my boy?" Elinor interjected.

Jeb turned his eyes to her, his gaze hard. "He's not your boy anymore, Ellie. Difficult as that is to accept, it's true."

Sam nodded. "Jeb's right."

Daisy shook her head. "You're both wrong. Jace is exactly the same as he was."

"Except for the undead part," Sam interrupted.

"You people need to get past what happened a century ago. You fight about bloodlines and the division of property and fuel a century long feud that started when one weak man fell prey to a vampire.

"It took Jace coming back into my life for me to realize everything our families have been fighting over is bullshit when the ones you love are sacrificed in the process.

"Matthews. Cochrans. We all come from the same two people. Eva and Noah. It's the same bloodline, and for the first time in however many generations, the proof of that is sleeping on the couch over there."

Daisy continued, shaking her head at the lot of them. "Jace is still Elinor and Carson's son. He's Jenny's father and the man I love, regardless what happened to transform him. If you can't accept that, then you're the ones who lose."

She gave Elinor a hug and then turned to scoop Jenny into her arms.

"Where are you going? You've been threatened too, Daisy. We need to hide both of you," her father questioned.

Daisy shook her head. "I thought that was best, but with your frame of mind regarding Jace, maybe it's better I handle things my way. I'm taking my daughter home, and then I'm taking her to meet her father."

Carson struggled to sit up, his eyes pained and sad. "No. Let your father keep her. He can take her to our beach house in Galveston. Jace doesn't know about it, so this

Violet won't know either. I'll be discharged tomorrow, and Ellie and I will join him while you, Jace, and Aimee figure this out."

He shot Sam a hard look. "If after all this is over, you still refuse to acknowledge my son, we're through, Sam. I mean it. You're my oldest friend, but you've never had kids of your own, so you have no idea what it's like to have them good as dead and then returned to you, even if they have changed."

"I'll tell Jace what you said, but I don't know what he'll choose," Daisy replied. "If he doesn't stay, this isn't over. We'll deal with Violet alone. But if he does decide to stay—"

Elinor put her hand on Daisy's cheek. "Don't give him a choice, sweetheart. Bring our boy home."

Chapter Ten

*T*he sun couldn't set fast enough as Daisy drove to the Riders' cabin. The last rays sunk below the horizon when she rounded the long dirt road from the main cut through.

Parking out back, she turned off the ignition and rushed for the screen door, but stopped with her hand on the knob.

The inside door was ajar.

Jace would never leave himself vulnerable during his death sleep hours.

Daisy looked back at the car, hesitating. Her purse and cellphone were on the front seat, but her UV flashlight was in her back pocket. Reaching around, she palmed the corrugated shaft just in case.

"Jace? You up?" Keeping her voice even, she pushed the door the rest of the way open.

The cabin was in shambles. Pieces of broken furniture and shattered glass scattered the wood floor from kitchen to living room, and a bloody swath dragged a path to the doorway.

"Jace?" she called again, but her plea was greeted by more silence and her heart sank.

Stomach clenched, she clicked on the flashlight. lowering the concentrated beam to the blood on the floor. The dark smear blackened and hissed the moment the UV waves touched the clotted mess, the air stinking the longer it held.

Tears flooded Daisy's eyes, blurring her vision. She sank to the floor and buried her face in her hands.

"I hate to trespass on this touching melodrama, but I'm going to anyway since you trespassed on mine."

Daisy's head jerked up and she blinked. A petite, redheaded woman with a short bob stared down at her. She was doll-like except for the blood smears on her clothing, making her resemble a deranged sprite.

Violet.

Pock marks scarred the hollows of both cheeks giving her white skin and underlying veins a silvery translucence in the dim light.

Daisy jerked the flashlight up aiming for the vampire's face, but the woman kicked it from her hand.

"You'll have to be faster than that, love. Inexperienced youngbloods fall for such tricks, but I haven't been a fledgling in almost a century and a half."

Daisy twisted to get to her feet, but Violet pushed her down. "You don't hear too well, do you, lovey?"

The vampire paused, straightening to listen to some unheard noise, and Daisy used the distraction to get to her feet.

The vampire was insane. Unstable, mean, irrational, so there was no reasoning with her. Talking was another thing. Aimee said most sociopaths have huge egos, so if Daisy got the woman talking, maybe she could buy some time.

She quickly scanned her options. Violet would rip her skin from her back if she tried to run. She needed a hook, something to get her to relax.

At least everyone knew she planned to meet Jace. If she wasn't in contact by morning, they'd come looking for her. That's if she lasted that long.

"Where is Jace?"

Violet turned her large amber eyes to her, tilting her head. "Wouldn't you like to know," she replied with a laugh. The tinkle was wrong, like off-key wind chimes.

Daisy watched the vampire pick at broken pieces of her hair. "Did you kill him?"

"Why do you care? Jace is mine to do with as I please." She sniffed, giving Daisy the once over. "If you think your prior claim gives you an edge, you're even more stupid than you look. I own him."

She danced backwards, running her hand along the broken spine of the couch. "What Jace and I have is magic, while the only thing you can offer is the eventuality of his changing your adult diapers."

Adult diapers? The dig was almost comical coming from a psychotic corpse.

Daisy bit her tongue and looked away. It didn't pay to argue.

"I'm talking to you, bitch!" Violet's lips peeled back in a snarl and she backhanded Daisy into the wall.

The air left her lungs in a bitter rush and prickles of angry pain radiated across her ribs and spine. Her eyesight blurred and something warm and sticky trickled from the back of her head. Daisy slumped to her side and vomited.

Violet's eyes dilated and she dropped into a crouch. "Your blood is polluted with his! I smell him all over you."

She tore chunks of brittle hair from her scalp, whipping her head back and forth.

"I see his mark on your throat! On your back, and if I stripped you bare, I know I'd find it between your legs!" She screamed clawing at her scalp.

This was it. If she didn't redirect this amount of crazy, Violet would kill her.

"Jace was in pain and needed to feed. He was starved."

She stopped her frenetic shaking and jerked her head around. The odd angle and her glazed eyes making her look like a broken marionette. "Starved?"

Daisy nodded.

"So you just let him feed from you?"

The woman's tone had gone from anger and accusing to childlike and singsong, and it terrified her.

Violet's head tilted toward the opposite direction as though considering other voices.

"Jace and I were school friends. No more."

"Were?"

Daisy's pain ebbed enough for her to slide her legs in, hoping to get to her knees. She bit back her nausea and tried to focus enough to crawl to all fours so she could shift. It was her only chance.

The screen door opened and closed. "I got the leather cuffs like you said—"

Disbelief clutched at her throat. "Seth?"

He dropped the black plastic bag in his hand to the table. "Surprised?"

His lip curled and he reached into the plastic sack and dragged out a set of leather BDSM wrist and ankle cuffs. He dangled them from two fists. "Fun, huh? I can't wait to watch."

"Why would you do this?"

"How else do you think Violet could take her final revenge on Micah's brats?"

"Micah? I'm not from Micah's line. You know that. Neither are you," she replied.

"You still believe that bullshit story I fed your dim father? His head is so far up his ass when it comes to your precious bloodline, he would have gotten down on his knees and sucked my cock to get me to marry you."

Violet snorted and Seth's grin widened. "Getting in good with him was easy. It was you who turned out to be the nut-buster, but Violet is going to let me bust *my* nut in your ass before she drains you dry. It's part of our deal."

Seth dropped the cuffs on the table and walked to where Daisy fell. His gate had a distinct limp from where Carson bit him.

He yanked her chin up, forcing her to look at him. "If you hadn't been such a cock-tease, I might have cut you some slack. I wasted a year chasing your ass, but now I get to watch as Violet cuts your wrists and ankles and lets you bleed out.

"Sloppy seconds aren't usually our style, but we'll make an exception this time. She's going to feed from your veins as I fuck your cunt dry."

Daisy puckered her cheeks and spit in his face. "You don't have the nuts to bust anything in anyone, you lying sack of shit!"

"Bitch!"

Seth backhanded her across the cheek and stars fluttered in front of her eyes. Blood gushed from her nose and the wound at the back of her head.

Her sight narrowed and her body went slack. She gulped in breaths against the looming blackness, and with the last of her consciousness, she summoned her wolf.

Every synapse fired, ordering her body to phase despite her pain. Her skin tingled with power and sinew heaved beneath her skin. Daisy dropped her head between her shoulder blades and her back arched, her spine undulating as her arms and legs reshaped into heavy-pawed quarters.

Thick fur rippled across her chest and back and her nose and jaw elongated. Anger and disgust flew through her mind and she bared her teeth, black lips peeling over razor-sharp canines.

"What the fuck!" Seth's eyes bulged at the sight of the large white wolf, his face incredulous, as though he thought Daisy weak and incapable of such fury.

He recoiled, diving for cover behind Violet, but Daisy was too fast. She launched for his throat, her teeth sinking deep into bone and cartilage. His neck snapped with one swift shake and she tossed him across the room, her white muzzle stained red.

Violet snarled, dropping to a low crouch and the two circled each other. Daisy thrashed her head, snapping and growling, keeping low and her eyes sharp.

Another howl rang out and Violet jerked her head toward the sound. An immense black wolf with blood red eyes crashed through the screen door. His paws hit Violet point blank, knocking her back.

Curved, saber-like teeth tore at her body, ripping chunks of flesh from her neck and chest. Gurgling noises bubbled up along with black, heart's blood, but Violet threw him off.

The vampire crawled to her knees and tried to stand, but the white wolf knocked her back, thick muscles coiling for a powerful release.

Daisy vaulted, twisted in mid-air as she phased to human. "Jace!" she cried, dropping into a crouch.

The black wolf rolled to his feet, his body shaking as bones and sinew snapped and reshaped to human. He ignored Daisy, his red eyes glowing with black rage.

He locked on his quarry. "I'm done with you, Violet. Your claim on me is over. I abjure you and no one will blame me for ending you here and now."

Violet scrambled despite her wounds, wheeling around to strike, but Daisy snagged a piece of jagged wood next to the fireplace and tossed the serrated spike to Jace. He caught it, driving the sharp end through Violet's chest as she lunged. Her own momentum sealing her fate.

The vampire stuttered to a halt, teetering on her heel before crumpling to the floor.

Nostrils flaring, Jace gave her head a vicious twist, ripping it from her shoulders, pitching the headless body forward in a pool of black blood.

Panting, he threw his head back, his face still mottled with rage.

Daisy didn't dare approach.

Jace dragged in slow, deep breaths and when his eyes finally met hers they were his normal brown with a red-hued ring.

"Are you hurt?" he asked.

She shook her head. "No. Are you?"

He lifted both hands in disbelief, still shaking. "I'm sorry, Daisy. This is my fault. I brought this to us, though I have no idea how Violet found me. We severed ties over a year ago, but I suppose it's my own fault for not publicly renouncing her." He exhaled, hard.

"She ambushed me in my death sleep. She's old enough to withstand some sunlight, so it's no surprise she was able to strike when I was at my most vulnerable. She bled me until I was so weak, I couldn't open my eyes once the sun finally set. The next thing I knew I was in a grave beneath our tree."

He shook his head. "I still have no idea how she knew about our cabin or our tree or especially, Jenny. I kept as much from her as I could, but even I didn't know we had a daughter until two days ago."

"Seth." Daisy pointed to the broken body on the floor by the wall.

Jace walked to the prone figure and rolled it onto its back. "Who did you say this was?"

"Seth Cochran. Supposedly a distant cousin of mine—ours."

"I don't know who he told you he was, but this is Bobby Sooner. He pretended to be your brother's friend the night of my bachelor party. Bobby sold me out to Violet. He was her blood whore."

Daisy sank onto what was left of the armchair. "Five years." She exhaled. "She consciously planned all this."

"I don't think Violet planned anything. I think it was Bobby. He took advantage and manipulated the situation for his own gain, convincing Violet it was the ultimate revenge."

Jace straightened, wiping his hands on his thighs. "The whole time I was buried, she used the maker's mind link to show me what she planned to do to you and Jenny. She left me there knowing I could see and hear everything, but too weak to stop it.

"What she didn't count on was my dormant Were genes or my own will to save my family. The full moon rose, and I felt your fear, your pain and the combination triggered my inner wolf. The force of everything was enough to heal me, freeing me to claw my way to the surface and get to you."

He shrugged. "It's the only explanation that makes any sense." He looked at Seth's body again. "You can't call the sheriff about him. There's no way."

She shook her head. "There's no need. Not after what happened today."

Jace eyed her. "I'm guessing, but you don't sound like you're referring to this." His hand swept the scene.

Daisy swallowed. "Seth tried to kidnap Jenny from preschool today."

Jace's jaw locked and his body stiffened. He paced, taking vicious strides until he turned with a snarl and ripped Seth's lifeless arms from his body, flinging them into the fireplace.

"Jace! Stop! Jenny's fine. Your father stopped Seth."

Jace jerked his eyes around.

"That's right," she replied to his unasked question. "Carson chased him down, phasing on the fly. He took a chunk out of Seth's leg, but as you can see, the douchebag got away."

Tension ebbed from the set of Jace's jaw, replaced by a silly, prideful grin, but one look at Daisy and he sobered. "What?"

"Your dad suffered a heart attack from the stress and the exertion—he's fine," she added quickly. "They took him to the hospital for tests. He had a minor episode and they're releasing him tomorrow."

Jace shoved a hand through his hair, pacing again. "And my mom?" He stopped, his eyes searching Daisy's face.

"She's with your dad, and they both know you're back." She watched the parade of emotions play across his face and her heart clenched. "They love you, Jace. They want you here no matter what."

Daisy waited before continuing. "Sam Fisher knows, too, although I don't think he was quite as receptive." She chuckled. "Weak as he was, your dad read him the riot act."

Jace stood staring until he stalked forward and picked Daisy up, whirling her around before sliding her naked body down the full length of him until his mouth found hers. He kissed her fast and then stepped back, keeping her hands in his.

"What about you? Do you want me, too?"

Daisy met his eyes, lacing her left hand with his. "I do."

He stepped back with a grin before gesturing toward the attached bunkhouse.

"Go see if there are a couple of blankets we can use for the ride home. Normally, I'm all for driving around with you buck-naked, but we need to torch this place and can't risk the distraction."

She looked at the shambles. "Years of happy memories ruined by one sociopath."

He ran a single knuckle over her cheek. "We'll make new memories." He swatted her bare ass. "Now scoot. I'll meet you by the car."

"Are you sure the fire won't spread?"

"I said, scoot."

"Jace—"

"We're out in hell's half acre, Daisy. It'll be fine."

Chapter Eleven

*T*hey sat in the truck far enough away and watched the fire engulf the cabin. The ranch was thousands of acres of private property, so the cabin would burn to the ground and no one would know.

"Violet's body disintegrated before I threw the first match, but we may have to come back for Bobby's remains," Jace said, watching the flames against the dark sky.

"I already called my dad. He's got it covered."

Jace leaned over and kissed her temple. "What are we going to do about him?"

Daisy cocked her head and looked at him. "What do you mean?"

"Is he happy I'm back?"

She blew out a breath and shrugged. "I don't know, but to be honest, I don't care. This ranch and its bad blood have cost this family so much already. I'm not willing to sacrifice another thing."

He pulled her close and she rested her head on his shoulder. "You still need to introduce me to our daughter," he said pressing a kiss to her hair.

She smiled, snuggling in closer. "That means a road trip to the beach. How much sunscreen do you think a vampire might need?"

⌒

Jace watched the moonlight dance on the water. The white sand a canvas of shadow and light as the waves crashed. Voices echoed from the house. Daisy's in particular.

His presence did nothing but exacerbate the situation, so he went for a walk leaving the rest to argue.

"You are so pig-headed! If mama were here she'd make you see reason." Daisy threw one hand in the air.

"Your mother, God rest her soul, would agree with me, and I will jerk a knot in your tail if you push me on this."

"You're being unreasonable, Jeb," Elinor interrupted. "Daisy's a grown woman."

"She's not your daughter, Ellie, so I'd remind you to butt out."

"Hey! Don't talk to my wife that way." Carson winced on the couch.

"Daisy is the mother of my grandchild, so I'll speak my peace regardless what you say. If she wants Jace, then you will have to accept it or face the consequences alone."

"Consequences? What are you jabbering about?" Jeb asked.

Daisy stood her ground. "It'll break my heart, but Jenny and I will leave if you don't accept Jace."

"And you will be alone, Jeb. Carson and I have every intention of going with them, wherever that may be. Search your heart. If the shoe were on the other foot, you'd move heaven and hell to keep Daisy with you."

Jeb exhaled. "For the last time, this has nothing to do with Jace staying or going. The boy can stay until the rapture for all I care." He got up and stalked to the kitchen counter for a beer, tossing the cap into the sink. "It's Daisy's wellbeing that concerns me."

"For God's sake, why?" Daisy interjected, trying not to lose her temper again.

"Why?" Jeb stared at her incredulously. "Forget the obvious logistics of keeping him sated and out of the sun, unless someone drives a stake through Jace's heart, he's going to live forever."

Daisy slapped her forehead. "And? I would've thought you'd be happy at the idea the ranch and the surrounding land were protected in perpetuity. You never have to deal with finding an heir to inherit. Ever."

Jeb turned to them watching him. "Daisy, you're not thinking this through. Brazos may be a large valley, but people still know people. Do you honestly think no one will notice that Jace never ages? How are you going to explain when you're eighty and he still looks twenty-five?"

She shrugged. "We'll keep to ourselves. Weres have managed to keep our dual nature hidden from the general human population for centuries. Jace and I will manage."

"How?" he questioned.

"We haven't figured that out yet."

Jeb rubbed his forehead. "I don't pretend to understand vampire politics, but I do know murdering one's maker is a huge no-no. How is he going to defend himself to their adjudicators?"

Carson gestured toward the Fed-Ex package on the table. "Darlin', will you bring me that box, please?"

Daisy carried the flat rectangle to the couch and Carson took it with a wink. "Thank you, honey."

He sat up and peeled back the stiff cardboard seal "Sam Fisher sent this overnight."

Inside was an aged file, cracked and faded from the protection of the inside plastic.

"These are the original pack archives documenting every death and the circumstances surrounding each case, including eyewitness accounts of the vampire Violet rubbernecking her handiwork."

Daisy slid in beside him, and Carson handed her some of the papers to scan.

"These are beyond belief. Aimee will need these documents sent ASAP. As soon as Francisco César takes one look at them, Jace will be in the clear for killing Violet. He's justified."

"Francisco César?" Jace's voice carried from the doorway, uncertainty shrouding his face.

Daisy looked up from the pages on her lap. "Yes. Aimee introduced us. Do you know him?"

Jace shook his head. "Only by reputation."

"I'm gathering the man's got pretty big boots, then," Carson mused.

Jace stepped through the threshold. "You could say that, Dad. Francisco César is not one to mess with. His word is usually final, and for him to offer his help, means he holds Aimee in high esteem."

Daisy got up and moved to the loveseat. "Sit with me, Jace." She patted the cushions. "You need to be part of the conversation. My father is going to mind his manners."

Humph.

Daisy shot her father a warning look. "Should I call Aimee to send a courier for these?" Daisy asked Carson, turning her attention back to the archives.

Carson shook his head. "I said these were the original documents. Sam already forwarded the photocopies to Aimee."

Daisy grinned, and she turned to peck Jace's cheek. "You're that much closer to being vindicated."

Jace inhaled, lifting one shoulder. "I don't know, Dais, but I certainly hope so."

She linked her hand with his. "I'm sure of it. Francisco was very upset when he learned the length and breadth of the crimes Violet committed against the Matthews pack.

"He said if there was proof to corroborate the claim, you would be within your rights to act, especially if Violet's threat endangered your natural child."

Jace leaned back against the couch cushion letting his shoulders relax. "Well, one good thing about being undead is once a thought is shared via a mind link, it's binding. I have Violet's sick intentions scorched into my brain, so much so, I may never let Jenny out of my sight again."

"Even when I go to the potty, Daddy?" Jenny asked, rubbing her eyes as she padded in from the bedroom in her pajamas and crawled onto Jace's lap.

He pressed his lips to the top of her head, her tiny, trusting hand in his as she curled up against his chest. She was asleep again in seconds, the soft rise and fall of her chest mesmerizing every adult in the room, especially him.

Eyes warm, Daisy pressed a kiss to his shoulder. "See? You're a natural."

Jeb nursed his beer, eyeing the little family. "It's clear y'all love each other, but I still don't get how you plan to make this work."

"So this is about me and not about the ranch," Jace remarked.

Jeb blew out a breath. "Forget the ranch and all that business for now. With you back, the pact is honored one way or the other, but yes, my issue is with you. There's no question you would kill to protect my girls. You've proven that. It's the day-to-day that baffles me on how you'll manage."

"Let me just say this." Carson cleared his throat. "I worked every day at the refinery while Ellie worked the night shift at the hospital. We managed, and so will they, and Jenny will be as right as rain as long as she knows her mama and daddy love her." He winked at his son.

"He's right, Jeb. The rest are just details, and the kids will figure it out as they go along, like everyone else," Elinor added.

"Please, Dad?" Daisy asked. "All I ask is you give Jace and me the chance to try."

Jeb let his breath out slowly, all eyes on him. "If you're that sure, I guess I don't have a choice."

With a happy shriek she got up and threw her arms around her father's neck. "If you were going to dig in your heels, I was ready to give it all up. The ranch, everything — even you, but I don't have to. Who says you can't have it all?"

Chapter Twelve

Summer in New York was muggy, and the air hugged the concrete saturated with a complex mix of scents.

Daisy wrinkled her nose as Jace held open the door to the club's private entrance. "This city is ripe in the summer and you can't stir people with a stick, it's so crowded. I'm glad we're only here for a pre-wedding getaway, although I'm not sure why we had to do this now. I have so much to plan."

"Relax. My mother is rivalling Martha Stewart these days. All you need to do is show up with Jenny for your fittings."

They went inside and Jace led her through the crowded tables toward the VIP section. The bouncer saw them approach and unhooked the velvet rope cordoning the stairs.

"Welcome back," he announced, giving Jace an approving nod and wink before stepping aside for them to pass.

"What was that all about?" Daisy asked.

"The vampire world is very small, and I suppose word has gotten around that Francisco cleared me of all charges based on the Matthews pack records. Violet wasn't well liked, even among our own. A lot of people are relieved she's no longer an issue."

"Amen to that."

"You look beautiful, by the way," Jace said, admiring the sway of Daisy's ass in her little black dress. He reached out, sliding his arm around her waist, letting his fingers dip to cup one curvy cheek. "Juicy enough to bite."

"You know it," she chuckled.

"That I do."

A dark haired woman waved from a back table and Jace grinned, giving her a quick chin pop.

"I invited some people to join us for drinks. Friends I want you to meet."

"When?"

He steered her toward the back bar. "Now."

The woman smiled, her short black bob gleaming as bright as her fang-tipped smile. "You must be Daisy," she said extending her hand. "I'm Bette. It's nice to finally meet the woman Jace hasn't shut up about for the past five years."

Astonished, Daisy looked across to Jace.

"Bette exaggerates," he said with a snort. "Let me introduce everyone else. This is Gehrig, Bette's boyfriend. And this is Abigail and Dash."

"Pleased to meet you," Daisy replied, nodding to each.

"Not as pleased as we are," Dash said with a chuckle. "It's hard enough being a Were in a city this size, but when the love of your life is a vampire, it adds a whole other level of wrong to the right." He winked, sliding his arm around Abigail. "It's nice our blended numbers are growing. Not everyone is as accepting of the change, and that applies to both sides."

Daisy looked at Abigail. "Wait, you're a vampire?"

She nodded. "It's a little hard to tell these days. Having a willing Were close at hand has its perks."

"That's an understatement, if I ever heard one. My skin hasn't been this flush or warm in nearly a century." Bette laughed, signaling the bartender to carry over a bottle of champagne and a decanter very similar to the one Aimee had prepared for Francisco in Houston.

"Of course, things are a bit easier for Gehrig and me," Dash began. "Our girls are older than Jace, so they have attained certain abilities that make for an easier time relationship-wise. Abigail is a day-walker and Bette can handle the early morning and the hour or so just before dusk. In that respect, age has its privileges when it comes to the undead."

"And it's not just the vampires who benefit," Gehrig pointed out. "A drop of vamp blood a day helps keep Father Time at bay for us as well. Not in an immortal sense, but it slows the aging process down immensely."

Jace handed Daisy a glass of champagne, pouring himself another from the separate bottle. "See?" he winked. "I bet this week alone I set your biological clock back ten years with all our blood play."

Daisy choked on her drink and Bette laughed. "Don't sweat it, honey. We all do it, and you're among friends now."

"Yes," Abigail added. "You need to enjoy the advantages while you can, especially while here. Not every club is owned and operated by vampires with certain rooms outfitted especially for the undead and their—guests."

Jace traced his finger along the edge of Daisy's bare arm and her skin tingled making her stomach jump in anticipation.

"Are you interested in seeing the surprise I have waiting for you?" he asked, bringing her fingers to his lips.

Daisy nodded.

"Good." He drained his glass, licking the corner of his mouth. He rose from his seat and took her hand.

"Have fun, you two," Bette called with a giggle.

Jace led Daisy in the same direction as their first night in New York, only this time he took her to a different door.

"How many exits and entrances does this place have?" she asked, trailing behind him.

He put his finger to her lips. "Close your eyes."

She did as he said and he took her hand, walking her through the darkened threshold.

The door closed behind them with a soft snick, and he slid his arms around her waist, from behind. He leaned over her shoulder and kissed the side of her throat behind her ear.

"Okay, open your eyes."

The room was large and dim, with a rustic feel and a touch of roadhouse. Polished wide-planked boards covered the walls and floor, complementing the rich Native American décor.

It could have been a hotel suite, with one exception. There was no bed. At the center of the room was a low saddle that looked as though it belonged on a very large mechanical bull. The tooled leather seat rested alone on a wide, raised platform set about one foot off the ground.

"What's all this?" she asked.

"You've heard the term rough riders?"

She nodded, swallowing at his sexy, low tone behind her ear.

"Consider this the vampire version." He kissed her throat, letting his tongue tease the tender flesh up to her ear. "And that—" He continued, nipping at her lobe. "Is called a Sybian."

"It looks like a saddle."

He chuckled. "And so it is, sort of."

Giving her a quick peck, he led her to the foot of the padded platform and bent to open a hidden drawer. Inside were dildos of every shape and size. "This saddle has one major difference. Instead of riding a bull, you get to ride your choice of these."

He reached into the drawer and took out a large, cinnamon-colored synthetic cock shaped like a wolf's erection. "I ordered this bad boy especially for your first ride."

Daisy took it from his hand and ran her fingers over the soft, faux flesh. The ridges in the molded shaft were so realistic she couldn't resist, and she brought the artificial head to her mouth and licked the underside.

Jace licked his lips, taking the phallus from her hand and rested it on a hand towel beside the saddle's base.

"First things first," he murmured.

He lifted her long dark hair to one shoulder and kissed her bare neck. "Strip for me, Daisy."

Jace walked to one side of the room and slid a chair closer. With his eyes on her, he unbuttoned his shirt, leaving it open to his chest and sat.

His eyes were dark and fathomless, and he ran a hand over the tight bulge behind his jeans, watching her.

Daisy reached behind to unzip her dress, rolling the fabric down from her shoulders to her waist. Her bra was sheer lace and her nipples puckered through the fabric.

She cupped her hands under each breast, sliding her thumbs over the stiff peaks, circling the full flesh before slipping her fingers beneath the dress's waist.

Jace groaned and unbuttoned his fly, freeing his corded length. He grasped the base, holding the hard member taut, watching Daisy wiggle the silk fabric over her hips and thighs until it puddled to the floor by her high heels.

She kicked the dress aside and stood wide legged in her shoes for a moment, her fingers teasing the low lace edge of her thong. She turned her back to him and bent over, running her hands up the back of her thighs and between her legs, snapping the thin thong string.

Still bent over, she unhooked her bra, letting it fall to the floor before turning to face Jace.

"Do you want the honors?" she asked, snapping her thong again, only this time she let her finger linger at the moist crotch.

"I'm so wet, Jace. Do you want a taste?" Daisy walked toward him, not waiting for an answer, pulled his hand to her crotch.

He eased her panties aside and slid his fingers into her slick sex, working her clit behind the wet silk.

Daisy arched back, jutting her tits forward, and he took the rounded flesh in one hand, squeezing as his finger curled into her spot between her legs.

"You want more?" he asked.

"Yes." Her words were a whisper as her pussy dripped in his palm, juicy and ready for a ride.

Jace pulled his hand away, tearing her panties from her body. He carried her to the low platform and laid her on the soft cover.

He pushed his pants from his hips and shoved them along with his shirt to the floor.

"Touch yourself, Daisy. I want to watch you work your pussy the way you're going to work this dildo," he growled, stepping onto the platform to screw the faux wolf cock into position.

The molded, plastic member jutted up from the center of the saddle with a protrusion at the shaft's base for a clit tease.

Holding out his hand, Jace helped Daisy to her feet. "Giddy up, cowgirl. It's time to mount."

She lifted her leg and hovered spread eagle above the large synthetic head.

"Hold the wide shaft tight and lower your wet slit onto its head, taking every hard inch. Work your pretty pink pussy. I want to watch that big cock stretch you until you scream."

Daisy moaned and slid onto the saddle, letting the hard, ridged synthetic plunge into her waiting sex. She sucked in a breath, arching at the full feel of it.

"Open, Daisy. Spread yourself wide."

Jace flipped a switch on the front of the saddle and the raised, rough protrusion at the front of the cock vibrated against her clit, the corded shaft rotating slowing inside her.

Daisy's eyes flew wide at the foreign feel and she lifted her ass, from the seat. He leaned in and kissed her, his mouth hungry and demanding until she moaned, sinking down onto the wide thickness again.

"Stroke me," he whispered against her mouth. "Take my cock."

He stood and faced the front of the low saddle as she rode. Daisy wrapped her hand around his member and slid her fingers from his base to his head and back again. A wet pearl of cum seeped onto her fingers and she rubbed the slick feel into his swollen ridge.

He broke their kiss and bit down on his wrist, spreading the pooling blood on his cock. "Taste me, Daisy. I want you to feel a little of what I feel."

She grabbed his hips, lapping at his cock, taking every drop. He moaned, and she lifted her face, letting him drip his blood onto her tongue. He lifted her chin to his lips and kissed her mouth before sealing his wrist.

"Ready to ride?" Jace didn't wait for an answer, he flipped the next switch and the saddle moved in time with the rotating synthetic flesh.

He knelt, dipped his head and teased her nipples, nipping and sucking, tongue working her along with the circular grind of the mechanical dick, forcing her higher and higher.

Daisy rolled her hips, her thighs shaking as she took every inch and pounded back. Her breath came in short pants, and when he turned up the vibration she cried out.

"Now!" he growled pushing his cock through her hands again.

The climax ripped through her, her inner walls quaking as she hung onto Jace's thick member, whimpering as the mechanical cock rung her dry, unrelenting against her pussy and her clit, until she wept in pleasure and pain as another climax hit.

"Jace!"

He lifted her from the saddle and set her on her feet beside it, but her knees buckled.

"Daisy," he whispered, holding her as he lowered her onto her back. Need raced through his blood, electric and demanding.

"You," she gasped. "I want you."

He groaned, kneeling between her trembling thighs. He lifted her hips, hungry for her sex, dripping and used. He dipped his head to lick her hypersensitive folds, savoring the flavor.

Daisy half-hissed, half-cried at the raspy feel, begging for more as he swirled his tongue over her clit.

"You're so swollen and wet," he muffled against her inner thigh, slipping his fangs into her endorphin-soaked vein. He pulled deeply, moaning as his organ jerked at the taste of her blood mixing with her spent essence.

He got to his knees and drove deep, burying his cock with a violent thrust. She cried out, her shaking legs locked around his back.

Daisy bucked against him and he pulled out, jaw clenched as he tried to contain his need. She protested. Clawing at him, urging him inside and with one powerful drive he took her, every muscle tensing as he came hard. Daisy's body crested toward climax again and he wrapped his arms around her as it crashed.

She whimpered against his chest and he held her as her trembling ebbed, her body relaxing after its final release.

"You okay, cowgirl? That was some ride."

She sighed, a soft smile spreading against his chest. "Don't talk to me. You planned this whole tortuous thing."

He chuckled, the soft rumble of his laughter beneath her cheek. "Guilty as charged, ma'am."

She toyed with the hair on his chest, fanning it through her fingers.

"You want to know why?"

She lifted her face, resting her chin on his chest. "Yes."

"It's because you were so wet and hot when you accidentally stumbled into the hog-tie room. If that got you hot, I knew this would make you come like a rocket."

"Hog-tie room?"

He chuckled again. "Well, that's what I call it, anyway."

"How many rooms are there? You never did answer my question."

Jace lifted her closer, bringing her mouth to his. "How about we find out together?"

The Red Veil Diaries

Bewitch Me

"For women, the best aphrodisiacs are words. The G-spot is in the ears. He who looks for it below there is wasting his time."

~ Isabel Allende, Of Love and Shadows

Chapter One

"*T*his place is off the chain, Laney! Holy beefcakes! Just look at all that man candy! Every size and flavor." Eve Kent licked her lips, practically bouncing in her seat in the VIP lounge. "Some friend, keeping this to yourself."

Lane Alden matched Eve's grin. "It's an underground vampire club for a reason, Evie. We know what's what, but the rest of the world?" She shook her head. "Not so much, and the undead want to keep it that way. A secret in plain sight. Technically, *we're* not even supposed to be here."

On the surface, the Red Veil was a trendy hangout for A-listers and wannabes who liked to think they lived on the edge. A mix of raw fantasy and kickass music wrapped in a big Goth bow. In truth it was also the seat of New York's Vampire Council, but that knowledge was on a need to know basis. A tidbit most hadn't a clue.

"I never realized vampires were so…so…" Eve trailed off, craning her neck for a better view of the main floor.

"Tempting?" Lane replied with a laugh. "Close your mouth, Eve, you're drooling."

With a sheepish chuckle, she wiped the corner of her mouth with the back of her hand. "Can you blame me? Talk about looking like you walked off the pages of a magazine." She took a quick breath. "I mean, I know the club is crawling with celebrity impersonators just for fun, but Holy Cinemascope! James Dean and Marlon Brando! Where did they find them?"

Lane wrapped her hand around her frosted mug and followed Eve's line of sight. "They're pretty amazing, but they're not impersonators."

Eve pulled her eyes from the crowd, her mouth dropping. "Wait, are you saying—"

"Yup."

Skeptical, Eve slid her gaze to the 50s icons again, before zeroing in on another celeb. "So, you're telling me, Patrick Swayze over there—" She gave a slow chin pop toward the end of the bar. "Mr. *Dirty Dancing* himself. *He's* the real deal? Big as life and thirty feet away from where we sit?"

"Depends on how you define *life*, but otherwise—" Lane nodded. "They are the original stars, with one major exception. They now drink blood to survive."

Eve blinked, stunned.

Lane lifted her drink toward her lips. "A bit of a shocker, I know. Back in the day, the Vampire Supreme was a huge movie buff. Intervention was a purely selfish move on his part, but when his favorite stars got sick or had a fatal accident, he made them an offer they couldn't refuse."

"Refuse? When you've got an indiscernible pulse, and you're lying on a slab with a tag on your toe, it's not a time to be choosy." Eve snorted.

Lane sipped her drink. "Sure, it is. But vampires don't worry about annoying credos the way we do."

"An it harm none, do as ye will." Eve's reply was a rote whisper.

"Exactly. Plus, the concept of personal gain isn't a problem for the undead, either. Still, it's kind of cool knowing our pop icons aren't really gone. Speaking of which, I ran into Alan Rickman a couple of months ago."

Eve exhaled a wistful sigh. "After all this time? *Always.*"

"I love that."

"Me, too." Eve nodded, finishing what was left of her martini. "Still, an undead Professor Snape is something I could believe." She paused holding the stem of her glass. "Laney, you said the 'Vampire Supreme.' Did you mean Sebastién DuLac? The one who just died?"

Lane bobbed her head. "Sebastién was a giant, condescending prick, but he was also a closet red-carpet groupie." She shrugged again. "Rubbing elbows with the elite fed his ego. Human or supernatural, he collected them. Especially if they had an ability he envied or found fascinating. He befriended Sean Leighton, Alpha of the Brethren of Were, just to get to his mate. Lily is a psychic, but Sebastién was convinced she could walk between worlds."

"Like between the living and the dead, or between our plane and Faerie?"

"Between the living and the dead," Lane replied, "but I wouldn't be surprised if he thought Lily could waltz into the Fae realm unhindered."

"Did Sebastién get her, or did the alpha rip him to shreds?"

Lane smirked at the gossipy look on Eve's face. "Sean Leighton is a powerful alpha, and the hottest shifter I've met, but Lily can hold her own. Sebastién couldn't lay a finger on her."

Eve slid her gaze back toward the bar. "Do you think he might—" Eve shook her head, not finishing her thought.

"Who might *what*?" Lane asked with a smirk.

She shook her head again. "Forget it. He's *Dirty Dancing's* Johnny Castle, and I'm a chubby witch with mousy brown hair and ordinary brown eyes."

"Evie, stop that."

"Laney, I've spent so much time cooped up in the motherhouse library, my ass now has its own zip code. If it wasn't for the rush of blood through my veins, my pasty skin could pass for undead. Hell, I'm surprised I don't hiss at daylight." She offered a soft shrug. "I'm not like you. You're fair and willowy. Members of the Circle of the Raven may be Fae-kissed, but I must have been absent when they handed out the *look*." Eve crooked her fingers into quotes.

"You don't give yourself enough credit, Evie. Forget dirty dancing with the vampires. Half the time the trace amount of Fae blood in our veins is too much of a distraction. They can't help themselves. Shifters on the other hand are a different story.

"You're a pretty girl, with just the right curves to drive the fanged and furry set wild. Focus on them. They love a little meat on the bone. As for your hair, it's a rich chestnut, and your eyes are more amber than brown." Laney reached for her friend's hand. "I mean it, Evie. No more self-deprecating. You're a Blood Witch about to join the Circle of the Raven, and we're a picky bunch of witchy bitches. Roll with that."

Eve sniffed, giving Laney a weedy smile. "At least I don't have pencils stuck in a messy bun or my nose in a book."

"Exactly. Now let go and relax. We're here to have fun. I'd say be careful, but you and I have nothing to worry about. At least not with the undead set. Vampires might have a hard time resisting our blood, but unless they want to chance the inherent risk, I think we're safe."

"What do you mean?"

Lane considered her friend. "Truth is, witch blood is poisonous to some vampires. It's a double whammy with Fae-kissed witches, because our blood is inherently alluring. Almost a drug. A plus for being a Raven if push came to shove in a dark alley."

"How come this isn't in any book I've studied? Believe me, I've combed through plenty."

"There isn't a spell for everything, Eve. We learn through trial and error. Witches need to adapt quickly. To cast on the fly and conjure when needed. Your initiation into the Circle of the Raven and our motherhouse is only the beginning.

"Anyway, I'm glad the Red Veil meets with your approval. Just remember, when it comes to the icy hot vampires, you look but don't touch. Like I said, Weres and shifters are a different story." Lane winked, turning an eye toward a sexy, wide-shouldered Were at the other end of the bar. "Touch all you want, as often as you want."

The crowd was thick and animated as they overlooked the main floor. A server approached with a smile and a small round tray.

"Can I get you ladies another drink?"

Lane nodded, draining the last of her mug. "I'll have another Moscow Mule. Extra ginger and lime this time."

"That one's my favorite," she said, before turning to Eve. "And you?"

"I'll try a dirty martini this time." She rubbed her hands together. "Three olives and heavy on the dirty."

The server grinned. "Got it. Coming right up, but I'll have to see some I.D. first."

"I showed the other server when we first ordered."

The server shrugged. "House rules. Sorry."

Eve grumbled, fishing in her purse. "I can't wait until they don't ask anymore."

"Yes, you can." Laney shook her head with a chuckle. "Trust me, it's as bad as the first day you get called ma'am."

The server looked at Eve's driver's license and then handed it back with another nod. "Thanks. I'll be right back with your drinks."

"Why couldn't you put the whammy on her the way you did the VIP bouncer?"

Lane glanced over her shoulder at the tall Were manning the velvet rope. "Because, proving you're over twenty-one is simple. Getting into the VIP section of the Red Veil, not so much." She smoothed the fresh napkin in front of her. "Magic is all about balance, Evie, and just because you *can*, doesn't always mean you should. The warning for witches about magic for personal gain is true, to a certain extent."

"So, getting the bouncer to let us into the VIP section isn't personal gain?"

Lane grinned. "Okay, so I bent the rules a little with that, big deal. I've been here a lot this past year. Is it *my* fault the bouncer recognized me? Technically, *he* allowed the perk."

"Yeah, right. With a little help from a handy compulsion spell. Was that what you meant about casting on the fly?"

"Wiseass." Lane smirked at the young witch.

The server came back with their drinks, setting them on the table. "This round is on the house." She turned with a grin toward the bouncer at the bottom of the stairs. "You must have made quite an impression on Kyle. He's usually so tight with money, he squeaks."

Eve stifled a snicker and Lane shot her a look. "Tell him we said thank you, and we'll catch up with him later."

The server walked away, and Lane turned to make eye contact with the bouncer.

"Watch and learn, little girl." Lane circled her hand in a small clockwise orbit, muttering in Latin under her breath. She maintained eye contact with Kyle, and in seconds he blinked as though confused, and then looked away.

"And that's how it's done. No harm, no foul." Lane picked up her drink, clicking her tongue. "Sometimes it's good to be a witch."

No sooner had the words left her mouth, than heat scorched her lungs. Her hand flew to her chest and she sucked in a painful breath.

"You okay?" Eve asked, lowering her drink.

Vertigo gripped hard and fast and she dropped her drink, fumbling for the edge of the table, taking short, sharp breaths.

"Lane!" Eve pushed back in her chair. "Help! Someone!"

The server rushed over, and they both moved to either side of Lane's chair. "What's the matter?" she asked.

"I don't know. She was fine a moment ago."

The server spared a look for the bartender watching from the sidelines. "Maybe we should call an ambulance. Is she allergic to anything? Asthmatic? Did she take…something?"

"She's not a druggie," Eve shot back, wrapping a hand around Lane's shoulder. "She's a witch, like you're a shifter, so help me get her out of this crowd so we can figure out what's happening."

The server straightened, surprised. "A witch? You're not supposed to —"

"Not supposed to what?" She glared up at the woman. "Are you going to help, or just stand pointless and watch?"

The woman scrambled, taking Lane's other arm. "Of course. Sorry," she replied. "The manager's office has a couch. Follow me."

Lane squeezed her eyes closed, ignoring the squabbling women. Something or someone in the club was messing with her senses. But why?

Clearing her mind, she focused on her breathing. In, out. In, out, until the vertigo ebbed. The music pulse still vibrated on her skin, and the air was thick as it skimmed her body, but she was in control.

"C'mon, Laney. Let's get you some place quiet with less nosy parkers." Eve hooked her arm inside Lane's elbow, but Lane shook her head.

She exhaled and then opened her eyes. "Give me a minute, Eve. I'm okay." Vodka and melting ice dripped off the edge of the table, chilling her fingers, and she let go for a moment only to grab hold again when she tried to stand.

"That's it. You need some fresh air and that means we're outta here. I'm calling an Uber."

Lane dragged in a steadying breath. "It's passing. Truly."

"Do you want me to call someone for you?" the server asked.

The three stood in the middle of a not so oblivious crowd. Lane shook her head again, letting go of the table for good.

"Thanks, but that's not necessary. I'm okay." Lane took another breath. "It's probably a backlash for tipping the VIP scales and then being so glib about it."

The server offered a tight smile, mopping up what was left of the spill. "I'll bring you some fresh drinks."

Plopping the wet bar towel into Lane's empty copper mug, she looked directly at Lane. "If you're sure you're okay."

"Yes, thanks. And a drink is just what the witch doctor ordered." She offered the woman a quick smile.

The server turned for the bar and Lane picked up Eve's martini, gulping a deep sip. "Talk to me, Evie. Tell me how your studies are going. Anything." She winced again, her hand going to her temple. "Any questions you want to ask?"

Eve threw a wet, crumpled napkin at her friend. "Questions? Yeah, I'd say I have a few. Like what the hell happened? One minute you're pulling a mind freak on the bouncer, and the next you're holding on for dear life. I may be a coven initiate, but I'm not stupid. That was no mere backlash. I mean, you're older and more skilled, but I can handle it. Tell me."

"Drink your martini, Eve." She handed the younger witch her glass. "It *was* a backlash. I played fast and loose with our Wiccan rules and ignored the whole personal gain tenet. Karma is a toothy bitch, and this time she answered in real time."

"You think?" Eve smirked at her friend.

Lane flashed a sheepish grin, but her gut still churned. If that was a consequence for nerve, then why did it feel so slick?

"I know you, Lane Alden, but I have no choice but to trust you. Just promise you'll fess up if we head into real trouble or something."

"Deal."

She smiled at her friend, but uncertainty bit at her belly. If that oily spin was a karmic bitch-slap, then so be it. But if it wasn't?

Chapter Two

The server returned with two fresh drinks and put them on the table. Lane gave the woman a quick smile and then picked up her drink, eyeing the younger Raven. Eve had gone quiet, but her eyes said otherwise.

"You look like you've got a question burning. You can ask me anything, Eve. Really."

"It's stupid. Just forget it."

Lane sighed. "C'mon, Eve. You watched me take a karmic thump in public, and I'm the elder at this table."

Eve gave her a droll look. "Twenty-eight doesn't qualify you for Crone, Laney."

"Very funny. Now spill."

Pulling her martini glass closer, she hesitated, smoothing the napkin under its stem. "Okay, but I told you it was stupid."

"I'm waiting."

"Do you think regular people sensed what was up with you? I mean, do they even know?"

"Know what?"

Eve inched closer, lowering her voice. "That this place is for real. As in *Original Gangstas*. Fangs and all."

Eve bared her teeth with a Bela Lugosi style hiss, and Lane lost it, sputtering on her drink. She grabbed her napkin to clean her chin, laughing.

"I told you it was stupid." Eve made a face.

Lane wiped her mouth and the front of her sleeve. "Oh, man. That was too funny. Still, I doubt vampires have ever been referred to as *Original Gangstas,* especially not when the Fae have owned the title since before time began."

"Witch 101. I get it. Dumb question." Eve fidgeted with her napkin.

"Every one of us has wondered the same thing from time to time. As clever as humans can be, they are still mired in a millennium of superstition and religious prejudice. They fear what they don't understand and hate what they fear. Even amongst themselves.

"So, as for your not-so-dumb question, if I had to venture a guess, it would be a hard no. I doubt regular people grasp the paranormal realities staring them in the face. Humans like to play with the idea of the supernatural, but most would freak if they knew what bellied up to the bar gauging their blood type."

Eve turned her gaze toward the dance floor. "Maybe they'd love knowing the supernatural exists outside the movies. I mean, talk about a fantasy come true, and—" Her mouth dropped, clipping the rest of her words. "Oh, my goddess. I think my ovaries just exploded."

Lane chuckled, licking lime juice from her thumb. "Looks like the idea of fantasies coming true isn't just for humans."

"Jeez. Is he for *real?*"

Lane tracked Eve's line of sight, watching a hunkie Were walk to the bar and order. "Oh, honey. That is *very* real."

"Be still my throbbing vagina."

Lane stifled a laugh. "Throbbing? Good word."

"Shut up, Lane. You should talk."

"No, I'm serious. The Red Veil is a place for guilty pleasures. The important thing is to be in the moment, right here, right now. Partake of all kinds, human and supernatural alike."

Eve licked her lips. "I'd like to partake of him, right here, right now."

Lane hid her smirk behind her mug's copper rim. She couldn't blame the girl's open-mouthed stare. There were panty-dropping hotties everywhere you looked. Perhaps the Veil's vampire owners planned it that way. A new strategy to lure in fresh blood. More bang for the fang.

"People should take a walk on the wild side from time to time. You should go for it, Eve."

The young witch jerked her eyes back to Lane. "And that's code for what, exactly?"

"To paraphrase Lady Gaga, when it comes to *love, if* it's not *rough it isn't fun.*" She shrugged. "Keeps things interesting."

"I bet. From what I've seen so far, I'm sure it's not hard to find a playmate."

Lane winked. "Easier still, if you have a certain magical skill set. Still, this isn't just about finding a fuckboy for hot monkey sex. Some of the best underground bands play here before they hit it big. Plus, the Veil makes the best Moscow Mule in the city."

"Yeah, nice try."

"Seriously, Eve. Vampire lust aside, the club part of this place is straight up legit. Real bands, real booze, and real bouncers who love to get busy on anyone trying to color outside the lines. The undead allow plenty of tease, but no follow through when it comes to blood sport. At least not out in the open."

"Now *that* sounds interesting." Eve scooted in, all ears.

Lane shook her head.

"Oh, c'mon. I know you know."

Lane shrugged, finishing her drink. "I do know, but that information is strictly on a need to know basis, and right now you *don't* need to know." She paused, letting a slow grin curve. "At least not until *after* you pass your initiation, little Raven."

"Party pooper."

They relaxed into the night, finally comfortable enough to enjoy the music and foreplay-in-motion out on the dance floor.

Lights flashed and the band went into a cover of The Cure's "Love Song." Eve bopped in her chair to the beat, singing low and off key with the rest of the crowd.

The simple lyrics spoke quiet volumes. Home again. Whole again. Lane closed her eyes. Those were anchors that eluded her, despite her magic. She never quite fit. Anywhere. At least not fully.

Not since—

She shook her head, dismissing the regret threatening to kill her buzz. Not here. Not now.

The Red Veil was her perfect escape. A blend of macabre and ethereal beauty wrapped in a veil of raw need. Its notorious backrooms were another story, though. They were by invitation only, and the only place on premises where people went to lose themselves between blurred erotic lines.

She'd been lucky to participate a few times, but there was no chance in hell they'd let a Fae-kissed witch and a coven initiate through those well-guarded doors tonight. No matter how eager.

Still, backlash or not, backrooms or not, Eve seemed to enjoy herself, and that was the point. Lane lifted her empty mug in salute. "To the first of your many milestones, Eve—and to the Red Veil. Our little secret."

"Secret?" Eve pulled her martini back from the toast. "Why?"

"Because it will cause a headache for me, and I don't want to deal with a headache," she explained without explaining

No wonder Caitlan said this crop of initiates was more difficult than the ones any other year. Too many questions.

"That makes no sense. Our coven is top heavy with females, Laney. And I don't mean in a big titty city kind of way. The Circle of the Raven is New York's motherhouse. As in the divine feminine. Read the subtext. It screams not enough men, in big capital letters."

"Don't make me regret bringing you tonight, Eve. You've got to swear not to say a word to anyone. I'm serious. If Caitlan finds out I brought you here, forget guys hot enough to burn, she'll break protocol and burn *me* at the stake. I'm already in her book as a bad influence. She'll light the pyre with one angry look, and then dance on my ashes if she finds out."

Eve laughed. "Dramatic much? Caitlan's not the kiss my ring type, so there must be a good reason you think she'd draw such a hard line. Maybe something to do with a bad influence's guilty pleasures?"

"Good witch or bad, it doesn't make what I said any less true. The undead that run this joint haven't exactly welcomed our kind, but truces are forming between unlikely supernaturals all over the place. Just look at the tentative peace between the Weres and the vampires. So, I figured why not?

"That truce was born out of literal necessity, Lane. HepZ was horrible. We're lucky the outbreak didn't reach the witchy community. It would have wiped us out in weeks. Being afraid of Caitlan and her rules or the club and its consequences are not the same thing."

So much for relaxing in VIP comfort. The club and its consequences? The witchling really hadn't a clue.

"You said you've been cooped up studying for weeks." Lane tried a different tack. "Blood Witch Lore is no joke. Back in the day, the only thing that kept my nose in the books was the guarantee of free-range magic once I passed."

"I know, but—"

The Circle of the Raven was the most powerful coven in New York, and the reason their supreme was no joke. Eve's obstinance was fallout from the stress of her initiation, but she'd rather deal with a rebellious Raven than their angry supreme any day.

Caitlan, on the other hand, was slightly to the left of the Wicked Witch of the West when it came to initiates hitting the books. But all work and no play made for a sad practitioner. Eve needed a diversion. A two-legged and hung like a horse kind of diversion. Even if it meant taking Caitlan's dagger-eyed stare.

Eve went quiet again, watching the purple light cast shadows along the poured concrete dance floor. Ambient light set the club's red boudoir feel to almost black. A perfect contrast to the bar's shiny steel and chrome.

"What does it feel like?" she asked, finally.

"What does what feel like?"

"To have all that power at your fingertips?"

Lane dug for the lime at the bottom of her mug, plopping it in her mouth. She chewed on the tart fruit before putting the rind on her napkin.

"You have power now, Eve. It's part of your DNA. An initiation simply assures the coven you're ready to wield it properly. Controlling your power instead of *it* controlling *you*. You'll find out what I mean soon enough. In the meantime, why not put some of what you studied into practice?"

"But—"

"Pfft." Lane dismissed the halfhearted argument. "You need a break, Eve. Why else do you think I risked my ass bringing you here, if not to try out some of your tricks?" She shrugged. "Who's going to know? And since I can't stop you from blabbing, at least there'll be something to show for my trouble."

"Wow, you make me sound like a brat."

"Well, if the broom fits, ride it."

"Hey!"

Lane chuckled. "Seriously. Do something for yourself tonight. I would, if I were you. In fact, I have. Many, many times. That shifter at the bar is yours for the taking. Hell, if I can smell the pheromones pouring off you, you know he certainly does.

"Well, Miss Ovaries Exploded? Do your stuff. Make eye contact and hold. Imagine the taste of his mouth. The way his fingers feel on your skin. Trust me, Eve. If you're in control, tonight might be a night you never forget."

Eve spared a glance for the handsome Were. "You think? I've never done anything like this before. I mean, he's definitely worth straddling six ways to Sunday, but—"

"No buts. We're not playing by the rules tonight. Focus your gaze and will him to turn. Once he does, he's yours. Go for it."

Taking a breath, Eve nodded. She stared at the man's back until his hand rose to the nape of his neck. When he turned, she locked eyes with his and mumbled a soft spell. In seconds, he picked up his drink and headed toward them.

"Holy shit! It actually worked." She swallowed hard. "What do I do now?"

"Don't break eye contact. When he stops at the table, *you* speak first. Tell him what you want and then visualize it happening. He'll get the picture in vivid detail once you put it in his mind."

The shifter stopped at Eve's chair with a confused look on his face. He stood holding his drink but didn't say anything.

Eve kept eye contact, but Lane had to smack her on the arm to get her to breathe. "*Uhm,* that looks interesting. What are you drinking?"

He blinked, but then glanced at the long neck in his hand. "It's called a Purple Haze. The brewery is in Louisiana."

Lane had to look away. Spelled or not, the boy didn't seem the sharpest knife in the drawer.

"I bet," Eve added. "The Mardi Gras funeral skeleton on the label is really cool."

He licked his lips but didn't say anything else.

"Are you visiting New York?" She bit her lip against a nervous giggle. "I'm Eve, by the way." She held out her hand, stifling a quick gasp when he folded her fingers into his palm.

"No, I'm from Long Island City. I'm Mason—" He paused, shaking his head. "You know, I'm not exactly sure how I ended up talking to you. One minute I'm sipping my beer at the bar, and the next nothing mattered except meeting you." He hesitated again, but this time with a smile. "Not that I'm sorry."

"Me neither," she replied. "You know—" She leaned in, giving him an eyeful of cleavage. "I love this place. The music rocks, and I really love to dance. You?"

A slow, grin tugged at the shifter's mouth. "I know exactly what you mean."

"So, do you like to dance?"

Eve murmured something more, and Mason's semi-perplexed look changed to a hungry stare. She nearly choked.

"There's nothing I'd like more." He chuckled then, rubbing a finger under his full bottom lip. "Actually, that's not true. If I told you what ran through my mind when I walked over, you'd slap me."

"That bad, huh?"

"No, that good. As in *X-rated* good." Mason hesitated again. "Look, I'm not always this forward. Not unless it's a full moon." He exhaled, still unsure. "I can't explain it, but I can't fight it, either." His gaze flicked from her face to her deep décolleté. "Not that I'd want to…God, you look good enough to eat."

She laughed. "Don't tell me. Wolf, right?"

"*Howl* you doing?" he replied, cracking a grin. "So, you're one of us, then. At least, I hope so. It'll save time explaining the unexplainable."

"We are—" Lane quietened a laugh. "Same tree, different branch, though."

"Mason, this is my friend—"

"Lane," she interjected. "Who was just about to head to the bar."

"Laney, no—"

With a dismissive wave, Lane pushed herself from her chair. "I'll be back. Just don't do anything I wouldn't do."

"Ha. That leaves things wide open, Miss I like to play rough sometimes."

Mason raised an eyebrow, glancing between the two witches. "Wow. And I thought tonight was going to be a bust. Lucky me. Two for the price of one."

He took a step back, giving Eve another suggestive look before sliding some of that steam to where Lane stood.

"Hold up, cowboy." Lane raised an eyebrow, shutting him down.

Eve's projection clearly overshot the mark. Either that or the horndog was truly as thick as a brick. Three was definitely *not* company, no matter what wolf boy thought.

"You've got the wrong end of the stick here, pup. So, unless you want to end up with a permanent tail, I suggest you keep your eye on one prize." She glanced at Eve. "Or do I need to conjure a rolled-up magazine and whack you on the nose?"

Mason burst out laughing.

"I think this was my bad." Eve winced, mouthing sorry to Lane.

"No worries, babe. I still make out the winner tonight." He lifted Eve's hand to his lips, skimming her knuckles. "Besides, I'm dying to see if the images in my head match what I see in your eyes."

Lane's phone buzzed and she dug in her back pocket, saved by the cell. "Shit. It's Caitlan." She made a face at the name on caller I.D. Their supreme had precognition, but damn she was good.

"What should I do?" Eve asked.

Lane waved the two of them down. "I have to take this or Caitlan will materialize or worse. Drinks are on me. Just don't go anywhere until I get back." Turning on her heel, she pressed accept call.

"Caitlan?" She kept her tone light, plugging her opposite ear as she walked from the table. "What's up?"

"Where are you?"

"I'm out, why?"

"Out where?"

Lane peered around a chrome pillar only to see Eve walking with Mason down the VIP stairs toward the dance floor.

"Shit," she muttered.

"Funny how one word can give so much away. What are you up to, missy?"

Lane frowned, turning her attention to the call. "Caitlan, did you call just to annoy me? I told you I'm out. I'm not one of your initiates, so go hound them."

"I would, but they're nowhere to be found. If this is one of your stunts, Lane Alden—"

"What makes you think missing initiates have anything to do with me?" She exhaled. "You know what, don't answer that. While I appreciate the backhanded vote of confidence that I could organize a Coven *coup de grâce*, I don't know what you're talking about, Caitlan. Your girls are doubtless holed up somewhere with a pizza and a cheap bottle of wine. That's what my friends and I did before our initiation."

"Exactly my point."

Lane scooted around the edge of the bar, trying to keep Eve in sight. "Caitlan, stop worrying. Your witchlings are all of age. If they needed to blow off a little steam, so what? Their test is at the end of the week. Every one of them will show up bright-eyed and bushy-tailed for their Dawning Ceremony. Have you ever known a Raven to miss their moment?"

"No, but—"

"Exactly," Lane shot back, watching Mason and Eve give each other a tongue bath on the dance floor. "Look, I have to go."

"Wait, Lane—*please.*"

That got her attention. She didn't hang up, but she wasn't sure she wanted to know what prompted their usually hard-assed supreme to be so imploring.

"You there?" Caitlan prompted.

Lane chewed on her lip. "I'm here. What's going on, Caitlan?"

"I need to talk with you." The supreme hesitated. "About a blood rite."

"A blood rite? You can't be serious. Why?"

"Word reached me about an hour ago. It's why I'm so frantic. There's an Unseelie in the city."

"Caitlan, there are any number of Sidhe, Seelie and Unseelie, in the city at any given time. Why is this a cause for alarm?"

"This one is a rogue, and he's looking to claim anyone with Fae-kissed blood."

"Claim? How? Why?" Lane sank into the nearest chair. "What did you hear?"

"There was an incident in the Dark Court. Some sort of power struggle or failed coup against the Unseelie king. I don't know all the details, but the Sidhe responsible was banished, accused of scandal. The price for him to regain his place at court is to seize a Fae-kissed witch and return with them to Faerie."

Caitlan's words came in a frustrated rush. Lane raked a hand through her long blonde hair. "For what purpose? I've never heard such a thing."

"Your guess is as good as mine." Caitlan exhaled on the other end of the phone. "Anyway, the why of it doesn't matter. We must do something. Dark Sidhe aren't known for kindness."

"Against humans. Not against their own."

Caitlan grunted, and the sound was both resentful and weary. "Despite the trace in our blood, we're not Fae. No court has ever claimed our lineage. In their eyes, Fae-kissed witches are a humiliation, only slightly better than humans. Maybe that's part of the so-called scandal."

The supreme was quiet for a moment before continuing. "I have no other choice, Lane. I am recalling all coven members to the motherhouse. Speculation is of no use, and we're wasting time. We need to protect our own, and the best way to do that is a lockdown and a blood rite. So, if you know the whereabouts of any of our initiates—" The leader of the Circle of the Raven didn't need to finish.

"I understand."

"Good." Caitlan paused again. "And Laney—"

"Yes?"

"Be careful, honey."

The supreme's voice softened, and for a moment it held the same gentleness Lane remembered from when she came to the motherhouse as a child. She had no memory of what came before, but all Fae-kissed witches were destined for the Circle of the Raven, and despite the supreme's penchant for discipline, Caitlan did everything she could to make their transition seamless and natural for every witchling.

Still, Lane was no longer a child, and over the years had given Caitlan and the other elders a run for their money. A black sheep.

"Lane, are you listening?"

She coughed. "Yeah…sorry. I was just thinking."

"Good. Despite you're reckless nature, you're a clever cookie. I know you don't usually like to play by the rules, but in this instance, you need to remember everything I taught you about the Sidhe to keep yourself, and whoever is with you, safe—at least until you're securely behind motherhouse doors. A rogue like this will do anything to regain their position at court. Shapeshift. Even kill." Her voice cracked. "I don't want to lose you. Any of you."

Lane chewed her lip. Caitlan knew Eve was with her tonight. The fact she didn't stop them from sneaking out spoke volumes. Their supreme wasn't quite the hard-ass she wanted everyone to believe. Black sheep or not, Caitlan loved her. And Eve.

"And Laney, if you don't make it home in time, promise you'll find some other kind of—sanctuary."

The word left no question Caitlan knew where she and Eve were tonight, but she also knew vampire council doors were iron clad. Talk about a clever cookie. If they had to face a rogue Sidhe, there was no better place to do so.

Lane closed her eyes, regretting the whole evening. "I'll do what I can, Caitlan. I promise."

Lane pressed end and locked her phone. She turned on her heel to head for the stairs, scanning for Eve the entire way. Caitlan's news explained what skimmed her senses earlier tonight. It wasn't a backlash. It was a premonition. She needed to grab Eve and get out before something happened.

Chapter Three

*T*he last thing Lane wanted was an undead frenzy. Fae blood was intoxicating to vampires, and the possibility of a full-blooded Sidhe in their private playground? Bad. Very bad.

It was enough she spelled their way into the VIP lounge, but to bring trouble to their doorstep was something else.

Vampires were imperious by nature, and not the most forgiving of beings. Especially not with those who disrespected their refuge. The Red Veil wasn't just a trendy underground club. It was *Le Sanctuaire*.

Sanctuary.

A place undead elders, Sebastién DuLac, Rémy Tessier, and Dominic De'Lessep, founded when North America was still the New World. It had evolved over the centuries, but here it stood in its modern incarnation.

Averting an incident in vampire country needed speed and stealth. She needed to work fast and stay as far under the undead radar as possible.

Pushing her way through the throng, Lane craned to peer past the sea of Goth humanity. The last she saw of Eve she was at the center of the pulsing crowd with Mason.

"Hopeless," she muttered, pivoting toward a back corner instead. She wasn't going to find Eve using ordinary means. She needed magic.

The back corridor opposite the bathrooms was quieter, and less likely for her to be interrupted. Leaning against a veil-draped pillar, she closed her eyes and expanded her senses. She concentrated on Eve and their shared bloodline.

Silence. Not even a blip.

Maybe a vampy ward blocked her search. Or maybe Eve's mind was so sex-soaked she didn't want to be found.

Opening her eyes, she exhaled an expletive. "You and your *'go for it'* attitude, Alden. Clever cookie, my ass."

Eve had teased her about their innate scrying ability, calling it a witchy version of Apple's Find My Phone. It was obvious the girl had turned hers to silent.

"I know you're getting your freak on right now, but I need a hint, sweetie. Where are you?" She physically scanned the area once more, hoping for something.

If Mason hurt her, that dumbass shifter would never see another full moon. Lifting a hand to her forehead, she exhaled. Most Weres were quick-witted as well as attractive. Leave it to her to pick the mental runt of the litter.

"Okay, Evie. I need you to answer me. Now."

For a witch not to answer a summons, it meant one of two things. Either she ignored the call, or she couldn't respond.

Worst case scenarios sprang to life and Lane clenched her jaw. "Stop it. We're not there yet."

Shoving her hand through her hair, she chewed on her lip. She needed to expand her range to the edge of the vampire sanctuary and their infamous backrooms before anything happened.

That's if you're not already too late.

I said stop.

Lane closed her eyes, pushing her guilt to the back of her mind. *We're not playing by the rules tonight.* Well, maybe bending the rules wasn't enough. Maybe she had to break them completely.

Her eyes snapped open.

Screw scrying the periphery. She was getting into those backrooms if it meant force feeding her blood to every vampire trolling the club.

She lifted both hands, her power on full charge, but before she could mumble a spelled word, pins and needles tingled at the base of her spine.

"What the fu—"

Her hands dropped as the tingle spread. It warmed, growing hotter and hotter until it spread through her extremities.

Lane arched away from the pillar. Almost of their own volition, rubbery legs pitched her toward the arched entrance to the backrooms.

Invisible hands trailed the length of her thighs, edging higher and higher. Her breasts ached and wetness slicked the lace of her panties.

Son of a bitch! Someone had answered her summons, but it wasn't Eve.

Her knees went weak, and she fisted the front of her blouse, fumbling for control. The urge to plunge her hands between her legs and self-satisfy nearly drove her to the floor.

The words 'Death by Sex' flashed through her mind, and she forced a breath, steadying herself against the edge of the entry way.

"Fuck you, you bastard!"

A soft chuckle stroked her mind. Except this wasn't funny. It was a taunt. Whoever this was, they wanted her to know they were in control. If it wasn't the rogue Sidhe, it was a minion, and she wasn't about to become a plaything.

What was it she preached to Eve? Witches need to cast on the fly and conjure when required?

Gritting her teeth, she threw a wall up against the invisible mind fuck and marshaled her focus. She reached for the pentacle at her throat and wrapped her hand around the silver and black tourmaline.

"Hands off, you pig!"

With a snarl, she reversed the attack, sending a bitch slap reply across the highjacked path. A painful hiss echoed in her mind, and she smirked.

"I hope that crushed your balls, you asshole!"

Message clear. Fuck with me and I will fuck with you right back.

She centered her strength before he found a way to retaliate, closing doors all over her mind. She couldn't find Eve without a wide search, but if this fucker kept messing with her mind, her chances were slim to none.

Maybe that was his sick plan. Dark Fae were known to be sexual predators. Death by Sex was a weapon of choice and a badge of honor in the Unseelie Court.

The invasive feel dissipated the moment she shut him down, and she steeled herself, disgusted at the damp feel in her panties.

Her body betrayed her, and she hated that someone had the ability to force her will. Still, score one for Team Witch. The big bad Sidhe bolted the moment she hit back.

"Coward." Drawing a cleansing breath, she used the energy from the crowd as a buffer and braced herself. A solitary witch couldn't go up against a rogue Sidhe alone. Especially not one with an agenda.

"Yeah, well. Two could play at that game, jerkwad."

She straightened her shoulders. No one touched her without permission, especially not an assailant too chicken to show himself.

The Fae bastard would get more than a bitch-slap when she got hold of him, but right now it was more important she find Eve.

Quieting her mind, she kept herself guarded and her power at low voltage. If opening her senses fully had tipped the bastard to her presence, she'd be damned if she gave him any more help.

"Come out, come out, whoever you are," she murmured. She cast a magical net across the club, pinpointing every supernatural by specific species and position.

Her underlying magic permeated the air, drawing energy from motion and sexual tension. The poured concrete floor shimmered like asphalt in summer, but most patrons moved in the surreal setting completely unaware.

Dread wound its way toward her, floating above the magic. Foreboding black tendrils grew as she followed the ominous sigil toward the entrance to the infamous backrooms.

"Oh God, Eve. No."

She stared at the steel and iron enforced door and her mouth wet dry. "Okay, well. Mason is a shifter. Maybe he has a season pass to a backroom freakshow and everything's all good."

"You really don't believe that, do you?"

Lane whirled on her heel at the deep male timbre. She blinked. The man standing behind her was not what she expected.

"Anyone ever tell you it's rude to eavesdrop on private conversations?"

Tall, gorgeous, and as dark as she was fair, he had supernatural written all over him, despite his cloaked glamour.

"Does it qualify as a conversation when one is talking to themselves?" He cocked his head, flashing a teasing grin.

"Look, I don't have time for whatever it is you think you're doing. I'm not interested. So, go away."

The half-smile on his lips sobered and he met her eyes with a steady, unnerving gaze. "You do realize you'll have to bargain your way through those locked doors. You won't find your charge otherwise. No witch has ever gained access alone. Not without help."

She lifted her chin, sliding into a defensive stance. "If the kind of help you suggest is what I think, there's more than a kick to the balls waiting for you if you take a step closer."

"I'm glad to see time hasn't tempered your devil fire, Laney. Can it be you really don't recognize me?"

Her eyes narrowed. The man's features were strong. With a full mouth and chiseled jaw. His hair was the color of rich dark chocolate, but it was the intense blue of his eyes that held her attention. Eyes the color of Blue Raspberry Crush.

Her chest tightened, and her mouth went dry.

It couldn't be.

He gave a little flourish, finishing with a courtly bow. "Now, love, tell me you don't remember slipping behind the hedgerow with me in Caitlan's garden. Or how we stole a bottle of her best mead and had our own Yule celebration, just us two."

"Gareth?" His name was an uncertain whisper.

Lifting his head, he winked, dropping his glamoured façade. "In the flesh."

Lane blinked again, stunned. "But, you're dead."

"Ah, my love. There's dead, and then there's dead-dead."

Past images flooded her mind as he closed the distance between them. If this was truly Gareth, he was as heady as ever, with the same underlying sensuality that used to make her mouth water.

"But how? I watched you burn." Her words faltered in disbelief, but there he stood. "Are you undead, then?"

It was the only answer that made sense, but there was no hint of vampire in the man. In fact, there was no hint of anything out of the ordinary, except for the fact she watched a pyre consume his body ten years earlier.

"Hardly undead, love." Gareth smiled softly. "You look great, by the way. Ethereal and as gorgeous as ever. You've grown into a stunning woman, Laney. Then again, I'm a little prejudiced. You were mine, so you were perfect. You still are."

"And you still dance around giving straight answers, if it's truly you."

Flashing a crooked smile, he touched the side of his perfect nose. "You were always smarter, but I'll give you a hint. Coveted blood has its advantages."

Her lips parted. "So, it's true then."

"Don't gape, love. It's not your style."

She snapped her mouth shut but slid back into a defensive stance, her eyes narrowing. "Sidhe can shapeshift, and they can help themselves to memories."

"Is this proof enough?" He rolled his shirt sleeve over his forearm, showing her the tender underside.

Lane stared at the mark. The same one she and every other Fae-kissed witch in the Circle of the Raven had upon their initiation. Not a tattoo. Not a brand. An inner mark that rose from their blood.

"Our mark is as unique as it is inborn. Granted by the Goddess Morrigan to the children of a witch and a full-blooded Sidhe and all their descendants. We carry the mark in our blood. Sidhe from either court can conceal almost anything with glamour, but not this."

Lane lifted the belled sleeve of her blouse, holding her forearm out as well. Intricate Celtic spirals twined over soft flesh, climbing ivy-like toward the elbow. Their two marks were identical, and when Lane's arm touched his, the patterns glowed. Like recognized like.

"Do you know how long I wondered and waited?" Her question was barely a murmur. "After a year, I figured the story was just legend. I mourned you, Gareth. For the longest time."

Gareth stroked the soft skin below her mark. "It took me a long time to recover, but yes, the Phoenix did rise."

"Phoenix Fae," she uttered the words almost reverently. "Does Caitlan know?"

He shook his head. "No. No one does." He shrugged. "Well, no one on this plane. Except you."

"This plane." She raised an eyebrow, still skeptical. "Are you saying—"

"Does it matter?" Gareth answered her question with a question. "You want to find your friend, and I want to help. Can't we leave it at that for now?"

She considered him. "Are you going to disappear for another decade, or at least stick around long enough to explain what happened and why you never let me know you were alive?"

Gareth clasped her arm, pressing their marks together. The air shimmered gold around them, soft magic tingling through their bodies.

"No one's making me go anywhere, love." He leaned in closer. "Not this time. Not without you."

The shared tingle spread, enveloping her body in delicious heat. Memories flooded their merged auras, leaving her even more stunned.

Gareth's face tense with need, his hips grinding deep as his thick length filled her. His teasing laugh when he surprised her with their first sex toy.

Her body hummed with pent-up need, and her lips parted again, but not to argue. "Gareth—" Next thing she knew, she was on tiptoe as though ten years never happened, ready to claim his mouth.

He pulled back. "Laney, I—"

She blinked, not sure which stung more. His rejection or her own stupidity. Mortified, she pulled her arm from their combined clasp, but he held tight.

"Laney, don't. Your impulse wasn't wrong. I've missed you. More than you can know. For ten years, you've occupied my mind and my heart." He exhaled, closing his eyes for a moment. "This is my fault. I shouldn't have tempted you from what's important."

"Tempted me?" Her eyes narrowed, distrust creeping in again. "Gareth, that wasn't you before?"

"Before when?"

With an expletive, her cheeks warmed even more, but she had to ask. "The invisible man touch…thing."

"You've lost me completely."

Self-conscious, she pressed her lips together. "Someone groped me with invisible hands when I tried scrying for Eve. It nearly had me on the floor with my hand in my panties, it was that strong."

Gareth's face tightened. "Fucking Leith."

"Leith." She watched him. "Is he the rogue Sidhe responsible for this mess?"

Nodding, he swore. "Don't worry. I'll show you how to deflect his magic. What he did will never happen again."

"No, it won't." She gave a satisfied snort. "I have a few tricks of my own and reversed it straight back to his balls. Hard."

Gareth laughed, cupping Lane's face. "Still my rebel Raven."

"Yep, only now I have a cause. Let's do what we have to and then blow this blood-pop stand. We have a decade that needs catching up."

Marianne Morea

Chapter Four

Gareth took Lane by the hand. Power surged between them, enough for her to taste their combined energy on the back of her tongue.

They stood at the entrance to the backrooms, and she held her breath. She'd been in this position before, but always with some Were taking the lead with his tongue down her throat.

"Do you trust me?" Gareth pulled a short-bladed athame from a sheath at his belt, his expression giving nothing away.

She blinked at the glint from the razor-sharp tip. "Wow. I only wanted to kiss you, Gareth. A simple no thanks would have done me fine."

He ignored her attempt at levity and held the athame steady. "Invoke a blood spell, Laney. Then draw the knife edge across my palm." He held the blade out to her hilt first. "You remember how to do that, right?"

"I don't like this, Gareth." She noted the carved handle resting in his palm, with runes and magical sigils she didn't recognize.

He urged the knife closer. "Take the athame, Lane. We're dealing with dark magic, and we need to fight fire with fire. There's only one way we're getting inside this undead citadel, and that's by enticing a vampire to open the door. We don't want to involve another innocent, so it's up to us. If my gut is correct, Eve's date paid a high price for the chance at a piece of witchy ass."

"Do you have to be so crude?" She exhaled a critical breath. Gareth voiced what she already thought. Eve and Mason were in deep shit.

She took the ritual knife from his hand with a less than gracious grunt. "What if this doesn't work?" The hilt buzzed in her palm, latent with power. "Do we have a plan B?"

He didn't answer.

"Blood is never used in white magic, Gareth." She stalled further. "The fates are funny about that. Plus, they never grant exactly what you want. They can be sneaky little beggars, twisting words. Like the Djinn."

"You're right. The fates can be difficult, but in this case, they owe me, Laney. Phoenix blood or not."

She puffed out the last of her indecision. "And you're sure there's no other way? What if we wait for someone to leave and then slip through the door unnoticed? People do it all the time all over the city, and it wouldn't directly involve an innocent."

"Lane, we need to do this on our own. Under our own steam." With a nod, he urged his palm closer to the athame's tip. "Don't be a chicken shit."

"If this goes south—"

"It won't." He nodded again. "Concentrate on what we need to happen, and then cast your best."

There were no more arguments. Lane held her breath and positioned the blade's sharp end over the center of Gareth's palm. Locking eyes with him, she began the summoning spell.

"Hear me in this witching hour, as I intreat the ancient power. Turn the tables, three times three, with banshee's cry reveal the Sidhe. Of Maid, of Mother and of Crone, blood to blood, and bone to bone—"

Gareth's eyes turned a golden hue as she dragged the razor tip across his flesh. A soft line of red formed, and she continued.

"Spirits from the misty veil, I summon forth and avail. From blooded blade safeguard and take, the sacrifice we now make. Magic pure combined and sealed, a captive's path now revealed."

Before he could stop her, Lane twisted the athame around and sliced her own palm as well. Blood pooled, and she clasped her hand to his, mingling their offering.

The ritual steel sandwiched between their palms glowed white hot, sizzling their wounded flesh. Lane hissed at the unexpected pain, instinctively jerking her hand back, but Gareth tightened his grip, keeping their blood fused.

"Don't let go." His voice left no room for questions.

Lane's throat constricted and she squeezed her eyes closed. Visions played behind her lids with seers' sight.

"Eve!" She winced, trying to sort through fragmented images, swallowing back at the thick smell of blood and sweat in her nose.

The visions ebbed before she could pinpoint anything concrete, but at least now she had a direction.

"Show me where she is, dammit!" With a grunt, Lane jerked Gareth's hand forward with hers, smearing their combined blood on the locked door.

The center steel panel buckled, as vampiric wards crumbled. In seconds, the heavy door swung wide revealing an angry vampire in the entry.

He looked first to Gareth and then to Lane, his nostrils flaring. "The backrooms are off limits to you lot! I don't know how you two managed to offset my wards, but—" The vampire paused midsentence, sniffing his best British highbrow sniff.

Shrewd red eyes flicked from the bloodied door to them and back before he paused, licking his lips. "Is this your best try?" he scoffed, dragging a single finger over the fresh, bloody smear.

Lane opened her mouth to argue, but Gareth pushed her behind his hip, shutting her up.

The vampire licked his finger clean. His red eyes glazed over immediately, and a silly smile replaced his stiff undead upper lip.

The veins in his pallid face glowed a faint blue, and he sighed, putting both hands flat on the door before leaning in to lick it clean.

"Oh, that's lovely. Brilliant." The vampire snorted, half sputter, half giggle, as his posh accent devolved. "Please, sir," he turned glassy eyes to Gareth, "I want some more."

"Listen, Oliver Twist. If you let us through, and then leave us to our business, you may have another taste." Gareth lifted their bloody hands for show and tell. "But only if you don't bother us."

The vampire simpered, resting his cheek on the door's cold surface. "There's much to be bothered with in here." He thumped the door with a limp fist. "Bother, bother, bother."

"Is he drunk?" Lane whispered, stunned.

"That was the plan." He tugged her around to his side, motioning for her to move slowly. "Your spell added power to the Fae trace in our blood, tripling its allure. The effect will wear off soon enough, though vamp-boy will have a doozy of a hangover. I think another little nip will give us the time we need to search for Eve."

Staring at the silly look on the vampire's face, she stifled a laugh when he wiped his nose on his shirt's frilly front brocade. "Oh man. He's drooling like a toothless bulldog."

"Exactly. One drop more and he should pass out completely."

"Gareth, if you're planning what I think, please don't. The undead can't be trusted around fresh blood. Drunk or not, I'm getting a distinct NatGeo Wild vibe. Pulling your wrist back will be like taking a juicy kill away from a starving animal."

"Way ahead of you, love." He winked, slipping a small, clear vial from his pocket. The tiny glass flashed iridescent in the light when he held it up for her to see. "I'm not letting his fangs anywhere near my veins, or yours for that matter."

Letting go of Lane's hand, he held the vial to his wound and folded his fingers into his palm. He squeezed, letting the narrow vial catch the calculated trickle before corking the glass.

"Hey, Dracula, do a witch solid, eh?" Gareth opened his palm and held it outward. "Seal the wound and then leave us be. If you do what we ask, then this is all yours to savor." He held the small glass container between the thumb and forefinger.

The vampire snatched Gareth's palm to his mouth, groaning as he tongued the wound. When finished, he turned red eyes to Lane, but she shook her head.

"No, thanks. I'm good."

Dracula smacked his lips. Defenseless or not, she flinched at his fully descended fangs. She scooted past, letting Gareth finish their transaction.

With all the times she'd been in the backrooms, she'd seen vampires come and go, but never courted one. Telling Eve to look but don't touch wasn't just lip service.

Wincing, she wrapped her injured hand with the black ribbon she wore around neck, using her teeth to pull the knot tight. The burn hurt like hell, but the thin cut had stopped bleeding. Still, she wasn't taking any chances.

"Worked like a charm." Gareth came up beside her wearing a shit-eating grin, gesturing toward the helpless vamp.

She followed his gaze only to see the vampire slumped against the closed reinforced steel like a drunk in an office doorway.

"Maybe we should have left the door open for a quick escape." She smirked. "We can add that to the list for later, along with the other thing."

"What other thing?"

"How you knew the spell and the blood would work." This time, she took him by the hand. "C'mon. I'm taking the lead now."

Despite the crowd in the main club, the backrooms' white marbled anteroom was empty. Telltale sounds from sex play drifted from various rooms, making her very aware of Gareth's proximity.

He was still the sexiest man she'd ever seen. That she used to know every inch of him intimately wasn't wasted on her, making his closeness even more visceral.

"Interesting place. Reminds me of the ancient brothels in Pompei." He let go of her hand to circle the mosaic floor depicting various sex acts.

She rolled her eyes. "Don't pull the prude card with me, Gareth Fairfax. You forget, I know you pretty well." She stopped herself. Heated memories were making her mouth go dry again. "Or at least I used to."

He slipped his hand into her palm again, careful not to squeeze too hard. "I haven't changed that much. A few scars here and there, but if you play your cards right, I'll let you connect the dots the same way I used to with the freckles on your cheeks."

Her gaze met his, and for a moment it was just the two of them and no one else mattered.

"That's not exactly how I remember that game," she cleared her throat, "but let's not go there right now."

"I wasn't talking about your face, love." He smacked her butt, letting his hand linger.

"If you're going to spank me, Gareth, you better be prepared for whatever comes next. I'm not an inexperienced girl anymore. I learned a lot in these backrooms."

Gareth stroked her inner elbow. "I've got plenty planned for you, love, and I don't care how many times you've been here. To be honest, it's a turn on." He leaned in, nipping the base of her ear. "Bring on the show and tell."

Lane's body burned with expectation. Her pulse raced and she had to stifle the urge to sink to her knees and lick Gareth's thighs and everything in between.

Clearing her throat again, she removed her arm from his caress and stepped back.

"You want me, Lane."

She met his eyes but didn't reply.

"I feel it in my bones, love. That pull between us. It hasn't changed. From the moment I sensed you, my cock was hard enough to cut diamonds, but your need is even more intense. Is your pretty pink pussy as sweet as I remember?" He nodded. "I plan to find out. When this is over, I'm going to spread you wide, lay you down and pound your soft mound until you scream for release."

"Gareth."

He shook his head, lifting her hand to his lips. "No, Lane. You need to hear this. I want to heal you and hold you and fuck you, because you're mine and I'm yours. The way it should have been before the fates fucked us over."

He kissed her knuckles and then let go of her hand, walking toward one of the tiled archways.

Lane didn't follow.

He glanced back at her hesitation. "If you expect me to apologize for my raw words, forget it. We have a second chance, Lane. I'm not sorry for grabbing it with both hands."

"I'm glad you're not sorry."

He blinked. "Then what?"

"You're going the wrong way."

His mouth opened and closed for a moment. "Why didn't you say something, then?"

"I would have, but you were on a such roll, I didn't want to interrupt." She smirked, stifling a chuckle.

He reached her in two strides, sweeping his arms around her waist. "Bitch."

"Gareth Fairfax, I do believe there's a chink in your perfect armor."

He tightened his grip, letting his lips hover over hers. "You have always been my weakness."

Before she could say a word, he took her mouth, crushing his lips to hers, hard and fast.

Heat zinged through her body and her breath caught in her throat. His kiss was harsh, as though ten years of want had suddenly found release.

She fisted the back of his shirt as his lips plundered her mouth. Lane moaned, meeting his fierce demand with her own. Pushing every reservation to the back of her mind, she reveled in his taste. It was raw and elemental. Conjuring the spirit of wind and rain, fire, and dark earth, filling her both with primal need and promise.

Gareth's hand dropped from the nape of her neck to caress the curve of her waist. Fingers trailed across thin fabric to seize the weight of her full breast.

"Gareth, stop," she murmured. "Eve—"

He left her vulnerable and wanting, so much so she pulled away. She barely had breath to rein herself in, but she had no choice. If this was where she and Gareth were meant to be, they'd find each other again.

Sliding his hand around her waist, Gareth held her before she slipped past. "Don't pull away, Lane. I didn't come back to hurt you."

"I'm not a fringe benefit, Gareth."

She turned to look away, but he cupped her chin, making her meet his eyes. "And I'm not an opportunist. I haven't changed that much, Laney. Neither have my feelings. You were never on the fringe of anything. Not for me. You were always special. I knew it then, and I know it now."

Lane didn't answer, but she didn't pull away either.

"If you truly don't want me. Don't want this—" He slid his hand to cup her breast again. "Then say the word, and I'll back off."

The choice was hers, and her jaw tightened with uncertainty. Even now, with her panties damp and her nether regions throbbing for his touch, she knew this had to wait.

She chewed on the inside of her cheek. Gareth was still the same gorgeous goofball she knew all those years ago. Of that she was sure. And he was right. She wanted him as much as he wanted her.

"I'm sorry, Lane. You're uncertain, and I should've expected that. Especially under the circumstances." He shook his head, hesitant. "Seeing you again. Knowing in my gut you've wanted me, the way I've wanted you."

Her breath caught at the need in his eyes. "Uhm, maybe we should talk more about this, sooner than later."

"Talk?" He nipped her bottom lip.

"You know what I mean."

His lips curved. "I do. Or at least I hope." He stepped back but kept hold of her hand. "Okay, Witchy Waze. Where are we headed?"

She pointed to the only red-tiled passageway in the antechamber and then took a step toward its entrance.

Gareth held tight, tugging her back.

"What are you doing?" she asked, confused at his hesitation. "This is what I saw in my vision."

He pointed to the inscription above the arch. "I read French, love, and *that* is definitely not welcome to Munchkin Land."

"I know what it means, Gareth. And no, we are categorically *not* in Oz."

The engraved inscription was akin to the warning at the entrance to Hell in *Dante's Inferno.* "Corrupted soul, blood and lust reside within. Enter at your own peril."

She nodded, impressed.

"Obviously, the undead have a penchant for melodrama."

"Not really. This passage is where the undead take the most debauched of their playmates, so it's anything but theatrical. Through here, anything goes. There's even an Oubliette for those that don't make it."

He frowned, staring at the inscription a moment longer. "I wonder if people know what they're getting themselves into. The threshold of no return."

"Plenty of people return, Gareth. They come back for more. Safe words aren't just for BDSM. Consent is key. Same as it is for regular people."

His face was unapologetic. "Regular people don't toss unfortunate partners into an Oubliette, never to be seen again."

She watched his shoulder muscles hunch. "Considering where we are, you might not want to voice your disapproval too loudly. Especially since the FC is that way." Her gaze tracked the length of the shadowed corridor.

"FC?"

"Fang Central. Otherwise known as the New York Vampire Council, to be precise."

His posture stiffened and darkness shadowed his face for a moment. She watched it war in his eyes and then disappear almost as quickly as it came.

"I didn't mean to give you the wrong impression, and for that I apologize. I've endured blood play for sport, Laney. It's not something I take lightly, regardless of consent."

Guilt slashed, sharp and fast, making her sorry for assuming. Sorry for being so condescending and glib. Ten years was a long time and she had no right to judge.

"I'm sorry, Gareth."

He inhaled a quick breath but managed a soft smile. "I'm in this with you for the duration, but right now my Spidey senses are going nuts, and I you need to stay behind me. I have a few tricks up my sleeve I can't explain, but if things go south, I'll need a clean line of sight."

Lane raised an eyebrow but didn't press. She squeezed his hand, and together they crossed the threshold into the dim unknown.

Chapter Five

"*H*e wants you." Bette stood in the doorway to Abigail's office, her eyes watching the elegant vampire as she studied her computer screen.

"He always wants me." Abigail waggled her eyebrows, still typing. "And I thought vampires were insatiable. Trust me, the fanged and furry got nothing on us — and not just at the full moon." She mimicked a growl.

"Not Dash, Abby. Rémy. He needs to speak to you."

She glanced at her assistant, frowning. "Can't you handle it? If these license renewals don't get paid, the Red Veil will be a G-rated juice bar by Friday night."

"Abby. He's not kidding."

She ignored Bette. "Fucking city bureaucrats. Licenses, my ass. More like extortion, yet we're the bloodsuckers."

"Abigail! Pay attention. A Were died last night. In the backrooms."

Abby's hands stopped mid-keystroke, and she turned, giving her full attention to Bette. "Fuck. Please tell me it has nothing to do with HepZ. We can't handle another breakout, Bette. Not so soon after everything."

"It's not the virus, Abs. It's worse. I think you'd better let Rémy explain. If you're worried about the club, those licenses are the least of it."

Bette moved to one of the chairs in front of Abby's large desk. "Look, I know you and Rémy prefer to handle things quietly, but this time —"

"This time, what?" Abby looked at her over the top of her laptop.

The younger vampire paused, clearly choosing her words. "This time, I don't think we have a choice to do things our way. There are other parties involved, and our usual means of disposal will," she hesitated, "raise questions we might not want answered."

With an indifferent wave, she went back to her laptop. "Donors know the risk when they sign up for the lifestyle."

"If you say so." Bette fidgeted with the end of her cuff.

Abby looked at her again. "Your fidgeting is screaming a different argument. What aren't you telling me? This incident was accidental, right?"

Bette pressed her lips together.

"Christ's blood on toast!" Abby snatched her phone console closer and buzzed her secretary.

"Yes?" The tinny intercom crackled.

"Calypso, I need you to call—"

Before she could finish her sentence, Bette waved both hands in front of her chest wildly. Abby put the intercom on mute. "What the fuck, Bette?"

"If you're asking her to call Dash, don't. Rémy doesn't want the Weres involved until we know more."

Exhaling hard, Abigail unmuted the intercom. "Never mind, Calypso. I'll take care of this myself."

"No problem, ma'am."

Bette hadn't been undead long enough to let innate vampiric hubris get in the way of common sense. Why else would the council keep her around, if not for the occasional reality check?

Resting an elbow on her desk, Abigail curled a finger over her lip. "Has Rémy seen the body? Be honest. How bad is this?"

The look on Bette's face spoke volumes.

"Lord love a dick." Abigail exhaled, chewing on her lip. She slid open a side desk drawer and pulled out a bottle of Jameson's Black Label and an insulated flask.

"Grab two glasses from the sideboard," she indicated the cherrywood cabinet by the couch. "I think we're both going to need this."

She poured them each a double shot of the aged Scotch before filling the rest with smooth crimson from the flask.

"Bottoms up." Abigail drained her glass in one shot. The warm, fresh blood and whiskey burned through her veins with a comforting feel.

She exhaled, raking a hand through her strawberry blonde hair. "What now?" she said, mostly for her own benefit. "I've never been one to shy away from difficulty, even if it means something unsavory."

"I know."

"We need this like we need our throat ripped out. If the body is as bad as your face says, fear is bound to follow once this gets out."

Bette put her half-finished drink on the desk. "I might as well tell. The body was found in the backrooms. The Carousel Suite in the red zone, to be exact. I had the area secured, but—" She puffed out a quick breath.

"Tell me everything right now. Rémy and I need all the facts if we're going to head off panic in the donor ranks. We haven't had a backroom death in ages."

"Just an observation, Abby. It's nothing."

"Well?"

Bette shrugged. "There was an unusual scent in the air. One I didn't recognize. It rode beneath the scent of residual blood, yet it was so potent it made my nips hard. I couldn't help it. I had to excuse myself and head to my room."

"For what? Did it make you sick?"

Bette shook her head, an embarrassed flush on her pale cheeks.

"For god's sake, Bette. Spit it out."

"Hey, don't shoot the messenger, Ms. Panic Pants. I'm trying to tell you, but this has me freaked out. The scent didn't make me ill. It made me ravenous. For blood and sex. I dragged the first guy I could get my hands on back to my room and fucked his brains out. It was a feeding frenzy topped with toe-curling, boneless, leg-shaking sex."

Abigail blinked at her. "You can't be serious. You're dating Gehrig. His Were blood should slake your thirst for months. Plus, Weres satiate other appetites better than most, so what the hell?"

"I know! That's what's so crazy disturbing." She exhaled. "Anyway, Rémy sensed the underlying peculiarity well. Or at least I think he noted the telltale lure. Maybe he's old enough to handle whatever sent me into a sexual feeding frenzy. Or maybe he's just old."

Abigail shut her laptop and grabbed her office keys. "Vampires don't exhaust donors to the point of expiring. Bleed them dry, sure, but we don't sex them to death. There's only two supernatural entities that do that, and neither are allowed into the Red Veil without clearing permission through me."

"You're not listening, Abby. The donor was drained. Every ounce. Yet this unusual scent wasn't on him. It was as if someone released an airborne drug that robs the undead of their senses."

"Don't be daft."

The clock on the wall chimed loudly as Abigail locked up her desk. "Where is Rémy now?"

"I'm here." Rémy stood in the doorway to Abigail's office. "I didn't want to waste time, so if the mountain won't come to Mohammed —"

"Rémy." Abigail put her keys down. "I was on my way. Bette was filling me in on what happened."

His frown deepened. "Did you call Dash?"

"No." She glanced at Bette. "Other than being drained, do we know who the victim was or what precipitated his death?" Abby asked.

Rémy moved to a chair in front of Abigail's desk and sat, shaking his head. "The victim was a Were, which complicates matters in the extreme."

"We'll need as much information as possible," Abigail added. "The Alpha of the Brethren and his hunters will want answers."

"I know." Rémy agreed. "We'll have no choice but to tell them eventually. Sean Leighton has every right to demand such. If the situation was reversed, we certainly would, though I would rather wait until we know more."

"I'll tell you what I think," Bette interrupted. "I think an outsider gained access to the backrooms without consent. I think they somehow found and manipulated the worst of our kind. Vampire dregs.

"Maybe one of the forbidden entities, like a demon or an incubus are responsible. From the look of what was left of that poor soul, whoever or whatever was responsible allowed the vampires involved to feed very well. Viciously well."

Abby shook her head again. "We have wards for that very reason. No one could get through."

"If the culprit is none of the above, then who?" Bette asked.

Rémy templed his fingers, his face like stone. "It was neither a demon nor an incubus. It was an entity we never anticipated."

"Why would you say that? Rémy, what do you know?" Abigail asked, stunned.

"My gut tells me it was a *Cinn ag Taitneamh*."

Bette looked from one to the other. "Wait, a Sin Egg Tat...what?" "

Abigail stood stunned, ignoring Bette.

He nodded, his expression tightening. "It's Gaelic, Bette. "Loosely translated, it means Shining Ones."

"Sidhe. Fae devils." Abigail sank back into her chair.

Rémy nodded again. "Yes, and if memory serves, it's not good. The Unseelie are powerful and innately magical. Malevolent, when it suits them."

Bette swiveled in her chair to face Rémy. "Are you telling us a Dark Fae killed a Were in our backrooms? How? If we have wards for other forbidden entities, how did we let this slippery sucker get through?"

"Good question," he acknowledged. "And one we need to answer sooner than later. An incubus, or a succubus or even a demon would have doubtless set off our wards. But this—" Rémy shook his head. "Someone invited this dark Sidhe into our world. There's no other explanation that fits."

Bette pursed her lips, unsure. "Wait. I thought the undead were the only supernaturals that needed an invitation to enter a private space."

"I don't mean that kind of invitation, Bette. What I mean is indications point to this dark Sidhe having help." He gave Abigail a dubious look. "Inside help."

"Don't look at me," she balked. "I certainly didn't let an Unseelie through our doors."

"No, but you oversee our wards. When was the last time their strength was confirmed?"

Abigail snatched her keys from her blotter and unlocked the top drawer to her desk. "Two days ago."

She pulled a black ledger from the narrow drawer and opened it to the center. Turning the book around, she tapped the latest entry. "I carried out a full test myself.

One of the newer sentinels was with me. It's part of their training program."

Rémy leaned forward to look at the logbook, but Bette caught Abby's eye, still confused.

"I thought the Fae only messed with humans, and then only when it suited them. What could they possibly gain coming here?"

"Dark Sidhe are caprice incarnate," Rémy replied, closing the book. "This could've been nothing more than sport, but when they crossed into our backrooms, they violated our sanctuary. Even the Sidhe know a vampire's lair is sacrosanct." He pushed the log back to Abigail. "Your records are impeccable as always. I apologize for jumping to the wrong conclusion."

She nodded once, but Rémy's sudden backdoor accusation left her nonplussed. Abby was old school, and would never question a master elder, but her eyes were daggers.

"Abigail." Rémy considered the tight set of her jaw. "We are creatures who live on a divided precipice. Ruled both by reason and by desire. Put yourself in my shoes. You would have considered the outside possibility as well, however upsetting. We are, after all, dealing with a Sidhe." He shrugged, unapologetic. "Occam's Razor."

"I don't understand." Bette bristled. "What does the Tinkerbell Club have to do with accusing one of our own?"

Rémy ignored the question. "You employ youngbloods as sentinels, yes?" he asked Abigail.

"It's been our policy for a while," she replied. "We've found their residual human blood makes it easy for them to blend with the crowds at the club. The fact they're also the strongest and most biddable of our kind makes them the perfect counterpart to the Were guard dogs we traditionally employ. Of course, once their lingering human blood dissipates, we dismiss them."

"Interesting."

Abby cocked her head. "The elders never concerned themselves with the details of running the club. At least Sebastién never did. What do my youngbloods have to do with any of this?"

Bette's mouth dropped, and her eyes jerked to Rémy. "Are you saying you think youngbloods made some sort of deal with a Fae?"

Abby's large office suddenly seemed small. Rémy reached for the desk phone and made a quick call, and when he hung up, he turned toward both sets of questioning eyes.

"I can't answer your question, Bette, because I no longer know." He shook his head. "I'm positive a Sidhe was responsible for what happened to this unfortunate shifter. What we need to find out is if they had help from a few traitorous youngbloods, and whether or not that help was compulsion or a pact."

Abigail sat in considered silence, sparing a glance for Bette. "I can't believe this was consciously done."

"Again, Occam's Razor. Until proven otherwise, we have to investigate."

"Well, sitting like three undead bumps on a log doesn't help anything. What do we do now?" Bette asked.

The clocked ticked in the background, making the tension seem worse. "We call the council," Rémy replied. "We can't handle this alone."

"Wait a minute." Bette raised an eyebrow. "We handle every other supernatural entity that crosses our threshold. Why not these puffed up pixies? Is there something you two senior citizens aren't saying? If I know Rémy, there's a history lesson in here somewhere."

He cracked a smile. "Since you asked so nicely, I'll tell you. With the help of the Druids, the Sidhe nearly enslaved our kind five millennia ago. Fae blood is both an aphrodisiac and addictive to vampires. It's very, very hard to resist. A thousand times more addicting to us than our blood is to the Weres. One taste and we are at their mercy."

"So, your guess about our youngbloods makes sense."

He nodded. "Unfortunately, yes."

She considered Rémy's words, but then swung her eyes to Abigail. "That unusual scent. It has got to be a telltale sign. Maybe it's a clue that'll help us get to the bottom of how this happened."

Rémy looked between them. "What scent?"

Abigail opened her mouth, but Bette beat her to it. "You were standing right next to me in the room, Rémy. Are you saying you didn't smell that sweet, underlying sexual current? It should have made the hair on your arms stand up, dude." She glanced to his crotch and then back again. "Among other things."

"Classy, Bette."

The younger vampire blew out a breath. "I'm sorry. Whatever lingered in that room was an unequivocal turn on, okay? The effect it had on me was unlike anything I ever experienced. I was so frenzied I did what was necessary to find release."

"An airborne aphrodisiac," Abby explained, giving Rémy an apologetic look. "

Rémy lifted an eyebrow. "If lingering magic had that kind of effect on Bette, imagine what actual Fae blood did to those youngbloods."

"Why weren't you affected?" Bette asked, curious. "Is that due to vampiric age? Because if that's the case, I'll stay a youngblood forever, thank you very much."

He let his eyes drift from Bette's eyes to her breasts and back again. "What makes you so certain I wasn't affected?

422

Perhaps quick release is the only option for those less experienced."

Rémy stifled a chuckle at the look on Bette's face. "We senior citizens can take our time and savor the moment."

"All righty, then. On that note…" Abigail pressed the intercom. "Calypso, I need a list of who from the vampire staff is unaccounted for this evening."

Rémy nodded. "Good start. I'll summon the remaining council. One of us will have to contact the Alpha of the Brethren once we gather our information."

Abby's phone dinged with a text message, and she glanced at the screen. "Dash is meeting with Sean today. He says the meeting should go well into the night."

"That buys us a little time. We'll reconvene in my quarters in an hour. My gut tells me that poor Were is just the beginning."

Chapter Six

Oil-stained torches lit the way, giving the setting a medieval feel. Their footsteps echoed on the stone tile, the staccato rhythm mingling with the sounds of pleasure and pain drifting in from various rooms.

Gareth's body language ignored the pleasant and not so pleasant, but a sharp yelp jerked his head toward the loudest of them.

His grip tightened on her hand, and a strong protective air enveloped her like a warm blanket. There was a time she hoped for that kind of consistency and strength in a relationship. A love to last the ages. Deep down she still did, despite every attempt to bury what she thought was lost.

Of course, now that Gareth was back —

You hope.

That one word scared her more than any rogue Sidhe ever could. She pushed the feeling away and concentrated instead on Gareth's wide shoulders and the way his muscled torso narrowed toward the gorgeous curve of his ass. Sex was something she understood. Primal. No thought required.

Hope.

Stop that.

Okay, how about hoping he's still as good in the sack as ever?

She put the brakes on her runaway emotional roller coaster. Eve, first. Sexy former, yet soon-to-be again lover, later.

She made herself stare at the spot between Gareth's shoulder blades, instead of his strong, muscular legs.

From there she cleared her mind enough to try and sense Eve. This was not a place her friend would have consented to go on her own.

Closing her eyes, she summoned her power. Energy rose, skittering beneath her skin so quickly it startled her. She opened her eyes, expecting the dim corridor to crackle blue with magic, but it was as dark as before, and Gareth was still a single pace ahead.

Their hands were linked, and when she concentrated on their laced fingers, energy flowed in a clear conduit. He had combined his power with hers again, giving her strength and solidarity.

If she could've kissed him then she would, but they had derailed themselves enough already.

Confident, she dove deeper, bringing their joined power to a head. The merger showed her glimpses from Gareth's mind. Images rushed forward. Pain he suffered. Death he suffered. She was about to sever the bond when she saw herself as he remembered…her face flushed with need…their bodies wrapped as her thighs shook…him gripping her hips, thrust after thrust.

Her panties dampened at the X-rated memories.

Would it be the same, now?

She imagined how he'd tease her, inch by inch, holding back just enough to make her beg.

"What's that, love? I can't hear you." His breathy whisper *making her nipples ache for his tongue. "You want this?" Him, fisting his cock, its corded length taut between her slick folds. "Hard and deep or slow and torturous?" Inch by inch, he'd*

tantalize, keeping her arms locked and her legs spread until she was ready to burst.

Fuck. She stifled a gasp. So much for derailing their mission. Lane took a breath to get a grip, only to hear him chuckle.

"Cut it out, Gareth," she ground out.

He glanced over his shoulder. "What? I'm just walking here."

"Give it a rest, Robert DeNiro. Put a lid on Memory Lane. I can't focus."

"Really."

"Gareth!"

He chuckled again. "That last one was all you, love. In fact, I'm having a moment myself. You certainly know how to put the F in fantasy. I'll never look at neckties the same way."

A self-satisfied grin tugged at her lips. "*Ties that bind* is more than just an old saying, and possibly something we should explore — later."

He groaned, squaring his shoulders. "You're killing me, Smalls."

Her heart squeezed at the movie quote. Memory flashed again, and she smiled at the sweet recollection. The two had broken Caitlan's curfew, sneaking downstairs to watch *The Sandlot* on a DVD player in the janitor's storage room. Cuddled up in a blanket, it was the first time they kissed. The first time they…and Gareth remembered.

"Can you sense her?"

"Her?" Lane coughed, startled from her musing.

"Eve. Remember?"

She shook off what was left of her reverie and called their shared power again. They were deep into the blood-play zone. This time Eve's trace hit full and in her face.

"She's here, or at least she was."

They stopped, and Lane turned toward a series of doors along the corridor. One by one she moved past each, holding that single thought like a divining staff.

The moans were loud, but most of the doors were either locked or warded. She hesitated at the last, stopping with her hand over the knob.

"Wait. I should go first," he said, moving her to the side before she could grab hold.

She wasn't about to argue.

The knob turned easily enough, and Gareth pushed it wide without hesitation.

"Anything?" she asked, craning to see around him.

"Plenty, but it's not what we hoped."

Lane pushed past him but stopped short just inside the room. "Oh, goddess. No."

Tied to a large, merry-go-round style platform was the shifter Eve had spelled at the bar.

"Mason." Her voice was a whisper as she walked toward the prone Were.

"You know this guy?"

She nodded slowly. "He was with Eve on the dance floor before I lost sight of them."

The round apparatus had no grab bars, just leather restraints at strategic points. The unfortunate Were was bound wrists and ankles, like Leonardo da Vinci's *Vitruvian Man*. His body was covered in torn flesh and random bitemarks.

Gareth moved to the platform's edge, reaching to check the man for a pulse. He looked up, meeting Lane's eyes before shaking his head.

He straightened from the shifter's lifeless form, the movement rotating the platform a few inches.

Gareth spared a look for Lane before bending to rock the platform back and forth. "Fucking thing spins, like a carnival wheel. They played goddamned spin the bottle with him." He kicked the wooden edge. "Fucking leeches made a game out of a gang feeding! Bastards!"

A single chair with silk fetters sat directly across from the rotating platform. Lane moved toward it, lifting one of the silken ties in her hand.

"They tied Eve to the chair, making her watch as Mason begged for his life." Lane winced, images flooding as her fingers twisted the silk.

"You have a choice, darling girl. Submit or your friend dies."

The Sidhe's hands clutched Eve's shoulders. Covetous and greedy. He wanted her, but she wasn't the prize.

"Where's your friend? I had hoped the idea of a threesome would be appealing. She frequents these hallowed halls enough, I thought she'd be game," he taunted, nipping her ear. "I could make you fetch her."

Eve's nipples hardened and he laughed. His hands hadn't moved from her shoulders, but her clit throbbed and with a single word, she came hard, crying out in her restraints.

"We can do this all night, my dear. I want Lane Alden. My raven will come home to roost, if I have to kidnap every member of your precious circle. Your supreme eluded me when I wanted her, but this time I will have my quarry."

Lane's hand went to her stomach and she doubled over, retching on the floor.

"What happened?" Gareth rushed to her side, ripping the silk from her hand, breaking the vision.

"There were three vampires, and they were all in some kind of thrall." She dragged in a breath before meeting Gareth's eyes. "Leith isn't kidnapping Fae-kissed witches to regain anything. He's looking for me. He wants me."

Gareth hesitated before nodding. "I know."

Straightening slowly, she wiped the back of her hand across her mouth. "What do you mean, you know?"

He waited, almost as if measuring his words. "I was sent."

"Sent? By whom?"

He pulled his hand back from between her shoulder blades. "Does it matter? I failed. Leith has Eve, and now you won't stop until you find her."

"Of course, it matters." She took a step toward him. "Gareth, please. Since I'm the one he wants, I think I deserve to know."

He exhaled, lifting a hand to his forehead. "Ten years has passed since you watched me burn, but for me it's been no more than a year. No more than that since the Unseelie untied me from the pyre in the motherhouse courtyard, waiting for me to rise from the ash. They burned me in our own backyard, laughing from a distance as they watched you and the others try to save me."

"I was there, remember. We were too late." She paused. "I was too late."

"You were spelled, Laney. You all were. They used a power the Seelie queen is still trying to decipher. All we know is it requires blood. Witch's blood." His eyes met hers. "Raven blood."

"Eve."

He didn't reply.

"How would they even know she's Fae-kissed? She hasn't completed her initiation."

Gareth looked at her. "They know. Almost as if they can smell the latency. They tried and lost with me, so taking a novice is the next logical step. The truth is, they can control a witch that hasn't fully come into her power, and a Fae-kissed Raven is even more of a prize.

"When they took me, they thought they captured a weapon. A rare Phoenix Fae, albeit a half-breed. One they could keep and bleed for their own purposes. What they didn't expect was me taking an iron sword to their throats three days later, giving it back to them three times over."

Lane's heart squeezed at the remembered visions she glimpsed. "Three times three. You have nothing to regret. You followed our rules. Whatever you put out, comes back threefold."

"Leave it to you to find poetic justice, courtesy of our Wiccan Rede." His eyes flicked to the platform again. "We need to find Eve before it's too late."

"We?" she asked. "You still haven't said how you know about all this. By your own admission you said you were in Faerie."

Gareth's eyes took on a gold hue, and Lane gasped, taking a step back. "You really are a Fae. Is there even any witch left?"

"I'm still very much a witch." He exhaled, shrugging. "I'm a half-breed, like you, but I've found acceptance and purpose in the Seelie Court. Light Sidhe can be capricious and impolitic, same as their dark Sidhe counterparts. They are quick to take offense and retaliate when given reason, unlike the Unseelie who are cruel for sport.

"The Seelie queen is kind and does her best to be just. Well, as much as a Fae can be. There's a tentative truce between the two courts. A common enemy will do that. Just look at the Vampires and Weres since the HepZ outbreak."

"You know about that?" Stunned, she looked at him.

"There's little we don't hear about. You forget, Faerie mirrors the mortal plane."

She snorted. "I don't believe that for a second. Soot, grit, smog. I don't think so. The only things we share are greed, ambition, and debauchery." She spared a pained glance for Mason.

He lifted his fingers to her cheek. "What about me? Do you believe me?"

The simple touch opened another cascade of memories and how Gareth was everything to her —

Once upon a time.

The way he looked now, with his lips parted, she angled her head to match his, primed for a kiss. She covered his hand, the urge to crush her mouth to his almost too much.

He pulled away slowly. Lane didn't fight him or say anything. Not because she had no words, but because she didn't trust herself.

"So, Golden Boy, how are we going to locate Eve?"

"Golden Boy?"

He was right. This was no time for humor.

"Sorry, Gareth. If you've found something that works to help you heal, then who am I to poke fun? Maybe I'm jealous, but that doesn't excuse the fact this entire situation is all my fault." Her regret was clear, and she glanced at her feet.

"No, Laney. This goes way beyond you. You saw the three vampires when you read the residual energy. Leith had help. From the inside. Both courts suspected as much. Why else would I be here? In this club?"

At that, her head jerked up. "Wait, vampires are working both sides?"

"Not exactly. But it explains why your shifter friend looks like a chew toy. It's all about the blood, Lane. Nothing works in this club without it."

"It's a vampire club, Gareth. Not exactly a trade secret. Despite the fact our blood doesn't do the trick." She lifted a hand. "Present company excluded, obviously."

"That's a fallacy. Witch blood may be poisonous to vampires, but the Fae trace in ours counteracts that anomaly. You saw the effects for yourself with the vampire at the entrance. Fae blood in its purest form is more than a temptation for the undead. It's addictive, the same way vampire blood is addicting to Weres."

She shook her head. "Not always. I know vampires and Weres who share blood and more, if you know what I mean. They consider themselves mates, and they're perfectly fine."

"Weres and shifters don't need blood for sustenance. Plus, they're basically human, despite their dual natures, and can choose moderation. Vampires don't discriminate when it comes to blood wants and needs. So, if a willing donor happens to be even more adept at manipulation than the undead feeding from their vein?"

"Like a dark Sidhe."

He nodded.

She wasn't convinced. "If our blood is safe, and our Fae trace so alluring, then how come we're not swarmed by trolling undead as if we're their next meal?"

"Two answers. One. Glamour. Two. The truth about Raven blood is a very well-kept secret. Purposefully well kept."

"This sucks." She exhaled, puffing her breath out in an agitated rush. "Pun totally intended."

"I agree."

Lane crossed her arms, scanning the mayhem once more. "So, what's our next move?" She hesitated, eyeing Mason's prone body.

"What is it? What do you see?"

Lifting a staying hand, she walked toward the platform and bent over the restraint holding Mason's right wrist.

"Well, well, well." She reached for the dead Were's clenched fist, and untangled a few strands of long, yellow hair from his fingers. "I think our unfortunate friend might not have died in vain." She held the glimmering strands to the light and smiled. "Bingo."

"You can't scry for a Sidhe, Laney. They don't respond to summonses."

She grinned. "Who said anything about a summoning? I'm thinking we use it to crush the bastard, but first we need bait."

"Oh, no you don't. The first thing we need to do is get you to get to the motherhouse. Caitlan will have the place warded better than Faerie itself. I'll take things from there."

"Not a chance." She met his blue-eyed gaze head on. "There's a dead Were in the backrooms of the Red Veil, courtesy of a dark Sidhe and his vampire minions. The bastard made it clear he wants me, so what better way to catch him than tempting him with what he wants?"

"Lane, no."

She wasn't taking no for an answer. "Look, I'm not suggesting I sit naked on a Faerie mound covered in laurels. We need a plan, and yes, that means Caitlan and the motherhouse library. If anyone knows why this Sidhe-tard wants me, it's got to be Caitlan, or at the very least she'll know where to look for the answer."

Lane moved toe-to-toe with Gareth, going up on the balls of her feet to press a kiss to his lips. "Think of how surprised she'll be when we show up together."

Yeah, right. Just like old times.

Chapter Seven

*L*ane's footsteps echoed in time with Gareth's along the cracked sidewalks. The city slowed its pulse in the hours before daybreak, the near quiet unnerving. Especially when you knew what might lurk in the shadows.

The motherhouse wasn't far, but at this time of night even a short distance seemed to take forever. A fixture in lower Manhattan, the motherhouse watched in serene detachment as history molded and remolded the surrounding city.

The house itself was an anomaly, a hidden treasure in plain sight amid diverse neighborhoods. Still, remnants of bygone days were evidenced in the cobbled streets that ran side-by-side with asphalt and rebar. Harkening back to the history that brought the witches to the New World.

"A half hour ago, you chirped with ideas. Why so quiet now?" Gareth asked, sneaking a look at Lane as they crossed the street.

"I'm preparing myself for battle."

"Good." He nodded in reply. "Forearmed is best. Especially when you already anticipate the worst."

Lane slid a glance his way. "I can't tell if you're being straight or snarky."

Gareth chuckled. "Both."

"Gee, thanks," she retorted, linking her arm with his. "You're the one the Sidhe royals sent as reinforcement. I should be confident, not worried."

"Now who's being snarky?" He chuckled again, but slowed their pace, his muscles tightening beneath Lane's hold. "Caitlan did a good job. I can feel her wards from here."

"Par for the course. Her protective vibe has been on overdrive for months. I wonder if she has had premonitions about this all along." Lane indicated the rich brownstone nestled inside a small fenced yard. "Home sweet home. The old girl hasn't changed that much since you left."

"No," he replied, taking in the elegant façade. "I'm surprised some developer hasn't bribed City Hall to press for eminent domain to put up some glass and steel monstrosity."

Lane pressed the intercom on the outer gate. "I meant Caitlan, but you're right about the real estate rats. They sic their lawyers and pocket politicos on us from time to time, but like you said, Caity Cat's wards are very good." She winked.

The gate slid seamlessly into its sheath within the decorative front stone wall. "In case you hadn't noticed, the gate and the entire perimeter are wrought iron."

Lane held out a hand, her delicate silver bracelets tinkling on her wrist. "Caitlan did that...after." She gave him a quick smile. "Anyway, the iron is by design. She wanted to ensure we never had a repeat of what happened with you."

"You can't put loved ones in a magic bubble, Laney. If someone is intent on harm, they find a way." He took her hand, kissing it before folding it with his. "Still, I can't blame her for trying."

The slate walk shimmered as they made their way to the front door. They climbed the wide stairs in awkward silence and stood on the porch.

"You ready?" she asked.

Gareth touched the raven-shaped doorknocker in reply, and the stained glass framing the sigil glowed.

"The house remembers you, Gareth."

He smiled. "I half expected Caitlan to imbue all kinds of cosmic nasties in case I went over to the dark side."

"If she did, the cosmic karma would be for me, not for you. She knows how much I like cookies."

He raised an eyebrow. "Cookies?"

"The meme? Come to the dark side. We have cookies?" She curled her fingers, teasing.

"Nope."

"I guess Faerie doesn't keep up with as much as they think."

He smirked in reply, watching her press her hand to the front door. "Witchy biometrics?"

The door lock clicked open, and she reached for the knob. "Layered spell work, but basically the same premise. Except ours makes the trespasser wish he'd never been born."

"I'll keep that in mind," he replied, but then hesitated as she turned the door handle. "Are you sure about this, Laney? I'm prepared to handle Leith on my own."

"This goes deeper than making a rogue Sidhe my bitch. I need to know my history, Gareth. Maybe that will explain why this happened in the first place. Whoever Leith is to me or to you, or whatever his relationship to either court, the truth needs outing. For Eve, but also for Mason. My gut tells me he was an innocent that got caught up in something he didn't understand."

"Okay. I know you've got skills, and that Caitlan has your back, but this is not going to be an easy fight."

The sobering thought forced her to glance at the street, and how different things were twelve hours ago when she and Eve set out for their night on the town.

The front door creaked open, pulling Lane's attention from the street. A woman with long silvery-pink hair stood in the doorway, her large blue eyes sweeping Gareth before she uttered a single word.

"So, the prodigal returns." The large onyx stone on her index finger winked in the hall light.

"Caitlan." Gareth flashed a close-lipped grin. "As welcoming as ever. Though I didn't expect you'd greet us yourself."

Her aqua eyes gave nothing away. "It's the least I could do, considering how forthcoming you've been over the years."

"And she's back," he replied with a short sigh.

Lane frowned at them both. "Give it a rest, both of you. Caitlan, you're as happy to see Gareth as I am, so cut it out. We were all traumatized by what happened ten years ago, Gareth especially, since he's the one that burned at the stake. I'm sure he has a long and interesting explanation for how he survived, and why he thought it best to keep that fact a secret, but right now we have bigger Fae to fry."

Neither said anything in reply, and Lane met Caitlan's considering stare, despite the awkward silence.

Lane exchanged an uncertain glance with Gareth. "Okay then. I'll take your no comment as a yes."

She took a step toward Caitlan, still blocking the entry. "Are you planning to let us in, or should Gareth and I strategize from a hotel room somewhere?"

Their Supreme stepped to the side, the motion an acknowledgment of the situation, not an absolution.

"Gareth, I had your old room prepared," she replied, closing the door behind them. "I'm sure you can remember the way."

Lane spared her quizzical look. "I didn't tell you we were coming."

"And I didn't bake a cake, so we're even," Caitlan answered with a dismissive wave.

"*How-ja do. How-ja do.*"

Caitlan flashed him soft grin.

"Okay, then. I'm sure that's a private joke of sorts, and one I haven't a clue about, but it only proves me right. You are happy to see Gareth, so cut it with the wicked witch stuff."

Caitlan considered the younger witch, giving her a half smile. "It's not a private joke, it's a hit song from the 1950s…*If I knew you were coming, I'd have baked a cake*…but I am guilty as charged. I'm glad you're both home, though I am a little insulted you doubted my powers of precognition."

She sighed, letting her gaze fall on Gareth again. "It's good to have you home, little frog, but don't think for one second you're excused from giving me a detailed accounting."

"Little frog?" Lane raised an eyebrow.

"Long story. Don't ask."

Caitlan winked at Gareth's quick blush, but then sobered again. "You two can play twenty questions once this dirty business is put to bed. My guess is you'll need our library, though I'm afraid you're on your own. We all are, as I've sent the rest of the initiates into seclusion. I will answer what I can, but without our archivist, I can't promise much."

"What happened to Grania?" Gareth asked. "Is she still full of piss and vinegar? I remember thinking she was so pickled sour, she'd live forever."

Sadness creased Caitlan's face, and Lane elbowed Gareth's side. "I'm sorry, Gareth. She died quite suddenly, last year. Caro has taken over, but a history like ours takes time."

Caitlan turned her eyes toward the stairs. "Go on up, then. Most of your belongings were put into storage, but I managed a pair of sweats and an old tee from a trunk I kept. They've been washed and folded and are on the bed in your room. I'll see the clothes you're wearing are washed and returned by morning."

She looked at Lane. "In the meantime, there are bottles of water and cookies on a tray in the hall. Take what you want and then meet me in the library in an hour. I'll brew a pot of coffee and scrounge up some real food."

They watched the willowy woman head toward the kitchen at the back of the house.

"I told you the dark side had cookies."

Gareth nodded absently. "With Caitlan, I believe it."

"Still, that went better than I expected." Lane turned with him toward the stairs.

"Is it me or did Caitlan seem a little too prepared for us? Do you think she knows more than what we anticipated?"

"Your guess is as good as mine, *little frog*," Lane teased.

"*Ribbit*. And no, I'm not telling you how I got the nickname. Let's just say the transfiguration scene in *Harry Potter* has nothing on Caitlan when she wants to make a point."

"She didn't! Why didn't you ever tell me?"

Gareth opened his mouth to reply, but something at the top of the stairs caught his eye. "I thought Caitlan said we were on our own."

"She did."

How many Ravens are in residence right now?"

"Nine, including me and Eve."

Gareth looked from the empty landing to where Lane stood at the bottom step. "A full coven."

"Twelve's better, but we do okay. Of course, most residents are initiates from all over. Only Eve and one other girl are true Ravens. Why?"

They climbed the stairs, past framed herbs and pressed magical plants. "Just curious."

Lane stepped onto the top landing first, pivoting toward a set of private doors off the second-floor hallway. Gareth followed, and the two stopped in front of a plain door where she waited for him to say something.

"Well, at least there's no skull and crossbones on the center panel."

Lane stepped to the side, giving Gareth the honors. "Believe it or not, she kept it as is for years. She only agreed to clean it out when the dust mites threatened a coup."

He cracked a grin, turning the knob. The door swung open and he stood for a moment staring at the dim interior. "Wow. Caitlan wasn't kidding," he murmured.

Lane slipped past to snap on the light. The room was immaculate, smelling of lemon polish and beeswax. Two wide pillar candles flickered from the dresser and the nightstand, bathing everything in soft light.

Gareth caught Lane's eye in the dresser mirror. "Feels like old times, huh."

"Wickedly so." She absently wrapped a hand over the smooth bedpost attached to the footboard.

"Wicked?"

A nostalgic grin tugged at her lips. "After what we did in here, right under Caitlan's twitchy nose?" She shrugged off a soft chuckle. "We'd have to be as naïve as we were then to assume she still doesn't know."

Gareth closed the door. "Are you talking about then or now?"

Without waiting for her to answer, he crossed the width of the room, moving in until the back of Lane's thighs pressed tight to the polished wood.

"You're as beautiful as I remember, Laney. Soft and luminous. With a mouth that begs kissing."

She met his blue eyes glittering in the candlelight. "We were so young."

"We were." He cupped both of her cheeks, letting his thumb trace the edge of her bottom lip. "But that doesn't mean we didn't have something real. We've come full circle, Lane. You and me. You bewitched me then, and you bewitch me now."

His thumb stopped its caress, and he held her chin as his eyes searched her steady gaze. "You know what I want, and I know you want it, too."

Her single word was all Gareth needed. He leaned in, taking her mouth. She moaned against his lips, and in seconds his hand slipped to the nape of her neck, urging more. Demanding more.

Breath mingled, hands tangled in hair, their tongues fought and plundered, hungry and exacting.

Gareth's hand slid to skim to her collarbone, trailing lower to tease the swell of one breast.

The candles were a dead giveaway their Supreme predicted this moment, despite her reserve at the door. Orchestrated it even. That Caitlan set the stage for a witchy booty call left her cheeks burning almost as much as Gareth's kiss.

Breathless, she broke their kiss with her hands still twisted in his dark hair. "Gareth—"

"You are so beautiful, Lane. Even more so when you're too stubborn to admit you're horny."

He shook his head, lifting a finger to her lips "Your eyes are wide and dilated, and your lips slightly swollen.

Your cheeks flushed. If I slipped my hand into your panties, my fingers would find you warm and slick."

"Gareth," she tried again, only to be silenced with another kiss.

She put her hands on his shoulders and pushed him back one step. Keeping her palm on his chest, she kept him at arm's length.

"What are you doing?" he asked, watching her loose the knit tieback from one of her belle sleeves.

Dangling it between them, a teasing smirk curved on her lips. "Remember?"

"You are such a tease. Fearless and sexy, but definitely a tease." He took the tieback from her hand and pulled its mate loose from her other sleeve.

"I'm going to take these as a yes," he said, holding the tiebacks in his palm, "but I still want to hear you say the word. You know how I feel, and I've made it very clear what I want."

"Graphically clear."

He waited, toying with the black knit ties. "Not good enough."

"The bedposts await, my lord." Lane bowed her head, lifting both wrists toward him.

Chapter Eight

Gareth held her chin, lifting her face. "What did you say, Lane?"

A soft gasp muffled the word as he cupped her breast through her blouse, giving her nipple a pinch.

"I'm sorry, what was that?" he teased.

"Please," she croaked.

"Please what?"

She licked her lips. This game made her clit throb and her pussy so wet, the slick warmth drenched her panties. Same as it did a decade ago, only more now that she'd been in the backrooms. If they ever settled this mess with the Sidhe Courts, she had a particular room she'd love to show Gareth.

"I'm waiting," he said, letting his thumb roll her taut bud again.

She sucked in a breath. "Fuck me, Gareth! Fuck me boneless so I come like rockets!"

He separated her from her blouse, lifting it over her head and tossing the sheer material to the floor beside the bed. Holding her wrists high, he unbuttoned her pants, releasing her hands only to push the pants to the floor, along with her lace undies.

"Mmmm," he smirked, letting his fingers graze her slick sex as he dragged his hand back to her waist.

Skimming even higher, he cupped her breasts again, only this time he pulled her bralette down to push her nipples up and over the edge of the lace.

"You have beautiful tits, Lane. You always did. So luscious. So inviting." Gareth's hands grazed the taut peaks, letting the bra's straps fall over her shoulders.

"I remember how I'd itch to touch you in class. To run my fingers over your nipples in secret." He dipped his head, flicking one pink peak with his tongue.

Lane inhaled deep, letting her head drop back. "I remember sex in the stacks."

"The library. Magical theory." He dipped his head again. "How many books did we knock off those shelves, rolling around in the dust?"

Her breath came in short pants, and she didn't answer. Instead, she cupped both breasts, arching them further to his mouth.

"Those books were as hard as my cock is right now." He bit down, grazing her sensitive flesh. "I'm so hard I could drill diamonds with the tip of my cock, but the only thing I'm going to drill is your pretty pink pussy."

The candlelight shimmered on her pale skin, and he took a step back, his gaze burning as it traveled her full length.

"Sit." He motioned to the edge of the bed. "Spread your legs."

"Wouldn't you rather me —"

He reached for her breast again, giving her nipple a hard pinch. She gasped at the mix of pleasure and pain. To follow delicious orders was a release from the day-to-day, knowing full well she could turn the tables on Gareth any time. And she would.

Her clit jerked at the thought of him on his knees, her hands in his hair and his gorgeous, talented mouth between her slick folds. Two could play at this, and she would keep her dominant side in check for the time being.

She slid onto the mattress, and as he pulled her toward the edge, her sensitive mound brushed the hard bar beneath his fly.

Her breath hitched at the rough feel of his fingers when he dipped a hand to her wet sex, his mouth to one nipple, drawing the stiff bud between his teeth.

Circling the puckered flesh, he teased and sucked, rolling the other between his fingers.

"Your pussy is so ripe, you're ready to burst. But I'm going to make you sweat for it. It's been ten years, so what's a few more minutes?"

Lane's fingers clutched the bedspread, but he didn't relent. She sucked in a breath as he worked the slick folds between her legs. He fisted her pussy, his fingers curling deep and punishing. She moaned, arching her hips to grind his hand closer to her clit.

"Not so fast, love," he murmured. Holding both her wrists in one hand, he pulled his other from her slick slit and pointed to the headboard.

Her skin was on fire, and her body hummed with need as she scooted backwards toward the pillows, watching him lick her essence from his fingers.

Scooping her knit tiebacks from the duvet, he walked around the side of the bed to the bedpost nearest the pillows.

"Do you remember our safe word?" she asked.

Their gazes locked, and he lifted her wrist to the post. "Fire." He bound her wrist tight before doing the same with the other on the opposite side.

Wispy feathers and silk flowers stood in a decorative vase on a side table. Gareth reached for a delicate plume and placed it on one of the pillows.

Lane watched, licking her lips as he stripped out of his clothes, grinning to herself when he pulled a clean handkerchief from his pocket.

"That for me?" she said, letting her lips slide into a smirk.

"Sexual sensory overload," he murmured, tying the handkerchief blindfold style over her eyes.

She felt weight shift on the bed, and then heard footsteps before the sound of running water.

"Gareth?" she called after him, lifting her head to try and see out the bottom edge.

When he came back, she felt the mattress dip again, and his clean, masculine scent, close enough to make her mouth water.

He spread her knees wide, circling her clit with his thumb. "You're already dripping, but I want to see what you do when something even hotter hits your spot."

He got up again, and this time when he came back, she heard a plastic cap snap open. She sucked in a breath as something very hot, but very silky, trickled over her belly and between her legs.

Gareth's hands smoothed the steamy lube, teasing her clit and folds. Her skin immediately tingled hot and cold, the feeling incredible and electric.

She gasped, the sensation aching for friction. Lifting her hips, he answered with something steaming and rough.

With a sharp intake, she bucked higher, but he held her off, letting the course edge of something rough and wet graze her flesh.

Panting for contact, her hands struggled against her restraints. "*Argh.* Gareth! What is that? I want it. Please! Give me something! My body is burning!"

"Amazing what a hot, damp hand towel can do." He chuckled. "How about a little of this?"

Lifting the feather from the vase, he trailed it over her taut nipples, teasing her again with the ghost of a touch.

She squirmed against the slow, sexy torment. He dipped his mouth to her lips, letting his tongue spar with hers, taking her higher and higher, but left her body screaming for touch and release.

Lane groaned against his mouth, her breasts aching for his mouth and his hands. "You suck, Gareth!" She gritted her teeth and arched her back.

"All you had to do was ask, love." He chuckled, dropping his head to her nipples, his tongue rasping and licking, sucking, and biting.

Slipping his hand to her pussy, he teased her wet slit with a single finger. Tracing the outline of her folds until she growled.

"Damn you, Gareth! Fuck ME!"

"You know, Caitlin never found our stash. Picture my surprise when I checked under the loose bathroom tile and found our bag of tricks. It was as well-hidden and well-preserved as if it was yesterday. Imagine how pissed she'd be if she knew we vacuum sealed sex toys with her foodsaver back in the day."

Lane felt his weight shift to the edge of the bed and when it evened out, he slipped something over each foot and then up her legs to the juncture between her thighs.

"Remember this?" Her clit jumped as current vibrated against her hard nub. "Madame Butterfly a la Silver Bullet. Ecstasy via remote control."

Electric jolts pulsed through her core and she cried out, lifting her hips. "I took the batteries from your TV clicker. I figured you wouldn't mind." He climbed over, straddling her waist.

"I called you butterfly for weeks, and your clit jumped every time I said the word."

Her mouth dropped open, and he pressed his cock to her lips. "Suck me now, butterfly. Ride the bullet and suck me deep."

With enough slack to lift her head, she licked his engorged head, circling its hard, ridged rim. She sucked him deep, flattening her tongue to milk his corded underside.

"God in heaven!" He drew a sharp breath. "Watching you suck my dick is so fucking hot! That's it, baby, more. Deeper."

He pulled the blindfold from her eyes, and he backed his cock from her lips. Holding the butterfly remote in one hand and his long, thick cock in the other, he watched her face as he pressed the remote again.

The pulses sharpened in intensity and then backed off to barely a whispered touch. The alternating vibration made her grit her teeth, crying out.

"What? You want to come?" He clicked his cheek. "Sorry, love, but I don't think you're there yet."

He lifted the candle from the nightstand and dripped a small amount of wax over her lower belly.

She hissed, arching her hips. "I want your cock, you bastard!"

"And I want your pussy, slippery and sweet, running wet and slick down my balls as I fuck you."

Gareth slid his hand across her stomach before shifting off her hips. He slid two fingers over her taut core before gliding the same two fingers inside her slick entrance.

Her sex was swollen and ready, and he watched her face as he worked her sex inside and out. His fingers drove deep, while his thumb worked her clit until Lane arched against her restraints, lifting her whole body in delicious agony. She was ready.

"GARETH! If you don't fuck me now, I swear I'll tie you down and ride you 'til your cock turns purple and falls off!"

He pulled his hand back, and she moaned in protest, but he silenced her with an unyielding kiss.

He pulled her knees up and slipped between her thighs, driving his thick length into her with a vicious thrust.

Without missing a beat, he pulled her restraints loose, locking his hands around both her ankles, spreading her wide. His balls smacked against her slick ass as he pounded hard.

She met him trust for thrust, both climbing closer to climax. Eyes blazed, and every muscle contracted, taut and ready. The air shimmered gold around them, same as it did at the Red Veil, only this time it was tangible.

Thick, and suffused with energy, it crackled as though alive. Her blonde hair rose, halo-like, and Gareth gathered her to him, burying himself deeper inside her tight shaft.

Lane's body spasmed, convulsing in delicious release and she cried out. Gareth's eyes glowed gold, and his skin shimmered the same, magical sheen.

Squeezing his eyes shut, he gasped, rigid as his body emptied deep within her. He held tight and taut, and when he finally lifted his lids, his breath locked in his throat.

"Laney, don't look down."

Seeing the stunned look on his face, she did exactly the opposite. "Holy fuck! We're levitating!"

She locked her arms and legs around Gareth's back as they hovered, entwined, five feet above the bed.

"What do we do?" she asked, trying to keep her voice calm.

"Kiss me," he replied. "Kiss me and empty your mind of everything but us and how we feel."

She pressed her mouth to his, letting herself get lost in his taste, his arms, and whoosh! A whirlwind swirled, clearing the air, and they dropped like a stone onto the mattress, breaking the frame with a loud crack.

Still wrapped, they didn't dare move.

"Laney, are you hurt? You okay?" Gareth asked.

Still shaken, she hid her head in the hollow of his throat. "I think so. What the hell was that?"

"I have no idea. Can you move at all? Are you sure you're okay?"

Slowly, she lifted her head from his chest, and moved her neck and shoulders. "I'm good, I think. You?"

He did the same, bit by bit. When he was sure they were both in one piece, he slid from her body and rolled to one side on the sloped mattress.

"Well," he chuckled, running a hand through his dark hair. "I always said every time with you was pure magic."

She smacked him on the shoulder. "Funny. Not funny, Gareth."

"You know," he grinned at the look still on her face, "we're going to have to do this over and over again to find out what caused us to levitate. Scientific method."

She gritted her teeth, struggling to sit up on the broken slope. "I doubt scientists ever use the words levitate and science in the same sentence. This was magic. Sidhe magic. I just know it."

He cupped her chin, making her meet his eyes. "This wasn't Sidhe magic. It was you and me. Plain and simple. If Sidhe blood had anything to do with it, it's ours. Combined."

"Gareth, we've been *here* many, many times before, and we never had magical fallout. I know that was ten years ago, but —"

He put a finger over her lips. "Maybe this was pent-up foreplay, or a sexual logjam that finally burst. We can look it up in Magical Theory in the stacks, maybe give it a go again there."

She rolled her eyes, watching him waggle his eyebrows. "I've had plenty of sex since you disappeared into Faerie. Nothing close to this ever happened."

450

"That's because it wasn't with *me*," he replied. "We've both matured into our own. Our powers and abilities are fully fledged. Think about that."

She curled onto her side, facing him. "What are we going to tell Caitlan when she sees this mess?"

"I'm sure she already knows."

Lane rolled onto her back again. "Nice. I have to live with the woman."

"No, you don't." He pulled her toward him, his face serious. "You can live with me. The way it should have been from the start. We can live here, or if you want, I can try to take you with me to Faerie."

He kissed her softly, and the air shimmered gold again. This time the feel was light and playful, skimming their skin with tiny prickles that made her hair rise again.

"Well, wherever we are, one thing is for sure. We're going to need serious homeowners' insurance."

She grinned, kissing him back until the gold shimmer thickened and she could no longer think.

Chapter Nine

Gareth scanned the library's dusty stacks. "This place hasn't changed at all." He walked past the old archivist's desk piled with volumes. "I can still feel Grania's eyes watching us over the top of her horn-rimmed glasses." He winked.

"She wasn't the cheeriest of people, but she certainly knew her stuff." Lane dragged a finger over a shelf, leaving marks in the dust. She turned toward Gareth standing with his hands on the back of Grania's worn chair. "This place is in such confusion. I don't even know where to begin."

"Me neither, though Caitlan seemed to think we'd figure it out. Where is she anyway? I thought she said Caro left references for us somewhere." He lifted a book from the closest pile on the desk and flipped a few pages before dropping it back on the pile. The soft thud sent dust swirling and he sneezed.

"Dust comes with the territory, but *God bless*, anyway." Wiping her hands on her pants, Lane moved to the large study table at the center of the room.

"As promised, I guess." She tapped the small pile of old books and papers on the worn wood.

Lifting a handwritten note from the top of the low stack, she gave it a quick scan. "It's from Caro," she said, continuing. "She says the books she left for us reference the Circle of the Raven and our relationship to the Fae courts. She apologizes, saying it's not much, but considering we're Sidhe bastards, we shouldn't be surprised."

"Sidhe bastards." Gareth repeated the words matter-of-factly. "Funny how I wasn't made to feel that way in the Seelie Court. The Summer Queen welcomes Fae blood, no matter what."

"When it suits her agenda, I'm sure." Lane tucked the note into her back pocket. She didn't dare look at Gareth. Other than what she was taught and had read, she had no real knowledge of the Sidhe. Right now, she didn't care. Gareth was proof her bias rang true. It didn't suit their agenda to send word he survived, otherwise she and Caitlan would have known the moment he rose from the ashes.

A rare Fae Phoenix was a keeper. A real find, and everyone knew Sidhe royalty loved to *collect* the wonderous and unique.

"Let's divide and conquer this lot. You take one half, and I'll take the other." He joined her at the study table. "Caitlan can referee once she gets here."

Lane didn't reply. Instead, she grabbed one of the marked reference books and opened it to a marked page.

Since dropping his glamour, she'd barely had time to wrap her head around the fact of him. Maybe she didn't want to. Especially since the only thing she was interested in wrapping were her legs around his hips.

I have a few tricks up my sleeve I can't explain. Gareth's earlier words ran through her mind and they stopped her cold.

His eyes were gold. Sidhe gold.

No. Gareth is Gareth. He's the man I loved.

Still love.

Exactly. Why else is it too hard for you to contemplate? He said tricks, and Sidhe are master manipulators.

Stop it.

He's a Raven. Not a Sidhe.

Death by Sex doesn't mean actual death. It means losing oneself completely.

Isn't that a definition of love?

Stop being thick. You know I mean losing your identity. Becoming a slave. Like those vampires.

I'm not listening.

Fine. At least ask the questions that need asking. If not for yourself, then for Eve.

Shut up.

She winced. Her inner voice was right. She had to know, regardless of the answer. Gareth had come back from the dead and rocked her world. Not just between the sheets, but by resurrecting emotions she'd long buried. In her gut, she knew Gareth was connected to what happened with Eve. She sent up a silent prayer it wasn't her worst fears.

"You okay?" he asked. "You look like you're a million miles away."

Gareth touched her arm, and she nearly jumped out of her skin.

"Laney? What's going on?" He turned her to face him, slipping his hands to her waist.

She bit her lip. Her head screamed ask him and get it over with, but her body wanted his mouth and his hands. Was her attraction one of the tricks he couldn't explain? Some kind of low wattage Sidhe glamour, or was this real?

"Before we start on the books, you need to tell me why you showed up unannounced when you did. You said you were sent, but you really didn't go into detail."

It was clear on his face he saw she wasn't kidding. "I was told to keep things on the down low unless things went south."

"By south, you mean if Leith got what he came for." Lane eyed him closer.

He nodded. "But he didn't. You're still here."

The reference book was still in her hand, and she dropped it onto the others with an exhale. "Leith took Eve. That's close enough, and considering you said you were still all Raven, it should have been enough for you to tell me the truth."

"I've faced horrors and death. I've lived and survived in a place where many don't share the Seelie queen's beliefs. They view me as a half-breed abomination rather than a rarity. I've faced all that, but I wasn't brave enough to tell you what you needed to hear."

Lane's jaw tightened, but her eyes stayed riveted. "Eve's dead. You knew when you spotted me and decided to drop your glamour."

"No. I mean, it's a possibility, but I don't know for sure." Gareth exhaled, turning from her to pace by the darkened window. "The Seelie queen got wind of what happened in the Dark Court. Whispers are second nature to the Sidhe, and once in the air are hard to resist. But what Leith tried struck home. The Seelie queen met the Unseelie king in the lands between and struck a deal. Neither wants Leith's plan to succeed, as it threatens their shared tenets."

"What tenets? How can a single Raven make a difference to a millennia old race?"

Gareth stopped pacing and walked back to the table to ruffle through papers. "Damn. I didn't expect I'd find it here."

"What?"

He looked at her. "Records of what really happened with me. It's here—" he picked up the accounting again. "But it's incomplete. The same power the Unseelie tapped when they tried to harness my blood, my power, is the same magic Leith is trying to obtain. He knows the Unseelie failed with me, but he believes he'll be the one to unleash a power so great none can withstand. He's mad.

But his genius is his determination. He won't stop until he's explored every possibility. And that includes you."

"My blood? Why? I'm nothing extraordinary. I'm a Raven, same as the rest. You were the unique one."

Gareth shrugged. "So, he thought. Now he's fixated on you. That's why I think it's more likely Eve is still alive. Killing her or letting her fall prey to his addicted vampires doesn't serve Leith's purpose. The answer has to be in these books somewhere. Raven lineage is a real thing, and there has to be a record of some sort hidden in this mess."

"If Leith is that sure of himself, then maybe he couldn't resist bragging about his plan. In his arrogance, maybe he shot off his mouth to add to Eve's terror. Scare her into subservience for my sake."

He considered her words. "Definitely possible. It fits the profile information the Seelie Court provided before I hopped realms. This all happened moments ago for them, while for us it's been hours and hours."

She took the recorded pages from Gareth's hand and put them on the table. "Let's try scrying for Eve. This is our sanctuary and her essence is strong here. It might work."

"I guess." Gareth glanced at the shelves of old books and stacks of papers. "We can't use smoke or flame in here, but we can outside."

Lane shook his head. "Caitlan secured the grounds, but she's yet to perform the blood rite sealing the wards. She needed us for that," Lane replied low. "We took long—" she caught Gareth's eye and winked. "*Upstairs.*"

Turning on his heel, he stalked out the library door. Lane stared after him. "Damn."

He came back a moment later with one of the oval mirrors from the wall above the hall credenza. "Clear a space. Fire is best, but I'm not taking any chances with you. In this case a reflective surface will do us just fine."

Lane moved the books and papers Caro left for them to a chair.

"—and as for taking too long upstairs," Gareth continued, placing the mirror on the worn wood. "I plan on taking whatever time I can grab with you, as often as you allow. Wherever and whenever."

Stifling an inner squeal, she turned for Caro's teaching crystals on the desk. Grabbing a handful of amethysts and Herkimer diamonds, she carried the lot to the table.

"Since we can't burn incense, these will help. I don't know if you remember, but Herkimer are double terminated quartz. They're powerful, high vibration crystals that boost clairvoyant and clairaudient abilities. They're Eve's go to crystal and might help direct us to her."

"Every little bit helps."

Lane finished placing the crystals and then took her place beside Gareth. "Ready when you are."

"The summons is best in Latin," he said.

"And?"

He shrugged "Dead languages were never my strong suit."

"Confidence issues, Gareth? Are you afraid you'll conjure something I'll have to clean up?"

"No."

"Then just say you'd rather I do the honors."

His lips pushed into a *gotcha* smirk. "Well, your pronunciation was always better than mine. Besides, Eve doesn't even know me."

"Bock, bock," she teased. "How you can still charm me into doing things is beyond me."

In one fluid move, he skimmed her waist, turning her so close their breath mingled. "I don't want to charm you into anything. I want you willing and wet."

Her lips parted, waiting for the crush of his mouth, but footsteps outside the library door caught their attention.

"I was afraid you couldn't do this without adult supervision," Caitlan said as she entered. "Do I need to separate you two?"

Lane stepped back from Gareth with a cough. "Why would you think that?"

The look on the older witch's face said it all and Gareth grinned, unhooking his arm from Lane's waist.

"Caitlan's no fool, love. She's right. Hard as it is to concentrate, *you* need to focus."

"Me?" Lane sputtered.

"Okay, you two. Enough. The walls in this house are old and thin. Especially upstairs. I don't need or want any more details than I already have."

Lane groaned, but Gareth countered with a smirk. "I should be grateful Caitlan didn't turn you into a frog again."

"I'm a prince, babe."

Caitlan shut the banter down, holding her hands out for them to grasp. "Good choice on the crystals. Three times three times three. Let's begin."

Chapter Ten

"You sure this incantation has to be in Latin?" Lane ignored Gareth's smirk.

Caitlan looked at them both. "Who said a beckoning has to be in Latin?"

"Uhm, *you*," Lane countered with a snort.

Gareth nodded. "Every class. Every day."

She dismissed them outright with a ghost of a smirk. "Even if I did, you should be grateful I was such a stickler or you two would never have broken into the old stacks back in the day."

"You knew it was us?" Lane asked, surprised.

Caitlan shrugged. "Of course. What did you think?"

"All righty, then." Lane closed her eyes, holding tight to both their hands.

"Clear your mind and focus solely on Eve," Caitlan instructed. "Her essence. Her magic. They live in the fabric of this house. Grasp the common trace and will the images forth."

Gareth mumbled something and Lane cracked one eye open. "I thought you said you were crap at Latin?"

"I am, but one phrase I know by heart. *Viam sapientiae monstrabo tibi.* I will show you the way of wisdom."

Eyes closed, Caitlan flashed a soft smile. "It's nice to know someone was paying attention."

"Wow, Gareth." Lane snorted again." What's the Latin word for brown-noser?"

"Lane—"

"Sorry, Caitlan." She inhaled a breath before beginning the slow intonation. *"Obsecro per velamen, in quo mihi quaero. Visus revelare et dirige in via, semita ut nunc mihi.* Through the veil I beseech, show me the one in which I seek. Guide my sight and reveal the way, show me now, the path to take."

Three sets of eyes focused on the silvered glass. Lane repeated the Latin words, a mere whisper at first, but her call grew in tone and urgency as the mirror darkened to a glossy black.

The crystals glowed, ringing the scrying surface in crackling magic. "Look sharp," Caitlan warned. "Whatever shown us could vanish in an instant."

The black glass rippled like still water disturbed, as the first image cleared the darkness.

"Eve," Lane whispered.

Her friend was curled on a low palette surrounded by rushes on a stone floor. Fat, drippy candles burned in brass holders, and when she looked closer, it was clear Eve suffered similar bites as Mason, though not fatal.

"Fucking Fae pig." Lane's voice cracked in anger. "He's let the vampires feed on her."

Caitlan studied the image as well. "The room looks medieval. Maybe he's got her holed up in the Cloisters over in Fort Tryon Park."

"It would serve Leith's purpose to keep this in our back yard," Gareth replied. "But truth is Eve could be anywhere. You forget the Sidhe can sift time. For all we know, the room looks medieval because it is medieval."

The glass rippled again. This time an image flashed of green hills cut by jagged, red cliffs. A dark sea battered the coastline, and Lane gasped at the accompanying sensation.

Desolation buffeted, but it disappeared as quickly as the image, leaving the mirror's surface cloudy and unreadable.

Black tendrils formed, swirling snake-like through the glassy murk. Lane shivered and gooseflesh spread across her skin. Her throat tightened as the dark harbingers rose.

"Gareth!" she croaked, squeezing his hand. "I can't stop them. What's hap...happen—" Her breath failed, and she pitched forward.

The crystals shattered, sending dirty gray fragments flying. Lane winced, blood trickling from where they bit into her flesh.

"Lane!" He twisted, trying to free his hand from Caitlan's grip, but she wouldn't let go. "I have to help her!"

"Gareth, no! If you break the circle, whatever holds Lane will take her completely. We are her only ground!"

Caitlan's words penetrated, and his jaw stiffened. Their blood mingled with Lane's and his eyes flashed liquid gold as the rivulets met. White hot power skittered over his skin, sizzling down his arm to his hand.

Hissing, Cait's muscles contracted against the surge, but she held tight. Iridescent energy spread, healing their wounds as it encompassed them whole, but pulled back when it swept toward Lane.

"He's stopping me from helping her!" With a snarl, Gareth ratcheted the surge, the intensity nearly bringing Caitlan to her knees.

"Save it, cowboy. Now is not the time for a power pissing match. Find another way!"

Lane whimpered, her veins straining in her throat as she tried to breathe.

"Show me what you see, Lane," Caitlan reassured. "Project the images like I taught you when you were a child. We can't help if we're fighting blind."

The encouragement was for Lane, but the arbitrating message was for Gareth. Don't poke the bear until cocked and ready.

"The bastard is using his power to—"

The supreme shot him a look, cutting off his words. "Brace yourself. I'm opening the channels!"

Caitlan withdrew the inner wards keeping the Fae magic at bay. They had to reach Leith before he reached them. It was the only way, if they wanted a shot at saving Lane from his grip.

Anger and dark lust flooded the open conduit to her mind, and the same cold, black tendrils clawed for her, but she was prepared.

Gareth gritted his teeth, fighting the attack as well, as Caitlan braced against the strike. Using all her skill, she isolated the intrusive sensations, redirecting to back-mind chambers.

The onslaught ebbed, and Gareth's relief was palpable. "Holy mousetrap, Batman, how did you do that?" He relaxed his grip, checking that Lane felt the temporary reprieve as well.

"Later. Right now, I need your power to help fight this bastard before he figures out my detour."

Gareth nodded, scowling. "I can taste his menace."

"Join the club. Weres got nothing on us when it comes to the tang of dark magic. When I give the word, send me everything you've got. Keep your grip tight on me and Lane, just in case."

His stony expression said it all. "Like iron. I want to see the bastard's face when we fry his Fae ass."

Caitlan's head yanked back and her body stiffened. She drew breath through her teeth, every muscle straining against an invisible force.

"Cait!"

Leith broke through her redirect, and a soft, cold laugh feathered through her mind. Painfully beautiful and unrelentingly erotic, he whispered in a language she didn't know, but somehow understood. Urgent and yearning, the murmurs buffeted her mind and teased her body, testing her reserve with hungry desire.

Supple and wet, the way you used to be. The way you wish to be. Want is swelling inside you, almost too much to bear. I feel it. You want my caress. My touch. You crave it. So easy to give in…to pleasure…to release. You know you have no choice.

Senses she thought long dead electrified her body, making her knees go weak. Invisible fingers stroked her nether flesh and the erotic punch left her breathless. She groaned, squeezing her eyes shut against the enticing sensations.

"He took Eve's power. She succumbed to him. Bastard seized her power when she…climaxed." Her words were clipped and tense. "Helpless and bound. I smell it through the mist. He's too strong."

Gareth gave her a vicious shake, bringing her back. "He's manipulating your senses, Caitlan. We're running out of time. We need to channel our combined power through to Lane. She knows what to do. She reversed Leith's magic earlier tonight at the Red Veil."

From the dark glass, black tendrils spread higher, climbing toward Lane's throat and down to her sex.

Panic touched the young witch's eyes, begging for help. This was it. Gareth steeled himself, and then lifted his face and arms toward the ceiling, keeping their hands locked in his grip.

"Forgive me," he whispered.

The air hung heavy and still, like the calm before a storm. Soft, yellow light emanated from Gareth's skin, expanding until it encircled the three of them completely.

It shimmered, warm and encompassing before spreading across the library.

Mad gusts tore at the room from nowhere, sending papers and books flying. The floorboards shook and glass panes splintered in the windows. The soft, buttery light surrounding them changed to an orange-gold, and Gareth's energy prickled across their flesh.

Power prickled with a thousand stings, narrowing tighter and tighter until it covered their bodies like a second skin.

"Caitlan! With me! Give it all to Lane! Now!"

Without hesitation, she lowered their linked hands, directing every ounce of power through to the younger witch.

Lane cried out at the unexpected flood, her flesh glowing bright and hot.

"Hold tight, love! We're fighting Fae fire with Fae fire. Phoenix style!"

Gareth's voice muffled in her ears. She knew he was there, but she could no longer feel his hands, or Caitlan's for that matter. She floated, her sight, and every other sense, blurred as she tried to focus on the dark glass.

Eve's image swirled in the murky depths for a moment, but then went black. Breathing hard, she tried to command the scrying glass, gathering the collective power swirling in her body.

"Show me what I seek!"

She had no sight, no voice, so the visions took her mind instead.

The mists cleared, only to show her friend was no longer alone in the stone room. A woman was with her, but who?

Ready power suffused her skin, but Lane froze as the woman turned. Her own face glanced back from the vision, and Lane nearly choked.

"Lane! Can you hear us?"

"Burn the bastard already!"

Gareth and Cait's voices barely penetrated as the image swirled and changed, but when she watched herself draw a short sword from its sheath beside the pallet bed, a silent scream ripped from her lips.

"Don't! Eve!" Shock and betrayal flashed in her friend's eyes as Lane watched the blade pierce Eve's chest. "It's not me! It's not true!"

Red anger bubbled hot, vibrating the amassed power waiting in Lane's chest. "No! You BASTARD!"

Collective energy exploded outward, its white heat incinerating the black tendrils holding her hostage. Lane collapsed in Gareth's arms as a loud hiss echoed in the chaos.

He held her tight, lowering her to the floor. "You had me worried there for a moment, kiddo. What the hell happened?"

Lane gripped his arms, her fingers buried in his biceps. "Leith had other plans for me."

Caitlan knelt beside her on the strewn papers. "We tried reaching you, honey, but your face...your eyes...they were blank and sightless. Where were you? What happened?"

She turned to meet Caitlan's worried eyes. "I was there. In the room with Eve. I killed her. Or I watched me do it."

"That's impossible. Even if you astral projected, you wouldn't be able to do anything but observe. You're not corporeal in that form."

Lane looked away. "I saw what I saw, Caitlan. I killed Eve."

"Eve isn't dead, Laney," Caitlan replied quickly. "I'd have felt it. When Ravens die, we all feel the weight of their soul leaving. It's part of our shared lineage."

Lane met her gaze but didn't comment.

"Cait's right. Leith is a dark Sidhe. He's taken power from witches for longer than anyone knows for sure. Don't you think he could manipulate the power he took from Eve to make you think you killed her? Maybe in a moment of weakness and fear, Eve—"

"What?" Lane blurted. "Blamed me for getting her into this mess in the first place? That Leith used her blame and my guilt to make me think I killed her?"

Caitlan nodded sadly. "Yes."

"Even if my hand didn't plunge that blade into Eve's heart, she's dead because of me." Lane grunted a derisive snort.

"She's not dead, Lane," Caitlan tried again.

Gareth stood, reaching to help both women off the floor. "C'mon. We have work to do. You did not kill Eve, Laney. She gave us a hint."

"Hint?" Lane took his hand and let him pull her to her feet.

He nodded, helping Caitlan next. "She turned Leith's own deception back on him, using it to give us a hint on how to defeat him. Permanently."

"I think I'm starting to see what Gareth means," Caitlan surveyed the mess in the library. "Though, the answer is going to be much harder to find in this clutter."

Bending to scoop up the pages on the floor around them, he straightened with a quick wink. "Not necessarily. Especially since we know what we're looking for now."

"Will one of you please explain to me what you're babbling about?"

He put the papers on the table next to the splintered scrying mirror, the spidery cracks distorting the normal reflection. "A sword."

Chapter Eleven

Caitlan crouched beside Lane, sorting through the scattered books on the floor by the study table. "If memory serves, there are only a handful of books that speak to the kind of weaponry resembling what you saw in your premonition."

"Well." Lane exhaled, tossing a book of random spells to the side. "They've got to be somewhere. The library's intact, just jumbled beyond recognition."

Caitlan snorted. "Tell that to Caro. Her categorization system is decimated."

"The sword in my premonition shined like polished silver. Maybe that's a clue and we should be looking for a book on metallic magical properties. The hilt has got to be a clue as well. It was even more ornate than your athame, Gareth."

He sorted books from the fallout on the opposite end of the room. "Silver is too soft a metal to be an effective weapon. The sword from your premonition was most likely carbon steel, which is iron ore based. I'd bet a testicle that's why *you* handled the sword in the vision and not Leith."

Caitlan nodded. "I agree with Gareth. We're looking for writings on a forged sword imbued with magical energy. Something a full-blooded Sidhe wouldn't dare risk touching." She paused, letting her gaze fall to Lane. "Try calling to it, honey. You're the one who saw the sword used. Visualize it. See it in the book that will tell us what we need."

"Anything's better than digging through this wreck." Resting her hands palm up on her knees, Lane rolled her shoulders and then closed her eyes. She muttered a soft spell awakening the part of her that knows, sees, and remembers everything.

"Silver moon, goddess wise, show me now within my right. Grant your blessing, three times three, show me now what I need. Crown chakra, knowledge bright, open now my third-eye's sight."

Power tingled her scalp, radiating through to her fingertips. They prickled as if already holding the book. She breathed slowly, in and out. Flashes formed, images flickering behind her lids as though the universe sorted the possibilities, discarding one after the other.

Caitlan stood, motioning to Gareth as a weak, winking glow peeked from beneath the bottom of one of stacks.

"Lane—" She kept her voice steady. "Whatever image is in your mind now, hold it. Expand it if you can, but don't let it go."

Caitlan moved toward the pile of books, bending to slowly remove each one until she stared at the glowing volume. Gold light shimmered from its spine and across its tatty cover. "Kids, I think we have lift off."

Lane exhaled, dropping her chin to her chest, murmuring a prayer of thanks to the universe. The image in her mind faded along with the tingle of power spiraling from her crown chakra, and she opened her eyes.

Unassuming in its design, the book had definitely seen better days. Its cloth cover was frayed along the edges, and time had rendered its title indiscernible.

Caitlan straightened with the book in her hand, turning to place it on the study table. She opened the cover with care, skimming the worn flyleaf before turning the first few delicate pages.

Lane and Gareth rounded the table to flank her on either side. "I wouldn't have given this a second glance," Lane murmured. "It looks too dogeared to be anything of significance." She reached to touch the delicate pages, but Caitlan smacked her hand.

"Gloves." The supreme nodded toward the desk. "In the top right drawer. The pages could be spelled or worse."

"*You* touched it," Lane grumbled, retrieving the gloves. "If the book was boobytrapped, you'd have been zapped the moment you skimmed a hand over the cover."

Caitlan rolled her eyes. "Don't be a baby. Privilege comes with age and experience."

Lane handed gloves all around and then stood by as Caitlan turned threadbare page after page. Illustrations rivalling the hand-copied books of old winked from nearly translucent pages.

"This should be in a museum, not moldering at the bottom of a pile of reference books in a basement library," Lane replied, running a gloved finger over the vivid gold and red ornamental lettering.

The illustrations depicted weapons of all shapes and sizes. From easy to conceal dirks to heavy claymores and thrusting longswords, along with techniques for block, swing, parry and thrust.

"So, the book the universe wanted us to find the medieval version of *Swordplay for Dummies*." Lane shifted the book for a closer look. "Okay, fates. What now?"

She skimmed the descriptions before gently turning the next few pages. "This is nothing but general descriptions of when and how to use the weapons. Plus, none of them fit what I saw exactly. The sword I wielded had Fae sigils in gold on the hilt, and other sigils I couldn't recognize engraved on the flat of the blade. On top of everything, we still don't know why Leith wants me in particular. I was hoping Caro's research could shed some light on that, but I guess not."

Caitlan walked toward the only shelf in the library with books still intact. They were so because they were encased in leather and glass. "Lane, how much do you remember from when you first came to the motherhouse?" Taking a key from a chain hidden in her cleavage, she unlocked the small bolt at the bottom of the case.

"Not much. I remember you and Grania. Gareth came later, but other than that—" Lane shrugged.

Caitlan lifted the glass lid to the case. "I'm not surprised."

"Does this have something to do with Leith and why he's wreaking havoc?" Gareth asked, his interest piqued as well.

"In a nutshell, yes." Caitlan took the books from inside the case, one by one, placing them on a chair. "You were brought here by your mother. Her name was Aislinn."

Lane's mouth opened but she snapped it closed at the look on Caitlan's face.

"She was a Raven, like you. Beautiful. Ethereal. Her one flaw was not knowing her own worth. She needed physical validation, and eventually it went way beyond sexual satisfaction. She fell prey to a Sidhe, and succumbing, eventually became enslaved." Her eyes were sad. "You know the type. Death by sex. Except your mother didn't die. She became pregnant.

"It was the life stirring within her, your life, that brought her to her senses. Aislinn escaped your father, never telling him of your existence. She did her best to raise you alone, but as you got older, she knew it was only a matter of time before he sensed you. Before puberty hit, and you came into your power.

"Aislinn showed up on our doorstep with you in tow. You weren't more than six or seven years old. Together we bound your Sidhe side, only allowing your witchy powers to manifest. It's the same with Gareth."

At Lane's sharp intake, Caitlan whirled on her heel.

"Relax, Gareth is *not* your brother. But he is a halfling, same as you. He has enough Sidhe blood to be claimed. Just as you do. Your mother didn't want that."

"So, she made the choice for me? From what you describe, I'm her polar opposite. I don't need validation from anyone but myself, let alone physical validation from sex. Hell, I frequented the backrooms at the Red Veil to get my freak on because it's what I wanted, not because I needed to feel good about myself."

Caitlan stood beside the empty case. "Not because you were trying to escape something?" Her eyes slipped to Gareth. "Memories of what might have been, perhaps?"

Lane didn't answer, and Caitlan took that as a cue to continue. "Your mother had good reason to choose for you. Gareth is male. And a rare Phoenix. It's why the Seelie queen accepted him into her court. You're female, so you'd have no choice but to be a concubine or a despised servant, especially since your bloodline hailed from the Unseelie court. Aislinn wanted you to have a choice in life, Lane. As a Raven, you could one day be a supreme, or more."

Gareth slipped an arm around Lane's slumped shoulders, supporting her under the weight of Caitlan's revelations. "Are you telling us Leith is Lane's father?"

"Yes." She nodded. "Earlier, I told you we needed a blood rite. I let you believe it was to protect the motherhouse and our coven, and I'm sorry for the lie of omission. The blood rite we need is to unbind Lane's Sidhe powers so the two of you can defeat Leith together. The blood rite will coalesce your powers and unlock your Fae side, but the only way to ensure you don't fall prey to what your father wants, you'll need to be claimed."

At that, Lane's shoulders stiffened, and her eyes jerked to Caitlan. "Claimed? By whom? How?"

"By another Sidhe."

Gareth spared a tentative glance for Lane. "Full-blooded?

"No." Caitlan met Gareth's eyes. "By you. You've been claimed by the Seelie Court, so by default you may claim a mate. Considering you were sent by your queen, I doubt she'll have much to say against the proposal. If we do the ritual correctly, Leith won't be able to resist trying to disrupt things."

Gareth looked at Lane. "You look like you're going to vomit. Bad idea?"

"No, it's what I've always wanted, it's just—" she licked her lips. "Not like this. Like we have no other choice."

He squeezed her shoulder, pressing a kiss to her hair. "Shotgun wedding, Fae style. Besides, you're the one who said you wanted to be bait."

Her head jerked around, and she met his eyes. "The vampires. We've completely left them out of the equation. They're going to want their pound of flesh, not to mention the Weres. Leith manipulated the three vamps he used to get to me, putting a very important truce at stake. Pardon the pun."

"If you're suggesting what I think you're suggesting, then I'm not sure I'm okay with it, Lane. The motherhouse has never hosted vampire guests, or shifters for that matter. I'm not so sure they'd be happy with the idea either."

"Then we'll have to rethink the plan of attack," Gareth interjected. "We still have to find the right weapon in this book and see what it has to say. In the meantime, we should contact the vampire council and the Alpha of the Brethren."

"Gareth's right. You've had enough for one twenty-four-hour period. I'll make the necessary calls. Leith is a consummate chess player, and this is a game for him. The board is ours for now. He can't make a move until we do, so get some rest. We can put together what we need for the ritual come morning. The house and grounds are completely warded, so sleep well." Caitlan winked. "I'll leave you two to it, then."

Gareth turned with Lane for the door, but Caitlan stopped them. "Just one more thing."

She waved a hand inside the empty glass and leather case, muttering a spell under her breath. A letter appeared, and she took it and the sword book and handed them both to Lane.

"It's from Aislinn. She left it for you to open when the time came for your powers to be woke. Read it and then look through the book. I have a feeling you'll find the all the answers you need."

Chapter Twelve

"Why don't you take a hot shower? It'll help." Gareth's fingers wrapped around her shoulders with a light squeeze. "Your head has to be spinning with what Caitlan revealed."

Lane inhaled, letting her head drop so his fingers kneaded more of the tension from her neck. "That's putting it lightly. Finding out my biological father is a Sidhe psychopath doesn't do much for my self-esteem. Especially since I've been the black sheep around here forever."

"Bending the rules doesn't make you a black sheep. You've never hurt anyone intentionally, and your heart was always in the right place."

"I suppose." She paused, cocking her head to glance at him from the side. "How come you didn't seem quite as stunned when Caitlan let my parentage out of the proverbial bag?"

He slid an arm forward, holding her against his chest. "Because I already knew."

His breath tickled the back of her ear, and she turned in his embrace to look at him eye to eye. "You knew?"

He nodded, cupping her cheek. "When word of Leith's attempt to bring about a coup reached the Summer Kingdom, the Seelie Court was a buzz. To be honest, I didn't pay much attention until I heard one name mentioned."

"Mine."

"Yes. At that point, I used every connection I had to find out whatever I could. The queen was the one who finally told me. Apparently, she knew about you from the beginning, including where you were all this time." He hesitated, letting go of her cheek. "She was the one who helped Aislinn get away from Leith. I guess she felt sorry for her in some small way, which is saying a lot because the Fae aren't exactly compassion incarnate. Just the opposite."

She pulled out of Gareth's grip. "Great. This just gets better and better."

"Laney, don't." He let her slip past but held onto her hand. "Which do you think holds more sway over who we become? Nature or nurture? You're still the same amazing woman you were twenty-four hours ago, right? Who cares if you've got Sidhe blood? I don't, and I'm in the same halfling boat as you.

"I told you before all this came to light. Before Caitlan even mentioned the possibility of us claiming each other. I want you. I've always wanted you. It's what should have been from the beginning and can be now." He paused, pulling her closer again. "Are you trying to tell me you don't want this? Don't want to be with me?"

His eyes searched hers, and the heat coming from his body and his gaze seared her soul and made her flesh ache for his touch.

"Uhm, I think I'm going to take that shower."

"Good. It'll help you relax. Maybe even help you sleep."

Lane shook her head. "A shower isn't going to do it for me, Gareth. I need something hard to work out these knots." She reached up and undid one tie at the top of her blouse, letting the soft fabric slip past one shoulder. "Something really hard."

She undid the second tie, letting her shirt slip to her waist in a silken fall. "How did you put it earlier? Hard enough to cut diamonds?" Reaching for the front of his pants, she hooked her fingers into his waistband. "Any ideas?"

"Plenty." Gareth slid his hands to her waist, letting his lips hover just above her mouth. "First off, you have too many clothes on," he tsked. "What are we going to do about that?" He reached for her blouse and tugged it over her head, letting the fabric fall to the floor. Unhooking her bra, he dipped his head to her jutting nipples, nipping them each through the lace until she moaned, arching her back.

He walked her backwards into the bathroom, leaving her bra on the floor with her blouse. There was enough ambient light from Lane's bedroom to set everything in warm, luscious shadow. His mouth crushed hers, devouring her lips and her tongue as he reached behind her back to turn on the spray. Steam rose almost immediately, bathing her exposed flesh in a gorgeous sheen.

Dragging his fingers over her full breasts, he circled her nipples with the wet condensation. "I want more than just your tits wet and on display, Laney. I want your pussy dripping. Spread wide for me to take and taste. There's something primal about fucking in water. Primitive. Ravaging. And I want it all. I want you wild with desire, your pussy so wet it slicks your thighs and drips over my chin and then later my balls."

Lane gasped and her nipples and clit throbbed from just his words. A single touch and she'd come like a rocket. Gareth's lips pushed into a smirk. "Strip, Lane. Leave on nothing but your panties."

She did as he asked, and he kissed her again but stepped back instead of escalating to the next level. Her mouth dropped to complain but stopped when she saw he went to the sideboard across from her bed.

"Lots of interesting things you've got hidden in the cupboard, little girl," he teased, resting a half-empty bottle of wine and a small, drawstring bag on the shower's tile floor. "Plus, I never let a good merlot go to waste."

He stepped back, untying the drawstring to his pants before slipping them past his hips. He did so slowly, teasing Lane completely as his fingers pushed the soft cotton past the sexy vee and tease of dark hair toward the hard length waiting below.

"You're killing me, Smalls." She flashed a smirk, quoting their movie as he did earlier.

His cock sprang free of the restrictive waistband, the hard bar thick and corded.

Lane licked her lips. *Smalls* was definitely not a word to describe Gareth. It never was.

His grin faded to an urgent slash and he scooped her into his arms and stepped over the edge and into the spacious open shower.

The water beaded on her skin, cascading in rivulets drenching her hair. He leaned down, taking one nipple between his teeth. He sucked the stiffening peak between his lips, letting one hand dip between her thighs.

Stroking her wet slit, he slipped two fingers into her cleft and curled them deep. He leaned in, taking her mouth as he circled her inner spot. "I want you on your knees, Lane. Your ass in the air. You're mine. Every inch of you."

He broke their kiss and pulled back his hand, licking each one before kissing her again. "The taste of you makes my cock want to burst. For years, I imagined how you smelled, your taste. Alone I worked my length to just your memory and every sense I could conjure. Now I have you here, in the flesh, and I want every inch of you."

Her heart pounded in her chest, but a secret smile stole across her lips as she kissed Gareth's neck, feathering tiny bites and kisses down his chest as she sank to her knees in front of him.

"Not so fast, love." He stopped her, pulling her to her feet again. "Me first."

His voice was commanding. Earlier it was just urgent, but now it was clear the sexy boy she loved, lusted for, and lost had grown into a man's man, with scars inside and out to match. Power rippled beneath her fingers as she explored his muscled torso and chest. She got to her feet, and the heat of his gaze locked her breath in her throat, nearly scorching her flesh. His eyes took in her full length, lingering at the way the spray glistened on her body, wet and bidding.

With one fluid motion, he swept her up again, sitting her on the marble bench at the back of the shower stall. He knelt and pushed her thighs apart. Dipping his face to her slick folds, he licked her slit to her hard nub. "You take my breath away, Lane. I could bury myself in you forever and never have enough."

She sucked in a breath, his words and the rough feel of his beard on her tender flesh pushing her higher toward climax. Closing her eyes, she let her head drop back as he slid his thumb between her folds. "So fucking wet," he whispered, letting his fingers slide further to circle her clit. "But we can do better."

He took the wine bottle from the floor of the shower and pull the cork with his teeth, spitting it to the floor. Pouring the wine over her breasts, it trickled to her pussy in purple rivulets.

Gareth sucked her tits, licking and nibbling his way to her slippery, wine-soaked mound. "Sweet musk and sweet wine. You intoxicate me, Lane. In all ways."

She arched back, moaning as his fingers and mouth drove her pussy. Gareth slid his free hand over her belly to cup her breast, and she dug her fingers into her dark hair, grinding herself farther into his mouth. She came hard as he sucked her clit deep, gasping as spasms shook.

He pulled back, wiping his mouth on the back of his hand with a satisfied grin. "So damn good, but now it's my turn." Pushing her knees wide, he got to his feet and wrapped his hand around his corded shaft.

Stepping between her thighs, he pressed the tip of his cock to her lips and Lane took his full length, no waiting. She wrapped her hands around his ass, working him with the flat of her tongue and her throat. Milking his corded length, she slid him even deeper before releasing him inch by inch until the ridged edge of his head bulged between her lips ready to blow.

A muffled gasp left Gareth's throat. "Woman, unless you want to swallow everything I give, you'd better spread yourself now!"

He didn't wait for an answer. He pulled his cock free and yanked her to her feet, crushing his mouth to hers, fierce and exacting. The salty taste of his essence was on her lips and it mixed with her nuance still on his tongue.

Breaking their kiss, he turned her so her back molded against his chest. "I want you on your knees, Lane. Your ass grinding my cock."

Nipping the back of her neck, he urged her to the tile. With a single thrust, he drove his member between her folds, his hips pumping hard and fast.

Gareth filled every inch of her core. Lane's breath locked in her throat as she came again, her hips meeting his thrust for thrust. Pleasure flooded her body as it quaked and squeezed.

He reached for the drawstring bag on the floor. "Feel like a walk on the wild side, little witch?" He drew a large dildo from inside the bag, curved with tiny nubs along the synthetic skin shaft. "You had quite a selection, but I thought this one looked like the most fun."

He pulled his cock back, taking a moment to spread her slick wetness back toward her tight hole.

Teasing her, he worked her ass with his thumb as he worked her pussy with the tip of the dildo. She moaned at the invasive feel as his fingers stretched her tight ring, readying her for his thick dick. He drew the fleshy plastic back from her sex and then helped her to all fours on the bench. Pressing the tip of his cock to her hole, he slid inside, inch by straining inch. She took him, sucking sharp breaths as her body hovered between pleasure and pain.

"So fucking tight," he whispered behind her ear as he teased her clit before slipping the dildo between her folds again.

With a deep thrust, he buried his length in her tight sheath, riding her ring as he worked her pussy. She moaned at the combined feel of his cock and the sexy toy, both filling beyond measure.

Every muscle tensed, suspended, until pleasure tore through her, radiating hot and fierce. Waves spread through her lower belly and down her thighs, penetrating her core as Gareth impaled her body over and over.

The tiled shower shimmered gold and white as power sizzled in and around them. It spiraled, sizzling on their skin. Gareth held tight. Every muscle coiled as her climax rocked through him. He let go with a cry, hot jets pulsing deep within her.

With a gasp, he let the dildo slide free. It splashed to the shower floor as he tightened one arm around Lane's waist. Cupping her pussy with the other, they rode the final waves together until they both slumped forward in the warm spray.

The two lay panting, their bodies entwined and sweaty as water cascaded around them. Gareth released her waist, slowly slipping his member from her tight ring. He reached for the bodywash on the shelf and lathered his hands, sliding the whip cream bubbles over Lane's breasts and between her legs.

She did the same, washing him as well. His lips found hers, and he kissed her soft and warm. "I love you, Lane Alden. I always have and I always will, and I am never letting you go."

Tucking herself beneath his arm, she wrapped soapy hands around his back, holding him tight. "Good, or I'll make Caitlan turn you into a frog for good."

He smiled against her hair, kissing the wet mass. "You'd kiss me into a prince again. I know you. You could never resist having the last word."

Lane slid her slippery hands around to his still thick member. "That's not the only last I couldn't resist."

Kissing her again, Gareth lifted her with a quick spin, pressing her back to the warm tile wall and his cock to her waiting pussy. He fucked her slow and languorous, teasing her with every stroke until neither could take anymore. They climaxed again, power surging between them, sending glittering light circling like constellations as they came.

He buried his head in her neck, a smile stretching across her wet skin. "I don't think we're going to need Caitlan's blood rite to waken your Sidhe side."

She laughed. "Why? You afraid of a little blood?"

"No. But it might be an overstatement at this point. Your skin is glowing gold, love. I think we accomplished the deed all by ourselves."

Lifting her arm, Lane grinned, watching her skin shimmer and sparkle. "Oh man, Caitlan's going to be so mad."

He laughed. "I don't think she'll care. She might even make us go through the motions just to be sure it's not a one off."

Cupping his wet face, she kissed him again, biting his bottom lip. "I am not a one off. You are not a one off. *We* are not a one off. Got it?"

"Yes, ma'am. Now let's get out of this water. It's going cold and my bits are starting to shrivel...and that's an *off* neither of us want."

Chapter Thirteen

Lane lay on her pillow, propped against the headboard. Gareth snored gently beside her, but she couldn't sleep. Too much had happened too quickly for rest to come.

She flipped through the channels on the television, but nothing interested her. Too preoccupied to give late night programming more than a cursory glance, her eyes swept to the desk across the bedroom, and the book and the letter sitting on top of Gareth's pile of clothes.

With a tentative breath, she swung her legs over the side of the bed and padded over to carry them back to the bed with her.

The letter had her name scrawled in big, looping script across the front, with a small heart drawn into the cursive letter E at the end of her name. She ran her fingers over the ink, wondering what her mother's thoughts were at the time. From what Caitlan said, she already knew her fears.

The generous handwriting and the drawn heart reminded her of commercials where moms hid tiny love notes inside their children's lunchboxes. Her heart squeezed at how she never knew what it felt like to have that kind of unconditional love. To have a mom.

Staring at the cursive heart, she knew now she had that all along, albeit from afar. Her throat tightened at the realization, and she didn't know whether to laugh, cry, or kill something. She'd been robbed, and it was Leith who was responsible.

Caitlan didn't say much more after her initial revelation. In fact, she didn't explain what happened to Aislinn after she and Caitlan bound her Sidhe powers. Maybe it was too painful. Or perhaps Caitlan didn't know. Maybe she thought the weight of the disclosure was enough for one night.

Either way, Leith was responsible no matter what happened. If Aislinn hadn't felt trapped and threatened, she'd never have been compelled to run.

"Like ripping off a Band-Aid," she murmured under her breath, and tore the envelope open across the top.

She pulled the thin cream-colored sheet from the inside and unfolded it to the same looping script.

My darling daughter,

If Caitlan revealed this letter, then your father has found you and I failed. Your safety and happiness are my only concerns, even if it means exchanging my life for yours.

You are my heart, my life and my hope, and the only reason I have to hold tether to this world. The choices I have made have been foolish and vain. I'm paying a heavy price for my mistakes by leaving you with the Ravens. It is the only way I know to guarantee your safety. By sacrificing my own weakness, I pray it gives you the courage and strength you'll need to make your life a success. My wish for you, my baby girl, is to find your true self and cherish who you are, and that in doing so you find love deserving of you. Never forget who you are, even when tempted. Know from this moment you were cherished above my own life. Loved and wanted.

Your father wasn't always a cruel being, but his Fae nature was corrupted and eventually his machinations and manipulations consumed him. He thought to make me a slave, and if he had an inkling of your existence, he would do the same with you. Me to do his bidding, and you to use as a pawn where he saw fit. I couldn't allow that. I sealed my own fate when I succumbed to him, but you, my darling, are an innocent. Fae blood may course through your veins, but you are a Raven, and that will give you the strength you need to overcome whatever poison Leith brings to your doorstep.

It is why I made the decision to bind your Sidhe side. Caitlan wasn't happy about the choice, but in the end, she knew it was the only way to protect you. Binding your Sidhe powers will buy you the time to develop as a Raven, and to find and cherish your inner strength and self-worth.

My only regret is I won't be with you to share in your accomplishments, to hug away your fears and worries, and to give you the mother's love you so deserve. I've made the choice to go back to Faerie. It's the second half of the sacrifice necessary to keep you safe. In my gut I know I'm not long for either plane, but if the fates smile on us and we meet again, I hope you can find it in your heart to forgive me.

Your loving mother,
Aislinn.

An ache washed through her along with grief so deep, the only thing large enough to fill the hole was anger. Lane folded the letter, slipping it into the envelope. Dropping it on the nightstand, she stared impotent at the ceiling.

"Fuck this," she muttered, and got up from the bed.

Pulling on a pair of leggings, she then pulled a sweatshirt over her head and shoved her feet into her sneakers. She took the book of swords from the bed and left the bedroom, careful not to wake Gareth.

Her mind swirled. Her mother gave her up to protect her because she wasn't strong enough to fight. Wasn't strong enough or maybe she simply didn't know how. That was about to change.

Lane headed back to the library. She knew the why, now she needed to know the how. The puzzle in her head was almost complete. The means to fight the bastard that robbed her mother of her will, and then robbed *her* of her mother, had been revealed in her vision. All that was left was to find the weapon and teach daddy dearest a lesson he'd never forget.

Light peeked from the bottom of the library door, and she paused to listen. There was no sound or movement and she sent her senses out to make sure.

Nothing.

Caitlan must have left a light on, knowing she'd read the letter and not be able to sleep.

She slipped quietly through the door and settled in a chair at the study table. Years ago, she'd sit in this very spot with friends, laughing in whispers at old Grania chewing on her dentures. Later, she sat with Gareth, both pretending to study while their hands explored hidden delights under the table.

Opening the book again, she skimmed every page. The ornate lettering was hard to read at first, but she focused on her quarry, hoping her new Sidhe senses would give her a little help.

She had no idea how to channel that power or even control it a little. The thought was disconcerting at the least and downright terrifying at most. She joked about the dark side, but being a Dark Fae halfling, could she fall prey to the same temptations that corrupted her father? Was it so easy? Part of her nature? Or was Gareth correct in that she had the best of both now, being raised as a Raven?

Focusing her senses, she pulled from the well of power deep within and pictured the sword and all its parts. The sigils on the pommel and the Fae wording on the blade.

She flipped to the center of the book and the most colorful spread in the volume. The painted illustration showed a hollow, with a sword depicted piercing what looked to be an ancient Faerie mound. The blade was the right length and breadth, but everything else was wrong.

Closing her eyes, she focused on the gold light that emanated from her skin in the shower. Let it bathe her mind, color everything with its sheen.

In that moment, the individual pieces of the image broke apart, reforming to show a labyrinth of trees and flowering bushes leading to latticed grotto. There was no mound in sight, but a rose-covered building similar to a gazebo sat at the end of the path.

She opened her eyes, and what she saw in her mind was depicted on the page, and inside the glass house was the sword.

"That looks very much like the Peggy Rockefeller Rose Garden at the New York Botanical Gardens. With one exception. It's completely enclosed and there are no doors."

She jumped, puffing out a startled breath as she saw Gareth peering over her shoulder. "Don't do that! Jeez."

"Sorry. I couldn't resist." He chuckled, pressing a kiss to her temple. "Are you okay? I woke up and you were gone."

She nodded. "I opened the letter."

"I saw."

Cocking her head, she eyed him from over her shoulder. "Did you read it? It's okay if you did, I mean I left it there in the open."

"No. Whatever it says is between you and your mom. You can tell me about it when you're ready."

His hand was on her shoulder and she pressed her cheek to it. "God, I love you."

One finger caressed the curve of her face. "Back atcha, love."

Lane breathed in his warm scent and then straightened. Refocusing, she tapped the book. "You said this looks familiar?"

Gareth inched the edge of the cover around to see better. "Yes. Like I said, the Rose Garden. But I don't remember this being in the book last night. Is it a different volume?"

"Nope. I zinged it with some newfound power and the page sort of rearranged itself. Must have been a spell that needed a halfling to work."

Gareth turned the book fully. "This is telling us one of three things. The sword is hidden here, or this is a Faerie mound or portal of some kind needed to find the sword, or it's both."

"Do you have your cell phone?" she asked.

Raising an eyebrow, he pulled his cell from his back pocket. "This isn't *Who Wants to be a Millionaire*, you can't phone a friend, Lane."

With a smirk, she snatched the iPhone from his hand. "You're cute, you know that?"

Snapping a picture of the image, she turned the camera horizontal to check. "Shit."

"I tried to tell you. Real magic can't be captured, even with today's digital knowhow." Gareth took the book from the table and tucked a placeholder into the crease marking the page. "The only technologies to even come close are Krilian Aura Photography, and the Ovilus for synthesizing EMF waves to speech."

"You've got to be kidding. We're the real deal, Gareth, yet you're talking cold spots and microwave interference. This isn't ghost hunting."

He chuckled. "Sounds like I hit a major sore spot. Of course, we're the real deal, but paranormal investigators aren't wrong. Things that go bump in the night are very much a part of our world." He slipped his arms around her waist from behind. "Although, I prefer our way of going bump in the night to theirs any day. Much more satisfying."

"Keep your head in the game, horn ball. We can play bump uglies again later. Right now, I want to head to the Botanical Gardens and check out this Rockefeller Rose Garden. According to Google, it doesn't open for a couple of hours yet, so until then we should research whatever we'll need to take with us in case it turns out to be a portal. The last thing I want is to get caught in a supernatural vortex between Faerie and here, and not have the sword."

"Vortex? I'm guessing you watch a lot of *Dr. Who*." He kissed the top of her head and reached for his phone on the table in front of her to double check the website.

She smirked, leaning back into his chest. "Hey, no hating on the good doctor. She's terrific."

"She?" he questioned.

"Yup. You don't have a problem with that, right?"

He chuckled behind her ear. "No, ma'am." Pausing, he crouched over her shoulder to better look at the website on his cellphone. "You do realize the Botanical Gardens closes at six pm."

"And?"

"We'll need to break in after dark if we expect to get anything done."

She nodded. "This time of year, it stays light until about seven thirty pm or so. If Caitlan called the Red Veil to fill the vampires in on what happened, they could help us big time once it gets dark. Until then, you and I can do a little recon to help set the stage."

In that moment, he spun her around and she immediately went up on tip toe to peck his lips. "So, big boy. Fancy a stroll through the park with me? Who knows, maybe you'll get lucky with a little afternoon delight."

Gareth smiled. "It's a date, but right now I think we need a little sleep. Yawning during a seduction is not exactly a turn on, so shut eye first. Afternoon delight with a little recon, later.

"Fine. I hope you know I expect spooning, right?"

He swung his arm around her shoulders and steered Lane toward the doors and their waiting bed upstairs. "If it means you in my arms…deal."

Chapter Fourteen

"What's all this?" Lane asked as she climbed into the cab.

Gareth moved the wicker basket to the opposite side of the back passenger seat, and then held out a hand to help her settle.

"I scavenged the larder for a picnic lunch. A romantic gesture, even if I say so myself." He clicked his cheek. "With the other initiates sequestered to safe houses around the city, the food just sat in the fridge. I thought why not pack it up and take it with us to the park?"

She closed the cab door. "Because this is a scouting assignment, not a date."

"Ha. Says the woman whose first thought when we planned this outing was public lewdness and a possible misdemeanor charge."

"Wow, Golden Boy. Way to suck the romance right out of an afternoon delight."

He swept her blonde hair behind her ear, tracing the curve of her jaw. "Sorry, love, but you can't call me that anymore."

"Golden Boy?"

He nodded. "You've conveniently forgotten that magical shimmer that rose to a gorgeous flush once you reached—"

"Ssh! Gareth!"

The cab driver glanced at them from the rearview wearing an amused smirk. "Where to, Mac?"

"New York Botanical Gardens, please," Gareth answered the man, trying not to chuckle.

The cab pulled into the street and began crosstown maneuvers to get to the West Side Highway northbound toward the Bronx.

"Great. Now the whole city knows I flush pink and gold in the heat of the moment." Lane hid her face in her hands.

Smirking, Gareth closed the small plexiglass divider between the front and the back of the cab. "*Thar* she glows, like a true Sidhe halfling."

"Funny. You make a Moby Dick analogy and I'm supposed think that's cute."

"It is cute, and so are you. Look on the bright side. If we don't get to the Bronx soon, the whole city will know you make my Moby Dick swell to bursting just by sitting beside me. Takes an awful lot of sexy to do that."

Gareth pressed a kiss to her temple, and she inhaled his clean, freshly showered scent, very much aware of his muscled thigh against her leg.

"I guess a picnic isn't such a bad idea. I mean, who am I to turn down an alfresco meal? We need to eat anyway, right?"

With a hand on her thigh, he let his fingers steal closer to the juncture between her thighs. "We definitely need to eat."

She turned to meet his blue eyes but didn't stand a chance as his lips claimed hers. He took her mouth with skill and command, but his kiss tasted as though he was holding something back. As if savoring a secret.

When he broke their kiss, she sat back with an uneven breath. "Damn, Gareth. Forget the Bronx. We might have to ward the cab and every place in between."

With a grin, he took her hand, pressing a kiss to her knuckles. "Not every place, Goldilocks. We'll find a spot that's just right. Not too hard. Not too soft."

She winced.

"That bad?"

"Awful."

He shook his head, but his teasing grin stayed widened. "C'mon. Admit it. That was cute. The whole fairy tale thing? Considering we're Faeries?"

"I'll give you five out of ten. With extra points for trying."

"Extra points?" He reached over, pulling her onto his lap. "How about I show you just how much extra I can be."

***

"Oh, man. You have got to be kidding me." Lane threw up a hand, as Gareth came up behind carrying two ice cream cones.

"What?" he asked, licking the edge of one before handing the other to Lane.

"That." She pointed to the Peggy Rockefeller Rose Garden, and the parade barricades and construction mesh blocking public access.

"Pardon our Appearance." She read the sign on the gates featuring a sepia-tone image of the Rose Garden from 1916.

With a curse, she leaned against the curved bluestone wall from the overlook above the Rose Garden. "Well, at least we know what we're up against."

"That green blob must be the gazebo." Gareth pointed with his ice cream toward the dull green tarpaulined dome peeking above the construction.

"The website didn't mention renovations. What do we do now?" Lane asked, squinting to better survey the area.

This area of the Botanical Gardens wasn't crowded, and now they knew why. Everywhere else, children walked in clusters as their teachers led class trips through the different exhibits. Others meandered the paved paths, but no one bothered with the cordoned off Rose Garden. There wasn't much to see. At least not for another month when the exhibit was set to reopen.

"June." Lane shook her head at the date posted on the sign. "We can't wait that long. Eve is still alive, at least that much we know. Caitlan and I scried for her again before you and I took off. We couldn't pinpoint her location, but we sensed her essence enough to satisfy she's still breathing."

Gareth took her hand. "C'mon." He tugged her away from the bluestone wall and steered her down the steps. "We need to take a closer look. We might be able to sneak in around the back. If the crew working this renovation is like other state-run projects, chances are they're milking the governmental cow. Wasted time and resources is the name of the game when taxpayers foot the bill, so we might have a shot."

They circled the path, but voices and machinery were muffled through the solid fencing, and Gareth swore. "The one time I need systematized laziness on my side, and everyone suddenly develops a work ethic."

"Did you honestly expect this to be easy? This isn't Hollywood meets the Fae version of *National Treasure*. We are going to have to break a few rules to get that sword and defeat Leith."

She stood with her hand half-raked through her hair. "You're not the only one who hoped we could do this now and be done, but it looks as if Caitlan was right. We need to come back tonight, and we're going to need the vampires for cover."

Walking twenty or so paces across the main grass, he left the paved path behind and stood for a moment listening, before jogging back.

"There's heavy traffic in that direction, so we can assume the highway is that way." He pointed toward the area behind them.

She nodded. "The Bronx River Parkway. Why?"

"Okay, then." He circled back toward the path again but this time he went in the opposite direction. "So, if the parkway is to the east, then the river running through the Gardens runs parallel."

"The Bronx River. It has the same name because, yes, it runs parallel to the highway, but what has one got to with the other, and why does it matter? We need a plan, not a topography lesson."

He jogged back, taking both her hands in his. "That's what I'm driving at. If we can't get into that gazebo in a straightforward manner, then we need to do so with stealth. This is a state park. Which means it has pretty tight security. The best way for us to sneak in is via the water. Flowing water carries magic. The Bronx River is all we've got. It's polluted, but it will still amplify vampiric glamour and whatever wards we conjure enough to do the trick."

Gareth's enthusiasm exuded confidence and strength, and she pictured him striding in the Faerie Courts like a magical medieval knight. The image was such a turn on, it left butterflies winging through her stomach.

"Uhm, speaking of warding large ribbons of ground and water." She rubbed her thumbs in sexy circles over his hands. "Aren't you hungry?"

She raised an eyebrow and his lips pushed to the side in a sexy crooked half-smile. "After all that foreplay in the cab? I'm surprised you even have to ask."

Without another word, he tossed her over his shoulder and jogged with her toward a cluster of secluded trees toward the back of the property.

"Gareth! Put me down!"

He let her down at the base of a large oak. "Pretty, huh?" Not waiting for her to reply, he turned and hiked a leg up onto a low branch.

"What the hell are you doing? Get down before you get us thrown out of here."

He climbed toward a narrow spread between two branches. "I hid the picnic basket up here. I balanced the wicker perfectly between two branches, and the leaves kept it hidden from sight."

"You do realize I wasn't talking about actual lunch, right?" She held her arms up, taking the basket as he lowered it toward the ground.

Jumping from the branches, he landed with barely a sound on the balls of his feet like a sexy, modern day Robin Hood. "If you were, I'd have changed your mind with a single kiss."

She rested the basket against the tree and then looked at him dryly. "And what makes you so sure you could change my mind? You've never seen me when I'm hangry. It's scary."

"Hangry," he repeated. "As in so hungry you'll rip someone a new one until they feed you?"

"Pretty much."

He strode toward her, walking her backwards until her back pressed against the tree. With both palms on the rough bark, he leaned in, letting the promise of a kiss hover above her lips.

"So, are you planning on feeding me or what?"

"Depends. I've seen you so starved you would have begged if I let you. But I'm such a nice guy, I didn't make you wait too long for *satisfaction*."

He traced the seam of her lips with the tip of his tongue, pulling back when she opened for a kiss. "I think you want me to make you beg. I think you want a mouthwatering, torturous wait before I feed you inches."

Her body hummed, and her panties were soaked at just his words. The thought of teasing torment, building until she clawed for release left her breathless.

She ached for him, yet he held himself in check, even as her chest heaved close enough to feel her heart pound.

"Fuck the risk." She licked her lips, straining for his mouth. "I want you here and now, Gareth."

He shook his head, leaving her panting as he moved to lift the lid to the picnic basket.

Food? He got her all hot and bothered and he'd rather eat a drumstick?

Rummaging underneath the Tupperware, he pulled out a nylon bag. "I told you this was a surprise."

With a sexy half grin, he untied the drawstring top and pulled a tiny dildo from the bag. "What do you think, Goldilocks? Hmmm? Methinks this one is too small and too soft."

He put it back in the bag with a wink before pulling another out with a flourish.

"Gareth, what the—" Lane's eyes went wide at the giant horse cock dildo in his hand.

"Too scary? Even for a hangry girl like you?" He tsked. "Well, perhaps this one *is* too big and too hard."

"Oh my God. You're nuts! What if they searched the whole picnic basket at the entrance?"

He pressed a finger to his lips and reached into the bag for a third time. "Let's see." Pulling a third dildo out, he palmed the synthetic flesh before walking with it to where Lane stood flabbergasted. "I think this one is just right. Don't you?"

His free hand reached for her breast as he pressed the realistic silicone into her palm. "This one is just the right length. The right girth. Smooth, yet fleshy and hard."

Taking her free hand, he pressed it to the hard bar behind his fly. "Almost like the real thing."

Lane gasped as his cock jerked behind the soft denim. She'd had him so many times before, but never enough.

"Tell me, Laney. Which would you rather suck? My thick meat or the thick silicone in your hand? Maybe you'll give me a smokin' hot visual and tongue them both."

Her heart jackhammered in her chest so hard she could barely form words. "The wards."

"I placed wards when I put the basket here. We'll have to strengthen them, but to do so we need to raise your power, and the only way to do that is for me to make you come."

She couldn't think as he lifted the hem of her spring dress, running his fingers between her legs.

"You're so wet, love. I can feel your slick sex through your panties and your clit is throbbing."

He slid the tips of his fingers under the top lace band and over her damp mound. "Against the tree, no one will see you groan and clench as my fingers work your wet slit."

He spread her slick folds, curling his hand deep. Two fingers, then three. Lane moaned at the rough feel, her breath catching when he circled her clit with his thumb, pumping his hand slowly.

Pinned against the trunk, Lane struggled for traction, trying to grind her sex deeper, harder into Gareth's hand.

He took her mouth, teasing her tongue and her lips with gentle kisses to match the gentle strokes on her pussy.

"Gareth!" she ground out.

He smiled against her lips. "I'm feeding your hunger, love, but obviously it's not enough. What do you want?"

A choked moan left her throat, raw and low.

"Say the words, Lane."

Jaw tight, she exhaled. "More, Gareth! I want more! Hard. Deep. I need it! Give it to me, please!"

Taking the dildo from her hand, he slid it between them, but she stopped his hand. Shaking her head, she held his wrist off.

"I want more, but I want *you*. Not synthetic flesh. *Your* flesh. I want you to fill me. Your cock. Your cum. In me now."

She took the dildo from him and tossed it toward the bag on the grass, not caring who saw or who came.

Gareth's eyes never left her hungry gaze as he unbuttoned his fly, freeing his member. Lifting her hips, he pushed her back against the tree, spreading her wide. Lane locked her ankles around his back, and he impaled her slick flesh with a single thrust.

Driving his hard length balls deep, she ignored the sting of the rough bark through her top. There was nothing gentle or slow now.

Gareth buried his head in the hollow of her neck, kissing her throat and the tender flesh of her jaw as he drove higher, deeper. He found her mouth and crushed his lips to hers, devouring her lips and tongue.

Their auras tingled, merging and flooding in and around their entwined bodies. Gold sparkles glinted as power rose between them and through them the closer they climbed toward climax.

With a sharp breath, he tore his mouth from hers. "My cock is ready to blow. Quickly, Lane! Reach for the knife in my back pocket. It's time!"

Not knowing what he meant, she fumbled blindly, sliding her fingers into the denim slit. Finding it, she wrapped her hand around the shaft and pulled it free.

Small enough to fit in the palm of her hand, she blinked at the ornate lettering on the handle.

"Open it and cut my palm. Do the same on your hand. The same as we did at the Red Veil."

"Why?"

His voice shook and sweat broke out on his forehead. "Do it, Lane!"

Every muscle in his body went rigid, so she dragged the sharp tip across his palm the same as she did the previous night.

"Now you. You have to trust me."

She did as he asked, and Gareth took her hand, pressing palm to palm. His leaned in, pressing his forehead to hers. His warm, sweet breath tickled her nose and mouth, and it tasted of power, of magic. Like honey sizzling on the tongue.

He pulled back, and his eyes found hers and locked. *"Root of my root, star spun lives. Bound in flesh and spirit light. Blood of my blood, bone of my bone, I claim thee now as we are one. United in life, transcended in death, the claim is cast on Danu's breath."*

Their blood flowed together, and his words teemed in her mind, expanding, shimmering like the golden force surrounding them.

Magic hummed in the air and in their flesh. Lane held tight as they spun, the world falling away. Body light, she floated with senses on fire.

Gareth filled her body and soul, and with a cry everything swelled. They moved together, seamless, boneless, climbing higher and higher until sheer power overwhelmed, and they exploded, climaxing into spasms.

Magic flowed, a river encircling them, pulling them under until it ebbed, leaving them panting as they clung together, the world returning.

Lane opened her eyes, expecting to see the earth spinning below then, only to find the sun winking through the leaves and her back still pressed against the bark.

Gareth lifted his head, still clasping their joined hands. "You okay?"

She exhaled a stunned breath. "Okay? What the hell was that?"

He let go of her hand and she jerked it close to see what caused such a tumult. "What the—"

The cut had healed, and in its place a white scar had formed at the center of her palm. Not a thin line as expected, but an intricate Celtic knot intertwined with the symbols for love and eternity.

"Don't worry. I have one, too." Gareth held up his hand. "It's a claiming sigil. It means you're safe now, no matter which plane we decide to roam."

She shoved at his shoulder. "Claiming sigil?!"

"Laney, you agreed. In the library, remember?"

"In the library? That was last night, Gareth! You could have warned me that's what was happening. I thought we died or something!"

He gaped. "More like died and gone to heaven. That was the single most intense sexual experience of my life. I can't believe you're saying it wasn't the same for you."

This time she punched his shoulder. "I never said it wasn't! It was fucking amazing. Fourth of July, Yule and Halloween all rolled into one. Fireworks and starbursts. But YOU SHOULD HAVE TOLD ME!"

"You agreed. Caitlan told you. The only way you'd be safe from Leith's master plan was for you to be claimed. You seemed thrilled when you realized she meant me. Happy even."

She exhaled. "I didn't say I wasn't. It's just — I would have liked to have been ready."

He laughed, pecking her lips with a quick kiss. "Trust me, love. You were *more* than ready. Dripping ready. It wouldn't have happened if you weren't. As for what to expect, how would I know?" He shrugged. "I've never claimed a mate before, so how could I tell you what would happen when I didn't have a clue?"

"Asking for a heads up in this isn't like ruining a surprise birthday party. It's a claiming. You could have warned me you were going to perform the rite. You knew the words. You must have looked them up or something."

"Those words aren't written anywhere except my heart. The only thing necessary for a claiming is sexual climax and the words, 'I claim.'" He shrugged. "The rest was all me." Taking her hand, his gaze dropped before he looked up again. "I'm sorry, Laney. I should have told you what I planned. I suppose I wanted it to knock your socks off."

Lane's heart squeezed. Gareth was her equal in everything. Her lover, her friend, her partner in crime and everything in between. How could she hold a Type A personality against him when she was the same? His actions and his words reflected something so beautiful, so surprisingly tender, and the feeling behind them far outweighed the rest.

"I'm sorry, too, Gareth."

"Sorry we're mated, or sorry for being such a pig-headed Raven about it?"

She punched his shoulder again.

"Hey! Ouch!"

"You knew what you were getting when you signed up for this rollercoaster. No backsies. I'm yours and you're mine. End of sentence. Just promise me you'll give me a heads-up next time something important happens that affects us both."

He kissed the end of her nose. "Deal."

"Good. Now let's get cleaned up before we really get arrested."

He stepped back, letting his still thick member slide from her body before gently helping her to the ground. "Careful, Lane. Get your legs first."

"*Oomph.*" She wobbled, holding on to his arm. "You're not kidding. That was really one wild ride, Mr. Toad."

"Please tell me you are not telling Caitlan to turn me into an amphibian simply because I claimed you sort of on the sly."

She laughed, snorting a little. "No, dummy. It's the Disney classic. *Mr. Toad's Wild Ride?*"

He shook his head.

"You have so been gone from this plane for too long. Once this is over, we are taking a trip to Orlando and the Magic Kingdom."

"Sounds like just the place for two Fae halflings."

Once she found her feet, she turned, showing him her back. "How chewed up are my shoulders and my dress?"

"Not at all, why?" He brushed a little crushed bark from her dress.

"I thought I'd be a scraped, bloody mess for sure."

He grinned, pulling Tupperware out of the picnic basket to hide the sex bag underneath. "We need to get back and fill Caitlan in on what happened, and then get the vampires onboard."

"Wait." She bent, stopping him from packing the food again. "There's hungry and then there's *hungry*. This is forever *our* spot, so why not spread the picnic blanket under our tree and enjoy the sunshine? Caitlan can wait. We joined ourselves in front of nature and the whole universe. I think this calls for a little happy before the hell begins, don't you?"

He straightened, pulling her into his arms. "Never a little happy. All happy. All the time."

Chapter Fifteen

"You sure Caitlan filled the vampires in on everything? What about the three rogue fangers involved in this mess?" Gareth asked, checking his watch again.

"She told them the whole story. In fact, she said they were already well aware of what happened on that macabre merry-go-round."

He exhaled a dubious breath. "I hope they're coming to help, and not just to take their pound of Fae flesh. Vampires are fickle, yet exacting creatures. In the absence of the true culprit, guilt by blood association suffices for them. I hope Caitlan took that into account when she arranged for us to meet them here of all places."

"If concrete could talk," Gareth added with a low breath, glancing at the stained walls outside the side entrance to the Red Veil.

Lane followed his line of sight. The discolorations on the wall and the asphalt below could be anything, but the look on Gareth's face wasn't wrong. It could be old blood. "I doubt we were asked here for a nefarious reason. The vampires specified this entrance because it's the only way into the Red Veil during the day. The others are sealed off for obvious reasons."

"Considering how much time you've spent here, if anyone knows the odd hours kept by the undead, it's you."

Lane's brows knotted at the obvious dig. "Wow. Snarky much? I thought you said my time here was a turn on."

"I did. And I meant it. But I'm back now, so—" He shrugged off the last bit as if it was taken as fact.

With a hand on her hip, Lane raised an eyebrow. "So, you're insinuating it's no longer acceptable for me to come here because you're back. Is that the subtext of what you just said?"

"I didn't say that."

"Good. Because if that's what you meant, I might have to practice my dick shriveling spells on your private parts." She looked at him, hoping the attempt at levity defused a potential argument.

"Gareth, picking up where we left off ten years ago is one thing, but regardless of how we still feel about each other, we've grown as people. If we have any hope of going forward, you have to accept I'm not the naïve headstrong girl I once was. I'm an adult, with ten years of living without you. I never was, nor am I now, the kind who likes to be told what I can and cannot do. Now…" she moved to put her hand on his arm. "If you meant you're back, and that you'd like to accompany me to the backrooms whenever the urge presents, that's another story."

He grumbled a response, and Lane bit the inside of her cheek not to laugh. Gareth may have come into his Fae power, but he was still Gareth when it came to her. Gorgeous, eager, and altogether endearing for being such a caveman, sometimes. Not that she'd ever tell him. Still, she was as much an alpha female as he was alpha male, and it made for interesting sparks all the way around.

"We should be meeting up at the Botanical Gardens. That's ground zero for us." He crossed his arms. "Hells bells, do you know how long it'll take us to get to the Bronx from lower Manhattan?"

At his ruffled posturing, she stifled a smirk and let her hand drop from his arm. "My guess is not that long, considering the time of night and the fact certain vampires can fly."

"Fly?" With a disbelieving look, he put up two hands. "Hell no. Undead Uber is not happening tonight."

She cracked a smile. "Whichever way we get there, I'm sure it'll be fine."

Mollified, his forehead relaxed, and he loosened the vise grip on his arms. "I shouldn't be so cynical about the fanged set. You're right. They have a stake in this, too."

"Hey, that was my pun." The smile on her face faded after a moment. "All joking aside. My Spidey senses are buzzing, but it's not from the vampires. I can't help but feel the fates are fucking with us from a distance. Maybe that's what you're picking up on."

"Fucking with us how?"

Lane lifted an uncertain hand. "I'm not sure, but something's blindsiding us. I can taste it."

"Because the Rose Garden is under renovation and closed to the public?" he asked. "We knew this was going to be tricky, Laney, but to be honest, all that tarpaulin blanketing the gazebo at the site might be a good thing. It gives us cover. Besides, every lesser Fae in that garden knows we're here. I caught them peeping at us all this afternoon. Even at the most inopportune moments, if you get my drift."

His look left no room for guessing, and she had to laugh. "Peeping. As in Peeping Toms?"

"More like Peeping Pixies, and brownies, and even a few phookas. At least I didn't sense any boggarts or sluagh. Gnarly buggers. The idea of those ill-begotten creatures watching us have sex is enough to cause erectile disfunction. We should be glad they don't show much during the day."

She burst out laughing. "Sloo-ah? That sounds like something you hack up after a chest cold."

"They're haggard and ugly, so you're not that far off. They usually skulk in the shadows and have been known to be the eyes and ears for the Dark Court, but the truth is they're more mercenary than that. Their aim is ripping souls from unsuspecting humans."

"Wonderful. The idea of Faerie just keeps getting better and better." She paused. "Wait. If they're mercenary, then they can be bought."

He nodded. "Exactly. While commerce with the Sluagh is always distasteful, it might come in handy at some point. And since the undead involved are at the mercy of a dark Sidhe, meeting the Sluagh's price might be an ace up our sleeve."

"I don't know, Gareth. I'd rather not bargain like that with Eve at stake. Or me for that matter. I'd like to keep my soul intact."

Shrugging, he checked his watch again. "Then we'll let the vampires negotiate with them if necessary. They're soulless, so it won't be an issue. I think we need to rally all supernatural species involved. Strength in paranormal numbers."

"I couldn't agree more, but I do argue the point that the undead are soulless. We are, in fact, not so."

Gareth wheeled around, instinctively pushing Lane behind him. Standing in the shadows across from them was an imposing vampire. Mysteriously beautiful, with long gold hair and one side of his face ruined.

"I apologize for startling you. Allow me to introduce myself. I am Rémy Tessier. Elder, and acting head of the Vampire Council. You must be Gareth Fairfax and Lane Alden, Fae halflings."

An elegant female vampire approached, rounding the corner as Rémy finished his introduction. "Ah, good. Right on time, as usual," Rémy said, lifting a hand to her.

The vampire smoothed the front of her vintage Chanel suit before moving to where Rémy stood with two strangers. She got within five feet of them and stopped. "Witch!" Her eyes flared crimson and her fangs descended.

Rémy's hand shot forward, grabbing her before she attacked. "Abigail, let me introduce our *guests*." He stressed the word. "Lane Arden and Gareth Fairfax. True, they are witches, but they are also Ravens."

She blinked, her eyes narrowing. "Ravens, as in the *Circle of the Raven*. As in Fae-kissed?"

He inclined his head. "Yes. They are halfling Fae to be precise, and they're here to help with this unfortunate situation. It seems an initiate of the motherhouse was taken last night from the Red Veil. The unfortunate Were we found dead was used to draw her to the backrooms. We believe the act was premeditated."

"Premeditated?" she questioned. "Bette told me the Were in question was found drained in the Carousel room. If he was part of a planned conspiracy, then why is he dead?" Abigail looked at the two witches.

"I saw what happened to him," Lane replied. "I don't mean I witnessed his death firsthand. I have second sight. I can't tell you much about him, other than his name was Mason. He was supposed to be a one-night stand for a stressed-out student." She looked to Rémy. "I'm sorry, but I have to agree with your vampire friend. I don't see how Mason was a part of this. Eve used a compulsion spell on him, so he'd take particular interest in her."

Abigail exhaled a cutting breath.

Lane turned an arched brow at the elegant, strawberry blonde vampire. "You sound as though you object. Don't vamps glamour their victims into exposing arteries and genitals and whatever else catches your fancy?"

She took it one step farther, sparing a look for Gareth. "Maybe we Ravens should leave the undead out of this completely and report the incident to the Alpha of the Brethren. Sean Leighton is a good friend of our Supreme. I'm sure he'd be interested to hear what happened to one of his own at the club *you* run."

"Lane—" Gareth's tone was a warning.

She lifted a hand. "No, it's okay. The undead are used to being at the top of the food chain. So, having wards they raised crumble at our fingertips, and their refuge infiltrated, must be upsetting. But we're not the ones they should be scrutinizing. Three of their own are at the heart of how this happened on their turf, so, Abigail...physician, heal thyself."

Bette joined them at that moment, rounding the corner the same way Abigail came. "What do doctors have to do with any of this?" she asked, stopping beside Rémy on the other side.

"It's Shakespeare, love," Gareth replied, keeping an eye on both Lane and Abigail.

"Lane is correct," Rémy replied with a wave, signaling Abigail to stand down. "We need to look within to find the guilty parties."

Gareth shook his head. "Not guilty. Just answerable."

"I think the witchy dude has a point," Bette chimed in, gesturing toward Gareth.

"Gareth," he said, giving her a quick nod.

"Go on," Rémy prompted Bette. "Have you pinpointed anyone from the work rota?"

She paused before bobbing her head. "Yes, but I also agree with Gareth. The undead involved were compelled, and a single vampire couldn't inflict the number of bite wounds we saw on that luckless Were. It has to be more than one."

"There were three vampires, to be exact," Lane interjected, keeping one eye on Abigail. "I saw them when I touched the restraints on the chair across from the carousel."

"Psychometry?" Rémy questioned.

Lane nodded. "It's a form of ESP, but in this instance, the residual energy was so thick I could taste it."

"Literally," Gareth added. "It made her retch."

Bette nodded, making a face. "I felt it, too. Not in the same way, but it was profound."

"Anyway," Abigail redirected. "We have been on high alert since the breach. I reviewed the tapes from the night in question. The Carousel Room, to be exact. We know who of our kind was involved, how long they stayed, and when they left."

"So, you knew all along who was involved?" Lane took a step forward.

"Sorry, I'm late. The city is packed with tourists tonight." They all turned toward Caitlan joining them from the street.

The Supreme's voice stopped Lane in her tracks, and she moved back to Gareth's side, ignoring the smirk on Abigail's face.

"Sean Leighton has been made aware of the situation, now that we're all on the same page," Caitlan continued. "He asked that the Raven motherhouse be permitted to deal with our issues first, before the vampires enact their justice. He also asked that Rémy contact him afterward, considering how and where Mason met his end."

"Agreed." Gareth nodded. "First things first."

Abigail balked. "First things first? Your kind *caused* the breach in the first place. Witches and Fae are forbidden entry into the Red Veil, yet you chose to use your powers to circumvent that rule. We are only here because your Supreme requested our presence, plus we need to see for ourselves the Fae responsible is taken to task."

"You can bet your sweet fangs, sister," Gareth replied. "The Sidhe responsible for this will die."

"Kill him if you must," Abigail added, but then spared a sly smile for Rémy and Bette. "But there are other, more satisfying ways to exact retribution."

Caitlan shook her head, in effect wiping the smirk from Abigail's face. "This particular Fae needs to die, and by Lane's hand. Besides, it's too dangerous for you to keep a Fae on tap, literally—and from the way your master is nodding, I can safely assume he agrees. I also believe the Alpha of the Brethren will want both Lane and Gareth at the sit down between the Weres and the vampires, once our business with this rogue Sidhe is concluded. After all, they were the ones who discovered Mason's body, and tracked the images and scents to the culprits."

"Indeed," Rémy agreed. "You'll have to forgive my indulgences. Abigail's heart may be silent, but it is in the right place when it comes to our kind. She is as protective of our own as you are of yours, and this situation has not presented her character in the best light. She is not as callous as she seems.

"In fact, she has learned tolerance beyond what most vampires are capable, especially in overcoming past taboos. I let her have her head at times, but in this case, I think it best to defer to you." He inclined his head. "Madame Raven, the Vampire Council of New York is at your disposal."

Chapter Sixteen

"*D*amn it! My pants are soaked to my knees!" Gareth grumbled as he climbed onto the east bank of the Bronx River. "Ugh, and I stink. That water is filthy, polluted."

Lane chuckled. "Be grateful Bette waited for you take your shoes off."

"I don't think that youngblood has full powers of flight. I'm lucky she didn't drop me at the deepest point."

Lane brushed off her pants before smoothing her hair back into a long ponytail. "Ha! That would have been practically unintentional."

"No thanks to you and your top of the food chain remarks." Gareth snorted.

She grinned, watching him squeeze out his pant cuffs. "Yet she somehow managed to place me on dry land."

"Beginner's luck."

"At least Rémy made Abigail stay behind with Caitlan. Things were starting to get ugly."

"Starting?" He laughed. "We're lucky Abigail can't fly, or she'd have dropped us onto the nearest garbage barge. If what Rémy said about vampires overcoming taboos is correct, your mouth single handedly set things back to naught."

"I did not," she shot back, reaching for the penlight and map in her back pocket.

"How far are we to the Rose Garden from here?"

Lane glanced past her shoulder into the gloom. "About twenty minutes via that path." She put the flashlight in her teeth, shining the soft yellow light on the map. "I know we agreed it's the fastest way, but now I think we should keep to the trees along the perimeter."

She traced the red outline on the map indicating a copse of cherry trees and then lilacs closer to the Rose Garden.

"We might run into lesser Fae there, but we should be fine," Gareth replied. "I wasn't able to learn much about the park's night security other than they patrol every hour or so. We didn't breach the fence, and there's really no buildings other than the greenhouse and one staff building, but I don't want to push our luck until we're at the site and can throw up a ward."

A whoosh caught their attention and they turned to see Rémy land soundlessly on the opposite bank across the water. With a single leap, he crossed to their embankment, walking with sure grace to where they stood waiting. "Caitlan thought you might need a hand keeping unwanted observers at bay."

Gareth grinned. "As long as you promise not to make a midnight snack out of the lesser Fae who reside in the gardens. If you get peckish, you can have the security detail."

The three kept to the shadows and the soft spring grass. The night was cool, but it had lost the winter chill that sometimes lingered in the early spring. Instead, there was a sweetness to the air that tasted of rebirth and the promise of summer.

"Rémy, what did you mean about Abigail and overcoming past taboos?" Lane asked, breaking their silence.

He considered her for a moment. "Abigail is superior, haughty. Impeccable in manner and dress, but ruthless in her desires. She was our former master's progeny, and his envoy before he fell from grace. When he met his final death from his own actions during the HepZ outbreak, it was hard on her.

"Then she met a shifter named Dash Collier. He headed the contingent of Weres the Alpha of the Brethren sent to help clear our shadow houses of the virus. Whatever Abigail threw at him…insults, jibes, even sex, he met her headstrong and head on. She had finally met her match.

"As you probably know, Weres and Vampires are natural enemies. Fraternization was taboo on both sides for centuries, until we needed each other in order to survive. In the aftermath of all that death, old prejudices no longer made sense. Abigail and Dash were the first to realize that and have been happy together since.

"You see, taboos are crumbling everywhere in our shared shadowed world. It's why I have chosen not to indict your breach at the Red Veil, despite Abigail's protest. It is true witch blood poses a problem for us, and Abigail's resentment stems from more than one undead friend meeting an ugly death because it. Even if those friends weren't discerning or careful about where or on whom they fed.

"Even with the risk, I'm willing to take the chance on a truce. And so is your Supreme. It's why I agreed to come with you tonight. With the right measures, I'm hopeful we can find a way to manage the situation, much in the same way the Weres manage theirs when it comes to vampire blood."

Blunt guilt slashed at Lane for jumping to earlier conclusions and she pursed her lips, watching the elegant predator move beside them with ease.

"You are obviously a remarkable man, Rémy Tessier," she offered. "I owe you an apology."

He grinned, and a hint of fang glinted in the moonlight. "So, you're putting us back at the top of the food chain then, eh?"

"Don't push it." She chuckled.

"And on that note, we're halfway there." Gareth stopped on the grass separating the copse of cherry trees from the early blooming lilacs. "We can either cut through here or veer over toward the path and bluestone circle just above the Rockefeller Rose Garden."

The full moon illuminated the small grove where they stood, and the grassy trail that cut through to Rose Garden. The labyrinth of gorgeous rose bushes was muted in the moonlight, as was the gazebo at the center of the lush landscaped architecture, covered in a dull green tarpaulin.

"Why risk the pavement when we're so close?" Lane gestured toward the soft slope ahead.

Gareth shrugged, non-committal. "It's six- and one-half dozen of another to me, but I thought you might want a break from the damp grass."

Together they moved toward the fragrant trees, but Rémy stayed put, motionless.

"Rémy? Is everything all right?" Lane asked.

"Something is barring my entry."

Before she could ask another question, a dull wince creased the vampire's face. "It's warded. With *Ferfaen*. The druid's plant."

"No unclean shall pass," a growly rasp croaked from the shadows. "How dare you bring an unclean to befoul our garden."

The rough voice came from the shadows, and Lane threw a hand outward, speaking a druid word for light. "*Soilsigh!*"

The little beast hissed, clamoring back into shadow, but not before they saw its squat, thickset body covered

516

with matted hair. Eyes blinked at them, glowing red and saucer-like in the refracted light.

Long prominent teeth showed behind thin lips, and skinny fingers armed with talons shielded its face.

"What manner of beast is this?" Rémy asked, taking a step closer to the creature only to have it hiss again. "If it thinks I'm unclean, then it hasn't looked in the mirror lately."

"Looks to be half boggart, half hogboon. Nasty mischief-maker mixed with a sweet-natured goblin," Gareth answered.

"A sweet goblin?" Rémy peered even closer. "Sounds like an oxymoron."

The creature snorted. "Ye thinks ye better? Ye defile the garden with yer unclean self. Begone! Before ye hurt more!"

"Hurt?" Gareth questioned, only to hear a clipped growl for an answer.

The creature scuttled forward, teeth bared, stopping short only when Lane stepped in front of both Gareth and Rémy.

"*Princesssss!*"

Its protracted hiss at the end of the word made her teeth hurt. "Who are you?" she questioned, raising another light spiral in her hand just in case.

"I be Xax, and I speak for the wee folk here. We folk mind our own, but ye and yers think it fun to hurt us for sport. Ye had yer help before, but don't think to be trolling for blood here anymore, missy. We banished the Redcaps when they chose the bloodsucking unclean that came with the new king. They've dipped their caps in our life's blood for the last time. You'll find no quarter and no help here."

Pixies divebombed like marauding flies, as two grimy-haired boggarts and a stray phooka came into view.

"*Jesus*, they're like a swarm on crack!" Gareth batted them away, but there were always more. "Ouch! They've got knives! Fucking mosquitos with swords!"

They didn't go near Rémy, but Lane ducked and twisted, waving her hands to fend them off as well.

With a wince, Rémy moved to Lane's side and the attack stopped immediately. He flicked one from Lane's shoulder with his thumb and forefinger. "Unclean, one. Psycho Tinkerbelle, zip."

A low moan caught Lane's attention and she turned toward the pained sound. She spoke the word for light again, only this time it showed a smaller version of Xax. A female, and she was injured.

Lane took a step toward the injured lesser, and Xax shot forward, blocking her way. "*Princesssss*, show mercy. I beg ye!"

The ugly belligerent creature was obviously the wounded lesser Fae's mate. Lane looked from him to Gareth. "Leith must have convinced these outcasts he defeated the Unseelie king and took over the court. That's what he meant by new king."

Her voice never moved above a whisper, but Xax heard her, nonetheless. He pulled himself to his full height, all two feet of him, and sniffed. "We be exiles, not outcasts. Thrown from our home in the roses because of the likes of ye and ye father."

"Leith is my father, but I'm no princess, and neither is he king," Lane replied. "The Unseelie king still rules. Leith is a liar and a murdering bastard, and he not only interacts with the unclean," she shot Rémy an apologetic look, "but he has them do his bidding against you and others of our kind."

The creature spit, and its saliva sizzled on the pavement leaving a pitted black spot. "A curse on his name!"

"Answer us this. Why can't our friend pass? Is the ground spelled?" Lane demanded.

The hogboon halfling turned with another sniff toward the shadows, clearly unwilling to play.

"Okay, Xax. I've got something for you, but only if you play nice." Lane dug in the canvas bag hanging across her chest, pulling out a handful of dollar store Marti Gras beads.

The creature turned, and eyes went wide as it stared at the colorful costume beads. Its thin lips parted, and it took an absent step forward.

Gareth looked at Lane. "Seriously?"

"When you said lesser Fae might live in the Gardens, I did a little research. Brownies and pixies like milk, phookas and boggarts like crops, goblins like shiny objects, especially jewelry."

"For Xax, *princesssss*?" The creature asked, pointing to his hairy chest.

She nodded. Opening her bag, she fished out an ear of corn and a container of heavy cream, placing all the offerings at the base of a lilac tree. "I have more, but I want answers."

They clamored for the offerings, sparing the three of them furtive looks before moving toward the shadows again.

"Wait," Lane stopped the goblin. "Why is my friend barred from the trees?"

The creature showed a wide set of long sharp teeth in a grotesque smile. "Because I warded his ilk, after those with the king hurt my Eesa. Ferfaen brewed thick and rich, and then poured into the earth that none who feed from living blood may pass."

"Eesa?" she questioned.

The hogboon goblin nodded once, and his red eyes seemed wet. "My mate." Xax lifted a clawed hand toward the injured female. "They found her in the roses gathering nectar, and they dragged her into—"

The little creature's voice cracked, and Rémy stopped him from explaining further. There was no need. The heartbreak on his face said it all.

With a hand on his heart, the vampire stepped forward and knelt to one knee. "Those that hurt your mate will be punished. You have my word."

"Are ye their king?" Xax's wide red eyes searched his for the truth.

Nodding, Rémy bowed his head and the hogboon goblin sniffed, giving him a nod back.

Waving a skinny, taloned hand, the ward barring Rémy from the grove crumbled with a low bell-like tinkle. Xax lifted a clawed finger and pointed it at the vampire. "Ye may pass, but ye won't enter the roses. The *princessssss* and her mate be the only two."

Rémy straightened, stalemated. "I'm out of my element here. Looks like you're on your own from this point. I'll do what I can from this side, but I cannot help if you get caught within."

"Salt and light," Gareth offered. "That should keep this lot at bay if they get too curious. Not that it's likely. The best thing you can do for us is keep unwanted human visitors away so we can do what we came to do."

"The false king expects ye through the roses," Xax interrupted. "He has one like ye. He feeds from her." The hogboon's chin dropped to his chest before he met Lane's eyes. "A friend, I think. She waits for ye to come."

Gareth put a staying hand on Lane's arm. "If Leith is expecting us through the roses, then the gazebo is a trap. There has to be another way."

"Xax will take ye through the tunnels."

Lane turned on her heel to watch Eesa struggle to stand.

"Eesa, no. It is forbidden."

"Xax," she coughed, "ye must take them. If the false king did this to us, what will he do to all the others?"

Lane dumped the contents of her bag at Xax's feet. "I'll bring you sacks of shiny jewels and as much cream as you can drink, if you can help us find a way to defeat the false king."

His saucer red eyes blinked, and when he cocked his head to watch her face, he looked like a demented cross between Dobby and a Gringotts's goblin from *Harry Potter*.

"The false king is yer father. How can we trust ye?"

Eesa coughed again as one of the boggarts helped her rest on a soft tuft of grass, and the small female's face winced with the effort.

"Gareth, can halfling Sidhe use their light to heal?"

He shook his head. "As far and I know, our magic is for defense and attack."

"Halflings might not be able to heal the small one, but I can." At Rémy's announcement, the grove went quiet.

Xax craned his neck to look at the tall vampire. His lips pulled back over his teeth in warning.

"*Uhm*, maybe that's not such a great idea right now," Gareth cautioned. "You're not exactly supernatural species of the month."

Rémy ignored him, taking a tentative step toward the hogboon goblin. Xax raised his hand, and blue magic sparked deadly. The energy bomb flew without warning and Rémy blurred out of the way.

The attack shattered a small bounder, sending rock shrapnel flying and the lesser Fae running for cover.

"Holy crap!" Lane and Gareth dove for the nearest tree.

Gareth covered her with his body as residual energy snapped and fizzed. "Goblins are no joke. They have abilities innate to their breed and pack quite a punch."

"I know you have no reason to trust me or my nature, but I speak the truth," Rémy tried again. "I promised with bent knee I would see justice done for you and your mate. She suffered when her blood was taken, and only fate knows what else."

"Do not speak of it! Ye lips are not worthy."

Gareth peeked his head around to watch the hogboon ready with another bomb. "Hang on, love."

Another ball grew in the hogboon goblin's hand.

"Vampires take blood, it's true." He ran for a tree, sparks singeing his cloak before the sizzling ball exploded in the grass where he last stood.

"But it's also true we have the power to heal!" Rémy lifted a surrendering hand and stepped from cover into the open. "I'm done running from you. As an elder, I take responsibility for the actions of the undead that hurt your mate. Attack if you must, but I'm telling you now my blood can heal. Will heal."

Xax's ears flicked and his red eyes narrowed, but the tilt of his head showed he was listening.

"Even a few drops will replenish and do no harm."

Eesa coughed again, struggling to sit up. "Xax, let him approach."

The hogboon looked from her to the vampire, uncertainty warring on his face with the need to protect.

"I will not touch her, if that is your wish. Eesa can take a few drops from my wrist directly onto her tongue."

Eesa winced, beckoning them both, and Xax glanced to the other lesser Fae before giving Rémy a nod.

The elder vampire knelt beside the small female. Using his thumbnail, he pierced the vein in his wrist and held it over her mouth.

The little hogboon goblin hesitated at first, but then licked her cracked lips as blood droplets fell. She grasped hold of Rémy's wrist and licked the wound, drinking directly from his vein until he gently moved her back.

Her ashen skin now held a lush brown sheen, and her flesh plumped. Dull eyes shined bright red with flecks of green and she took her first easy breath. Holding her hand out to Xax, he helped her to her feet.

"Thank ye," he said, offering the elder vampire a stocky bow.

Eesa tapped him on the shoulder and then pointed toward a nondescript boulder at the edge of the lilac grove.

He nodded, and then closed his eyes for a moment. When he opened them again, he lifted his mate's hand to his formidable mouth. He kissed her knuckles, and then wrapped his long, clawed fingers around her hand.

"Come." He gestured for Lane and Gareth to follow. Sparing a look for Rémy, he placed a fist over his heart.

Rémy copied the move. "Don't worry, my warrior friend. I will protect your mate and your friends until you return. Those that did this to you will meet their final death either by my hand, or by the hand of the Fae halfling at your side. Though I hope she saves the honor for me."

"If I can, I will," Lane replied, tapping the canvas bag strapped across her chest.

"Godspeed...*princesssss*." Rémy winked, mimicking the hogboon goblin's speech, and he and the lesser Fae watched the three disappear into the unknown.

Chapter Seventeen

"*A* concealed portal right in the middle of a State Park." Lane watched as Xax cut a narrow ribbon in the shimmering membrane warding the entry from prying eyes.

The jagged edge of the rock face seemed monolithic in size and shape, and she wondered if it was naturally occurring or if the *Cinn ag Taitneamh* had placed it here by design.

A crack spread, wide enough for a man to squeeze past sideways, and Xax stepped through the opening first. When he gave the signal, he stepped to the side, allowing Lane and Gareth to follow.

Lane's skin tingled as she stepped through the entry and her body shivered. Once through, she wiped her arms and legs with her palms, smoothing her hair as if a film had somehow stuck.

"Ew, that's got to be by design," she said, wiggling around.

"Lane, what the hell are you doing?"

She made a face, still smoothing her hair. "You don't feel that?"

"Feel what? The transition?"

"Is that what you call it? God, it's like walking through a spider's web, soft but instinctively icky. Man, if the wards don't stop you, that creep factor totally does the trick."

He laughed. "You'll get used to it."

"Ugh, no thanks."

The hogboon goblin turned, lifting a hand to the crevice from the inside to begin the incantation to close the portal.

"Xax, don't. Leave it open for now."

His ears flicked. "I cannot. Ye can't enter further into the Middle Course if the portal be open to the human plane."

"Middle Course?"

Xax bobbed his furry head. "Yes, mistress. Be what this is. Middle Course. Neither Earth nor Faerie. It be in between."

"Xax, I understand your predicament, and we appreciate everything you've done for us so far, but if you close the rock portal and we get separated or something untoward happens, Lane and I will be trapped."

Gareth swung an arm toward the myriad tunnels facing them ahead. Xax seemed to consider his point, his red eyes gleaming in the semi-dark.

For a moment his eyes flickered orange and then he smiled a sharp-toothed grin. "Do ye know the *Ballad of Tam Lin*? Tis a long poem."

"Yes, why?" Gareth nodded, but raised an eyebrow at the odd question.

"Have ye a silver blade? Best with runes and sigils."

Gareth nodded, sparing a perplexed look for Lane.

The hogboon goblin tapped the side of his heart-shaped head. "Clever it is, and magic it holds. Say the final lines of the lament and trace a five-pointed star in the air. Any portal ye want will open." He nodded, giggling to himself. "Tis Goblin magic so be afeared. The portal once opened can suck ye straight through to the other side and keep ye hostage. Tricky it be but use if ye must."

Xax then closed the rock portal and then turned with a little skip. Since they entered the Middle Course, the little hogboon had energy and his skin seemed to glow even in the dim light.

"You like it here, Xax?" Lane asked.

He bobbed his head, holding his palm toward a wall torch. The end flamed immediately, and Xax motioned for Gareth to take it.

"All Fae folk take sustenance of spirit from Fae-kissed ground. The Middle Course is as close as we exiled can be to our home."

The tunnels spread in a labyrinth, dark and wet, and Gareth handed the torch to Xax, motioning for him to take the lead.

Lane opened her senses, looking for any sign of Eve. She exhaled hard, shaking her head.

"What's the matter?"

She puffed out another breath into the damp. "I can't seem to focus. I need to sense Eve, or we'll end up going in circles."

"That's because you're relying on your witch side. You're a Raven, but you're also a halfling Sidhe, and being where we are, you'll do better tapping into that half."

She snorted. "I don't think this is the place or the time for us to get down and dirty, Gareth."

"I claimed you, love. Your power is right there under the surface for you to try whenever you want. You don't need me anymore." He paused with a gorgeous crooked grin. "Well, not to use your magic anyway. For everything else and for toe-curling, mind-shattering —"

"La, la, la, la…I get the picture," she said singsong, giving him a *shut up now or else* look.

Xax glanced over his shoulder with a long-toothed grin and a snicker on his lips. Lane cocked back, punching Gareth in the shoulder.

"Ow!"

"See?"

He rubbed his arm. "Don't be so uptight. Middle Course is halfway to Faerie, and everyone knows the Fae do it magically."

"Gareth, I swear."

He laughed out loud. "Okay, okay. To save myself some unnecessary bruising, how about you practice your magic. Try an energy ball. Open your hand and concentrate on your palm. Focus. Imagine heat and magic in a blue and white swirl."

She opened her palm as they walked, and a tiny spark formed, but then went out.

"That's a good start. Try again, only this time expand it. Hold the thought."

Lane focused again, and this time the spark held. It swirled in her palm like a tiny blue pulsing galaxy. She blew out a breath, and when she did it spiraled up, growing and coalescing into a sphere.

"Holy shit! Gareth! Look!"

He nodded. "See, I told you. Now wing it at the wall and not my shoulder."

"Ha. Ha." She cocked back, hurling the energy ball against the wall. Rock crumbled in a scorched mess and Xax yelled.

"Are ye crazy? Do ye want to bring the entire substrate down on our heads?"

She flashed what she hoped was a sheepish apology but squealed when Gareth swung his arm around her shoulder.

"Now try a repelling light." He let go of her long enough to palm a handful of rocks from the explosion. "Just concentrate like you did earlier, but instead of thinking destruction, think prevention. The light should be pure yellow and should buzz in your palm rather than pulse."

She held her hand out again, and this time chanted the word repel over and over in her head. A white light formed, and as it grew it took on a buttery sheen.

It hummed across her skin, and she grinned. "Like holding a glowing vibrator."

"Yeah, well. Don't even think about using it the way I know your dirty mind is thinking. You'll burn your lady bits off."

With a silent wince, she nodded. "Gotcha. Not a toy." Holding her palm up, she barely had time to react when Gareth lobbed a rock at her head.

"Hey!" Instinct kicked in and she ducked. "Send up a smoke signal or something to give me a heads-up there, Golden Boy."

"Nope. What would be the point of that? An opponent isn't going to telegraph his intentions. You have to be ready."

Without warning, he threw another, but this time she recalled her power and changed the rock's trajectory toward the wall instead of her head.

"Very good. Your Sidhe nature is kicking in on a core level. Now try to use that same intuition to sense Eve."

Gareth whistled, grabbing Xax's attention ahead. Xax stopped, and he and Gareth waited while Lane focused her Fae gifts to sense the witch.

She closed her eyes and held both hands out to the side, elbows close. A dull white light emanated over each hand, and it spiraled, circling her skin. The power spread up her arms and across her chest and down until it covered her whole body.

She cocked her head, listening. As though moving on autopilot, she turned on her heel, walking like a glowing Halloween ghost until she stood in front of a stone expanse.

Gareth moved to her side, taking her hand. He hissed as her power surged, clinging to his skin as it merged with his underlying essence.

If ever Xax's fearsome grin could seem approving, it was now. "Warded it be, but tis no wall. Tis a room."

Lane's eyes snapped open. "Eve's inside."

"Our combined blood crumbled the wards at the Red Veil, so maybe we should give that a try."

Gareth fished in his pocket for the mini ritual knife. With a flick, he unfolded the jackknife and held it over her hand.

"I'm really starting to hate this. I'm going to look like a teenage cutter." She winced and held open her palm.

"Stop grumbling. With your Fae abilities, you'll heal even faster now." Gareth sliced her palm and then did the same to himself.

Lane snatched the blade from him. "I'll hang onto this, thank you."

They clasped hands and like before, power sizzled and burned between them. She mumbled the same spell she used at the vampire club and the two let go of each other to smear the wall with their mingled blood.

The stone groaned and cracked, and then dissolved to nothing. No explosion. No earth fissure to swallow the rock expansion. Just poof. Gone.

"Well, that was anticlimactic." No sooner did the words leave Lane's mouth than Leith's undead trio stepped from the shadows.

Hissing, they attacked, the first backhanding Xax, sending him flying into the tunnel wall. The little hogboon goblin hit with a sickening crack, slumping to the ground.

"Eve! She's shackled to the bed! Gareth! Grab her!"

Eve screamed, but Lane kept her eyes on the three vampires as they advanced. Her body shimmered with power, attracting them like moths to a flame.

With a snarl, the first advanced. He moved in a weird shuffle with lips curled over stained fangs.

"Lane! Watch out!"

Gareth raced for the sword on the wall. He yanked it from its bracket, cracking the pommel. "Damn it to hell!"

He fisted the crucifer grip with both hands. Sigils sparked to life despite the crack. He lifted it high with a battle cry, and the blade swung with a spark slicing through Eve's chains.

Freed, she clamored to the corner of the room while he pivoted around to help Lane.

"Over here, leeches!" He sliced the blade over his hand, letting the blood well and drip to the floor in a crimson path. "You want Fae blood, come and get it!"

They turned in unison, their eyes yellow and streaked with black veins.

"It's like an episode of the fucking *Walking Dead*," Lane circled around the other way.

"Yeah, except with fangs."

Gareth gripped the hilt tight, holding his ground until the first vampire closed in with a snarl. He swung the blade, severing its undead head from its shoulders. The others shrieked but kept advancing.

Lane dug in her canvas bag, pulling out a thin metallic net. It glistened in her hand like liquid silver. She swung the precious metal over her head high and wide before throwing fishing net style over the remaining vampires.

They crumpled to the ground, their pallid flesh sloughing in gray ribbons under the silver net.

"Is there anything else in that bag I should know about, Mary Poppins?" Gareth exhaled.

Resting the sword against the wall, he dragged them into the tunnel corridor, leaving them for Rémy. The other had already turned to ash, but at least he'd have these two to use for amends with the Weres.

"Check Xax. I'll get Eve," she said, scanning the room's shadows for her friend.

The room was suddenly alight, and her hand flew to shield her eyes as she squinted, blind.

"Hello, Lane." The voice that spoke her name was definitely male and definitely not Gareth's.

"Who are you?" Her eyes adjusted to see a tall, blond, ethereally beautiful man standing over Eve with his fingers twisted in her dark hair.

He stared at her the same way she stared at him, assessing and wondering. There was no question who he was. They had the same eyes. The same lithe frame.

"Leith." His name was a whispered curse on her tongue.

He inclined his head. "I knew it was only a matter of time before you figured out how to find your friend."

Letting go of Eve's hair, he gave her a rough shove toward the far corner. Her friend cried out, and the sound of her pain tightened Lane's jaw.

Outside, Xax got to his feet despite a small red trickle from the gash at his temple. He shook his head, holding onto Gareth's arm, but the two turned at Eve's cry.

"Lane!" Gareth let go of the little hogboon goblin, rushing for the room again.

Leith's eyes jerked toward the broken wards, and in seconds white fire shot from both hands, knocking Gareth back toward the tunnel wall.

"Gareth!"

Leith waved one hand, the motion sending Lane crashing toward the pallet bed. Another blitz of pure white fire pinned Gareth to the wall. Then the flash grew, as though feeding on Gareth's own power until there was nothing left. He was gone. No scorch marks. No ashes. Nothing.

"No!"

Pain sluiced through her veins and a shriek ripped from her core. Rage as white hot as Leith's blitz coursed through her veins. She turned for the sword against the wall.

"I wouldn't if I were you, my dear." Leith tsked, holding a short blade to Eve's throat.

Her fingers curled around the hilt. Anger and fear swelled. What should she do? With a snarl, she lifted the sword and plunged it into the dirt. The ground rumbled, opening into a deep crevasse. Dirt and rock crumbled into the gap, but Leith simply laughed. A wave of his hand closed the rift, the ground swallowing the sword with it.

"Little girl, there is so much you need to learn. So much I will teach you once you're at my side."

Her body shook with rage and pain. Heat scorched her palms and she hurled two fireballs at his head. He deflected them with ease, smirking as they barely singed the walls.

All the magic she thought she had at her fingertips was useless against a full Sidhe. Gareth was gone. Her mind rebelled against the thought. This was *not* happening. Yet, here she stood. Facing her father, alone.

Another wave of his hand reset his wards, and just like that, she was cut off from the only way she knew to get home.

Lane steeled her jaw and lifted her eyes to the man who ruined her life. The man responsible for taking everything she loved. The fire Leith used to kill Gareth had hardened her to the core. If he wanted a protégé, he'd get one in spades. At least until she could turn the tables and burn his ass the same way he had the man she loved.

"You took a life. Now it's time to relinquish one," she said, finally.

"You are in no position to bargain, little girl."

"Let Eve go."

He sheathed the knife from her friend's throat and Eve's shoulders slumped.

"Not good enough."

He cocked his head. "Convince me, then."

"Eve served her purpose. She got me here. Now let her go."

He shrugged, and then snapped his fingers. Eve disappeared with a shriek, but it was his laughter that jerked her gaze back to his ice blue eyes.

"Where is she? I said let her go."

"Ah, yes. But you didn't specify *where.*"

Lane clenched her fists, ignoring the burning in her palms. She itched to burn his ass, but right now it was futile and a waste of energy. She needed to conserve her resources and feel out the situation.

"Why are you playing games, Leith? You wanted me here, but really, isn't the cost a little high?"

He shrugged. "The cost isn't mine, my dear." He smoothed the front of his velvet coat. "Still, Eve may prove a bargaining chip yet. I sent her to my castle. But don't worry, she has at least three friends there who know her intimately."

If the bastard meant his three bloodsuckers, then obviously, Leith didn't know everything. Not when his vampire mafia was down one head, literally, and the rest were tied up in silver.

Xax would have found Rémy by now, letting him and the others know what happened. Not that they could help.

"Asshole, haven't you heard you catch more flies with honey than vinegar? You want me so badly, you arranged this elaborate scheme, yet instead of trying to entice me, your first instinct was to frighten and bully me. Dude, it's Machiavellianism 101 in reverse. You always try the sweets before the sour. Then again, my mother said you were good looking. She never said you were smart."

"So, you knew about me."

She shook her head. "Not until yesterday. But I wasn't wrong all these years. You were just a sperm donor."

A slash formed on his lips and his fingers curled. The energy that crackled, though, he extinguished as quickly as it sparked. "You can blame your whore of a mother for that. I was robbed of the chance to be your father, but that is something I plan to remedy."

She nearly laughed in his face. "Well, daddy dearest, you're off to one hell of a start." Lane watched his face, and in that moment, she knew she had him. Not exactly where she wanted, but it was a start.

"You want me for a protégé or whatever? I'll bite, but I have a few conditions."

She'd just learned the hard way about not being specific, and she wasn't about to make the same mistake. She had to out-cunning the master.

"Name your price."

"First, I want Eve safely returned to the motherhouse, unharmed, in one piece, with her mind and body intact as it was before you took her from the Red Veil.

"Second, I want Gareth restored and returned to the Seelie Court, also unharmed, in one piece, with his mind and body intact before you hit him with your fire ball.

"Next, I want to get a message to Caitlan, the Supreme of the Circle of the Ravens. I want her to know I'm well and staying in Faerie with you of my own volition, and I want the message to be timely. That means Earth time, not Faerie time."

He smirked. "You sound like you've had dealing with the Djinn."

"More like dealings with the cocksucker who sired me. I trust no one and nothing, Leith. From here on in, it's all about me and what I want."

534

Pride seemed to spark in his eyes, and the smile creeping on his lips made her ill. She dismissed the feeling. There was no time to indulge anything but revenge and getting the hell out of here with the people she loved.

"Oh, and one last thing, Leith."

He inclined his head, waiting.

"I have reason to believe my mother is still alive, and I think you know exactly where she is. I want to see her. Not in a scrying surface or in a memory, but for real, face to face — and she better be healthy and hearty, or hell will reign."

He chuckled, impressed. "How I got you off that wilted rose of a Raven is beyond me. You inherited your mother's pretty face, but there's much more of me in you than you think. You're quick and resourceful, as well as adaptive. Do well to hone those traits." He turned with a flourish. "Very well. If you wish to see your mother, then so be it." He clapped his hands, and in that moment everything went dark.

Chapter Eighteen

*L*ane woke to slatted light winking in from a shuttered window. Blinking to adjust, she tried to sit up, only to wince back against a lumpy pillow.

A dull throb pounded the top of her head in time with nauseous waves in her stomach. She dragged her arm across her eyes, hoping the counterpressure would help.

"Easy now. Give yourself a chance. It'll take a bit for your body to shake off Leith's touch. Gentle isn't a word in his vocabulary."

At the soft feminine voice, Lane pulled her arm back. "If you mean what I think you mean, then he's more of a sick fuck than I thought."

The woman flashed a shy smile. "I haven't heard that accent or that kind of language in a very long time."

Her hand was soft as she brushed Lane's hair back to place a cool towel on her forehead. "He didn't touch you, sweetheart. Not in that way, anyway. He saves that particular cruelty for me."

The woman looked to be in her mid-thirties, with flawless skin and long, sandy blonde hair that fell to her waist in a thick braid. Her eyes were dove-gray, but dulled, as if all the hope had gone out of her life.

There was something familiar about her, but Lane couldn't place it. Not until the sad woman leaned over to adjust a pillow.

Her pendant came loose from her bodice and swung forward. Lane gripped the woman's arm, all pain and nausea forgotten.

"Is your name Aislinn?" she asked, her eyes taking in every detail of the woman's face.

She nodded but didn't offer anything more.

The door opened and Eve came in carrying a pitcher and washbowl, with a white cloth over her arm.

"Lane!" She rushed forward, water sloshing. "Thank God! Oh, Laney! I knew you'd never give up on me!"

The pitcher and the rest clattered as she dropped them on the nearest table and rushed to give Lane a hug.

Aislinn's eyes went unblinking as the realization hit, and Lane stared at her from over Eve's hug.

"Laney Belle?" She froze with her daughter's hand still on her arm.

Lane's throat tightened against any kind of words, so all she could do was nod.

Eve backed off and stared at the two. "Wait, are you saying this is your...I mean Laney is..."

"Yes, child. To all of the above." Aislinn's voice was barely a whisper as disbelief changed to fleeting joy, but it was regret and censure that took control. She looked away, slipping her arm from Lane's grip.

"No. Don't do that," Lane said, sitting up. "This is not your fault. I chose to be here...and I made him agree to certain conditions. One of them was you."

Aislinn sniffed hard. "You chose to be here. That tells me I failed. Miserably."

Shaken, she got up from the bed and walked toward the window. Pulling back the shutters, she let the room fill with overcast light. "You chose to be here, where it's always either winter or fall."

Aislinn kept her gaze outside. "Caitlan must have given you my letter if you thought to demand anything of your father, let alone to see me."

"That megalomaniac is not my father. He's a sperm donor."

Turning, Aislinn shook her head with a self-disdaining snort. "Then how can I be your mother when I abandoned you?"

"Don't. You did what you did to protect me." Lane got up from the bed, not caring about the cold, damp floor on her bare feet.

"Caitlan did give me your letter. But only because Leith was sniffing around. I know leaving me with the Ravens was the hardest thing you ever had to do. That you stayed with me all that time told me you tried. You weren't wrong about binding my powers."

"But?"

Lane looked at the way the breeze blew loose tendrils around her face. The simple image brought so many memories

"No buts, just a question."

With an inhale, Aislinn lifted her chin, as if bracing herself. "What do you want to know?"

"My only question is why didn't you stay after you and Caitlan bound my Sidhe side? The Circle of the Raven was your home, too. The motherhouse would have protected you as well."

Aislinn looked at the floor. "Seven years on the human plane is barely seven days here in Faerie." She looked up again, her eyes were dry. "Any longer and Leith would have gotten suspicious. I could risk a week, but no more. To be honest, I still can't believe I managed it. Those years with you were the happiest of my life, and the memories have sustained me since."

She moved to crouch by a stone slate near an inside wall. Wiggling the loose rock, she took a metal box from a hole behind the slate.

Aislinn lifted the lid, pulling out a clear plastic bag. "My most precious possessions," she said. "Pictures of you and me."

Lane looked at the mementoes in her mother's hand, and then stared at the woman she remembered, but barely knew. "Stored in an iron strongbox."

"Yes. Hidden but unlocked, because no Fae would dare touch it."

Eve moved to look at the pictures through the Ziplock bag. "Laney, you were so cute. You look just like Aislinn. Even now it's easy to see you're her daughter."

Lane wasn't paying attention. Her eyes hadn't moved from Aislinn's face. "If you knew how to escape home, why didn't you do so beforehand?"

"Leith wasn't always the way he is now. I was happy with him. Happy being here. I barely noticed the changes in him until it was too late. Truth is, I didn't want to leave until he became so cruel and hungry for power there was no way I could let him know about you."

"Then how did he find out about Lane?" Eve asked, handing the pictures back. "Did you tell him?"

Aislinn's eyes went wide. "God, no! He'd have to kill me first."

"Then how?" Eve asked again. "Because his plan to find Lane, and lure her here, was pretty elaborate for something he'd just learned about. I was taken by mistake. I think he and his cohorts thought Lane would be in that backroom. The club where it all went down is one of her favorite haunts, but he got me instead. Still, everything I suffered is nothing compared to the lives lost in this mess."

Aislinn's eyes welled. "I don't know how he found out about Lane, and I'm so very sorry for everything you two have endured."

Lane unfolded her arms from her chest. "Leith's machinations are not your fault. He's the one responsible. Any normal person who found they had a secret daughter would have contacted me in a normal way. Met me for coffee. Bought me dinner. Not try and kidnap me."

Raking a hand through her hair, she took in the layout of the room. Her gaze moved from the window to the door and then back to both women.

"Eve, you came in with that pitcher and stuff from somewhere outside, so we obviously have the freedom to move around."

"We are at *dun Sliabh Creagach*," Aislinn replied. "It's the seat of Leith's ancestral home. Loosely translated, it means jagged mountain." She swept a hand toward the window.

"Look outside. We're perched on a cliff facing the sea. We have free roam because there's literally nowhere else to go."

Lane moved to the window beside her mother. Aislinn was right about that. The water was dark and beautiful, but despite its majesty, the rocks around the shore were deadly.

She turned abruptly, taking Aislinn's hand. "There has to be another way. Think."

"I don't see how. The portal I used to get home has been sealed since I returned. Leith must have suspected I was testing out an escape, so he had it destroyed. The only other portal is from here to the Seelie Court. We might be able to open it, but they'd never let us through."

"Not even for sanctuary?" Eve asked, nodding as she looked at Lane. "Contrary to what Caitlan thinks, I actually paid attention in class. We could ask for asylum."

Lane dropped her eyes for a moment. "I lost someone dear to me in the Middle Course when we came looking for a way in to rescue Eve. He had sanctuary at the Seelie Court."

Eve moved to Lane's side to take her other hand, and the three of them stood in the stone window overlooking the tumultuous sea.

"I saw what happened during that fight. Who was he, Lane?"

Lane looked up with a sniff. "It was Gareth, Eve. He was the love of my life. Someone I thought lost to this godforsaken plane and this so-called superior race. Leith wasn't the first of his kind to become drunk on the thought of power." She filled them in on Gareth's story.

"I watched Mason die, too," Eve said, her voice barely a whisper. "It was horrible. And to think I used to think the undead mysterious and sexy. They're nothing but coldhearted predators."

Lane squeezed her hand. "I know, honey. And the undead bastards that helped themselves to his life are getting their hearts and fangs ripped out by their Master Adjudicator. Or at least I hope so. There are a lot of moving parts to this thing.

"We can talk later about the miles of therapy we're facing after we get out of here, but first; we need a plan. We have each other, and we're not without skills. Three Ravens form a circle of three times three times three."

Eve smiled and even giggled the way she used to before this mess. "And you're a halfling Sidhe. So, hell yeah. I'm in."

"How?" Aislinn voiced. "I just said there's no portal open to us, even to the Middle Course. Only the Seelie Court."

Lane nodded. "Exactly. And I'm wearing Gareth's claim." She lifted her palm, showing them the sigil. "When he was alive it shimmered translucent gold, but since the Middle Course…"

Her voice trailed, and she let go of Eve's hand to run a finger over the dull white scar. "Well, at least it's still a pretty design."

"It's beautiful, Lane." Eve took her hand again.

"Yes." She nodded again. "Let's hope it's also our ticket out of here. Maybe it'll give Leith a stroke that someone laid claim to me first." She smiled.

Aislinn loosed her hand from their strategizing. "If we're really going to do this, then we don't have much time. In this castle, servants' eyes and ears are everywhere. Eve and I managed to ward this room to give us some privacy, but only just barely. The manor is like a trip wire. Anything but a gossamer touch sets off alarms."

"God, that man is not just a megalomaniac, he's paranoid as shit." Lane exhaled a disgusted grunt.

"He is what he is, Laney Belle. We can't worry about that now. He has plans for you. I know him, sweetheart. He won't want to wait. The servants have most likely let him know you've stirred from the portal's magical backlash. Everyone thinks it's so easy for the Fae to abduct unwilling victims. It's not. It takes as much out of them as it does the abductee."

"You sound almost sorry he suffered dragging me and Eve here." Lane paused, sparing a look for Eve.

"Aislinn, if you have any doubts, you have to voice them now. We can't have you go all Stockholm Syndrome on us at the last minute."

Her mother shook her head. "I'm in. If only to get you two back where you belong. I don't really care about me."

"You should. Just because your lover changed course mid-trip doesn't mean you're obligated to ride the crazy train with him." Eve nodded. "Besides, you look amazing.

You left the human realm twenty years ago, but you don't look like you've aged at all."

Aislinn patted Eve's arm. "I've aged all right. Mentally and emotionally. Even if the packaging is well preserved."

"Good genes." Lane slipped her arm around Aislinn's shoulders. "Like mother, like daughter."

Lane pecked her mother's cheek and then left their huddle to hunt for her clothes.

"They're not here, honey," Aislinn said. "Leith wants us all to dress in Fae fashion."

She sat on the end of the bed, scrubbing the heel of her palm into her eye. "Great. So, we all look like extras from the Lord of the Rings."

"I thought Renaissance Festival, but either works," Eve said, opening the wardrobe. "C'mon, Laney. At least they're pretty. Think of it like playing dress-up."

Lane exhaled, but then squared her shoulders and got up from the bed. "Maid Marion does manslaughter," she mumbled.

Dressed and ready to play their parts, the three women sat in the manor's courtyard. Leith hadn't showed yet and waiting ratcheted the tension for everyone.

"Maybe he knows and isn't coming," Eve whispered, holding her needlepoint. "And what the hell is it you've got me sewing? I'm a twenty-first century witch, not a homespun hack."

"Shut it, Eve. Until we have lift off, just play the game. He thinks this is a cat and mouse, but he's about to find out he's up against a pride of lionesses and he's lunch." Lane gripped the wooden frame of her needlepoint so tightly it cracked.

The overcast sky had broken into a dull sunshine. A cool breeze off the water stirred the sheer trim on Lane's dress, and she frowned. Under any other circumstances, she'd love this level of cosplay. But this gave new meaning to the term ladies-in-waiting.

Footsteps echoed from the main house, and Aislinn looked up from her sewing, giving a nearly imperceptible nod.

"Lane, I'm heartened to see you dressed as a lady of your station. You are of house, *dun Sliabh Creagach*, and all will know you as such." He frowned, turning his attention to Aislinn as she helped Eve pull a stray thread.

"Don't grow too contented with your daily comforts, you unworthy whore. You are only here because my daughter wishes it. That's right, you taint-blooded slut. *My* daughter. The one you hid from me and then abandoned."

He walked behind her, giving her hair a vicious yank, pulling her from her chair. Aislinn winced, but she didn't cry out.

A servant took a step toward her as she lay on the ground beside her chair, but one look from Leith sent the girl running. He waved his hand and every servant fled.

Lane flung her broken sewing at Leith and rushed to Aislinn's side, motioning for Eve to follow. The two crouched beside her, helping her to her feet.

"I guess you didn't take my hint about flies and honey, did you, asshole? What an absolute waste. Like Mama said, you might look like a sexy, real-life Legolas, but you're no Lord of the Rings. You're nothing. Not to me and not to her."

"Really, dearest. I expected more of you."

Lane straightened, keeping her hand linked with Aislinn's. Eve stood on the opposite side, her fingers laced as well.

"Are you addressing me or my mother? She was your dearest once, but that all changed when you decided to try for glory. I've got news for you, bucko. For glory you need guts, and you are nothing but an insecure little boy trying to fill a man's shoes."

"Rail all you want, Lane. In time, the lure of your Sidhe blood will be too strong to resist." With a snort, he turned on his heel. "I'll leave you to your happy reunion, but come morning we have a war to plan, and I expect my daughter to be at my side and do and say everything I ask, or this reunion will be a funeral pyre."

"Time's up, dude. My Sidhe blood is calling and it wants you!"

The three Ravens lifted their joined hands, with Lane at their center. Power grew, circling and swirling in and through the circle of three.

Leith growled, lifting his hands, but his palms were empty. His eyes flashed to Lane and she pushed her lips to a vengeful smirk. "Your biggest flaw is hubris, Leith. Not mendacity. Not avarice. But pride and overconfidence. You left the three of us to our own devices, gave us freedom to walk the halls of this manor. What you forgot is we're witches, and when you get three of us together, we can open a whole can of whoop ass."

Aislinn smiled. "All those years you kept me sequestered didn't dull my witchy powers. I practiced alone. Honing my skills. Hoping one day you'd grow so complacent, so sure of my yolk you'd forget the rule of three and unwittingly bring other witches here. I should thank you, Leith. Not only did you bring me witches, but you brought Ravens, and no one masters the power of three times three times three better."

Lane nodded. "There's one other tidbit you should know. The rules also ricochet. Whatever you put into the universe will come back threefold."

Eve giggled her sweet laugh. "Basically, dude, you're fucked."

Aislinn turned, blowing in the direction of the crystals they placed in a circle ahead of time. The exact circle where Leith stood.

The pure quartz blazed with white light, and he turned in a rush, but he was trapped.

"Tsk, tsk, Dad. Game's over and you lose."

"I am an immortal! You cannot kill me!"

They gripped hands even tighter. Their words catching power, it eddied within the bound circle.

"We call the realms of space and time, unlock the gates, release the prime. From fiery breath, world's first light, fire burn and candle bright, invoke the fates, set wrongs to right, burn baby burn, our foe now smite!"

The courtyard's bluestone slates shook and split. Leith fell to his knees as around him the ground gave way. It crumbled like it did in the Middle Course, only this time Leith couldn't seal the rift. Fire spewed all around him as he knelt on a small outcrop of rock.

Lane pulled loose from Eve's grip, keeping her other hand laced with her mother's hand. They'd do this together.

She lifted a hand toward the fiery rock, and mumbled words she didn't know she knew. Wind ripped and swirled and in the midst of the maelstrom, the sword rose.

Calling to it, she gripped the hilt and with every ounce of strength, hurled the iron clad steel into Leith's chest.

He screamed as the iron ore flamed, engulfing his body in the one fire no full Sidhe could withstand. He fell to the depths, white flame sealing his fate. Lane waved a hand over the pit, and it sealed.

"Huh. I guess like father like daughter."

Aislinn squeezed her hand, before pressing a kiss to her daughter's cheek. "Let's not build on that, okay?"

Lane laughed. "Like mother like daughter."

"Uhm, can we make like a banana and split? I don't want to be here when the minions find out we toasted their boss."

Aislinn nodded. "C'mon. The portal to the Seelie Court is down by the water."

"The water! You mean down those rocks?" Eve stopped short.

"Did you think Leith would make any part of this easy?" She tugged Eve's sleeve. "We'll be fine. I know a shortcut."

Chapter Nineteen

"Gareth claimed you." It wasn't a question. Still, it didn't bode well to ignore the Seelie queen. Not in her own court, anyway.

"Yes, your Grace. He did." Lane lifted her hand to show the queen the mark on her palm.

The queen beckoned her closer, and when in reach she touched the dull white mark softly. "That's quite a sigil. Gareth must have loved you very much."

Lane nodded, swallowing against the lump in her throat. "As I him."

The queen considered Lane, waving her back to her place. "A claiming rite is a varied and personal thing. It can be simple and perfunctory or elaborate and heartfelt. It requires only two things, of which I'm sure you're aware."

Lane bobbed her head, not trusting her voice.

"Do you recall any of the words spoken when Gareth claimed you?" She gestured toward the sigil. "The words he used ensuring the rite."

Gareth's words were a tattoo on her heart, even as the sentiments behind them were evidenced on her hand. "Every word, your Grace."

"Can you repeat them for me?"

Lane stifled a recoil. The woman wasn't just the Tiana, Queen of the Seelie, Sovereign of the Summer Court. She was *all* Sidhe. As selfish and thoughtlessly forbidding as Leith was cruel.

"I'd rather not, your Grace. Gareth's words are still too painful to remember, let alone speak aloud."

The queen looked at her, but then lifted a dismissive hand. "Indulge me."

Jaw set, Lane glanced away for a moment. Every eye in the court was on her now, and she dare not refuse. Not if she wanted the woman on the throne to allow her, Eve, and Aislinn to return home in one piece.

She sucked in a breath, ignoring the anger and hurt stinging her eyes. *"Root of my root, star spun lives. Bound in flesh and spirit light. Blood of my blood, bone of my bone, I claim thee now as we are one. United in life, transcended in death, the claim is cast on Danu's breath."*

"Thank you, Lane. Your lover's words were as I suspected. He was and is a very clever halfling. It's why I welcomed him to my court. Aside from the fact he's rather yummy to look at."

Flummoxed, Lane blinked at the regal woman. "Was and *is*, your Majesty? Gareth is dead."

She smiled, showing perfect white teeth behind full lips. "Ah, there's dead and then there's dead-dead."

Lane's pulsed raced in that moment. Tiana had uttered the exact words Gareth said when she first saw him at the Red Veil.

"I see by your eyes you understood my meaning, or at least partly. When Gareth spoke the words, *united in life, transcended in death*, he unwittingly found a loophole. He spent enough time in Faerie to know we are cunning creatures, and unless requests are made comprehensively, it leaves room for less exacting interpretations. Wiggle room, to use a human phrase, that the Sidhe employ at their whim."

Lane licked her lips, afraid to ask the million-dollar question biting her tongue. Leith had played the same game when she demanded he let Eve go. She assumed he understood she meant home to the motherhouse. The bastard was true to his nature and played her.

When the queen didn't elaborate, Lane plucked up the courage and asked, "Are you telling me Gareth is alive?"

Tiana lifted a hand again. "Not exactly. Not yet."

She motioned for Lane to approach again, and when she was close enough, the queen took Lane's hand, holding it palm up. She beckoned one of her ladies-in-waiting forward and took a silver and jewel encrusted dirk from the woman's belt.

Without preamble, the queen slit Lane's palm below the claiming sigil. Blood rose in a red line, and Lane didn't dare move. Tiana then did the unthinkable. She pricked her own finger and held it over Lane's palm.

The collective gasp that rose from the court earned a stern eyebrow from the queen, and it quieted immediately.

She curled her finger inward, waiting. "You'll have to forgive the court, my dear. They are not used to witnessing my aid to halflings and Ravens, but if we are to survive the new millennium and continue to thrive, that needs to change.

"My counterpart, Lachlan, King of the Unseelie and Sovereign of the Winter Court, wholeheartedly agrees. It's the reason Leith attempted his coup. He knew that with you and your mother, he had an ace up his sleeve. Who better to rule a new dynastic Faerie than one who had…what is it you humans say? Skin in the game?"

The queen then uncurled her finger. "Do you know where Gareth fell?" she asked.

Lane nodded. "In the labyrinths of the Middle Course near the abandoned spring portal."

"Very well. Picture him there. Not as he was when Leith set him aflame, but as you wish to see him. Virile. Handsome. Whole. Keep the image vivid, and do not pull away from my hand." Her eyes met Lane's and her gaze held.

Lane nodded and then closed her eyes as instructed. Without hesitation, Tiana squeezed the tip of her finger. A drop of royal blood mingled with the blood in Lane's palm.

Immediate pain shot through Lane's hand, scorching worse than any burn from a hot stove.

A strangled cry died on her tongue as she gritted her teeth against the reflex to jerk away. Lane didn't dare open her eyes, betting her flesh had crisped, charring as the agony spread toward her elbow.

Panting, she concentrated on Gareth, forcing her mind to a place of cool water and refreshing breezes. She pictured Gareth's sexy crooked grin, and the way his raspberry blue eyes flashed with laughter. The way those same blue eyes darkened with need as his body tensed with desire. The image expanded, and memories of him flooded her mind and heart, augmenting the picture in her head, making the pain subside.

In that moment, the queen released her hand. Lane opened her eyes, expecting worse than third degree burns, only to find her skin smooth and unmarked.

"I'm sorry, my dear, but I had to test you. I actually got the idea from a Sci-Fi book decades ago." She waved her hand dismissively. "I can't recall the title, and it doesn't really matter, though I admit, the method is quite effective."

Lane's mouth dropped. "You gave me a Fae version of the *Bene Gesserit* box test from *Dune*?

"Gareth proved his love for you by sacrificing his life for yours. If I am to help bring him back from the dead, I need to be sure you are deserving of my help. Though you professed as much, I needed to satisfy you truly love him as you sat." She smiled. "You passed the test."

Lane rubbed the phantom burning still in her hand. "Well, thanks. I guess."

The queen inclined her head again.

"So, your Grace. What now?" Lane threw caution and propriety to the wind. If Tiana was psycho enough to magically duplicate a fictional torture device, then nothing was certain. "How do you help bring Gareth back? He's a Phoenix, so his DNA might prove helpful. The last time it took ten years."

The queen shook her head. "Much less than that. A month in Faerie, and he was sitting up in bed. Of course, it took many months for him to fully regain his strength. His DNA, as you put it, allowed him to return from the ashes because he was killed with human flame. This time he was killed with Fae fire. It's a little trickier."

"How long for him to recover this time, your Grace? Just give it to me straight."

The queen raised an eyebrow, but the smirk tugging at the corner of her mouth said she was impressed.

"Very well. The images you held in your mind during your trial are all that was required." She motioned to Lane's palm. "Your sigil. See how it glows iridescent, instead of the flat white as when you arrived at my court? Your trial had you endure simulated Fae fire, but it was your strength of will and your love for Gareth that sustained you. Not only did you prove your faithfulness to me, you proved it to the fates. Gareth lives. He will need to recover but seek him where last you saw him. He will be there."

Lane's heart pounded with every word the queen spoke, and every fiber of her being twisted to bolt for the nearest portal, but she didn't dare turn and run.

As if reading her mind, Tiana lifted a hand. "What are you waiting for, girl? Go!"

Lane pivoted on her heel, but then stopped, circling back to offer a curtsey. She caught Eve and Aislinn's faces in the flurry. How could she go anywhere knowing they were still stuck?

Holding her breath, Lane straightened. "Your Grace," she began haltingly. "What about my friend and my mother?"

"It is my wish they stay at court a little longer. Rest assured they will be restored to you in due time." The queen turned her eyes to Aislinn. "I believe there is much to learn from your mother about resolve."

Lane hesitated, but then plunged ahead. "Would due time be in Fae time or *our* time?"

The queen laughed out loud, her eyes flashing gold. "Do you really want to ask that question of me?"

"No, ma'am. I guess not." Lane shook her head. "I'll have to trust you and your word."

Tiana gestured to one of her guards. "Ilar, escort Mistress Alden to the spring portal. You will follow her to the Middle Course, but no farther. Report back to me once you return."

The guard's fist hit his breastplate. "As you wish, your Grace."

Lane curtsied low, mouthing the words thank you before turning for the door with the guard. She followed him down the palace steps and into the palace park.

The gardens were wild and beautiful, with every kind of tree and flowering plant known and unknown in an endless summer. No wonder the Sidhe picked the New York Botanical Gardens to hide portals and ex-pat fae.

Ilar led her to a spring at the center of a temple-like garden. Water lilies floated on thick green stalks in the dark depths. Trees reflected on the surface gave all who looked a magical mirror image.

"This spot is beautiful and all, but what do we do next?" Lane waited for Ilar as he stood by the silty edge, silent.

"Are you telling me you don't know how to work this inter-realm thingamajig, because I certainly don't. Gareth and I had a hogboon helping us—" she broke off mid-sentence as Xax's words to Gareth came flooding back.

She met the guard's eyes. "What's your name again?"

"Ilar, mistress."

"Well, Ilar. Do you guys know the *Ballad of Tam Lin*?"

"Of course, mistress," he replied. "It's a well-loved tale."

She nodded, chewing on her lip. "Okay, then I think I know how to start our engines here. I need the words to the last lines of that poem, and a silver blade."

He stood blinking, as if unsure what to do next. "Chop, chop!" She clapped her hands. "Pen and paper, or quill and parchment. Whatever floats your Faerie boat. I don't know this ballad, so I'll need you to dictate the exact words so I can write them down."

Ilar turned on his heel and jogged in the direction of the palace. When he came back, he had a rolled piece of parchment and what looked like Gareth's ritual jackknife in his hand.

"Will these suffice, mistress?"

Lane took the knife from his hand. It was Gareth's all right. "Where did you get this?"

Her voice cracked at the thought of Gareth's belongings traded for bets on dice games in some dank garrison.

"The queen gave it to me earlier. She said if you asked for a blade, I was to give you this. The parchment I had to procure."

He held out the scroll. "It is the ballad in its entirety. My mother wrote out the poem for me when I was a lad."

554

Guilt bit at her for thinking the worst. "I'm sorry for snapping at you, Ilar. I appreciate the help. I promise I'm not keeping the poem. I just need to recite the words."

He nodded and unrolled the parchment, holding it up for her to see. "Whenever you're ready, mistress."

Lane issued a silent prayer to the universe and ran her thumb over the delicate runes and Celtic scrolling on the jackknife's handle.

"Here goes everything." Opening Gareth's blade, she traced a five-point star in the air as she read the last lines of the *Ballad of Tam Lin*.

"Oh, had I known, Tam Lin," she said, *"what this knight I did see, I have looked him in the eyes and turned him to a tree."*

The water in the spring rippled then swirled until it settled again, showing clear as glass. At the bottom was the torchlit passage where Gareth shielded her from Leith's energy ball.

Her chest tightened at the memory, and dry tears scored her throat. She blinked back the sting, peering into the crystal water for any sign of Gareth.

Blue and white flame had consumed his body in seconds. The ball of energy left nothing behind. No scorch marks, and no ash.

"He's not there," she murmured to herself.

Ilar stepped to her side, rolling the scroll before sticking it into his breastplate. "Are you sure this is the place you last saw him?"

She nodded. "We had come down that passage, there, with Xax." Gesturing toward the stone tunnel, she shrugged. "The hogboon helped us."

"Then perhaps the exiled goblin found your mate and is tending him now."

Lane went up on tip toe and pecked the man's scruffy cheek. "You, Ilar, are a genius." She gripped the guard's hand and stepped to the edge of the spring. "Let's go. I have a hogboon goblin to find. On the count of three, jump."

Chapter Twenty

*L*ane held tight to Ilar's arm. The membrane between realms was translucent and thin as they crossed the boundary from Faerie into the Middle Course. The feel was gossamer as they passed, the same filmy consistency as when she crossed with Gareth from the human plane through the rock portal near the lilac grove.

Ilar landed without noise or disturbing the soft ground, holding tight to Lane to keep her from pitching forward into the stone.

She caught her breath and found her feet before letting go of his arm. She looked around at the ground, and the telltale signs of the fight that ensued a week ago. Or was it a day? Leith had killed Gareth in this spot, but Lane had no clue if time in the Middle Course ran concurrent with Faerie or with the human realm.

"Is it always so cold here?" Ilar asked, brushing residual film from his arms.

Lane didn't reply. There was no sign of Gareth or Xax, and that meant she needed to look for them. Or at the very least, find her way to the rock portal and hope she found her happy ending.

"Look," she said, turning toward the Fae guard. "The spring portal won't reseal itself with the spell I used. I can close it now, but then you'd be stuck here. I know you have to get back to Faerie and report to the queen."

"Couldn't you use the same spell to reopen the portal once you've found your mate?"

She shrugged. "I don't know. To be honest, the fact it worked at all was a shot in the dark. Fact is, we both can't leave the portal unattended. I need you to stay here. Guard the opening against gatecrashers. I'll go ahead and find my hogboon friend. I'm sure he can help with portal magic."

Ilar shook his head. "The queen ordered I accompany you."

"I know, but the portal is wide open. Anyone could enter and I don't want to take the chance. The queen's new philosophies regarding halflings and Ravens didn't strike me as popular among her courtiers. Stay here. Guard the portal. I promise, I'll be back."

She hesitated, turning back with Gareth's knife. "Take this. It belonged to my mate, and it means the world to me. Keep it until I get back."

He looked at the small knife and then nodded, his face telling her he understood it was collateral.

She pecked Ilar's cheek again and then took off through the tunnel, hunting for anything Xax left behind for her to follow.

The hogboon had dropped cherry blossom petals Hansel and Gretel style the first time they passed this way. Lane flicked her palm open, and a ball of light swirled, illuminating the passage.

Xax's petals were still there, brown and mushy, but still fragrant enough in the rock enclosure.

Giving Ilar Gareth's blade meant she didn't have it to trace a pentacle in the air if she needed it to open the crevice in the rock portal. Xax would never leave it open, not with Eesa still weak.

The walls of the stone labyrinth seemed claustrophobic, and she needed to stop and recheck the ground or risk losing her way in the maze. The petals Xax left were crushed into the dirt, making them hard to see.

"C'mon, Lane. You're a halfling Sidhe and a Raven witch. Double the power. The Fae are connected to nature, do something. Think."

She closed her eyes and mumbled an improvised rhyme. It was juvenile, but perhaps it would do the trick. *"Light of day in the midst of night, Petals soft white and bright."*

Cringing at the half-assed spell, she waited with the ball of light pulsing in her hand. Sparks broke off in a swirl, floating to the dirt floor. One by one old petals plumped, their tender white satin glowing in a definite line leading to the outer portal.

"Damn! It's good to be a witchy Sidhe!"

Not wasting another second, Lane took off running. Her footfalls echoed off the stone, and her breath puffed in short cloudy pants. She rounded a corner only to skid to a stop when she saw Xax waiting at the open crevice.

"I'm not sure what ye did, mistress, but the whole of the grove is alight with magic. Blooms across cherry trees and the lilacs both are aglow, so I knew ye'd returned."

He made a tight flourished bow, and she couldn't resist rubbing his dobby-like ears. "You, my friend, are a sight for sore eyes. Please, tell me…is he…is…" her throat tightened, and she couldn't bring herself to ask.

Xax took her hand, careful to keep his taloned fingers loose. "He's here, mistress. Weak. But whole again and aching for ye." He pulled her toward the opening. "Come."

"I—" She hesitated, glancing over her shoulder. "The queen sent someone to help me. He's watching the spring portal. I know you have reasons not to cross paths with the queen's guard, and after all you've done for me, I won't bring trouble to your doorstep."

Xax's ear's flicked toward the direction she came, and his nose twitched. "I have nothing to fear, mistress. Not on this side of the portal. My exile is not the queen's concern. It was the Unseelie's doing."

He lifted her hand, giving it another tug. "Leave the guard be and come see your love."

Heart pounding, she let the Hogboon lead. When they exited the crevice, the entire lesser Fae population was there to greet them. Gareth stood at the center of the throng. Tall and gorgeous as ever and wearing a sexy crooked smile.

"Gareth!"

Jerking free of Xax's hand, Lane ran toward him, not caring the lesser Fae had to jump or risk being flattened.

"You're alive! Thank God!" She flung herself into his arms, the force sending his breath from his chest in a soft whoomph.

He laughed, wincing from the vise grip hug. "Easy, love. I'm not quiet one hundred percent."

Crying, Lane buried her face in his chest. "Don't you ever do that to me again!"

His chest vibrated with a soft chuckle. "What? Die or save your life?"

"Just shut up, Golden Boy, and kiss me!"

His mouth crushed hers and he lifted her off her feet, spinning her around. Lane poured everything into their kiss. Fear, anger, worry, sadness, joy, and most of all, love.

Putting her down, he stepped back when her feet touched the ground. His eyes took in every inch of her tearstained face. "I knew you'd figure it out," he said, wiping her cheeks.

"I didn't, actually. It was Tiana. She's the one who knew you'd be smart enough to find a loophole to cheat death by Fae fire."

He smiled. "She's really something."

"I guess. Even if she's decided to keep Eve and my mother in Faerie a bit longer. She says they can teach her a lot about human resolve."

"Resolve?"

Lane nodded. "She's adopting a new policy on inter-Fae relations."

"Uh oh," he winced, but not from pain.

"Uh oh is right. To be honest, she's a little scary. Fickle and unpredictable."

Gareth cocked his head, surprised. "What did you expect, Lane? A straight shooter? Tiana is the Queen of the Sidhe, and that makes her queen manipulator."

"I know, but I didn't expect her to be so stereotypically Sidhe one moment and magnanimous the next. I still can't believe she helped bring you back. She even sent a personal guard to ensure I got here from Faerie in one piece. He's still at the spring portal watching for gatecrashers. I had to give him your jackknife as collateral or he wouldn't stay put. The last thing I wanted was for him to scare Xax or the other exiles."

Gareth glanced past her shoulder to the open crevice at the rock portal. "Then we'll have to go back together and show your friend it's mission accomplished. You need to close the portal anyway after he leaves, and if I know Tiana, she's already waiting for her detailed report."

"Well, you certainly know Tiana. And she knows you."

He looked at her funny. "What's that supposed to mean?"

Lane chewed her lip as the lesser Fae dispersed back to the grove. Gareth nodded to Xax as he and Eesa stood by their tree. Lane blew them a kiss, touching a hand to her heart as Gareth took her hand to walk down the slope to the narrow crevice in the rock face.

"Gareth, you were one of the queen's favorites, right?"

He shrugged. "Tiana has many pets, but I suppose she liked me well enough. She helped me return from the dead so you and I could be together, so yeah."

"Did you and she, you know—" Lane let the question just lay there.

"So that's where your last comment came from. Did Tiana and I, what? What is it you're stumbling over your tongue to ask?"

Lane felt her cheeks flush, but seeing Tiana, she had to know. "After everything we've been through, you're really going to make me spell it out?"

He didn't reply, and she growled low in frustration.

"Fine. I'm a big girl, so I'm just going to ask. I want to know if the Seelie queen took advantage of her position and made you do her—"

"What? Bidding?"

Lane let go of his hand. "No, you big jerk! *Her*! Did you do HER?"

"Oh, man. You're jealous! I die and get brought back from the ether and all you're worried about is if I slept with the Faerie queen?"

"I am not jealous." She sniffed. "Tiana is a beautiful sovereign who's used to getting everything she wants the moment she wants it. No one tells her no." She looked at him. "So, did you?"

"You didn't wonder about my connection with the queen when you knew she sent me to help with Leith, so why now?"

Lane folded her arms tight. "Because she gave me the Fae version of the *Bene Gesserit* box test!"

"Like from *Dune?*" His mouth dropped.

"It's not funny, Gareth! I thought the woman deep fried my hand!"

Gareth tugged her close again, but she kept her arms crossed even in his embrace.

"I'm sorry, Laney. Tiana can be capricious and even cruel sometimes, but she's better than most."

"She handed me some bull about being sure I was worthy of you. That my love for you was just as fierce as yours was for me." She sniffed again, before lifting her face to his. "Was it torture for sport, or compensation for letting you go? Or just for shits and giggles to see how much I would withstand to have you?"

He kissed the top of her head, resting his cheek on her hair. "I don't know, love. It could be all of the above, or nothing at all. Fae who only know their own realm are a funny lot. Maybe Tiana keeping Eve and Aislinn is a good thing. Either way, your suffering got the job done. Even from nothingness, I felt every emotion. As strong as they are right now with you in my arms. I knew whatever you poured into that magic, it would work."

Lane exhaled an acquiescent breath. "I suppose I should be grateful you were favorite enough for her to want you to be happy. Now if we could only parlay that into her letting my mother and Eve come home. They're Ravens, not lab rats."

He lifted her chin so he could see her eyes. "We can."

"How? I love you, Gareth, but I'm not doing the fry daddy thing again."

He laughed for a moment, but then his face softened. "We go back to the Summer Court, together. We ask the queen for an indulgence. Tiana might insist we stay in exchange for Eve and Aislinn, but then they have the choice to either stay with us or return. Either way, you and I will be together. And if we stay in Faerie, that together is a very, very long time."

She grinned up at him, loosening her arms to fit around his waist. "Long. As in forever, right?"

"My bewitching love, anything is possible with you."

Epilogue

"Lane, seriously hope this isn't some macabre, visit-the-scene-of-the-crime, fetish thing."

"Trust me, Gareth. You're the one who said that thinking about the time I spent in the backrooms was a turn on."

"Yeah, that was before I saw what they did to that poor Were kid."

Lane nodded. "I know. From what Rémy said, Sean Leighton was not happy at all. He nearly ripped up the truce because Rémy kept it from him so long."

"I don't blame him, but there were extenuating circumstances, plus the Vampire Council gave Sean his due. He watched as they sent those two demented vampers to final death, without their fangs."

"I don't want to talk about it anymore. It's over. Eve and my mother are visiting Caitlan, while you and I are here. So, let's enjoy ourselves before we head back."

"Remember we promised Xax and Eesa we'd stop at the bakery for them."

"I know. Chocolate croissants in gold foil paper. I don't know which Xax wants more. The pastry or the wrapper."

She stopped in front of a silver door with a spray of rhinestones. "Yay! We're here."

"Where? Elvis's dressing room?"

Up on tip toe, she pressed a kiss to his lips, letting it linger. "No, babe. It's my favorite fantasy room of all. Glitter Kink. Sexy burlesque with a twist."

She stepped back from him and let her long, thin leather coat puddle to her ankles.

"Holy fuck-me pumps! Lane, what the—? You wore that under your coat on the subway!" He licked his lips at the strappy, crotchless leather and rhinestone bikini and stiletto heels.

Before he could say another word, she took the feather boa from her neck and wrapped it around his waist, tugging him toward the door.

"Leather and sexy, glittery toys enough to make any woman spread wide and wet and sigh..." She smiled, crooking her little finger. "Come play, Gareth. I promise, it'll be something you never forget."

"Bewitch me, baby. All the way."

Note from the Author

The *Red Veil Diaries* is an offshoot of my paranormal romantic suspense series, the *Cursed by Blood* saga. The underground vampire club, The Red Veil, was first introduced in *Twice Cursed*, book two of the *Cursed by Blood* series, and many of the characters from the Diaries are there as well, their lives unfolding and entwined throughout the eight-book series.

If you enjoyed *The Red Veil Diaries* and want more romantic suspense with a twist of paranormal, I hope you'll check out the *Cursed by Blood* series, too!

Available in KINDLE UNLIMITED!

About the Author

 Marianne Morea was born and raised in New York. Inspired by the dichotomies that define 'the city that never sleeps', she began her career after college as a budding journalist. Later, earning a MFA, from The School of Visual Arts in Manhattan, she moved on to the graphic arts. But it was her lifelong love affair with words, and the fantasies and 'what ifs' they stir, that finally brought her back to writing.

If you enjoyed the story, please feel free to email me. Reviews are always welcome, especially on Amazon and Goodreads!

Here's a Special Treat!

CHARACTER INTERIEWS!

Let's welcome Dash Collier, from Marianne Morea's Erotic Urban Fantasy, Tempt Me ...

1. *Interviewer:* Tell us about yourself, Dash…

   [Chuckling, Dash raises an eyebrow] "What's there to tell, really?" [He runs a hand through his hair, exhaling, a sexy half smile teasing the corner of his mouth] "I'm a wolf shifter, someone blessed with dual natures. Other than that, I grew up not much differently than you. I have a mother and a father, I went to school, learned how to shift, I have a pesky younger brother, Gehrig, whose sole purpose in life is getting laid.

2. *Interviewer:* "You still haven't said a word about Abigail. Trouble in paradise?"

   "Abigail's middle name is trouble, so I would tread very carefully if I were you. As to my relationship with her: she's headstrong and hard to handle, yet compassionate, super smart and fierce…not to mention beautiful…she's everything I never knew I wanted and I wouldn't change a thing. Trouble in paradise? With Abby, it wouldn't be paradise unless there was trouble. I mean, she's fanged and fabulous, so it comes with the territory. Old taboos are sometimes hard to overcome, but as long as Abigail is willing to take the heat, then so am I. *[he growls low]* MORE than willing, if you get my meaning. We're talking hot!"

3. *Interviewer:* "As a child, what did you want to be when you grew up?"

    [Shrugs] "I never really gave it much thought. In my world you are born into your dual nature, and automatically part of a pack or pride or whatever grouping is specific to your animal nature. I knew I was destined to be one of our Alpha's hunters because of my blood line. Blood fight challenges are far and few these days, so Sean Leighton was our alpha hands down, despite the inside bullshit that went down. But never in my wildest dreams would I have thought I'd be a Hunter in something as unusual as the Brethren, or that our Alpha's nutty idea of uniting the Weres would work. And now we have a truce with the vampires. So win-win!"

4. *Interviewer:* "Does Abigail fly? I heard some do. Do the two of you ever race the moon together?"

    [A sheepish grin spreads across Dash's face] "Abby does fly, and she leaves me in the dust every chance she gets. It's infuriating, but she always makes up for it. *[wink]*

5. *Interviewer:* "What are you passionate about these days?"

[Smiling broadly now, he glances over his shoulder at the pretty strawberry blonde vampire sitting off to the side of the interview set] "Abigail. She's my whole existence now. That and keeping the tentative truce between the Weres and Vampires. We are trailblazing new ground for the races. Her and I and Gehrig and Bette…it's been tough. Old taboos die a hard death, but we've managed to make it work. Hey, she's my old lady, so… *[He chuckles, winking]* "Like two-hundred and fifty years old."

[Abigail blows a razzberry at him off set.]

6. *Interviewer:* *[chuckling]* "Well, you know what they say about blondes having more fun…"

[Raising an eyebrow, Dash cocks his head to the side] "With Abigail, you never go right to fun. *[He winks at her.]* But it's definitely a rollercoaster ride worth taking."

7. *Interviewer:* "What is your favorite meal?"

"You're kidding, right?" *[With a sly grin, Dash leans forward in his chair, letting a bit of a growl rumble in his throat for effect]* "I crave what any four-fanged carnivore would…a very, very, succulent…" *[The interviewer scoots back in her chair and Dash laughs out loud]* "Sorry, I just couldn't resist. I learned that from the vampires. I guess my favorite meal is a big, juicy steak. Rare, of course.

8. *Interviewer:* "What do you do to unwind and relax?"

"I run in wolf form through the forest. It calms me, and helps me to put things into perspective or clear my mind." *[Looking over his shoulder again, he smiles, shaking his head]* "Like I said, Abby likes to leave me in the dust."

9. *Interviewer:* "If you could apologize to someone in your past, who would it be?"

[Dash takes a deep breath, letting it out slowly] "I'm not really sure how to answer that question. I guess I would have to say, the vamps I never gave a chance to. Being a Were, I was brought up to think one way, and it took accepting my feelings for someone my roots reviled to really see the big picture."

10. *Interviewer:* "What is something people would be surprised about you?"

"That unlike Hollywood stereotypes, Weres are not bloodthirsty, mindless beasts come the full moon. We can shift any time, any day. We are as comfortable and as cognizant in our animal forms as we are when we're in our human forms. We're really not that different from anyone else—just like humans, we have our good days and our bad days. We get angry and vent, we laugh, we cry, we bleed when we're hurt, we have prejudices that we need to rise above…we're just trying to find our way in this world just like you."

11. *Interviewer:* "Thank you, Dash, for taking the time to meet with us this evening."

Let's welcome, Daisy Cochran, heroine and main character from Marianne Morea's Taste Me ...

1. *Interviewer:* Taste Me, is yours and Jace's story. Tells us a little about how your story started.

   [Daisy shifts in her seat, her lips softly closed.] "That's a hard topic. My story begins a long time ago when I fell in love with the shifter of my dreams. My involvement with Jace was meant to be. Our families had known each other for generations. Our union was the answer to everyone's prayers, including mine. It just didn't happen the way everyone expected.

2. *Interviewer:* "Tell me, Daisy…most of the ladies think Jace is quite a hunk, is it true that when you first met him, all you could think about was licking his thighs?"

   [Daisy blinks, open mouthed.] "Boy, they told me you were direct…but *jeez. Umm, yeah.* Jace struck me immediately as a hottie. But when I bumped into him at The Red Veil after he had been turned, he was entirely predatory, and he oozed sex appeal—I couldn't help myself. I guess to answer your question, yes—he was, and is, mouthwateringly handsome."

   [Chuckling off set, Jace winks] "Back attcha, babe."

3. *Interviewer:* "There are some who have commented that your ethereal connection to Jace happened after you had your daughter. What do you have to say to that?"

    "There are many readers who have made that comment, but my answer to that is simply this…when you are dealing with grief and guilt and all the emotions that go hand-in-hand with those, it's not hard to cling to something that makes you feel safe, regardless of how reckless it seems. Jace and I fell in love before our lives were blindsided, and that love endured. Our baby girl is what made us realize that and accept though things had changed…we had changed…our feelings and our destiny did not. Regardless of who accepted us or not.

4. *Interviewer:* "When Jace left you at the altar, we all know how difficult that was for you, yet we really don't see you cry. Where did you channel all that pain you so obviously felt?"

    [Daisy closes her eyes and exhales sadly before opening them again.] "When something like that happens, you're numb at first. You don't know what to feel because the situation is just so unreal. I did cry. But my anger at the situation was just too overwhelming at the time. Anyone who picks up the series knows that. I did cry, but just not where anyone could see. I ached for Jace, and having no word for five years nearly killed me. It was our daughter that kept me going. And Jace's mom and dad. They never let me go."

5. *Interviewer:* "How are you adjusting to being together with a vampire?"

[Smiling, Daisy glances over her shoulder at Jace.] "Adjustment...that's the perfect word to describe it. Things haven't been smooth sailing for us since we got together. We didn't just ride off into the sunset together. We've had quite a bit of fine tuning and many heated moments. Trouble seems to find us, and of course there are Weres in our pack that won't accept Jace now that he's a vampire, but he's still a Were and can still shift, so they need to get over their tired selves...so for the most part it's all good."

6. *Interviewer:* "Why do you suppose Ms. Morea titled the book Taste Me?"

[Daisy tilts her head, thoughtfully.] "I asked her that once. She told me it was because Jace was a vampire, yet he was still a Were. You see, Weres are born dual natured. We are just another race akin to humankind. Marianne said that vampires were once human and so cursed into their existence, and that for them, all the answers are in the blood. That for Jace and I to realize we belonged together, we needed to taste our love again. Him through my blood and me through how he made my body...well...you know. *[Blushes fiercely]* Not a bad answer, huh?"

7. *Interviewer:* "Do you think your best friend, Aimee Dunne, will get her own story? She knows vamps and

Weres inside and out. Plus she's an Avian shifter. Is there love for her on the horizon?"

[Daisy smiles softly.] "I certainly hope so. There is still a divide between the races, and she certainly knows her way around both. Aims is a smart cookie. Sometimes too smart. She has to learn to let go and open up. Life isn't all sex and go. There's love, too. Personally? I think she's a little too clinical, and that makes her afraid. Of course, she'd psychoanalyze the crud out of it and *me* for saying it out loud, but there you are. Perhaps we'll all find out at some point during the Diaries. There's so much more to unfold…"

8. **Interviewer:** "And my last question has to be…do you ever think you'll choose pack life or will you and Jace form your own hybrid world?"

[Daisy shrugs, slyly] "I don't know yet. Guess we'll both just have to wait and see."

9. **Interviewer:** "Thank you, Daisy, for sharing so much with us, and yes, there is much more to come, and I can't wait!"

Other Books by Marianne Morea